Patrick Donahoe

An Exposition of the Apocalypse of St. John the Apostle

Patrick Donahoe

An Exposition of the Apocalypse of St. John the Apostle

Reprint of the original, first published in 1858.

1st Edition 2023 | ISBN: 978-3-37513-868-4

Verlag (Publisher): Salzwasser Verlag GmbH, Zeilweg 44, 60439 Frankfurt, Deutschland
Vertretungsberechtigt (Authorized to represent): E. Roepke, Zeilweg 44, 60439 Frankfurt, Deutschland
Druck (Print): Books on Demand GmbH, In de Tarpen 42, 22848 Norderstedt, Deutschland

AN

EXPOSITION

OF THE

APOCALYPSE

OF

ST. JOHN THE APOSTLE.

By a Secular Priest.

Verbum enim Crucis, pereuntibus quidem stultitia est: iis autem qui salvi fiunt, id est nobis, Dei virtus est.—1 Cor. i. 18.

BOSTON:
PUBLISHED BY PATRICK DONAHOE,
No. 23 FRANKLIN STREET.
1858.

CONTENTS.

PRELIMINARY NOTES.

I.—From a wish to avoid prolixity, the author has, perhaps, presumed too much on the patience or diligence of the reader. In some instances, what has been only suggested for his reflection, might have been expressed more plainly, and the reader thereby spared an unnecessary labor. It was intended, by the First Seal, chap. vi., verse 1, that he should contemplate our Lord in his office of Creator, or as Christus Creator. In the second, Christus Redemptor. Third, Christus Remunerator. Fourth, Christus Pater futuri sæculi. From these attributes of his Divinity, we pass to those of his Humanity; from the Action of the Son of God, to the Passion of the Son of man: which passion is manifested under the Fifth Seal in his creatures, afterwards in his own person; as is set forth in the proper place.

II.—Chap. ix. verse 2. The reasoning to prove, that Protestantism is not a heresy, and that it is the revolt, is incomplete; and the conclusion, so far forth, is rash. It should be remarked: that, while the reformers took care to avoid a name, which implied heresy, or infidelity, they fell upon the very term "protest," which is equivalent to revolt; and which so entirely commits them to opposition of the truth, that, if the Roman Catholic Church were for a moment removed, Protestantism would cease to exist. If it is not always permitted, even in human affairs, to protest the authority of a supreme tribunal, much more in divine things, a protest, or appeal, or demur, is a plain rebellion; and, therefore, Protestantism, as applied to the divine rule of faith, is an offence, a revolt. Whether it be only a revolt, or something more than this, that is to say, the revolt, will depend upon the alternative which stands thus: Is it only a single instance, of dissent from the Catholic Church; or is it a general rule, for diversity in the interpretation of revealed truth? Does it, by accident, vary from the Catholic discipline; or does it, by its essence, challenge and subject every authority to itself? Does it plead any apology for its especial necessity; or does it set up a claim for universal license, in forms of religion? Is it an exception, or is it a law, of resistance to the Church?

III.—Chap. ix. verse 12. The metaphor of the dying body, is of course to be referred to human society, not as it uses, but as it abuses, the gift of Christianity; not as it admits, but as it resists the influence of the Church, the health of the race.

IV.—Chap. ix. verse 16. The number of the army, is not supposed to include any definite or integral part of the Catholic peoples as such, but rather the masses which are infected with revolutionary principles, and which are the instruments of their propagation throughout the world; and these are dispersed among the nations of either continent, whose form of civilization is distinctively Latin.

V.—In the same connection as the above, where allusion is made to the guilt of the Jewish people, it ought not to be insinuated that popular guilt is necessarily the most grievous of all. A national crime is, so to speak, perfunctory and impersonal; but that of an individual, is intentional. The woe which the Divine Master denounced upon his apostate disciple, was never affirmed of the Hebrew people. Hence also, as a corollary of the above, and which is not without some significance in the argument of this work, it might be added: That, when we institute comparisons with the Jewish nation, it should be, not to their detriment, so much as to our own discipline; for, however we may magnify the sin of the unbelieving Hebrew, the sin of the apostate Christian is incomparably greater.

VI.—Chap ix. verse 19. Whereas corruption is imputed to Christendom, it will be observed that Christendom is not a synonyme for the Church of Christ. It is the region, or geographical circuit, of the nations who claim the Christian name. An equivalent term is wanting in the Latin, or other languages than our own; and therefore, theologically speaking, it is to be called the generation of the Holy Ghost only in a restricted sense: not as his hereditary and organic body of the faithful, but as a creation or an inspiration, which may, or may not, be perpetuated.

VII.—So far as the Apocalypse relates to future events, this Exposition does not pretend to pronounce upon them categorically; but is to be left open to those variations which may be prompted by prudent conjecture, or other good reasons. The Twelve hundred and sixty days of the Antichristian empire, chap. xi. verse 3, which have been interpreted literally as days, may also perhaps be reckoned as twelve hundred and sixty years; and the period thus defined be substituted throughout the work, for the shorter one which has been adopted in conformity with the more common tradition. It will be found that the change indicated, will not interfere with the plan of the work, nor require any material abridgment of its details; but, since the sense of some passages must be enlarged or otherwise qualified to meet the proposed variation, the following hints may serve to clear the way, and make room for the days to be taken uniformly in their widest sense of years. In chap. xi., the Temple being the Church, the Court may be Christendom, or the Christian countries; the Holy City, Christianity or the Christian republic; which is trodden under foot by the Pagan nations, when they shall become associated to the modern civilization. The two Witnesses may be the Christian and the Hebrew religions, of the New and of the Old Testaments. It is written, I will give to them: because the hearts of the Hebrew people will be converted to the truth, as it is in Jesus Christ; and to the Church, will be given a new grace, that together they may publish the truth, with an energy and certainty, more luminous than ever before. Verse 6., These have power to shut heaven, that it rain not: when they withhold their countenance and sanction from the political or social institutions of the times, men will find their schemes of prosperity abortive, their political devices graceless and impotent to secure the tranquillity of the State. These two witnesses may be said to be killed, verse 7, in the persons of their representatives; as if the Sovereign Pontiff being removed by death, the Church should remain for a time without a visible head. And this time will be three years and a half, or twelve hundred and sixty literal days; being another forty-two months of days, within the forty-two months of years —time within time—abomination of desolation within desolation. The Beast of those days will be the hereditary Antichrist of twelve hundred and sixty years, and the personal Antichrist of twelve hundred and sixty days, who then fills the throne. And their bodies shall be in the streets, and they shall see their bodies for three days and a half: that is, they shall see the Christian religion, tô which may have been associated the testimony of the Hebrew race, (presignified, perhaps, by the united authorities of St. Peter and St. Paul,) extinguished, as it were, in the persons of their respective heads; and so remaining for those days, without any signs of life; the faithful being distracted among themselves, and impotent to recover the order which is essential to authority; and exhibiting none of those sensible proofs of an overruling Providence, which, at other times, have uniformly and incontestably attended the tribulations or disasters which have fallen upon the truth. Verse 9, The people will not suffer their bodies to be laid in sepulchres, because the faithful then on earth, can find no consolation nor discern any sufficient reason, how they may defend and account for their being abandoned, by the divine Master, to a season of such darkness and sorrow; that is, there does not remain to them the sad consolation of discovering a certain propriety and order in the disposition of events, as tending in any way to the greater glory of God. But, verse 11, after the three years and a half are ended, there is a manifest interposition of the divine Head of the Church. The spirit of life from God entered into them; the faithful with their pastors everywhere rise up as if inspired by God; and stand upon their feet: confessing boldly the Word of the Cross. And they heard a great voice from heaven, saying to them, Come up hither: they receive miraculous gifts from heaven. And they went up to heaven in a cloud: they are exalted by the divine Goodness to a preternatural immunity from the ills of the flesh; or they are so elevated by heavenly favors, that their enemies see and confess that they are the sons of God. But whereas it is written, In a cloud: this may be, because their enemies do not, themselves, discern plainly the truth, nor come to the same light of sacred wisdom.

The time and times and half a time of the woman's flight to the desert, chap. xii. 6 and 14, will be the same twelve hundred and sixty years of desolation, when religion is deprived of that due establishment in society, which constitutes her as a city; with her own walks and stores, and vested rights of house and home; thronged by her peaceful lineage and faithful domestics.

If the forty-two months, chap. xiii., verse 5 and 18, be taken for twelve hundred and sixty years, the idea of the power and universality of the Antichristian empire, over every tribe, and people, and tongue, and nation, seems to be much amplified. But because it is written: His number is the number of a MAN, we must still suppose a personal Antichrist, in whom this empire at length terminates.

It is said of the Beast, chap. xvii. verse 10, he must remain a short time.

And, chap. xx. verse 3, that Satan must be loosed a little time. How then can the thousand years of the saints' reign bear a literal interpretation, and yet the days of Antichrist be magnified to years? It might be answered: that all the days of the wicked are but a little time, and do not deserve to be counted by thousands, nor as years, but rather as "an hour, a day, a month, or a year." And for the Saints, their blessedness so nearly approaches to the eternal state that they are above the conditions of time, or are to be reckoned by no measure less noble than the full thousand years. The prosperity of the impious is to be compared, not with the beatitude of the just, but only with the tribulations of the same; for the joys of the bad, and the sorrows of the good, both endure but for a short time, and alike they vanish as the smoke. Finally, the intrusion of the Gentiles, Gog and Magog, verse 7, into the sphere of civilization, and their time of trampling under foot the truths and traditions of the Christian religion, may be commensurate with the same twelve hundred and sixty years.

VIII.—The signification of many of the symbolical terms, is not fully disclosed till the work is nearly ended; but such as it is, the same is presented according as it occurred to the author himself. Besides what has been suggested in other places, it may be added: Fire, chap. xv. verse 2, is so apt and so familiar a symbol of liberty, that it is a common form of expression to describe certain characters of mind, as fiery. Every thing else may be handled or moulded, but the fire must not be touched: check it, and it dies; compress it, and it ceases to exist. Even thus, the Creator himself respects the liberty of his creatures, and this is proved more excellently in divine things, than in any other way: for he will suffer sacrilege in his most Holy Sacrament, rather than expose the secret guilt of the unworthy recipient.

In the same connection: Water may be considered an emblem of life, by reason of its activity; of the life Human, because it is deciduous and transient; of the life eternal, inasmuch as it is continuous and constant. And though there is an infinite difference between these two, yet there is also a certain ontological affinity, because there can be no life whatever, inverse from that which is always and absolutely good; but according as it departs from, or is opposed to, that which is eternally good, it ceases to be life, and becomes death. Again, life proceeds from being, action from intelligence, the eternal life from the eternal ens: then the entity of life and action, is truth; which also is like a sea for its breadth, and like crystal for its simplicity. And because truth, or pure intelligence, is immutable both in time and in eternity, the same is compared to a sea of glass or crystal, and only then, indirectly: "as it were," a sea of glass. While, on the other hand, life is compared directly to the waters; because (unlike the truth) life is found to be itself a creature; not only Increate, but also a thing created. For there is one life that now is, one that is to be, and one that has always been. In chap. xxi. verse 1, where it is written: The sea is no more, this may be understood of the present life, in respect of its intermedial or separate existence, which, so far forth, pertains neither to heaven nor to hell, having nothing constant nor determinate in itself. But the river, chap. xxii. verse 1, implies unition, as well as communication, of existence; and thus, the river of life may always be an emblem of the eternal procession of the Third Person of the Blessed Trinity.

INTRODUCTION

AND

DIVISION OF THE WORK.

It is designed, in the following treatise, to furnish the devout reader with a commentary of the Apocalypse of Blessed John the Apostle, subject to the authority of the Roman Church, in harmony with the teaching of the Holy Fathers, and in accordance with the ordinary Gloss of the English Vulgate. The subject is so sublime, so many holy and learned men have already been occupied with it, and, at the same time, the curious and irreverent have so often made it an occasion of scandal and derision, that it would seem, in a manner, presumptuous, to add another to the catalogue of learned labors and various conjectures now on record. But, on the other hand, as the meritorious works of earlier writers are a great help in the study of this sacred book, so, for the modern observer, there will be a double advantage: because the march of events must afford a better insight of its profound meaning, and some progress must accrue to its interpretation, from only the added experience of successive years. It is not intended, however, to depart from the ordinary routine of former authorities, nor by any means to elicit a meaning diverse from the general sense of ecclesiastical traditions; but rather to obtain the consent, and to render the spirit of the same, so far as they concur in a direct application to the requirements of the age. Wherefore it is hoped that the apology for this work may be found in its plan, if not in its detail and execution.

Commentators usually divide the Apocalypse into Seven Parts, and though they do not agree upon the points of division, the custom may be observed for the reverence of that sacred number. For since, in the Holy Scriptures, numbers and signs are often employed to convey a deeper meaning to the attentive reader, we can well suppose that, in this book of mysteries, there may be an intrinsic propriety in pursuing such an arrangement. Accordingly,

The First Part, commencing with the first chapter, ends with the third. And, because it relates wholly to things then present, and neither to the future nor to the past, and moreover, is as a mirror, wherein all may compare their own spiritual state in all ages, now as then, it may be entitled The Present Time. The consideration now advanced, is of itself sufficient to show that the Apocalypse does not relate exclusively to things future in time. With the advent of Christianity, prophecy was somewhat eclipsed of its greatness. This single book of the apostle supplies, for the Christian people, the many volumes of the prophets; and, though it is of a kindred spirit, with like figures and language, yet the blessed apostle appears not to be bounded by temporal events, or limited by the transactions of earth; but rather he discourses of heaven, and earth, and hell, of the throne of the Lamb, of the seat of the Beast, and of the prison of Satan. As the gospel contained the fulness of truth, so here the plenitude of mystery is emblazoned for the fear and love of men.

The Second Part, commencing with the fourth chapter, ends with the eleventh. This part describes all time, from end to end. That is to say, the imagery of the text may be so applied, without doing violence to the interpretations of others. To take an example, (chap. vi. verse 4,) the metaphor of the horse, is commonly understood to signify war;

but, while we understand it of Christian times, nothing forbids our contemplating war as a dispensation of divine Providence, by which, in all times, he admonishes every one that he must do battle for his sovereign Lord. Again, there is mention toward the close, (chap. xi.,) of the two witnesses, or Henoch and Elias; who are taken from the beginning and middle of the world's history, and are brought out again in the end. Now these names, if they are in the future, belong also to the past; we may say then that the ages of ages, and the ends of the earth, are here met together, and this part may be entitled, TIME UNIVERSAL.

PART THIRD extends through the twelfth and thirteenth chapters. Describing, first, the Church, and afterward her adversaries, from Satan to antichrist, this part may be styled THE CHURCH MILITANT BEFORE THE SECULAR POWER OR THE WORLD.

PART FOURTH, commencing (chap. xiv.) with the harvest-time, or the ingathering of the elect, and ending (chap. xvi.) with the outpouring of the last vials of wrath, is here designated, THE LAST DAYS OF THE CHURCH AND OF THE WORLD.

Chapters xvii. and xviii. describe the fall of Babylon. The apostle glances incidentally at her pomps, but the burden of the narration is her mournful end and utter destruction. Babylon is taken to be this world, in respect of its blandishments. As the Beast is the brute force of the secular arm, so Babylon is the lust of pleasure which beguiles the souls of men. Now as we approach the end, the reverse of this world's pageant comes more plainly in view, and we begin to look back on its empty joys as if already withered; wherefore the FIFTH PART is named, THE RETROSPECT OF THE WORLD'S DESTRUCTION.

PART SIXTH, which includes the nineteenth chapter, announces the song of triumph for Christ's victory over his enemies, discloses their slaughtered bodies on the field of battle, and the vultures flocking to their prey. It will be entitled, THE RETROSPECT OF CHRIST'S VICTORY.

PART SEVENTH embràces the remaining chapters, viz., xx., xxi., and xxii. It shows the just judgments of Almighty God, or his retribution of reward and punishment. Beginning with the fallen angels, it makes manifest the temporal and then the eternal chastisement of Satan: the first, and afterward the second, or eternal death of all whose names are not written in the book of life. It also declares the present happiness of the saints in heaven, and promises that, for the just, there shall be no more sorrow nor death, but eternal beatitude in the Paradise of God. It may be called, THE DAY OF JUDGMENT.

*** The chapters of the interpretation will correspond with those of the sacred text.

EXPOSITION

OF THE

APOCALYPSE OF ST. JOHN, THE APOSTLE.

PART I.

THE PRESENT TIME.

THE beloved Apostle, Saint John, the Evangelist, now hoary with years, the Virgin, unscathed by the fires of martyrdom, being banished to the island of Patmos, and shut out from all part in the affairs of earth, is summoned by the Spirit of God, one holy Lord's-day, to look in upon the divine mysteries, and to be the messenger to men of sacred and hidden truths. Inspired by God, he reaches through the height and depth of the ancient Beauty ever new, leading us among the choirs of the blessed, and through the prisons of hell; and marking, in distant ages, that controlling Hand which disposes with unerring certainty, of every vicissitude in all the course of time. He strikes terror upon the heart of the impious, but imparts courage to the weary pilgrim, toiling "through a land of drought and the image of death,"[1] where virtue is oppressed and vice triumphs, where the light of truth is obscured, and error makes dark his way.

[1] Jeremiah ii. 6.

The heart of the wise man is in the future, and never without apprehension. Holy Daniel was praised, because he was a man of desires; and was blessed, because, with prayer and fasting, he remained watchful and inquisitive for the end. Now here is provided for the Christian understanding, a fountain of mystery, noble and deep; and, at the same time, free, generous, and accessible; and thus the church of God, like the householder, rich in things old and new, supplies the immortal soul, trained in the fulness of truth, and in the science of the saints, and thirsting for the eternal life, with a well of sweet waters, a fountain of fair visions. Fons hortorum, puteus aquarum viventium, quæ fluunt impetu de Libano.[1]

[1] Cant. iv. 15.

CHAPTER I.

1 The revelation of Jesus Christ, which God gave to him to make known to his servants the things which must shortly come to pass; and signified sending by his angel to his servant, John.

This revelation, or Apocalypse, is from God the Father, "of whom all paternity in heaven and earth is named," through his Son, our Lord. It is written, "shortly," because to him who meditates eternal things, all time is short. Or because it is purposely contrived by the Master, that his servants shall be ever watchful, and apprehensive of his instant coming. And he tells them plainly, that the end shall come as "a snare, upon all that sit upon the face of the whole earth." Wherefore, as St. Thomas[1] observes, there is for every one a double uncertainty; inasmuch as the hour of his death is uncertain, and again, the day of the last judgment may be nearer than the space of a man's life. Because one and another of the angels are declared, at different passages, to have instructed the apostle, it need not be supposed that one particular angel is here intended, but the mode of communication is signified, that is, by angelic ministration.

2 Who hath given testimony to the word of God, and the testimony of Jesus Christ, what things soever he hath seen.

As an apostle and evangelist, St. John was a teacher of the word of God: and, as a martyr, he had borne witness to the divinity of Jesus Christ.

3 Blessed is he that readeth and heareth the words of this prophecy, and keepeth those things which are written in it; for the time is at hand.

Even the humblest of the unlearned seems invited to read, or to hear and meditate these things.

[1] Sum. Theol. Supp., 88. 3.

4 John, to the seven churches, which are in Asia. Grace be unto you, and peace from him who is, and who was, and who is to come, and from the seven spirits which are before his throne.

According to St. Gregory and others, by seven churches, may be understood, one Catholic church, full of the seven-fold spirit of grace. The title, "who is," is synonymous with the sacred name of Jehovah, and thus the apostle employs the language of the ancient dispensation, and of the times old and new, because this prophecy reaches, as it were, throughout the mysteries of the kingdom of God. By the seven spirits, may be understood seven angels, the patrons of the churches, to whom he writes, or, seven principal spirits at the throne of God. The sacred Scriptures exercise variously the intelligence of the reader, sometimes by images, as if picturing the sentiment, at other times by numbers. For even as the mother now hides, and now discovers her face, for the divertisement of her babe, so our feeble minds, by diligence, shall be quickened to a livelier sense of the divine sweetness But, most of all, it is difficult for the human intelligence to comprehend the nature of pure spirits; and it may, perhaps, be said, that harmonious and perfect numbers convey the best idea of their lofty state, which the common understanding is capable of receiving. And, that even this much apprehension of the celestial order, is no insignificant step in knowledge, may be inferred from the reflection, that he who could number the glories of heaven, would know them

5 And from Jesus Christ, who is the faithful witness, the first begotten of the dead, and the prince of the kings of the earth; who hath loved us, and washed us from our sins in his own blood;

6 And hath made us a kingdom, and priests to God and his Father; to him be glory and empire, forever and ever. Amen.

He is the faithful witness, who is Himself the strength of all the martyrs. He first has turned back the tide of death, and hath made us a kingdom and priests to God, since he has chosen the Christian soul for his temple, where He, the

King, and Priest and Victim, is pleased to dwell. "He that eateth my flesh and drinketh my blood, abideth in me, and I in him."

7 Behold he cometh with the clouds; and every eye shall see him, and they that pierced him. And all the tribes of the earth shall bewail themselves because of him. Even so, Amen.

If we consider how few are the inhabitants of the earth, who have not, at some time, heard the name of Christ, we may well suppose that there is hardly one, but will recognize him in the day of judgment, for him of whom they had heard in life. And they that pierced him, and that persecuted him in his members, shall behold him in his sacred Humanity, through the Divinity they shall never look upon; and they shall mourn for themselves, when it is too late, because they had no compassion for him in the day of grace.

8 I am Alpha and Omega, the beginning and the end, saith the Lord God who is, and who was, and who is to come, the Almighty.

These words are often repeated in this book, to lift up our minds to the things that are above; or, because the Prophet of the church reads not only the future, but all times, far and near, from the eternal decree, to its final consummation.

9 I, John, your brother, and sharer in tribulation, and in the kingdom and patience in Christ Jesus, was in the island which is called Patmos, for the word of God, and for the testimony of Jesus.

10 I was in spirit on the Lord's day, and heard behind me a great voice, as of a trumpet.

In the times of the former testament, men looked forward to a promised good; but, as the apostle heard the voice behind him, so now, in Christian times, they who love the truth, must look not forward, but back upon the same, as fully accomplished. The sentence of divine truth falls upon the soul as the voice of a trumpet, because there are none who can endure its scrutiny without emotion; no human heart which must not throb under its perception.

11 Saying: what thou seest, write in a book, and send to the seven churches which are in Asia, to Ephesus, and to Smyrna, and to Pergamus, and to Thyatira, and to Sardis, and to Philadelphia, and to Laodicea.

As St. Paul addressed his epistles to the Corinthians, or Thessalonians by name, so here the divine sentence being addressed personally to the Bishop of Ephesus and the others, serves to arrest more forcibly the attention of every prelate and pastor in all the church.

12 And I turned to see the voice that spoke with me, and being turned, I saw seven golden candlesticks.

13 And in the midst of the seven golden candlesticks, one, like unto the Son of man, clothed with a garment down to the feet, and girded about near the paps with a golden girdle.

The seven golden candlesticks aptly represent the church of God, which gives light to the world; in the midst of which, abides our Lord Jesus Christ, who is clothed down to his feet, with robes flowing with the plenitude of grace, and girded with golden charity, ad mamillas, even to his inmost heart. As St. Gregory [1] observes, the law of Moses required the loins of the flesh to be girded, but the law of Christ constrains even the thoughts of the heart, with the bonds of love.

14 And his head and hair were white, like white wool, and as snow, and his eyes were as a flame of fire,

15 And his feet like unto fine brass, as in a burning furnace, and his voice, as the sound of many waters.

His sacred head is white with the lustre of eternity, and his eyes read the secrets of the heart; his humanity, though submitted to the furnace of affliction, endures incorruptible as fine brass; and his voice, like many waters, is that of the Redeemer of all the nations and tribes of the children of Adam.

[1] Moral, xxiv. 26.

16 And he had in his right hand seven stars; and from his mouth came out a sharp, two-edged sword; and his countenance shined as the sun shineth in its full strength.

He upholds the pastors of the Church by his strong and sure right hand. The word which proceeds from his lips, pierces and divides between good and evil. Or St. Gregory[1] upon the text, Heb. iv. 12, "For the word of God," etc., shows that, by the joints, are understood the thoughts of the heart, involved, complicated, and overlying one another; and, by the marrow, or inmost part, the intention; between which perplexity of thought, and unity of intention, the sword of truth infallibly and irresistibly divides. His countenance shines as that of him, who is "the true light, which enlighteneth every man that cometh into this world."

17 And when I saw him, I fell at his feet as dead. And he laid his right hand upon me, saying, Fear not: I am the first and the last.

18. And alive and was dead, and behold, I am living forever and ever, and have the keys of death and of hell.

If the prophet Daniel "languished and was sick" because of the revelations made to him, consider how was the heart of John ravished, with joy and fear, to behold the Master, whom he had known in human mould, now clothed with the majesty of God. He holds the keys of death and of hell, to rescue men from the temporal and the eternal death, to secure them against the loss both of body and of soul.

19 Write, therefore, the things which thou hast seen, and which are, and which must be done hereafter.

The things beheld in prophetic vision are not necessarily future; but all that which is hidden and inexplicable by human means, may be subject-matter for the inspired prophet.

20 The mystery of the seven stars, which thou sawest in my right hand, and the seven golden candlesticks: the seven stars are the angels of the seven churches: and the seven candlesticks are the seven churches.

[1] Ezekiel xi. 9,16,17.

The candelabrum or branched candlestick, stands for the plurality of the congregation ; and the star, for the unity of its prelate. The bishop is well named a star, and an angel; the guide and examplar, as well as the guardian of his flock. His mind and heart are fixed on high, and his work is that of a ministering angel.

And thus, even now, as we enter this temple of truth, do we find the sound and sense accord: the name plainly spoken, the owner strictly marked; "I know mine," he saith, "and mine know me." Qui numerat multitudinem stellarum, et omnibus eis nomina vocat.[1]

CHAPTER II.

1 To the angel of the Church of Ephesus, write: These things saith he, who holdeth the seven stars in his right hand, who walketh in the midst of the Seven Golden Candlesticks.

As the faithful Sentinel slumbers not, but walks his round, so the Lord moves among the churches, visiting the hearts of his people, with joy for the diligent, and fear for the negligent.

2 I know thy works, and thy labor, and thy patience, and how thou canst not bear evil men; and thou hast tried them who say they are apostles and are not, and hast found them liars.

3 And thou hast patience, and hast borne for my name, and hast not failed.

The Bishop of Ephesus is said to have been St. Timothy. Many were his good works, and long his patience, and with holy David he could say, "Have I not hated them, O Lord, that hated thee? I have hated them with a perfect hatred."[2] Yet it is added:

4 But this I have against thee, that thou hast left thy first charity.

[1] Psalms cxlvi. 4. [2] Psalms cxxxi. 21

5 Be mindful, therefore, from whence thou art fallen, and do penance and do the first works. Or else I will come to thee, and will remove thy candlestick out of its place, unless thou shalt have done penance.

The first works are those which are animated by the first charity, the early love, which pleases God, and which has deserved for some, that "He hastened to bring them out of the midst of iniquities."[1] But for him who is left in this life, if with the lapse of time, failing, it should at length wholly expire, then his good works are unprofitable, and have lost their salt; it is time that he be rejected, and another be called to fill his place. As a man, the Bishop of Ephesus may have had his faults; as a saint, he doubtless corrected them with holy zeal. Says the Prince of the Apostles, "The time is that judgment should begin at the house of God;"[2] and thus presently do we find it, with the first voice we hear from this revelation of the divine will.

6 But this thou hast, that thou hatest the deeds of the Nicolaites, which I also hate.

The Nicolaites permitted fornication; and because he hated and pursued with rigor, so detestable a heresy, he deserved praise; and that this, his zeal for purity, should cover a multitude of his infirmities.

7 He that hath an ear, let him hear what the Spirit saith to the churches. To him that overcometh, I will give to eat of the tree of life, which is in the paradise of my God.

Who is there, in his early or his riper years, has ever read these warnings without fear; and that has not been ready to exclaim, "If the just man shall scarcely be saved, where shall the ungodly and the sinner appear?" With burning cheek and throbbing heart do we seek the testimony of our conscience; and, with concern and grief, hasten to compare it by this light of divine justice. But if the judgment

[1] Wisdom iv. 14. [2] 1 Peter iv. 17.

be strict, the promise is sure; he that toils through a long life, and multiplies his works, and preserves to the end the merit of his holy labor, needs and deserves to be refreshed with the fruits of eternal life in the paradise of God.

8 And to the angel of the church of Smyrna, write. These things saith the First and the Last, who was dead and who liveth.

9 I know thy tribulation and thy poverty: but thou art rich; and thou art blasphemed by those who say they are Jews and are not, but are the synagogue of Satan.

He who has been most high in heaven, and abject on earth, who has known the glories of eternal life, and has been acquainted with the sorrows of the temporal death, assures his beloved servant, St. Polycarp, that, in the midst of poverty and tribulation, his state is nevertheless blessed and abundant in the true riches. Insignificant in the midst of unbelievers and haughty Jews, yet he was venerable before the Church of God.

10 Fear none of those things which thou shalt suffer. Behold, the devil shall cast some of you into prison, that you may be tried; and you shall have tribulation ten days. Be thou faithful unto death, and I will give thee the crown of life.

11 He that hath an ear let him hear what the Spirit saith to the churches: He that shall overcome, shall not be hurt by the second death.

They were to prepare themselves for a persecution of ten days, or the heat of the persecution would endure for that time. In which they are exhorted to be of good courage; and while the message tenderly evades the harsh menace of death, it rather reminds them how glorious is that crown of life, which is the reward of blessed martyrs; and how, with their short sorrow, no second death should ever hurt them after.

12 And to the angel of the church of Pergamus write: These things saith he that hath the sharp, two-edged sword:

13 I know where thou dwellest, where the seat of Satan is; and thou holdest fast my name, and hast not denied my faith. Even in those days Antipas was my faithful witness, who was slain among you, where Satan dwelleth.

Antipas, the former Bishop of Pergamus, had already suffered for Christ, under the persecution of Domitian. This wicked city is said to have been given to idolatry above all the cities of Asia.

14 But I have a few things against thee; because thou hast there them that hold the doctrine of Balaam, who taught Balac to cast a stumbling-block before the children of Israel, to eat and commit fornication:

15 So hast thou also them that hold the doctrine of the Nicolaites.

Balaam, the soothsayer, taught Balac, the king of Moab, to seduce the people of Israel, by means of his women, to eat of their idolatrous offerings. So there were, among the Christians of Pergamus, some who, by favoring the doctrines of the Nicolaites, acted the same accursed part, and betrayed the souls of their frail or ignorant brethren.

16 In like manner do penance; if not, I will come to thee quickly; and will fight against them with the sword of my mouth.

The penance should be like the offence, that is, one of bodily austerities. Otherwise, they would receive sentence of divine reprobation, more to be feared than the sword of any corporal chastisement.

17 He that hath an ear, let him hear what the Spirit saith to the churches: To him that overcometh I will give the hidden manna, and will give him a white stone; and in the stone a new name written, which no man knoweth but he that receiveth it.

In this city, so full of dangerous allurements, whoever was victorious should taste the hidden sweetness of celestial joys, and become adopted to a spotless heritage, by the title of chastity; whose excellence cannot possibly be understood by any but the pure in heart.

18 And to the angel of the church of Thyatira write: These things saith the Son of God, who hath eyes as a flame of fire, and his feet like unto fine brass:

19 I know thy works, and thy faith, and thy charity, and ministry, and thy patience, and thy last works, which are more than the former.

Great was the virtue of the Bishop of Thyatira, who ever advanced still higher in a holy life, since his last works were more than the former. But there were tares in his fruitful field.

20 But I have a few things against thee; because thou permittest the woman Jezebel, who calleth herself a prophetess, to teach and to seduce my servants, to commit fornication, and to eat of things offered to idols.

21 And I gave her time to do penance; and and she will not repent of her fornication.

22 Behold, I will cast her into a bed; and they that commit adultery with her shall be in very great tribulation, unless they do penance from their deeds.

23 And I will kill her children with death; and all the churches shall know, that I am he who searcheth the reins and hearts; and I will give to every one of you according to your works.

A fearful denunciation of some woman, who seems to have had an appearance of sanctity before the Christians of Thyatira, but who was, like Jezebel, stained with the worst crimes, and obstinate in her wicked courses. Her bed was now ready for her in hell, as well as for her children, or immediate disciples. And they who committed adultery with her, or had been, in any way, defiled by her example, were in danger of very great tribulation.

24 And to the rest who are at Thyatira: Whosoever have not this doctrine, and who have not known the depths of Satan, as they say, I will not put upon you any other weight:

25 Yet that which you have, hold fast till I come.

They doubtless veiled their doctrines with a show of mystery, calling them depths, *altitudines*, full of profound meaning, beyond the comprehension of the vulgar; into which the imprudent, impelled by presumption and itching curiosity, fell headlong. These were the depths of Satan, rather than of truth. They who were clear of this heresy should have no other new afflictions to try them; but such as they were exposed to, they must receive patiently, and persevere therein to the end.

26 And he that shall overcome, and keep my words unto the end, to him I will give power over the nations:

27 And he shall rule them with a rod of iron; and as the vessel of a potter, they shall be broken;

28 Even as I received from my Father; and I will give him the morning star.

29 He that hath an ear, let him hear what the Spirit saith to the churches.

They who, in humble virtue, withstand Satan and his pomps, shall be exalted to a heavenly authority, even like that of a son of God; and shall come to those self-same heights, from which Lucifer, the arch-rebel, fell. As the just Judge is terrible to the impious, so is the virtuous man formidable before this world. When holy Job went forth, "the young men hid themselves, and the old men rose and stood up." Here is the true wisdom, the sovereign honor; lovely before heaven, mighty before men. Fortitudo et decor indumentum ejus.[1]

CHAPTER III.

1 And to the angel of the church of Sardis write: These things saith he, who hath the seven spirits of God, and the seven stars: I know thy works, that thou hast the name of being alive, and thou art dead.

2 Be watchful, and strengthen the things that remain, which are ready to die. For I find not thy works full before my God.

[1] Prov. xxxi. 25.

3 Have in mind therefore in what manner thou hast received and heard, and observe and do penance. If then thou shalt not watch, I will come to thee as a thief; and thou shalt not know at what hour I will come to thee.

"God holds in higher estimation," says St. John of the Cross, "the least degree of purity in thy conscience, than any other great work whatsoever, with which thou canst serve him." Many there are who multiply the good works which are admired by men, but take no care for that secret devotion of heart which is loved by God. If distracted by temporal cares, they keep no watchful eye to the light which God has placed within the soul, the flame of charity at length expires, and death surprises them as if in the slumbers of the night.

4 But thou hast a few names in Sardis, which have not defiled their garments; and they shall walk with me in white, because they are worthy.

5 He that shall evercome, shall thus be clothed in white garments; and I will not blot out his name out of the book of life: and I will confess his name before my Father, and before his angels.

6 He that hath an ear, let him hear what the Spirit saith to the churches.

Others, unregarded by the world, treasure up silently the true riches in heaven; and deserve to walk in the white robes of angels; and their hidden beauty shall in another day be made manifest.

7 And to the angel of the church of Philadelphia write: These things saith the Holy One and the True One, who hath the key of David; He that openeth and no man shutteth: shutteth and no man openeth:

8 I know thy works. Behold, I have given before thee a door opened, which no man can shut: because thou hast a little strength, and hast kept my word, and hast not denied my name.

9 Behold, I will bring of the synagogue of Satan who say they are Jews, and are not, but do lie: behold, I will make them come and adore before thy feet: and they shall know that I have loved thee.

The angel of Philadelphia was beloved, because, however few his talents, he had kept them well, and gained good fruit to God. In this mortal pilgrimage, where souls come and go, where the gates of life and death are ever clanging upon the portals, where one is called and another is rejected, one lost and another found; the Lord, the Holy and True, himself holds the key, and disposes all things. For his reward, it should be the happiness of this holy Prelate, to receive into the bosom of the Church many elect souls; and even the proud Jews should come and adore before his feet; as Christians ever delight to do before the vicar of Christ.

10 Because thou hast kept the word of my patience, I will also keep thee from the hour of temptation, which shall come upon all the world, to tempt them that dwell upon the earth.

These are gracious words. We take hope from them, that in this, our day of many and marvellous conversions, the evil hour of temptation for all the world may be somewhat removed.

11 Behold, I come quickly; hold fast that which thou hast, that no man take thy crown.

The sole and singular power of God is seen in the conversions of these days, which are of individuals, rather than of nations, or of families. One out of his kindred is taken, and another left. "The man of his peace, in whom God trusted," is cast out, and the stranger called in to take his crown. Now the elated convert, stored with heavenly gifts, suddenly falls; and the prodigal son of the Church comes back, weeping, to regain his heritage. Now the parent fights manfully for his reward, and the child turns coward and deserter; and again, the father is reprobate, but his offspring, or spouse, are found with burning zeal, to appear in judgment against him. "And behold, they are last that shall be first, and they are first that shall be last."

12 He that shall overcome, I will make him a pillar in the temple of my God; and he shall go out no more; and I will write

upon him the name of my God, and the name of the city of my God, the New Jerusalem, which cometh down out of heaven from my God, and my new name.

The constant soul, which holds its steady course through this troubled existence, entering at length into its rest, shall be established like a rock. To behold the blessed Trinity, is a happiness unchangeable and eternal, out of which his will, once mutable, shall not be withdrawn, nor diverted forever. And he shall be numbered among the sons of God; and his place shall be in the city of God; and the name of Jesus will be the title of his inheritance.

13 He that hath an ear, let him hear what the Spirit saith to the churches.

14 And to the angel of the Church of Laodicea, write: These things saith the Amen, the faithful and true witness, who is the beginning of the creation of God.

The Amen, it is remarked in the annotations of our English Bible, is the True one; and the beginning, because the efficient cause of creation.

15 I know thy works; that thou art neither cold nor hot; I would thou wert cold or hot:

16 But because thou art lukewarm, and neither cold nor hot, I will begin to vomit thee out of my mouth.

Thus may be described one who has neither unction within, nor shows good works without; who may have some regard for propriety and the opinion of men, but intends, before all things, his own ease; who is never kindled to indignation toward the vicious, nor to praises for the virtuous; who trims so nicely his course, that the good need not rebuke, nor the bad deride him. While no one trembles at his tone of authority, no heart is touched by his words of entreaty.

17 Because thou sayest, I am rich and made wealthy, and I have need of nothing; and thou knowest not that thou art wretched, and miserable, and poor, and blind, and naked.

18 I counsel thee to buy of me, gold, tried in the fire, that thou mayest be made rich; and mayest be clothed in white garments, that the shame of thy nakedness may not appear; and anoint thy eyes with eye-salve, that thou mayest see.

They who live in affluence and honor, possessed of refined tastes, with abundant means of enjoyment; if they lack the one thing necessary, the sovereign love of God, are of all others the most miserable. What tender nursing do they require! What soft and delicate clothing, what warm and tranquil shelter! Therefore, none need, more than they, the true riches; none are more naked, nor less able to meet the jeers and arrows of the malignant; and no eyes are so blind as theirs to the beauty of heaven. Yet they are not forgotten; cold and impenetrable may be their hearts, but kind counsel is given, and warning words follow them to the end.

19 Those whom I love I rebuke and chastise. Be zealous, therefore, and do penance.

The most fatal piece of ill-fortune of all others, is to be left to ease and plenty. The chastisement of God is better than the tenderest caresses of men. Nam virtus in infirmitate perficitur.[1]

20 Behold, I stand at the door and knock; if any man shall hear my voice, and open to me the gate, I will come in to him, and will sup with him, and he with me.

21 To him that shall overcome, I will grant to sit with me in my throne; as I, also, have overcome, and have sat with my Father in his throne.

Consider the sweet importunity of the Shepherd of our souls. In all ages, and in every condition of life, he asks to be admitted to the hearts of men, that he may grace their honors, and adorn their wealth, or partake of their sorrows, and divide their poverty. For this poor entertainment here, they can share his throne hereafter. Qui habet aurem, audiat quid Spiritus dicat ecclesiis.

[1] 2 Cor. xii. 9.

PART II.

TIME UNIVERSAL.

We now approach more arduous heights. To attempt them might be rash, but that the path is well beaten and accommodated for the willing disciple. If there be a progress in the definement of truths of dogma, so with the process of time do we reasonably look for a clearer perception of the pages of prophecy. It need not be objected, that many seem to have lost their way, or that venerable authors have been divided upon the meaning of the sacred text, for its signification is ample enough to embrace them all. If they have been found premature in the literal application of some points, it does not follow that they were wholly mistaken, but rather it proves the power and verity of the figure, when a resemblance has been found sufficient to render probable their argument; for it is as certain that there have already been antichrists, as that antichrist is yet to come. But if this point be still insisted, then it may be said, that we can profit even by their errors; which, joined with their rich stores of erudition, and with the continual unfolding of events, furnish fresh advantages both old and new.

As, in holy Scripture, many things are purposely hidden, say the Fathers, that we may search them out with labor, and thus come to relish more highly the fruit of knowledge as if it were that of our own industry; so here, it seems, is a vast field of mystic wisdom, equal to the researches, not of a life-time, but of successive generations; the ancient prophecies affected one nation or one time, but this concerns the whole generation of Christ to the end of days. Moreover, it will suit the most cultivated as well as the rudest age. A simple and childlike people are more susceptible to impressions; monsters, possessions, and other manisfestations of diabolic power, or even the narrations of the same, subdue their docile minds to that holy fear which is the beginning of wisdom. But in a sceptical and searching generation, which would scatter every cloud, and rend every veil of mystery, the same unchanging truth remains clear, and yet more resplendent; though her ancient barriers be prostrate, and men will no longer reverence her rod, her inquisition, or anathema; even so, these may be laid aside, and the church be found fair and vigorous as of old. And thus it will be seen, perhaps, that, by simplifying the interpretation, the warnings of this sacred book will apply with new force to the age in which we live. It is written that the end shall come as "a thief in the night," like "lightning," and as in "the days of Noe;" it appears, therefore, that the divine economy is sparing of signs sensible, but furnishes abundant help for the spiritual discernment and application of such tokens. The dragon that punishes the body, is less terrible than the one that destroys the soul; the prodigy which strikes the senses, is of less moment than that which searches the spirit. Either the philosophers would go forth to analyze the material phenomenon, and so divest it of all preternatural or spiritual import, or else it must be supposed so enormous, as to stun and crush the hearts of men, even in the highest intoxication of intellectual pride. But this is not in accordance with the course of God's dealings with man, and least of all, with the arrogant infidel. "A wicked and adulterous generation seeketh after a sign; and a sign shall not be given it, but the sign of Jonas the prophet. And he left them and went away." It may be set down, then, for a rule, that the literal meaning is to be restricted, and the moral sense amplified; as if the material image were designed to attract strongly the attention to hidden and portentous truths, affecting the welfare of society, and principally intended to aid us in the attainment of more lively apprehensions of the delusions of the unseen adversary, and of the perils of the immortal soul.

The Outline of this Part, which commences with the fourth chapter, and ends with the eleventh, may be described thus: The apostle is supposed to glance at the whole compass of time; that is to say, his prophetic sight, not being bounded to one given period, is free to range over the full measure of the universe. Beginning, (chap. iv.,) at the throne of God in heaven, whence proceed all things, he describes the celestial Court. Herein, (chap. v.,) is found the Book of seven seals, the volume of the mysterious decrees of divine Providence, which can only be loosed by the Lamb of God; wherefore Him, the crucified, do all the company of heaven praise and adore. One after another, the seals are opened, (chap. vi.,) and the method of divine government is gradually unfolded. But, chap. vii., before the solution is finished, or the last seal is opened, the elect are numbered and marked out from all the ages of time. The last seal is opened; (chap. viii.;) the whole mystery of grace and mercy is declared; and thenceforth there remain seven angels, with trumpets, to publish the warnings of divine justice. They successively fulfil their office, (chap. viii. and ix.,) but before the seventh and last summons is ended, a mighty angel, (chap. x.,) who foretokens the end of time, cries aloud, and seven thunders, which follow at his voice, are sealed up, as if too high and awful for human comprehension. But he gives to John his book, and tells him he must prophesy again. Thereupon follows, (chap. xi.,) as if in episode, a history of the two witnesses who will be found on earth in the last days. Then the seventh angel sounds his trumpet, and the end is come; time is finished, and eternity is begun.

CHAPTER IV.

1 After these things I saw: and behold, a door open in heaven, and the first voice which I heard, was, as it were, of a trumpet speaking with me, saying: Come up hither, and I will show thee the things which must come to pass hereafter.

It was the privilege of blessed John, to look in upon heavenly things as by a door; but, in the end of this Part, it is written: "The temple of God was opened in heaven, and the ark of his testament was seen in heaven;" (chap. xi. v. 19,) as if to proceed from the beginning to the end of things, when the inmost and holiest court is opened to the elect. The voice, as of a trumpet, calls him with the tone of authority to survey all future time. Here it may be remarked again, that though the principal matter of the Apocalypse relates to the future, yet every item of the same, is not, therefore, necessarily restricted to some one particular date, subsequent to the times of St. John. A term, to which pertains the attribute of eternity, may be placed in the past or present, as well as in the future, (examples of which follow in this chapter,) and an amplitude of signification in this kind, seems to be authorized by those words in a previous chapter: (chap. i. v. 19:) "Write the things which thou hast seen, and which are, and which must be done hereafter." And, furthermore, a maxim or established principle of jurisprudence may be found in early, as well as in later, periods of divine government, so that some passages seem not only to admit, but to demand, that the analogy be extended in either direction indefinitely, so long as proportion and fitness are observed.

2 And immediately I was in the spirit: and behold, there was a throne set in heaven, and one sitting upon the throne.

3 And he that sat was to the sight like the jasper and the sardine stone: and there was a rainbow round about the throne, in sight like unto an emerald.

He beholds the throne of God, filled by the presence of the Father Almighty, the Creator of heaven and earth. The jasper, of various colors, may denote the many works of the Creator, and the sardine stone, red, may signify the justice of God. The rainbow, the sign of reconciliation, and, like an emerald, or the color which signifies benignity, shows that "mercy and truth have met each other; justice and peace have kissed."

It is proved by theologians, that though man, while he lives this mortal life, cannot see God, yet he may be so elevated or abstracted from the flesh, as to attain even to the vision of the divine essence. Thus the apostle of the Gentiles was wrapt to the third heaven, and "heard secret words which it is not lawful for man to utter;" by which is understood the vision of the Blessed, which cannot be participated by those in the natural life. Now St. Thomas[1] shows, that this vision can only be by the intellective power, and not by any species or similitude whatever. Accordingly, he ranks this vision of the Apocalypse as the *visio imaginaria,* and below the intellectual vision. John was in the spirit, in ecstasy, but *raptus* superadds to this, says the angelic Doctor, a certain violence. It seems, therefore, that the apostle does not, in this revelation, behold the essence of God in itself; nor would it be in place, for then, there would remain the "things unutterable," which are no matter for tradition nor discourse.

4 And round about the throne were four-and-twenty seats: and upon the seats four-and-twenty ancients sitting, clothed in white garments, and golden crowns on their heads.

A type of the twenty-four ancients was the order of twenty-four courses of priests, called princes of the sanctuary; as instituted by king Solomon in the temple. The apostle would naturally employ much of the symbolism of the ancient dispensation, which was fulfilled, but not destroyed, by the new testament. Another instance is obtained, by add-

[1] Sum. Theo. 1,1, 12, 11; et 2,2, 175, 3. St. Aug. De Gen. 12, 26.

ing to the twelve patriarchs, the princes of Israel, the twelve apostles the princes of the church. Or, if the four gospels be multiplied by the work of six days, the time of this earthly pilgrimage, we have the number twenty-four: which may represent the sacred Doctors who labor in the word of God.

5 And from the throne proceeded lightnings, and voices, and thunderings: and there were seven lamps burning before the throne, which are the seven spirits of God.

From the throne of God proceed the light of truth, the counsels of wisdom, and the fearful warnings of judgment. The angel Raphael, as is related in the book of Tobias, is "one of the seven who stand before the Lord." As the king is always attended by the officers of his household, so like lamps ever burning the angels wait at the throne of their Lord.

6 And before the throne there was, as it were, a sea of glass like crystal; and, in the midst of the throne, and round about the throne, were four living creatures, full of eyes before and behind.

The assemblage of the heavenly hosts is spread before the throne of God, like a sea; whose pure intelligence admits no shadow nor doubt, but reveals, in its crystal depths, the light of absolute, unchanging truth.

Much has been written about the four living creatures, who are described also in the prophecy of Ezechiel. Some would have them to be angels, and object to the interpretation which would refer them to the four evangelists, because St. John was yet living, and therefore his place was elsewhere. But hereupon they fall into another difficulty; for, in chap. v., verse 9, the four creatures adore the Lamb, saying, "Thou hast *redeemed* us;" which is the language of the human, rather than of the angelic, race. If those described by Ezechiel will apply to the four evangelists, so John, in prophetic vision, might see the same thing; and we could suppose, either in the simplicity of his heart, he was ignorant of his own honors, since he observed the precept, "Let not thy left hand know what thy right hand doeth," or, if conscious of them, the "grace of God was sufficient" to preserve him from motions of pride.

7 And the first living creature like to a lion, and the second living creature like to a calf, and the third living creature having the face, as it were, of a man; and the fourth living creature was like to an eagle flying.

Sublime was the office of the holy evangelists, because, in the four gospels alone, are recorded the words spoken by our Lord Jesus Christ in his divine person. Therefore they may be said to be in the midst of the throne, because he himself occupies the substance of their labors; and round about the throne, because it was their immediate office to record and publish his divine acts. Having the face of a man, because they describe the Creator as a man in the midst of his creatures; of a calf, as the emblem of sacrifice; of a lion, as one who cries in the desert, warning men of the judgments of God; of an eagle, because they lead to the vision of God. Others have extended the analogy to the four doctors of the Latin Church:—St. Gregory, like a man for his condescension and human kindness; St. Ambrose, a lion for his fearlessness; St. Jerome, laborious as the ox, was also a victim for the love of penance; St. Augustine, like the eagle, soars in intellect, and gazes upon the sun of wisdom. So in the beginning, we may call Adam the man, the type of all his race; Noe, the lion, who fought single-handed a wicked world, and summoned it to penance. Abraham, as a priest, was ready to shed the blood of his own son. Moses came to the heights of Sinai, where it is written, "The Lord spoke to Moses face to face."

8 And the four living creatures had each of them six wings; and round about and within they are full of eyes. And they rested not day and night, saying, Holy, holy, holy, Lord God Almighty, who was, and who is, and who is to come.

To follow, however, the tradition which is sustained by the authority of the Roman Breviary, in its office for the evangelists, the four living creatures are no other than they who were inspired to record the words spoken by the lips of the living God. By the dignity of their office, they are among the prophets like winged seraphim at his throne. Through them is his fourfold virture declared; of temperance, in mercifully condescending to bear, in the flesh, the load of our human infirmities; of fortitude, in vindicating lowly virtue and rebuking hypocrisy; of justice, in shedding his sacred blood for the sins of men; of prudence, in imparting to the rational soul the light which may lead it to eternal life. In their pages is found the eternal truth, from which nothing can lie hid; whose all-seeing eye reads the secrets of the heart within, and the works without; which is watchful to every good, which is vigilant against every thought of evil. St. Matthew, therefore, beginning with his human generation; St. Mark, with the loud summons to prepare the way of the Lord; St. Luke, with his priestly dignity; and St. John, with his divinity, are they who proclaim the thrice holy Lord God Almighty.

9 And when these living creatures gave glory, and honor, and benediction to him that sitteth on the throne, who liveth forever and ever,

10 The four-and-twenty ancients fell down before him that sitteth on the throne, and adored him that liveth forever and ever, and cast their crowns before the throne, saying:

11 Thou art worthy, O Lord our God, to receive glory, and honor, and power: because thou hast created all things; and for thy will they were and have been created.

Through these four, the revelation of the Most Holy Trinity having been published for the four quarters of the whole earth, the multiplication of these numbers, three and four, gives twelve; which may signify, therefore, the vocation or instruction of the Creator to his creatures. And, as the holy child Jesus was twelve years of age, when he first sat in the temple and instructed the doctors; so his apostles, our teachers in the faith, are twelve. But again this vocation of the

Creator is twofold, being both old and new, a former and a latter testament of his holy law. Accordingly, the company of his prophets (leaving apart the four, whose copious writings are adorned with historical or didactic matter of inspiration) are counted as twelve. And thus their united numbers, the foundation of the apostles and prophets, upon which the people of God are built, may be represented by twenty-four. While, then, the four living creatures declare the glory of God, so the united company of our fathers in the faith, render to him of whom all paternity in heaven and earth is named, the homage of their crowns, the gifts which they have received from his bounty, and praise him, because he hath created all things, and because he doth, and ever will, dispose of his creatures in a manner worthy of his paternal love, or glorious to his sovereign majesty.

CHAPTER V.

1 And I saw, in the right hand of him that sat on the throne, a book written within and without, sealed with seven seals.

In God's own hand, is the eternal law, by which are ruled all things in heaven, on earth, and in hell; which "reacheth from end to end mightily, and ordereth all things sweetly." The book is written within and without, because of the overflowing multitude and magnitude of his works. Quam magnificata sunt opera tua Domine![1] It is sealed with sevenfold mystery, for "how incomprehensible are his judgments, and how unsearchable his ways!" He is full of benignity and compassion, and yet hatred and cruelty are found in his domain. Wide as the heavens is the difference between good and evil, and yet souls, made in his image, know not the one from the other; but call good evil and evil good. He is omnipotent, and yet his power is trampled in the dust. He is a Father, who loves even to death,

[1] Psalms xci. 6.

and he looks on while his creatures are sinking in the pit of hell. Who shall answer for this mystery? Where is the account of this strange contradiction?

2 And I saw a strong angel, proclaiming, with a loud voice: Who is worthy to open the book, and to loose the seals thereof?

3 And no man was able, neither in heaven, nor in earth, nor under the earth, to open the book, nor to look on it.

A strong angel asks this dread question, for no common intelligence is able to contemplate it. But too often it happens that reason perishes in the attempt; is tossed, shipwrecked, and lost, only for approaching it rashly.

4 And I wept much, because no man was found worthy to open the book, nor to see it.

By no skill or power, of created wisdom or virtue, shall one be able to read the inscrutable judgments of God; much less to translate them for the common discourse. And in this lonely and desert land, the just man cries: "My tears have been my bread day and night, whilst it is said to me daily: Where is thy God."

5 And one of the ancients said to me: Weep not; behold, the Lion of the tribe of Judah, the root of David, hath conquered to open the book, and to loose the seven seals thereof.

In the ancient dispensation, it was the office of the Precursor, to announce the Lamb of God who taketh away the sins of the world; which sacred function, however, was fulfilled in the latter dispensation, by the Prince of the Apostles, who first plainly confessed the divinity of Christ among men.

6 And I saw: and behold, in the midst of the throne, and of the four living creatures, and in the midst of the ancients, a Lamb standing as it were slain, having seven horns and seven eyes; which are the seven spirits of God, sent forth into all the earth.

"Omnia in sapientia fecisti; thou hast made all things in wisdom. Therefore,[1] says St. Augustine, thou hast made

[1] Psalms ciii. 24.

all things in Christ. He, the despised one, the buffeted, spit upon, crowned with thorns, the crucified one, in him thou hast made all things." The cross of Christ is the answer to every sorrow, and every scandal. The wolf rends the lamb, and the lamb is more dear to the memory than ever before. Innocence is oppressed, and cold hearts are kindled to fervent zeal and love. Virtue proved perfect by adversity: and good wrought out of evil: this is the divine merit, and the reason of all that is done under the sun. And this pure reason of things human, appeals so powerfully to the soul, that in every one there is a response to that eternal truth of the cross. Silent, neglected, half suffocated it may be, but in the secrets of the conscience, it will not be belied. It is the most precious and sacred, the most divinely blessed, among all the emanations of the wisdom of God. It is the key of heaven, the spring of merit, the salt of eternal life; the contradictory of every possible appearance of false joy, of empty honors, of perishable treasures. Searching out, from the depths of his riches, this precious gift, God has given it to fallen man for his ever-present consolation, and infallible remedy in all this vale of tears. And then, as if ravished with the beauty of his work, he has stooped down to earth, and has made himself a folly to all the sons of pride, that he might seize it for his own, and bear it back to heaven, with new honors and a greater glory. In the midst, then, of the throne, and in the heart of all the saints, stands, all lovely, the Lamb of God; who sends through all the world his heavenly messengers of truth and grace, to break the pride or melt the heart of man. Conquassabit capita in terra multorum.[1] Oculi ejus sicut columbæ, super rivulos aquarum.[2]

7 And he came, and took the book out of the right hand of him that sat on the throne.

8 And when he had opened the book, the four living creatures, and the four-and-twenty ancients fell down before the Lamb, having

[1] Psalms cix. 6. [2] Cant. v. 12.

every one of them harps, and golden vials full of odors, which are the prayers of the saints.

The book is opened by him that was crucified; and the fruits of the cross, the songs of the saints, and the sweet odor of their virtues, outweigh all losses in the wreck of this dull earth.

9 And they sung a new canticle, saying: Thou art worthy, O Lord, to take the book, and to open the seals thereof: because thou wast slain, and hast redeemed us to God in thy blood, out of every tribe, and tongue, and people, and nation.

10 And thou hast made us to our God a kingdom, and priests: and we shall reign on the earth.

This is a new song in heaven, when the most high God is praised for his lowly obedience; and because he has proved, by his own example, that nothing which befalls the just man, can be degrading to him, nor detrimental of his true good; and that, in all his universe, there is no scandal nor condemnation for the soul which keeps his grace. It is a new song, because it is as if some new thing were invented for the delight of heaven, when the souls of the just are by his redemption received into the society of the angels; and thenceforth obtain a royal authority and a sacerdotal dignity, to bestow celestial graces, and from heaven to rule the hearts of men; guiding their lives in the communion of the saints, and governing their acts to the greater glory of God.

Thus far, the account of the seeming contradiction in the works of God, is plain to the common understanding. But, if one would go farther, and think to search out that divine reason of things, which transcends the measure of human intelligence and of the common consent; then, does he not thrust himself rashly into that presence of which it is written, "The searcher of majesty shall be overwhelmed by glory"? The natural religion teaches the omnipotence of God. The Christian revelation teaches his infinite goodness; for, by the Cross is proved, not so much the difficulty of salvation, as the infinite love with which a God desires it for his creatures.

Now these premises being given, of the power and good-will of the Creator, if, at the same time, the happiness of his creatures does not follow, what is the conclusion for a rational mind? That there is no reason in the works of God? that he creates some absolutely for their own torment? that, like a despot he acts without any order and method? Or, on the contrary, will he not rather conclude, that there is, in the wisdom of the Creator, a higher and a better reason, than he, in his littleness, can comprehend? Here is the difference between the believer and the infidel. The one confesses all and more than he can understand; the other imputes a defection to his Maker, and so renounces what little understanding he himself possessed. The one, obedient to the grace of God, is satisfied that there must be, and is, a motive so good, so infinitely wise and holy, that it passes all the thought and imagination of man; the other, being abandoned to his folly, knows even less than before, and his natural capacities are thenceforward contracted, darkened, and defaced.

But again, it may be argued: Suppose there is this higher reason or motive in the ordination of the works of God; yet the Apostle of the Gentiles plainly teaches that this motive itself is the will of God; and the will of God itself is the principle and the cause of his absolute decrees. But, even so, the will of God is infinitely good, and therefore all which is conformed to it is good, and all which contradicts it is bad; and hence, if one would not be at variance with it, let him first take care that he do not injure it, even by a suspicion; lest it be, to his intelligence, like the iron rod against the potter's vessel. But furthermore, the man of understanding, who seeks not to divide the truth but to hold it in its integrity, cannot forget that the will of God, is the goodness of God, as well as the power of God.[1] That its infinite

[1] The will of God is the cause of things. And of his will there is no cause; as also of his knowledge, or power, there cannot be a cause. But as, by one act of his intelligence, he knows all things, so, in his goodness, he wills all things. In human acts, the knowledge is the cause as directing; the will is the cause as commanding; the power is the cause as executing. But, in God, all these are one. (Sum. Theo. i. 19. 4 & 5.)

virtue reaches from end to end, and is extended to the meanest, as well as the best, of all that is in existence. That it cannot be divorced from his wisdom, nor from his justice, nor his mercy, nor his knowledge, nor his sanctity, nor his glory; but that, whatever proceeds from it, must needs redound to his own sacred honor, or to the happiness of his elect, or even in hell, to be constrained by it is something better than the reprobate have deserved.

Now this has been abundantly proved for our instruction, by the passion and cross of the Lamb of God. He, the Word of God, has laid aside his omnipotence, to prove to men the very excess of his love. He, the Wisdom of God, has become the victim of the ignorance or malice of his creatures. He, the just Judge of men, is himself our Advocate: "And he is the propitiation for our sins; and not for ours only, but also for those of the whole world."[1]

11 And I saw and I heard the voice of many angels round about the throne, and the living creatures, and the ancients: and the number of them was thousands of thousands.

12 Saying, with a loud voice: Worthy is the Lamb that was slain to receive power, and divinity, and wisdom, and strength, and honor, and glory, and benediction.

What is salvation for man is joy for the angels; and the full chorus of heaven joins to praise, as is due, the divine Redeemer of our race.

13 And every creature which is in heaven, and on the earth, and under the earth, and such as are in the sea, and the things that are therein, I heard all saying: To him that sitteth on the throne, and to the Lamb, benediction, and honor, and glory, and power, forever and ever.

14 And the four living creatures said, Amen: and the four-and-twenty ancients fell down on their faces, and adored him that liveth forever.

The mystery is ended. All blessings have come to men; the joy of angels is consummated, and every created thing

[1] 1 John ii. 2.

receives new lustre from the Lamb of God, and the union perfect and indissoluble, of the Creator and the creature. Thus, to the Lamb of God, is here ascribed, in the unity of the Father Almighty, the supreme worship of the created universe. And all the praises of the ancient psalmist, calling upon angels and men, upon the beasts of the earth, the mountains, and the deeps, and every element, to praise the Lord, all which is due to the Sovereign Godhead, is here rendered, with solemn form and purpose, to the majesty of our blessed Redeemer; who, with the Father and the Holy Ghost, liveth and reigneth one God, world without end. Amen.

CHAPTER VI.

IT has been already observed, that the book of seven seals is the volume of divine mysteries; a relation, or a vindication of the administration of the eternal decrees; such as creation, redemption, and election; or, in a word, the story of God's dealings with his creatures, in respect of their salvation. Also, it is manifest that Christ crucified, or the Lamb slain, is the key of this sacred enigma; thus common tradition pictures it, from the lofty cathedral window, to the humble print of the Christian cottage. In this chapter, the book is opened; and because it was written above, (chap. v. verse 8,) "when he had opened the book, etc.," it need not be supposed that there is any discrepancy in the historical account of the action. But it may be observed: The grand difficulty of the rational soul is sin, and its adequate solution is the blood of the Lamb. A fact of such dignity is plainly sufficient in itself, and deserves to stand alone, as we find it in the chapter just past.

But, if we would view the same thing under other aspects, and would subject it to a more detailed examination, we naturally divide the argument into its three terms, the beginning, middle, and end; or the preparation, the consummation, and the consequences. And this division is also warranted by the disposition of the sacred text. The book, or volume rolled up, is sealed with seven seals. Not without labor, nor instantaneously, but with reverent preparation, and with due delays, are the seals unloosed; and when, at length, the last is opened, (chap. viii.,) there is the silence of a crisis, a consummation of import awful and unutterable; afterwards follows the conclusion of this mighty scene, and the end of all things.

1 And I saw that the Lamb had opened one of the seven seals; and I heard one of the four living creatures, saying, as with a voice of thunder, Come thou, and see.

One of the four living creatures, or the first one, is he who, with the loud voice, as of a lion, cries, "Prepare ye the way of the Lord;" who heralds "the Lion of the tribe of Judah;" "the Lord strong and mighty."

2 And I saw, and behold, a white horse; and he that sat upon him had a bow, and a crown was given to him; and he went forth conquering, that he might conquer.

In the beginning is Christ, the sovereign Lord of angels and of men; who is white with the lustre of eternity; and is crowned with victory. "The Lord hath reigned; he is clothed with beauty; the Lord is clothed with strength, and hath girded himself."[1] St. Augustine, in his City of God,[2] considers an interesting question, in this wise: How shall we say that the Lord God was ever Lord (*Dominus*,) when as yet there was no creature or subject in his dominion? If before heaven and earth were created, we suppose some time, not marked by hours and days, but depending on some mutable movement, mutabili motu, of which the priority passes, and the sequel follows, so that they are not at one and the same time, and if thus the angelic beings were constituted; it would seem that they have been in all time, since with them time itself was made. And if they have been in every time, why

[1] Psalms xcii. [2] L. xii. c. 15.

not say they have always been? But hereupon it may be asked: Why then are they not coeternal with the Creator, if they and he have always been? Perhaps it may be answered, they have always been, and yet have been created. As the times themselves have been made, and yet in every time there have been times, so, in every time, there may have been angels, who were made with the times, and without whom there was not any time. It cannot be denied that, in every time, there has been time, otherwise there would be a time, when there was no time, which is absurd. And there can be no times where there are no creatures whatever, whose mutations mark the time. If then they have always been, they have been created; nor, because they have always been, would they be coeternal with the Creator. For he has always been from eternity immutable. But they are said to have been always, because they are in every time; now time which passes with mutation, cannot be coeternal with eternity which is immutable. Wherefore, if the Lord God has always had creatures or subjects under his dominion, he was yet always before them, and preceding not by any space of transition, but in enduring perpetuity. The Holy Father [1] admits that this is a question too lofty for our human understanding; but it may help us to form a better idea of the sublimity of God's creation, and while we consider how vast and ponderous are the ages of ages which rest on us, we shall, with deeper reverence and awe, weigh well that formidable end, for which Christians have watched, with sleepless vigilance, in every generation. To return: Christ, the Sovereign Lord, crowned King of angels and of men, who rides forth in spotless purity, himself pure, his own works pure; who, with far-reaching bow, sends his mandate through all the bounds of time, and who conquers the conquerors, ever victorious; this one, is here before us in the

[1] Some suppose that the creation of the angels is intended by the word *light:* "And God said, Be light made," others, by the word *heaven:* "In the beginning God created heaven;" which latter interpretation is the one most favored by St. Augustine.

first opening of the Book; as if to signify: "Thou hast given a warning to them that fear thee; that they may flee from before the bow." [1]

3 And when he had opened the second seal, I heard the second living creature saying: Come thou, and see.

The second living creature, like to a calf, or victim for sacrifice, announces Christ the Savior of men, himself the High Priest, and Victim for their sins. For the fallen angels there is no sacrifice, nor shedding of blood, nor any redemption; but for fallen man there is abundant atonement, and full satisfaction for every soul.

4 And there went out another horse that was red: and it was granted to him who sat thereon to take away peace from the earth, and that they should kill one another: and to him was given a great sword.

Truly this is no other than he of whom it is written: Quare rubrum est indumentum tuum — "Why is thy apparel red, and thy garments like theirs that tread in the wine press? I have trodden the wine-press alone, and of the Gentiles there is not a man with me: I have trampled on them in my indignation, and their blood is sprinkled on my garments." [2] And who saith: "Do not think that I came to send peace upon the earth: I came not to send peace, but the sword." [3] Because there can be no friendship between truth and error, because, however ready the world may be to patronize virtue, virtue herself has no word of praise for folly; because right and wrong will not be reconciled; blood must flow. This earth is the battle-field; and he who did not interpose when angels fought in heaven, who is the Lord of Hosts, "mighty in battle," has chosen it for his place of combat, and watered it with his own blood. And while it is the most grievous of crimes to shed innocent blood, so to suffer in a just cause unto blood, is the most glorious and heroic of meritorious works. Thus is divine justice satisfied; and thus is the judgment of

[1] Ps. lix. 4. [2] Isaiah lxiii. 2. [3] Matthew x. 34.

men convinced; and whereas, before, their mind rusted in sordid peace, with the noise of war, it is restored to the freshness of youth; a noble ardor, and a generous purpose inspire the heart; and while life itself is sacrificed, there is occasion for the man of good will to pay, unto the Sovereign Lord of Life, an act of supreme worship, the most lovely and sublime of all, after that of the Divine Sacrifice.

5 And when he had opened the third seal, I heard the third living creature saying: Come thou, and see. And, behold, a black horse; and he that sat on him had a pair of scales in his hand.

The third living creature, having the face of a man, describes him who was seen among men, as the "Man of sorrows," in whom there was "no beauty nor comeliness: and we have seen him, and there was no sightliness that we should be desirous of him."[1]

6 And I heard as it were a voice, in the midst of the four living creatures, saying: Two pounds of wheat for a penny, and thrice two pounds of barley for a penny; and wine, and oil, hurt thou not.

The prices and measures here mentioned, signify what would be strictly sufficient for the support of a man, after the just labor of a day's time, so that he might have exactly what were enough and no more. Thus he, who "hath ordered all things in measure, and number, and weight," before whom "the whole world is as the least grain of the balance," when he comes on earth, appears in the dark robe of poverty. He was able to multiply the little loaves to be the food of thousands, and yet he gathers up the broken fragments that there may be no waste. Here again, in this Master of the house, the divine Œconomus, do we find the cardinal virtue of temperance illustrated in his own labor and his scant reward. Thus, too, the good pastor, his disciple, as a voice from the midst of the four living creatures, or by the common testimony of the holy evangelists, is found in sombre garb before the world; merciful and indulgent, but

[1] Isaiah lxiii. 2.

just at the same time, and dispensing, with a guarded hand, the treasures of divine grace. Again, the divine Providence which distributes to each one according to his necessities, and divides rigorously his rewards, according to the deserts of those who observe his precepts, deals liberally with them who love his counsels of perfection; and, if he is careful of his coarser goods, most tenderly and jealously does he guard his wine and oil, the precious and abundant merits of his saints.

7 And when he had opened the fourth seal, I heard the voice of the fourth living creature, saying: Come thou, and see.

The fourth living creature, like to an eagle flying, designates the divinity of Christ; or the things which are above and beyond the testimony of sense, whither no man can come but by the way of death.

8 And behold a pale horse: and he that sat upon him, his name was Death, and hell followed after him; and power was given to him over the four parts of the earth, to kill with sword, with famine, and with death, and with the beasts of the earth.

Our divine Savior is the living God, in his death, as well as in his life. And he is able to endure persecution and poverty, and the name of death itself, without loss. Or, it may be said, that, of all accidents, this of death, the "maximus terrorum," is eminently in his own power. In this dispensation, is the great lesson of prudence manifest. He who remembers it will never sin. To suffer in war is honorable, to suffer in poverty is a more humble lot, but in pallid death all distinctions are swept away, every light of consolation, or of human estimation, is quenched; "the death of man and of beast is one, and the condition of them both is equal."[1] The power of death is seen over all the earth and over all men. In forms innumerable, in shapes cruel and fearful, in times and manners doubtful and sudden; but inevitably and decisively, the sentence falls at last on every

[1] Eccle. iii. 19.

one. The entrance to life is difficult and uncertain, but for the egress what facility, what trifles give the opportunity! And yet how inexplicable! for, of all the human race, there is not one who has solved this mystery, nor has given us any account of it, except the One who overrides death, and drags hell itself captive after him.

9 And when he had opened the fifth seal, I saw, under the altar, the souls of them that were slain for the word of God, and for the testimony which they held.

If the dispensations of divine Providence, by which he appoints suffering and death, are marvellous, much more do we wonder in considering the cruel torments with which he permits his chosen ones to be tried, above all other men. Having suffered in testimony of the truth, their place is nearest to the cross, as if under its shadow; that is, their merits are joined with those of their divine Master, and are contained, as it were, in the altar of his own sacrifice.

10 And they cried, with a loud voice, saying, How long, O Lord, holy and true, dost thou not judge and revenge our blood on them that dwell on the earth?

St. Paul, the apostle, says, "The expectation of the creature waiteth for the revelation of the sons of God."[1] If the natural instinct even groans and sighs for a sign from heaven, how much more does the blood of holy martyrs plead for justice, and for the vindication of insulted truth! Kindled with indignation at the obstinacy of the Samaritan city, the disciples said, "Lord, wilt thou that we command fire to come down from heaven and consume them?" But it was answered to them; "The Son of man came not to destroy souls, but to save."[2]

11 And white stoles were given to each of them one; and it was said to them, that they should rest yet, for a little time, till their fellow servants and their brethren, who were to be slain even as they, should be filled up.

[1] Romans viii. 19. [2] Luke ix. 54.

If thus we can be instructed in the unbounded goodness and long-suffering of God ; if, in any way and at any cost, men can be brought to meditate his unwearied patience and mercy, the lesson shall even be repeated ; and he is able to furnish others of his servants, who will with joy fill up the number of his martyrs. Blessed are they who are not scandalized by these wonders of divine Providence, and whom "the benignity of God leadeth to penance ; " but much more they who resist temptation unto death, whose heroic merits obtain the heavenly honors, and abound to the welfare of their fellow-servants on earth.

12 And I saw when he had opened the sixth seal ; and, behold, there was a great earthquake ; and the sun became black as sack-cloth of hair ; and the whole moon became as blood.

According as the seals are loosed, the crisis approaches ; the mystery deepens, and wonder rises. It is a homely saying, that the greatest wonder would be if there were no wonders. Even so in divine things ; miracle answers miracle ; and by prodigy is prodigy solved ; and the inquisitive mind is put to silence by the exhibition of truths still more impenetrable. All the cries of suffering man are hushed before the sorrows of Jesus Christ. Can God permit his own creature to be afflicted ? Christ answers with his own tears. Can he suffer cruel injustice to strike the innocent man ? He shows his own bleeding side. Which is better, the benefactor's kind word, or his precious blood ? His strong arm and swift rescue, or his own sacred heart and his life for his friend ? Truly it is strange that man can fight against his brother, or rob the poor, or stone the prophet ; but that he should defy the most high God, and despise him in his need, and laugh at his agony, O dreadful thought ! Can we think the sin of mighty angels so grievous as this of man, the last of God's works, the poor little child of dust, with whom the Creator had thought to find his delight and sweet divertisement ?

If, by this sixth seal, be understood the passion of Christ, the words will bear even a literal interpretation. "The earth quaked, and the rocks were rent."[1] "And there was darkness over all the earth." "And the sun was darkened."[2] So that the wise pagan[3] (blessed by God) exclaimed, "Either the God of nature is in pain, or this earth is falling to destruction." Or, allegorically, it may be said, the sun became black when the light of divine goodness seemed extinguished, and "Jesus cried, with a loud voice, Deus meus, Deus meus, ut quid dereliquisti me." And the moon, or the Jewish Church, became as blood, when it was desecrated by the people who said, "His blood be upon us and upon our children."

13 And the stars from heaven fell upon the earth, as the fig-tree casteth its green figs when it is shaken by a great wind.

Thus, with the first blast of that dreadful storm, the disciples "leaving him, all fled away." And St. Peter, that rock and fortress of the truth, suddenly crumbles to the earth, and denies him even as do the others.

14 And the heaven withdrew as a book rolled up together, and every mountain and the islands were moved out of their places.

When, having descended upon earth to converse with men, the voice of God was drowned in the shouts of the ungrateful people, crying, "Crucify him," all heavenly communication was made void, and truth itself seemed to have failed on high. While on earth, every mountain and island, every pillar and refuge of salvation, seemed to be disturbed from its foundation.

15 And the kings of the earth, and the princes, and the tribunes, and the rich men, and the strong men, and every bond man, and every free man, hid themselves in the dens and in the rocks of the mountains.

As soon as our Lord was born in Bethlehem, the cruel Herod began to be transported with fear; the wife of Pontius Pilate saw terrible visions, and he himself with anguish

[1] St. Matthew. [2] St. Luke. [3] St. Denis.

desired to wash publicly his hands of the sin of blood; and all the multitude who witnessed the passion of Jesus Christ, and "saw the things that were done, returned, striking their breasts;" and only with the hearing of such things, Felix, the governor, was "terrified," and sent Paul away from his presence. Thus have we seen how every heart, in every age, from the mightiest king to the poorest slave, will quail before the cross of Christ; and, if not aided by divine grace, will shrink back into the den, the darkness of its own guilty conscience; and harden itself in gloomy pride, or cold despair.

16 And they say to the mountains and to the rocks: Fall upon us, and hide us from the face of him that sitteth upon the throne, and from the wrath of the Lamb:

17 For the great day of their wrath is come; and who shall be able to stand?

In their miserable delusion, how fearful to the wicked, is the presence of him who came to save them! In their insane terror they fly from the very haven of safety. Thus the sufferings of Jesus Christ smite the disobedient with the dread of speedy judgment and deserved wrath.

CHAPTER VII.

AFTER night, cometh the morning. Ad vesperam demorabitur fletus: et ad matutinum lætitia.[1] The sorrows of our blessed Lord have gained for men light and joy everlasting. From the noble tree of the Cross, is obtained fruit for heaven, how fair and various, how abundant and perennial! Nulla silva talem profert, fronde, flore, germine. In this chapter are described the children of God begotten in Jesus Christ, who take their life from his merits, and who, therefore, follow and depend upon his sacred passion. The sixth seal

[1] Psalms xxix. 6.

being the passion, and the seventh, the death of Christ, here is the place for their enumeration, because the former being the sufficient cause of our salvation, the latter is not the cause by way of merit, properly speaking, but by way of the effecting it, per modum efficientiæ, as St. Thomas[1] shows; salvation being gained by his passion, and whatever remains contrary to its adeption being removed by his death; such as our own deaths of body and of soul.

1 After these things I saw four angels standing on the four corners of the earth, holding the four winds of the earth, that they should not blow upon the earth, nor upon the sea, nor on any tree.

By the ministration of his angels, God tenderly guards his elect, and defends them against the storms which malignant spirits would raise up on every side.

2 And I saw another angel ascending from the rising of the sun, having the seal of the living God: and he cried with a loud voice to the four angels, to whom it was given to hurt the earth and the sea.

3 Saying: Hurt not the earth, nor the sea, nor the trees, till we seal the servants of our God in their foreheads.

Yet another angel is added, as if to make their safety still more assured. Men are astonished at the multitude of human ills, but are insensible to the thousand perils, from which they are incessantly rescued only by the goodness of their Creator and his holy angels. This is the region of storms, a land of wild disorder, and, so far forth, it is not the work of God, but rather it is by his restraining hand, that the tempest of evil passions does not sweep all into perdition. The earth, the sea, the trees, may signify that no perils, by land or sea, nor any temptations will overcome the elect soul, however frail, if he have the grace of God. Or the earth may be the circumcised, the sea, the baptized; the trees, which are the first to suffer in the storms, the prophets and prelates of the people of God. There is a tradition that St. Francis of Assissium was revealed in the angel having the seal (*stigmata*) of the living God.

[1] Sum. Theol. iii. 50. 6.

And there can be no doubt that his office was, like this of the angel, to stay the divine anger, so that allegorically, at least, the application is just. But it would seem more congruent to understand, by the angel ascending from the rising of the sun, some heavenly spirit, the vicegerent of the Orient from on high; who marks his servants with the sign of the Redeemer, which is that of the cross, or the *signaculum gratiæ,* [1] prefigured by the letter *Thau,* as described in the prophecy of Ezechiel. [2] And in their foreheads: as being manifestly to others and consciously to themselves, the servants of God. And St. Michael, the patron angel of the people of God, seems to be thus indicated in the Breviary.[3]

4 And I heard the numbers of them that were sealed, a hundred forty-four thousand sealed of all the tribes of the children of Irsael.

Some writers have labored to find a special application for the numbers here mentioned, as if their place were in the primitive times of the church, or in its last days, when the Jews are to be converted. But as we read this lesson (from the second to the twelfth verse) in the Mass of All Saints, who doubts that the whole company of the elect, from all ages, is intended? In the former dispensation, we naturally, if not necessarily, conceive of the faithful as a marked and chosen race, a given number, so to speak; but, in the latter, as a multitude indefinite.

5 Of the tribe of Juda, twelve thousand sealed; of the tribe of Reuben twelve thousand sealed; of the tribe of Gad twelve thousand sealed.

6 Of the tribe of Aser, twelve thousand sealed; of the tribe of Nepthali, twelve thousand sealed; of the tribe of Manasses, twelve thousand sealed.

7 Of the tribe of Simeon, twelve thousand sealed; of the tribe of Levi, twelve thousand sealed; of the tribe of Issachar, twelve thousand sealed.

[1] Sum. Theol. iii. 63. 3. [2] Ezechiel ix. 4.

[3] Sep. 29. ant. Dum sacrum, ad magnificat.

8 Of the tribe of Zabulon, twelve thousand sealed; of the tribe of Joseph, twelve thousand sealed; of the tribe of Benjamin, twelve thousand sealed.

As was remarked above, the people of God, before the year of grace, were as if a limited number. The numerals here employed, are such as signify, withal, the perfection or totality of the chosen race. The number one thousand stands for perfection, because ten are the commandments; and the ten being squared (cubically) or carried to perfection, gives one thousand. Three are the persons of the blessed Trinity, which, multiplied by four, gives twelve; and, in the faith of the Trinity, either implicit or explicit, are the elect called, from out of the four quarters of the earth. Thus the one hundred and forty-four thousand is the universality or perfect whole of the saints in the first ages.

9 After this, I saw a great multitude which no man could number, of all nations, and tribes, and peoples, and tongues, standing before the throne, and in sight of the Lamb, clothed with white robes, and palms in their hands.

Who can declare the number of those who have been predestined from eternity to immortal life? It is written of that life: "Few there are who find it."[1] But, on the other hand, how fruitful are the merits of the omnipotent Redeemer, the Father of the world to come! "His work is praise and magnificence."[2] This is the seed of Abram, to whom the Lord said: "Look up to heaven, and number the stars if thou canst. And he said to him, So shall thy seed be."[3] Therefore the mind is lost in considering the numbers, the purity, and the glories of the saints.

10 And they cried with a loud voice, saying: Salvation to our God, who sitteth upon the throne, and to the Lamb.

As here, in this life, the just man makes an offering of himself, and of all that he has, to him from whom all has been received; so in heaven do the saints render back to

[1] St. Math. vii. 14. [2] Psalms cx. 3. [3] Gen. xv. 5.

Almighty God, that salvation which is the infinite gift of their beatitude; of which gift, also, he himself, the Divine Redeemer, is the essential principle; Tecum principium in die virtutis tuæ, in splendoribus sanctorum.[1]

11 And all the angels stood round about the throne, and about the ancients. and about the four living creatures; and they fell before the throne upon their faces, and adored God,

12 Saying: Amen. Benediction, and glory, and wisdom, and thanksgiving, honor and power, and strength to our God, forever and ever. Amen.

Thus, in the Apocalypse, are revealed not only things future, but the present happiness of the saints, the songs of the angels, and heaven itself is brought before us.

13 And one of the ancients answered, and said to me: Who are these that are clothed in white robes; and whence are they come?

The question thus interposed attracts the attention, and gives weight to the answer. In like manner, is related a vision which appeared, at the death of St. Benedict, to his disciples in a distant place. They saw a pathway from his cell, reaching into the heavens, by the way of the Orient, bespread with robes, and glittering with lights. A man of noble and venerable appearance, standing above it, asks them, "Whose path is this?" They, professing that they knew not, he says: "This is the way by which Benedict, beloved of God, ascendeth to heaven." Thus, by question and answer, are we best instructed in the things of God, which are "hid from the wise and prudent, and are revealed to little ones."[2]

14 And I said to him: My Lord, thou knowest. And he said to me: These are they who have come out of great tribulation, and have washed their robes, and have made them white in the blood of the Lamb.

15 Therefore they are before the throne of God, and serve him day and night in his temple; and he that sitteth on the throne shall dwell over them.

[1] Psalms cix. 3. [2] St. Matthew xi. 25.

16 They shall not hunger nor thirst any more; neither shall the sun fall on them, nor any heat;

17 For the Lamb, which is in the midst of the throne, shall rule them, and shall lead them to the fountains of the waters of life; and God shall wipe away all tears from their eyes.

According to the gospel, which is so beautifully joined with this lesson on the feast of All Saints, these are they of whom it is written: "Blessed are the poor in spirit, for theirs is the kingdom of heaven.[1] Blessed are the meek, for they shall possess the land. Blessed are they that mourn, for they shall be comforted. Blessed are they that hunger and thirst after justice, for they shall be filled." These are the merciful, the clean of heart, and the peace-makers. These are they that have suffered persecution for justice sake, "for theirs is the kingdom of heaven."

CHAPTER VIII.

1 AND when he had opened the seventh seal, there was silence in heaven, as it were for half an hour.

What dread event in all the bounds of time, could cause silence in heaven? What awful catastrophe could reach even to the throne of God, and hush the songs of paradise? Surely no other than the death of our Lord Jesus Christ.

It would seem to be the part of discretion to copy this sacred silence, and pass on; as does the apostle. But perhaps an attempt to satisfy some objections which might be raised, will make the justice of this interpretation more evident. It may be asked, why distinguish between the passion and the death of Christ, since the former was in the way to, or tended to, the latter? It may be answered, that no violence nor wounds could be the cause of his death, except by

[1] St. Matthew v. 3.

his own will; according to the words of the gospel: "No man taketh away my life from me, but I lay it down of myself." And in the second place, the sufferings, even of Christ, are less than his death. That the son of Mary should suffer persecution, appeared not impossible; but that the Lord of Christians should utterly fail and sink down visibly in the overwhelming waves, like the unfaithful prophet Jonas, this extinguished the last hope of his disciples, and they said mournfully: "We hoped that it was he who should have redeemed Israel." Death is the contradictory of life, and how could there be life in death? or how could death be the death of death? This of course is utterly inexplicable except by virtue of his divinity, indefectible and ever present with the dead, as well as the living body.

The martyr suffers, but dies at last the common death. St. Thecla was cast into fire, was exposed to wild beasts, was lashed to bulls, and drawn by them, and then thrown into a pit full of serpents, and yet was preserved by God, and lived unto her ninetieth year. But at length she dies and is seen no more of men. On the other hand, the Lord of martyrs suffers abundantly, and without any remedy, for the sins of men; and because this is not enough for his love, and that there may be no room for doubt, he lays down his life also, and is dead, and buried; that, as his sacred wounds were the satisfaction for the guilt, so his death should be the destruction of the death of his people, and their mortality be swallowed up in his victory.

The blessed martyrs prevail against every manner of fearful torment, except death; but this One alone, marvellous to relate, prevails over death itself. Therefore, to return, as every suffering is less than death, the passion of Christ, is less than the death of Christ. And if it be a noble thing to meet and prevail against the fire and the sword, it is of virtue sublime and infinite, to conquer death itself, and rise victorious over the grave. Thus by the miracle of miracles, terrible and lovely, is the Book of seven seals wide open laid.

Allegorically, the silence may represent the interval between the old and new Testaments; that Sabbath when our Lord rested in the grave, and when there was no visible appointed organ of religion, or established tribunal of truth.

Morally, the silence may signify the time of grace, "the acceptable time," when Heaven waits for the soul, balanced between good and evil, to make its choice of heaven or of hell; while divine Providence condescending to the delays of our human discourse, suspends the sentence of justice, and gives time for repentance. This, it may be suggested, is the rationale of certain portions of the office for St. Michael's day, which allude to his combat with the dragon, the adversary of the soul of man. In either case, the half-hour signifies some imperfoct or broken interval of time, as St. Gregory shows.

2 And I saw seven angels standing in the presence of God; and to them were given seven trumpets.

What is the relation of the seven trumpets, to the book of seven seals? Are they the contents, so to speak, of the volume, and flowing from it? or do they correspond severally to the seals? or what coherence, if any, is there with all that has gone before? It is to be observed: that, with the opening of the seals, certain ordinances are discovered to us, by which men are disciplined, instructed, and enabled effectually to attain unto eternal life. Now these are the contents of the volume, and with the unfolding itself of the same, they are discerned; and with the grace of God, they are both apprehended and appreciated. And all this grace of salvation is secured to us by the blood of the Lamb; this is the plain and sufficient solution of all the troubles of the human race; the key and the sum, the without and the within, of sacred mystery. And yet man is not contented and docile to the sweet yoke of truth, as the event has proved. What therefore remains, what can follow after the effusion of mercy, but the reprisals of justice? Knowing, as we do, that, with this generation of Christ, all things are to be fulfilled, the future of this transitory scene is a fruitful source of fears to the Christian. The worldling, indeed, infatuated with the foolish hope that it contains, in fact, the fleeting good he will one day grasp, promises progress and better things. But the believer already possesses the true good as a reality, a fact accomplished; even as blessed John heard the voice behind him, and looked back rather than forward, to behold the source of life and truth. The other waits upon it as yet to come, and is confident in the future; but, as his presumption mounts higher, so is his downfall nearer; and his boast is the wise man's terror. Therefore, it is to be expected, that now the heavenly communications shall come in louder and in trumpet tones; and from this forth, it can be no matter of surprise, if the voice of prophecy be portentous of danger, and of woe to a guilty world. Thus it seemed in apostolic times, it was so in the middle ages, it is the thought of many in this day.

Again, the seven trumpets are divided from the seven seals, by the personal interposition of the divine Redeemer, and both are to be referred respectively to him, rather than reciprocally among themselves. Domine, opus tuum, in medio annorum, notum facies.[1] He is the middle by right, in respect of which all else is merely relative. Wherever his age might fall in time, he is the centre and source, and all beside is either before Christ, or after Christ, on this side or on that. To borrow an illustration from the modern astronomy: The sun is the centre; whether our land be found in light or darkness, in heat or in cold, he is the enduring centre around which all others revolve. It seems, therefore, unnecessary to trace the analogy between the seals and the trumpets farther than to remark, first: That the number seven comprises the fulness of the divine dispensations, whether preceding or following upon the mystery of the cross. And secondly: That the latter are the counterpart of the former, inasmuch as the seals signify purposes obscure and indistinct, the trumpets open and public proclamations; the former veiled in mercy,

[1] Hab. iii. 2.

for the "times of ignorance," the latter published with manifest penalties; the former being such chastisement as might proceed from a father to a beloved son; the latter are the visitation of justice upon ungrateful subjects; the one in order to discipline, and without sin, such as the Son of God might share in person; the other in retribution of malice; the one corporal, the other spiritual, evils.

Thus, the opening of the seven seals, leads to the trumpets which peal the alarm of justice with seven-fold warning; and, if the transition appear at first to be abrupt, yet it is not without preparation, as is seen in what follows:

3 And another angel came and stood before the altar, having a golden censer; and there was given to him much incense, that he should offer of the prayers of all saints upon the golden altar, which is before the throne of God.

That is the golden altar, upon which has rested the ever-blessed, and alone-holy Victim, the Lamb of God. And it is written: the prayers of all saints, for every worthy and acceptable prayer and oblation of every creature, is offered up to God, through his creative Word. He hath drawn all things to himself, when he has been lifted up on the Altar of his Cross; for by this alone, are all things, from the utmost bounds of his created universe, restored to the porportions of Absolute Equity, and engaged to render endless glory to his divine Majesty. This is that altar, which from all eternity was designed to reconcile things new and old, things of good report and of evil report, things assured and things lost, the high and the low, the abject and the glorious. Verily, the cross of Christ is exceedingly honorable, and in it there is no stain or disgrace. Its sacred word is God's creature forever good and innocent, which he has embraced with the most tender affection of his divine will. Of itself, it had no power to oppress; the nails, the thorns, the lance, had no force to pierce nor wound; they were his own creature. But if guilty wretches had liberty to crush their Lord, to drive the nail, and to hurl the lance, these acts were none of his.

Alas! they were their own veritable and proper work; and by their own infamy, must the reprobate also bring to the Cross, glory and honor; as the saints by their sanctity, so the malignant by their malice, forever and ever.

4 And the smoke of the incense of the prayers of the saints, ascended up before God, from the hand of the angel.

So precious before God are the merits of his saints, that they are offered up by angels, as incense on his own altar in heaven; that is, in union with the merits of his divine Son, and as the sweet odor of his Holy Cross. And as if this ministration of the holy angels deserved chiefly our grateful veneration, the church repeats in their office this passage more frequently than any other: Stetit angelus juxta aram templi, habens thuribulum aureum in manu sua.

5 And the angel took the censer, and filled it with the fire of the altar, and cast it on the earth; and there were thunderings, and voices, and lightnings, and a great earthquake.

Besides the sufferings of their Lord, the injuries done to his saints are a further occasion of chastisement to this world. The saints are given for our consolation, and to delay the just judgments of God; but, on the other hand, according as they are despised, their merits are increased, and our guilt is aggravated. Not altogether like beasts of burden for the service of insolent men, do they suffer in silence and in patience; a grace to the well disposed, they are, "in the way of scorners, a deep pit."[1] They are described, in holy scripture, as heaping coals of fire on the heads of their enemies; and the hot indignation of Heaven falls at length upon their persecutors the more heavily, for the reason that they took it not upon themselves to revenge their wrongs. Sacred and terrible, therefore, is the fire which conveys their prayers on high, and which falls back upon the earth with thunderings, and with voices, with terror and conviction to every creature in all the world, where their sound has gone forth.

[1] Proverbs xiii. 15.

6 And the seven angels who had the seven trumpets, prepared themselves to sound the trumpet.

If it be right to attempt any interpretation of what now follows, we must be governed by the facts of history, and the testimony of experience. Since it is very manifestly taught by the Fathers,[1] that these two points are certain: first, that the end of the world may be close at hand, and again, that it may be very distant; and yet both propositions are strictly correct; it seems that the exposition ought in justice to be so adapted to the past and present history of the church, that the same may be fairly covered, and the sense of the signs given be fully occupied; except that the last of all may be left partially indeterminate. Farther than this, it does not, perhaps, concern us who are now on earth, but thus far it certainly deserves careful and devout attention. Incola ego sum in terra; non abscondas a me mandata tua.[2]

7 And the first angel sounded the trumpet; and there was made hail and fire, mingled with blood; and it was cast on the earth; and the third part of the earth was burnt up; and the third part of the trees was burnt up; and all green grass was burnt up.

By hail or snow is commonly understood[3] the coldness of the impious, the hard, frozen hearts of the obstinate; the reverse of which is the fervor of charity, which endures even to death. Or, if the mingling of blood changes the ordinary signification, and it should be regarded, not as the fervor of charity, but the heat of persecution, either way, the result is this: that the advent of the church of Christ on earth was greeted with the cold hatred of the Jew, and the fiery persecution of the Gentile. Prœ fulgore in conspectu ejus nubes transierant; grando et carbones ignis.[4] Before the brightness of the gospel, the clouds of prejudice and of error are scattered; while hail, and coals of fire, hatred and fiery persecution, mark their passage.

The third part of the earth signifies a great proportion of

[1] St Augustine, Epistle 199. [2] Psalms cxviii. cxix. [3] St. Gregory, Mor. 29, 20. [4] Psalms xvii. 13.

the multitudes to whom the gospel was preached; the trees, the body of believers, or the pastors and prelates of the same; and the grass, all tender and timorous souls. Now, "Without the law sin was dead. But, when the commandment came, sin revived."[1] When, therefore, the truth was first published in the early age of the church, there was new and fearful danger to the souls of men. How miserably did every weak and cowardly heart fall before the persecutions of those days! How many, who stood high in the church, or were eminent for their gifts of nature and of grace, then were made castaways! And how vast was the number of perverse souls in all the world who heard the tidings of salvation, and were summoned to penance, but neglected the kind offer, or hardened their hearts, and blasphemed against the Holy Ghost!

To take the moral to our own hearts: great is our danger so often as a new grace is offered to us, and we hesitate to choose the best part, and to follow the counsels of piety. And great is the peril of every soul, when, the truth being set before it, he debates, in the recesses of his heart, whether to declare for God or for Satan.

Mystically, the seven capital sins may be distributed among these seven periods of the latter times. The new religion, with its doctrines of penance and self-abnegation, provoked the pagan world to Wrath; and, for three hundred years, they pursued the Christian people with fury unrelenting and vindictive to the last degree. Thus Satan thought to extinguish the truth; but, as it is written, "Quare fremuerant gentes, Why have the Gentiles raged, and the people devised vain things? He that dwelleth in heaven shall laugh at them, and the Lord shall deride them."[2] Opposed to the rage of the heathen was the Meekness of the faithful; whose gentle and patient submission to all their injuries, at length gained the victory; and the Cross was exalted, by the emperor Constantine, to receive the homage of the world.

[1] Romans vii. 8. [2] Psalms ii.

8 And the second angel sounded the trumpet, and, as it were a great mountain, burning with fire, was cast into the sea; and the third part of the sea became blood.

Such is the frailty and perversity of human nature, that no sooner is one evil relieved than a new vexation appears. After the persecution from without, Christians began to be afflicted by heresy within their midst. Heresy, inflated and proud, would lift itself like a great mountain even to heaven; overbearing and aggressive, it burns not with the fervor o charity, but with the fire of ambition. Restless and discontented, its continual occupation is to multiply lies, and to kindle the flames of discord and rebellion. By the judgment of God, it falls upon Christendom, the sea of the Baptized; and a third part of it is defiled with blood, that malady of the intellect which is most directly opposed to the safety of the rational soul; wherefore the psalmist cries, Libera me de sanguinibus,[1]—"Deliver me from blood, O God, thou God of my salvation." For then the tongue shall be free to confess the truth in its integrity: et exultabit lingua mea justitiam tuam.

9 And the third part of those creatures died, which had life in the sea; and the third part of the ships was destroyed.

Many souls which once lived by faith were then lost; and many churches, which had been appointed, like good ships, to carry souls safely over the billows of this stormy life, then perished—pastors and people—in one common wreck.

Who could count all the injuries which were heaped upon the truth by the numberless heresies of those days? Down to the seventh century, there was hardly one of the sacred mysteries spared by the false doctrines of the Donatists, Arians, Pelagians, Nestorians, and the like. The blessed Trinity, divine grace, the mother of God, and the holy church, his spouse, were insulted; innocent people were persecuted often to death, and holy doctors driven like vagabonds over the earth.

[1] Psalms l. 16.

Mystically, the second period is marked by Pride. This sin is one of the first returns the creature makes to his beneficent Creator. Lucifer, in his first glory, thought to be like God. And men, considering the mighty opposition over which their constancy may have triumphed, ascribed not the honor to him to whom alone it was due. The pride of the heretics was met by the Humility of the faithful; and long after the follies of the former were forgotten by men, the virtues and the wisdom of the latter still adorn the walks of holy church.

10 And the third angel sounded the trumpet, and a great star fell from heaven, burning as it were a torch; and it fell on the third part of the rivers, and upon the fountains of waters.

There have been two nations in the world's history, the Greek and the Roman, illustrious above all others, by their endowments, physical and intellectual. Both were called by God, and adopted into his holy inheritance, and together they served him as obedient sons for many years. But, like Esau and Jacob, as if the one were hated and the other loved, the time at length came when the first made little account of his honorable estate, and, abandoning his pleasant home, went forth, wayward and lonely, to make his habitation in the wilderness.

Many were the tribulations of Christendom from the irruptions of barbarians, and by the terrors of the impostor Mahomet and his followers; but all these were less than the fall of the Greek Church. To him who has faith in the Divine Sacrifice of the Altar, the scandals and sacrilege consequent upon the Greek Schism, are fearful beyond expression. This great evil, long threatened, and often initiated, was at length consummated in the eleventh century, and the Greek was excommunicated by the Latin Church. And, like a great star, of beauty and of magnitude, it was separated from the Catholic Church, and lost its place in the kingdom of heaven, the firmament of the saints. Burning as a torch: because being manifestly possessed of the sacraments, and of sees of high dignity, it was able to dazzle and mislead the souls of men. And it fell on the third part of the rivers: not upon the sea, but upon the tributaries of the same, local and particular churches. And upon the fountains of waters: the prelates, and their metropolitans, with the Patriarch, are the fountains of authority, and, by right, should be the source of life to their flocks.

11 And the name of the star is called Wormwood: and the third part of the waters became wormwood, and many men died of the waters because they were made bitter.

It is said of wormwood, that, for its bitterness, all animals pass it by, and leave it untouched. Thus, the Greek Church remains alone, without fellowship with any other; shunned alike, by Saracen and Crusader, by Heretic and Catholic.

A third part of the waters being thus converted to bitterness, many men died: many, to whom was given the greater grace, could not live with a safe conscience in obedience to that Church. The scandals and contradictions of such a system, form one of those anomalies in the moral order, which we may suppose are to be found only in the sphere of humanity, of man fallen and redeemed; sanctified, and yet desecrated. But though many, it seems not that all die, nor, as it were, one integral portion, but an obscure, indefinite number; while others, in their simplicity and pardonable ignorance, may receive the veritable sacraments even unto eternal life.

Morally, the way to heaven leads through many tribulations. And often it seems longer and more difficult to one than to another. But if he goes forth in the joy of charity, all his labor is light; otherwise, the sin of Sloth must weigh upon his soul, and in sadness and disgust he deems his task insuperable and unprofitable. Thus the Greek's sadness in divine things, is betrayed by the Iconoclast heresy; and this sadness, joined with his restlessness, and inconstancy of mind, caused him to draw back from the good work, and to fall into the bitterness of *Acedia*.

The fourth trumpet, or the central one of the seven, brings us to the heart of the middle age; the age which is the enigma of human history. The world calls it the dark age; the scrupulous, the middle age; others deem it the age of faith, by excellence. The first supposes Christendom to have lapsed into a kind of lethargy, shameful and degrading. The second regard it as the transition state of Christianity; as if, yet in its nonage, it were germinating the full vigor of manhood; or preparing, from the wreck of Paganism, the new structure of fair truth in the beauty of holiness. The third, believe that the sway of true religion over the heart and mind of man, had then attained the highest rank which is consistent with the present relations of God and man. The first opinion is the most heretical; and this is a presumption that the third, its contradictory, is the most Catholic. The second, if fairly stated, is at the same time favorable and injurious to the honor of holy church. If not fairly stated, perhaps a bolder examination, or a more explicit statement of the same, will at last determine it to the one side or the other. For all agree, that the middle age was a crisis, or turning point, in the tide of Christian events. Now did the current turn on the flood, or on the ebb? There appears to be no other alternative; and the middle opinion must sail either with the first, or with the last, or else be left to the jeers of the one, and the pity of the other; for it is impossible, in the nature of things, that these can ever be persuaded to keep in company.

Many of the embarrassments of this question may be disposed of, by elevating it from the plane of the material, to that of the spiritual order. The highest happiness for the rational soul in this life, is, through the deductions of reason, to approach the source of wisdom. Certain divine truths being given, such as: Blessed are the poor in spirit; or, He that loveth his life shall lose it; or, What shall it profit a man if he gain the whole world, and lose his own soul; man finds, to his unspeakable joy, that, according as he proves these, and, aided by divine grace, carries them out to their logical consequences, so in the same proportion does heaven open before him, and eternal wisdom illuminate his soul. Accordingly, with the communication of these sacred maxims, it has been seen that this earth began to run into decay; men would rush to martyrdom, as to the gate of heaven; or they left all things, and went forth to the desert, to the caves and dens of the earth. Presently, Europe was covered with monasteries and churches; and thousands and tens of thousands rose in the night watches to praise God, and ceased not till the day was ended. The science of the saints, the manner of their lives, the inventions of penance, the divine rewards, and the castigations of Satan; this was their study, their occupation, and their recreation. This divine wisdom had come to be a part of the grand pursuits of human society; a part of its language, of its habits, and modes of life; pervading and possessing its philosophy, literature and arts; so that there hardly remains any account to be given of men in such times, except that they loved and served God. "One thing is necessary;" and the marvellous unity of that age is the sublime expression of this sacred truth.

The true wisdom, that which relates to eternity, the infinite treasure to men, which fills the page of holy scripture, this must needs be brought to its last perfection in the church of Christ. And so it is found to be in the Middle Age. All the scattered wisdom of past ages, both human and divine, was then collected, fitted with exquisite adaptation, and reared up a glorious temple for the joy and contemplation of the people of God. How can this be proved to the common mind, to one that has no sense of any wisdom, but that which is of the earth? To shew him the pages of St. Thomas, or St. Bonaventure, would be to tell the blind man of colors, or of the stars of heaven.

But in another way, it may be observed, that it is no more than reasonable to conclude, that since, in all the works of God, there is an infancy, a beginning, which progresses steadily to maturity; so the Church, beginning in weakness, must advance to perfect strength, with absolute certainty and infallible success. Now the time when the wisdom of the cross attains to its highest lustre, may be determined with the same probability as other historical facts. The doctors of the church, as well as the world's heroes in arms or science, are often distinguished by titles, which, approved by after generations, and enduring the test of time, mark out the different periods of history, and become landmarks of traditional truth, which none will dispute. Now, in the age of which we speak, there were those who, for their sublime wisdom, deserved the titles of the Great, the Angelic, and the Seraphic; as if human discourse, inspired by grace, could no farther go; and as if, in the providence of God, it were neither necessary, nor intended, that, in this mortal state, the mind should have any higher range, than what is thus given in the Catholic Church.

Another argument, ad hominem, to him who rejoices in material progress, is, that he may easily trace back the beginnings of his boasted lights, step by step, to that very age. Now how can light have its source in darkness? How can ignorance and superstition be the principle, the seed of enlightened science, and of true liberty? Oculi ejus ut palpebræ diliculi. Well did St. Gregory[1] prophesy of the last days, when Leviathan, the monster of the abyss, coming in antichrist, his eyes are likened to "the eyelids of the morning;[2] quia sapientes illius simplicitatem veræ fidei quasi transactæ noctis tenebras respuunt, et ejus signa mendacia quasi exsurgentis solis radios ostendunt. Because they scorn the simplicity of the true faith, as if the darkness of a night passed away; and they display his lying wonders, as the beams of a new rising sun."

And this leads to another consideration of the Middle age, by which we survey that aspect of the same, which, as in all human things, is the adverse and mournful one. It is a condition of human infirmity, corpus aggravans animam,

[1] Moral. xxxiii. 33. [2] Job xli. 9.

that, however elevated it may be by the divine goodness, it is always falling, and sustains not its honors. If, in the Middle age, the sun of wisdom attains his meridian, then, also, he turns downwards. The navigator knows well how brief is the transit—a moment, and then the morning is passed forever; the evening is come. To return to the text:

12 And the fourth angel sounded the trumpet, and the third part of the sun was smitten, and the third part of the moon, and the third part of the stars, so that the third part of them was darkened; and a third part of the day shined not, and of the night in like manner.

Thus, at the very time, when the sun of truth shone forth in his noon-tide splendor, presently the holyday is overcast. The clouds of error, the delusions of paganism just scattered, began to gather and threaten again the souls of men. For here is the beginning of what the world calls the revival of learning, the renaissance; when pagan wisdom began to be preferred above that of the saints; when men began to be weary of the yoke of Christ, and to lust after the vanities of the world. Wherfore the third part of the sun was smitten: by their spiritual adultery the purity of truth was wounded, and the moon, the Church, began to be diminished and to lose the love and reverence of men; and the third part of the stars: many of those who were eminent in holy church, were swept away by the blind enthusiasm for heathen studies and arts. Thus, day and night, the greater, as well as the lesser lights, were alike obscured. Profane and unclean men, solely for the sake of their mundane talent, began to be once more patronized by the great, and lauded by the multitude. Earthquakes, plagues, and floods admonished them of the divine displeasure; and, what was most appalling, the Church was as if rent in twain by the Western Schism. Accordingly it follows:

13 And I beheld and heard the voice of one eagle flying through the midst of heaven, saying, with a loud voice, Woe, woe, woe, to the inhabitants of the earth, by reason of the other voices of the three angels who are yet to sound the trumpet.

At the same time there appeared in Christendom, by the mercy of God, certain holy preachers, who, in a new and extraordinary manner, warned men of their danger, and exhorted them by word and example to despise the world, and to embrace the cross; whose united testimony was like the voice of one eagle, calling men away from earth to the things that are above; flying, or with active charity moving rapidly through the midst of the Church, and in the sight of all the servants of God. Thus did holy friars threaten woe to the earth; and, as early as the thirteenth century, with the apprehension of evil days to come, many began already to watch the signs of antichrist. The symptoms of apostasy, and of the hatred of authority, became daily more manifest; and if, in earlier periods, men thought the world was falling into dissolution, they witnessed now what was far more terrible; not the downfall of the earthly fabric, but the upheavings of rebellion.

In attributing one predominent vice to an age, it is not implied that the others are not also present, but rather, as time passes on, new sins seem to be superadded, till all at last are accumulated in the man of sin. In the midst of plenty, ingratitude is most manifest. Reared up in the midst of the Church's beauty and holiness, like the first parents in Paradise, men Gluttonously longed after forbidden fruit, and desired to be as gods. As in the former Jerusalem, "pride, fulness of bread, and abundance, and the idleness of her and her daughters,"[1] was the beginning of sins, so in the latter part of the Middle age, Prodiit quasi ex adipe iniquitas eorum.[2]

CHAPTER IX.

1 AND the fifth angel sounded the trumpet; and I saw a star fall from heaven, upon the earth; and to him was given the key of the bottomless pit.

[1] Ezechiel xvi. 49. [2] Psalms lxxii. 7.

Protestantism was so long in preparing, that it has been a vexed question, both among its friends and opponents, as to when and where it did begin. In truth, the cockle is sown nearly as early in time as the good seed; and, from the first, there were many antichrists. But this renders plausible a familiar argument, which the indifferent bring against every supposed change or deterioration of one age as compared with another, namely: That human nature is always the same. To which it may be answered, that, whatever be the secret malice of man, the outward manifestations of the same are by no means alike in kind or degree. And besides that the above argument would prove too much, and make vain the admonitions of revelation; it may be further replied: that, if human nature be always the same, it is always inclined to evil, and always tending downwards; and therefore, in some sense, is not so much always the same, as never the same; since there is nothing in existence, as we may suppose, so variable, inconstant, and full of dangerous hazard. But however uncertain may be the origin of Protestantism, it is plain that no period of history is marked more forcibly than the decisive outbreak of this woe, in the sixteenth century. The common mind of Christendom seems instinctively to have agreed, that this was the "revolt" intended by the apostle St. Paul; and naturally it watches the fallen star, as if it denoted no other than Martin Luther. He might be called a star, because at first his place was, as a consecrated friar and priest, in the kingdom of heaven. He was, therefore, one of the lesser lights, the Prædicatores; and, as such, not without eminence by his gifts of intellect. And for the abundance and force of his words, even the church condescended to treat with him, and to seek to win him to the side of truth. Or, if the star is to be interpreted of a church rather than of a person, the Anglican Church was most conspicuous among those which lapsed into Protestantism, and her fall was the most marked and decisive. As in another chapter, (xx. ver. 1 and 2,) we read how an angel, having the key of the bottomless pit, laid hold on Satan, and bound him in the pit; so here, by the ministration of the angel, the prison doors are set open for the adversary of man; according to a just judgment of God, who now constrains, and again permits evil to appear, for the reproof of the impious, or for the instruction of the wise.

2 And he opened the bottomless pit; and the smoke of the pit ascended as the smoke of a great furnace; and the sun was darkened, and the air, with the smoke of the pit.

It may be observed that, in the fourth period or trumpet, given above, the sun began to be darkened. Men began to be weary of the ancient wisdom, and to be infatuated with the follies of Paganism; and, as the evil grew daily worse, at length it resulted in the open contempt of the Church, the example being given by Luther and his disciples. Europe was now profoundly darkened, and the air was as if tainted with their blasphemies and ribaldry. Formerly, sordid and discontented minds had expressed themselves in language pharisaical and sanctimonious; but now all restraint was thrown aside, and, surprised with the novelty of the infernal sport, multitudes began, for the first time in Christendom, to greet, with shouts of applause, the ridicule of holy things. Ancient practices, venerable institutions and places, which had been held most sacred, being suddenly presented in a ludicrous attitude, silly people and impious wits abandoned themselves, like feeble children, to all buffoonery and mockery of divine authority.

Or if, on the other hand, men addressed themselves, with any serious purpose to learned research, this was in order to explode some ancient verity; to prove, not a truth, but some error; not that their ancestors were right, but that they were wrong. Human science was valued according as it militated successfully against revealed truth. Galileo has been immeasurably praised for his obstinacy, more than for any discovery he ever made. But the kind of wisdom which is levelled principally against authority, is substantially negative. These are the altitudes of Satan, which bring no light to the soul, but suffocate it as with the smoke of a furnace.

Protestantism, therefore, was not so much a heresy as "The Revolt." That it was not a mere heresy, in the ordinary sense of the word, may be inferred from the fact that Protestantism is not, nor has it ever been, commonly called a heresy. As if by common consent, that name is neither generally given nor taken. But it is certain that, in time, people must and will call things by their right names. Ask what is Arianism or Calvinism, and there is ready an answer, perfectly distinct; but Protestantism defies definition, and whoever would attempt to classify or expound it, is confounded with the smoke of the abyss.

3 And from the smoke of the pit there came out locusts upon the earth; and power was given to them, as the scorpions of the earth have power.

Thus was the revolt initiated, amid the sneers of the learned, the buffoonery of wits, and the ghastly terrors of fanatics. And then began to appear the evil generation of locusts, which, bred in this womb of rebellion, came leaping and swarming over Christian lands. These were the infidels, who attacked not Catholicity alone, but the religion of Jesus Christ, as such. There may have been heresies and schisms before; there may have been errors and follies in paganism, but never in Christian Europe, nor in heathen Athens or Rome, never before was it heard of, that men should dare publicly to revile the religion of the state, the universal belief, and the common object of worship, held in pious veneration by the race then and there in being.

Power was given to them: for they were not without mental ability, with which they corrupted souls, in a hidden and subtle manner, like the scorpion. It is said that the scorpion attacks indirectly, and stings with the tail. Thus toward the end of the sixteenth century did they begin to make their approaches, unsuspected till the sting was given, and the heart was poisoned, with the hatred of the cross, and with the disgust of heavenly wisdom.

4 And it was commanded them, that they should not hurt the grass of the earth, nor any green thing, nor any tree; but only the men who have not the sign of God in their foreheads.

It is evident that they could not harm the simple and uneducated, who remained in ignorance of their impieties, and who, even if they listened to them, would not apprehend the real meaning of their subtleties. Besides these, all those of a tender conscience, such for example as the devout female sex, and also the trees, men of sound judgment, and truly eminent for greatness of soul, would likewise be left uninjured. Only those who had not the sign of God, who loved not the Cross, who hated the lowly way of virtue and obedience, these fell everywhere a prey to the modern philosophers.

5 And it was given to them that they should not kill them; but that they should torment them five months; and their torment was as the torment of a scorpion, when he striketh a man.

By the tender mercy of God, whose strong love reaches even to the third and fourth generation, the faith was not yet so wholly eradicated, but that these wretched men would at last be glad to receive the consolations of the religion they had ridiculed. And uniformly the life-giving sacraments, or at least that of Baptism, was administered to every one born in Christian lands or of Christian parents. Five months was the time of the flood. It is written:[1] "And the waters prevailed upon the earth a hundred and fifty days." But from the time that the deluge commenced, till Noe came forth from the ark, was more than a twelvemonth. If we understand, by the five months, a hundred and fifty years, it may be remembered that for about that time the infidels flourished, although the date[2] of their commencement may be somewhat

[1] Genesis vii. 24.

[2] There may be reckoned about 150 years thus: In the intellectual order, from the birth of Bayle, to the death of Voltaire. Cotemporaneously in

ambiguous, and the traces of their devastation may linger in society for long after, or even till the day of judgment. The torment of the scorpion is that of a poison, slow, but grievous, and causing an inextinguishable thirst.[1] Thus, however pleasant and easy may be the approaches of infidelity, in the end the soul is stung with remorse and terror. And, though the sting of ridicule upon holy things is a weapon, sharp and powerful, and he who handles it, may for a short time be flattered, and admired by the world, and may be intoxicated by its praises, yet, in the end, his heart is lonely, and wrung with anguish for the loss of the celestial refreshment, while in his flesh rages the fever of concupiscence, which no waters of pleasure can assuage.

6 And in those days men shall seek death, and shall not find it; and they shall desire to die, and death shall fly from them.

Multa flagella peccatoris. In proportion as they disturbed the peace of society, they aggravated their own wants. With the lust of pleasure, the excessive ambition for fame, and the thirst of riches, men began to be weary of life, and many desired to die, rather than to endure physical pain, or the loss of reputation, or the reverses of bankruptcy. This is proved by the practices of duelling and suicide, which began to prevail after the revolt of the sixteenth century. It shows what would be his desire, only that the infidel is a coward, and cannot find the death he would wish, an escape from every pain. For having some remains of the Christian faith, while they ridiculed penance, and detested pain above all other things, yet, at the same time, they were held in check, by the irresistible apprehension of the future torments; which had been implanted in the years of their childhood, and had sunk deep in their minds, in the days of their first innocence. And, therefore, though they, of all men, may have the most hated suffering, and would gladly escape it by

the political order from the English, to the French revolution, or from the murder of Charles I., to that of Louis XVI.

[1] Pliny, quoted by Cor. a Lep.

death, and would wish they had never been born; these, withal, were the very ones who could not throw off the conviction, that after death was instant judgment. So it is that the apostate or the impious Christian is most cruelly divided between the earthly delights, and the pains of hell; and no other human being seems so far removed from the attainment of his ends as he; for he hates chiefly the cross, and thereby does to himself most unnatural violence; since the cross, impressed upon him in baptism, is the very life of his soul.

7 And the shapes of the locusts were like unto horses prepared for battle; and, on their heads, were, as it were, crowns like gold; and their faces as the faces of men.

The locust is an impure animal; voracious, restless, impudent, and noxious. Coming in swarms, they bring terror to the husbandman, and desolation to the infested land. Their manner of skipping or leaping, denotes vain glory, as is observed by the holy Fathers. In a word, St. Augustine describes the whole signification: Locusta est malitia ore lædens, infideli scilicet testimonio[1] The malice which hurts with the mouth, to wit, the words of the infidel. The excessive vanity of the sophists of the last two centuries, their insatiable thirst for the popular glory, their malice, their impudent, volatile, and incoherent manner of impugning the truth, are hereby aptly expressed. Like horses before the battle, they are impetuous, libidinous, and full of confidence. They are crowned with the praises of the multitude; which, if like gold, are nevertheless empty and unprofitable; for, though they toil hard, impious authors are left, after all, with a scant reward, perhaps to poverty and starvation. They have the faces of men, because they profess to be the best friends of humanity; to desire most earnestly the enlightenment of ignorance, the elevation and happiness of the human race.

8 And they had hair as the hair of women: and their teeth were as the teeth of lions.

[1] Ennar. Ps. lxxvii.

They are smooth and unmanly in their appearance, and effeminate in their lives; and while they persuade to every softness and voluptuousness of manners, they rend, with cruel and biting words, the Lamb of God, and, as if from the jaws of a lion, is heard their horrid cry: "Crush the Wretch."

9 And they had breastplates, as it were breastplates of iron: and the sound of their wings was as the sound of chariots, of many horses rushing to battle.

Hard and impenetrable are their hearts to the voice of reason, and to the language of affection; cold and insensible to the endearments of home and of family, to the gentle and soothing associations of religion, to the noble traditions of piety and of patriotism; while their malignant pens astonish all far and near, and Christendom trembles before the clamors of the multitude, as if at the rattling of the cars of Antichrist.

10 And they had tails like unto scorpions, and stings were in their tails: and their power was to hurt men five months.

Again, it is written, that they sting like scorpions. If they have a show of reason, or if the poison of their impiety is not on the surface, still it lurks below; and the unhappy soul which receives their advances, which would temporize with them, is inevitably stung at last. However fair they may promise, always in the end is woe.

If by the five months, or one hunderd and fifty days of the deluge, we understand an analogous period of a hundred and fifty years, in which prevailed the flood of infidelity; the beginning of the same may be placed near the middle of the seventeenth, and the end near the close of the eighteenth century. The beginning is more obsure than the end; naturally, the freethinker was at first timorous and cautious like Montaigne, toward the commencement of the seventeenth century; but, about the middle of the same, we have bolder names, as Hobbes and Bayle; and the work of extermination, once in motion, there follows a crowd of poets, philosophers, and heretics, whose baleful influence manifestly culminated in the days of Voltaire. The latter point of time may accordingly be considered the end of the first woe, because then there commenced a reaction in favor of Christianity. Not that there are no revilers nor infidels still remaining, but they have not the same power to torment men; for there is now a noble company able and willing to meet them with their own weapons, of wit, of eloquence, and of learning. And whereas, before, men were ashamed of wisdom, or were not unwilling to leave her in some obscurity; since that time there have been many, distinguished as statesmen, soldiers, and artists, or accomplished in literature, and in science, who have rendered brilliant testimony to the ancient wisdom, and have made fair and plain to men her honorable walks.

11 And they had over them, a king, the angel of the bottomless pit; whose name, in Hebrew, is Abaddon; and, in Greek, Apollyon; in Latin, Exterminans.

As the title of our Blessed Lord was written "in Greek, and Latin, and Hebrew," in like manner is recorded that of his adversary, the evil spirit of the abyss, whose advent in the man of sin is foretokened in the revolt and its generation of infidels, his pioneers. Their office is manifestly one of simple destruction. It has been exercised in the destruction of churches, monasteries, hospitals, and the shrines of the dead; in the destruction of sacraments, of rites and ceremonies, civil and religious; in the destruction of authority, moral and ecclesiastical, secular and domestic; in the destruction of logic, of tradition, and of the memory of great and good men. This is that pure mischief of radicalism, which exterminates festivals, recreations, and the repose of holidays, and of rustic life; which blackens and corrodes the supererogation of every heroic act of charity, of every loyal and chivalrous deed of mercy; which extirpates true patriotism or self-sacrifice for the public good, and rends old attachments of place, of family, of spouse, and of the paternal hearth. These are the bitter fruits of infidelity; it is true, that any other error will beget disorder, and is more or less destructive; but with this difference, that the latter may be so by accident, but the former is so by essence. After the renaissance, men, having turned away from the ancient and catholic wisdom, were, necessarily without a foundation to build upon, without a purpose or any definite aim of a high order; therefore, if anything was to be done, they must pull down, instead of building up. And, from the first may be found in literature, authors, otherwise amiable, who thus employed their talent; who seemed to think they had a work to do, but the work was always destructive, and not creative; and their moral was not a utility, but an apology; not a generous gift, but a hungry petition. On the other hand, if they seem to have a purpose, it is a futile one. Thus the vanity of the new learning is exemplified in the metaphysician, who, discarding the definitions of an Augustine, or an Anselm, and throwing down the ladder, as it were, of his science, thought to obtain some enunciation of the truth, more lofty and complete than if he had availed himself of the abundant aids already on record.

But these evils are light, as compared with those in the moral order. There were authors as early as the fourteenth century, whose obscenity is revolting; but, compared with those of the last century, they are but as silly youth to the full grown ruffian. The former were seduced by the beauty of the flesh, but the latter embraced the dung: amplexati sunt stercora.[1] Treating of some of the prophecies which relate to the last days, St. Augustine declares frankly, that he cannot understand them. Now, the Saint was once a man of the world, and was, moreover, endowed with a lofty intellect; but could it ever have entered his mind that, in after years, a Christian man should conceive and indite a work like the infamous poem of Voltaire? and that, the same being multiplied by the press, thousands on thousands of copies, should be scattered throughout Christian Europe, and be hailed with delight? God forbid! that holy sage, or blushing penitent, ever thought it. A like calamity never happened before, nor

[1] Lam. iv. 5.

could, by any possibility, have been a topic of induction for human experience.

Again: in the latter days, men have exploded the terrors of the inquisition, have destroyed their racks and dungeons, have uprooted the stake, and stripped the executioner of his mask and squalid fear; they boast of their mildness, in wars without sacking, burning and hanging; and, if men will endure these things no longer, it would be wrong to enforce them; but it is not, therefore, a matter for self-congratulation, but rather for humiliation and wholesome reprehension. For all this is the result, not of any robustness, but of infirmity of character, since they have come to consider corporal chastisement, or physical pain, as the greatest of evils; when it is, in truth, the least evil, of which we have any knowledge. Tell the one whose soul is in anguish by reason of injustice or dishonor, that his sorrows are less than those of his neighbor, who is in corporal pains, and he is insulted. A little child receives a casual hurt, and laughs at it: it is the testimony of a rational nature. But that grown men should hold physical pain or chastisement in horror, this is the sophistry of the revolt. Compare with this the household of St. Louis[1] in the thirteenth century, who resolutely branded a man on the mouth for blasphemy; or the castle of De Joinville, where, because the name of the devil began, in those days, to be used frequently in discourse, it was appointed that, for every such offence, a man should receive a blow or the ferule. "The rod and reproof give wisdom;" saith holy scripture. The language of those times is in accordance with that wisdom, breathing of simplicity and innocence as if inspired by God. The Church's calendar records their merits; their own words confirm it; their monuments prove that their words were good, and from the heart.

It is charged to the former times, that they were stained with many dark crimes; but those who believe the record

[1] De J. Life of S. Louis.

of their crimes should also believe that of their virtues, and of the manifest interposition of Almighty God, in their human affairs; for the one belongs as necessarily to the history of a people of God, as the other. It is plain, that the bad man must be made worse by the non-resistance of his victim; accordingly, when Christians act up to their faith, when they are unwilling to take vengeance into their own hands, when they appeal to the ecclesiastical authority, and avoid a resort to the secular tribunal, the malice of the reprobate man abounds indefinitely; hence he runs a desperate course, unchecked, till, by a sudden judgment of God, he falls into some terrible calamity, or into manifest perdition. But, in the times when every man can find a speedy vengeance, and immediately calls upon the secular arm in every possible emergency, it follows not by any means that there is less iniquity, but only this: that the monster does not make head, and does not reveal himself for the salutary instruction of the prudent, while divine Providence does not interpose, because they do not leave any room for the interposition. Now such is not the normal condition of a people of God; on the contrary, it belongs neither to the natural, nor to the supernatural order. It is the horrid rule of material force, which reaches not the soul; which is not, nor ever can be, a curb for the secret corruption. And now men begin to be convinced, that it cannot preserve for them even common propriety, nor secure them against the full measure of public depravity.

But since the propositions now laid down may be disputed; since all the virtues of other times may be assumed for the latter days, and all the modern vices may be ascribed to the former ages; since it is absurd to trust the professions of men when the good and the bad may equally pretend the same thing; how is the difficulty to be cleared up, and what is the test which is to distinguish truth from the error with which it is so grievously confounded, in human affairs? The remedy is simple, if men will condescend to use it. It is the testimony of the Cross, the plain, evangelical truth, which searches not the profession, but the motive; and which convicts the false glory, because it proceeds from a totally contrary principle, to that which constitutes the true happiness of a people. In the former ages, for example, slavery was extinguished, and a reasonable equality obtained, because the maxim, Blessed are the meek, was the belief and practice of both lord and subject. In the last days, the same Christian prerogative of liberty is demanded, because every one disdains to own a master. Then Holy Scripture was studied for the love of one true religion; now the Bible is praised, because it is a cloak for a thousand errors. Then much alms was given, because of the belief, Blessed are the poor; now much wealth is bestowed, to train the youth in the hope of becoming rich. Then the trades were honored, because no one was ashamed of his honest work; now the mechanic arts are cultivated, because of the ambition to rise above one's rank in life. The age of faith was the age of humility; the age of infidelity is the age of pride; in the one, the Cross was loved; in the other, the Cross is hated. Therefore the modern times, when compared with the former periods of Christianity, may justly be distinguished as days of woe.

Morally, the fifth period is marked by Luxury. Chastity was never more despised by men. Formerly it had been recognized and reverenced even by pagan nations; but the histories, the literature, and the arts of that age betray their unbridled lust; to punish which, divine Providence sent them a loathsome disease, which is so transmitted by fornication as to make manifest inexcusably the rottenness of sin. On the other hand, the ecclesiastical orders were reformed to a more rigid purity of manners; and according as the scrutiny of the infidel was bold and malicious, so were their humble virtues proved and refined.

12 One woe is past; and, behold, there come two more woes hereafter.

Coming now to the second woe, it may be asked: Where is the beginning of the same, and where the end? or why may there not be an interval between the first and second woe? Also, what is the relation of the three woes one with another? what with the appointments of the whole seven trumpets? It is to be observed: That causes and effects in human history are so involved, and especially in Christian history, that no eventuality remains alone, but, like the meshes of a net, is interwoven with all before and after. And, as the ravages of the deluge remained on the earth long after the flood was ended, so the effects of the first woe are still visible in the present time; and therefore it does not seem necessary nor convenient, to suppose any interval between the first and second woe. There is, however, some exception to be made in respect of the third woe, because, being the end of time, it is abrupt and decisive; it is said, it will come "quickly." Thus, by the first woe, men are tormented; by the second, they are killed; and the third, which is the eternal or final destruction, is the consummation of every woe. The malady which terminates in death, beginning, as it were, with the extremities, gains at length upon the vital parts, and all is ended. Thus the first trumpet denoted outward persecution; the second, inward disorder; the third, the languor of sadness; the fourth, the darkness of a crisis; the fifth, the paroxysms of a malignant disease; the sixth, the last agony; the seventh, the end which engulfs all.

Again, it may be objected: That the same proportion of years is not observed in the latter, as in the former periods; the fifth trumpet, or the first woe, extending over less than three centuries, and the second not yet having reached one hundred years. But it is written: Unless those days had been shortened, there should no flesh be saved; now it would hardly seem probable that some seven or seventy days at the end of time is here intended, but rather that years are to be deducted out of the average, so to speak, of the last ages. And if the last, that is, the present period, were to be shortened by centuries, as the last but one appears shortened by scores; who could complain that any violence is thereby done to holy scripture? It is true, indeed, supposing we are now in the midst of the last period, (the third woe is the end itself,) that the difficulty of making a fair estimate of the same is very great, and second only to that of unfolding future events; forasmuch as no one can be an impartial judge in his own cause. It is like the snake in the grass; we can see one and another venomous fold, but neither the beginning nor the end; and we cannot determine whether it is nearer, or farther, from our feet, only with some new transposition, or perhaps with the sudden, but always dreaded catastrophe.

13 And the sixth angel sounded the trumpet; and I heard a voice from the four horns of the golden altar, which is before the eyes of God.

As the last days draw nigh, voices are multiplied, time is shortened, Satan rages, and works, both good and bad, abound. Even as the inspired writer spends many words upon the times of woe; so is the mind of man therein exercised to marvellous activity of discussion, of investigation, of thought, and of action, in modes spiritual and material. By the interposition of the voice from the altar, the announcement of this second woe is rendered more emphatic; for it proceeds from the horns of the golden altar, as if from that Most Sacred Victim, who is ever before the eyes of God, as the divine motive of mercy and of just retribution.

The golden altar being our refuge and our salvation, its horns being appointed to yield protection, and to extend the benediction of Heaven to the four quarters of the world, would it not seem now that men have exhausted even the patience and clemency of the Redeemer? For he himself demands that they be abandoned to their desperate courses; instead of the solid and prosperous science of the cross, which, like an anchor, was to hold them fast in the hope of eternal life, that they be cast loose to the storm of evil passions; to be the sport of those illusions, which, from every quarter of the earth, mock them with the foolish imagination of temporal felicity, with the insane ambition of earthly grandeur, or with the hatred of a heavenly guidance, and with the despair of a celestial inheritance.

14 Saying to the sixth angel, who had the trumpet: Loose the four angels, who are bound in the great river Euphrates.

Because the four angels were bound, and because they bring damage to men, it might be supposed they were bad angels. But it is to be remembered, that an angel is a minister of God, appointed to execute his ordinances of justice, as well as of mercy. It is sufficient, however, for the present purpose, to consider them as representative of the principal passions of the soul, which are four in number, because all the other passions may be reduced to these, viz., joy, sorrow, fear, and hope.[1] Of themselves, the passions are good, or indifferent, and, so far as they are mere natural causes, they may well be administered by good angels as their higher causes. Again, the Euphrates being an emblem of tranquillity, or of a condition which in itself is good, it need be no reproach to the good agent that he is controlled by, or subjected to, a good influence. In chapter vii. v. 1, the four angels, or the four winds which blow from the four corners of the earth, and which agitate the human order with diverse passions, as if of heat and cold, of wet and dry, these, in the first instance, and in respect of the predestination of the elect, were prohibited absolutely from doing hurt. Moreover, it may be gathered from the present text, that, in the course of times succeeding, or at least for a certain indefinite time, they are still constrained by incidental causes, and as if with difficulty. But now at last they are cast loose, and the passions are abandoned to their natural issues, uncontrolled by divine grace; so that the mind of man is tossed grievously by the impetuous motions of joy and sorrow in the present, of inordinate fear or hope about his future estate; and society is seen drifting before the impulses of blind instinct or morbid sentiment, urged this way or that, by the agitation of sophists,

[1] St. Thomas, Sum. Theo. 1. 2. 25. 4.

fanatics, or demagogues. As for example: when it yields sympathy to the culprit, whereas, it should render indignation; or commiseration for the stranger in distant lands, while it is cold to the claims of those at home. As when it overacts one virtue to the detriment of another: exalting temperance at the expense of justice, and so doing evil that good may come; or exaggerating its tenderness for the weak and helpless, at the expense of piety, the father of the family being committed to shipwreck and death, that his wife or child may be rescued before him; as if the members should take precedence of the head itself, in point of actual existence. But most especially does society veer and quake, when it touches upon a point of order, when there is question of authority on the one hand, or of obedience on the other; as when it bows before the rights of the people, or when it dictates the duties of its rulers. Now as far as they may be human operations, there can be in all these instances some element of good, and so far they may pertain, at least remotely, to the administration of angels. But, because they are deprived of the evangelical character, because they lack the motive of right reason, and the principle of order, they are, notwithstanding, ghastly deformities, and hideous symptoms that the reason itself is crazed, the vital principle impaired and disorganized; and so dissolution cannot be far off.

To resume: The four angels may signify the universality of passions, which hold the four quarters of the earth. The river Euphrates, the joy and the strength of the city of Babylon, implies plenty and security. At first, the human passions are constrained, and their fervor assuaged by the bounty of divine Providence. Afterwards, that bounty is weakened of its benign influence, or is perverted by ungrateful men, to be the occasion of lust, of insolence, and of mutiny. Thus toward the close of the last century, while men were abandoned to every license of impiety and debauchery, while princes and philosophers were left to the undisturbed enjoyment of power and of pleasure; suddenly the multitude of evil passions engendered in that state of godless ease and plenty, was let loose. And all the traits of a vicious sovereign have passed into the manners of the people. The arrogance, the power once his, is now theirs; his vanity, his avarice, his caprices, his thirst for pleasure, and his means of indulgence are theirs. As he was once courted and worshipped, so now are the people glorified. The age of rationalism is inaugurated, and the rights of man are set up against those of God. Revolution follows upon revolution, and Christendom is convulsed with the heavy woe of Democracy.

There is no question here of the political merits of Democracy, nor whether it may not be as good a form of civil government as another; but by the word Democracy is intended that error which attributes to the common humanity a sovereignty inherent and supreme, and, therefore, divine. After the thought, comes the deed; after the free-thinker, comes the free-doer. The license and anarchy of the understanding, which prevailed in the last centuries, have passed into the political and domestic relations of life; and the natural and sacred duty of obedience has become, in the last days, surrounded with difficulty, disturbed by a storm of disputation, and involved in the smoke of the bottomless pit. And why is it that the minds of men are thus troubled, but because they have rebelled against the church, and are meditating treason against the Most High God?

To consider briefly the argument, they pretend: That, granting the original source of authority to be divine, yet, because the powers that be, or the secular power, is not conferred directly from heaven, therefore it must be derived through the people. But when was the power bestowed upon the people, either mediately or immediately? Do we find it in the nature of things, that the child governs the parent, the scholars their master, the soldiers their captain, or the herds their leader? But the sophists would have it for a law, that the power is not delivered down from above, but proceeds upward from beneath. Otherwise, why is there any question of the rights of the multitude? Unus Dominus: There is one Lord, as there is one truth, and his power is one, and indivisible; and, if it be communicated to another, not therefore is it divided or abstracted from his dominion; but he who resists it resists God. Therefore there can be no question about the divine right of the powers that be; for there is no other right; and, in this sense, as able writers have shown, rights belong not to man, but to God. Consequently, the rest is a simple question of fact, and not of right. Sometimes, the power is derived from the king to one whom God, not men, made to be the king's son. Sometimes one, gifted with a prudent understanding and a stout heart, gifts which he received from God, and not from men, takes in his own hand the sceptre: and, if God prosper, and men obey him, who shall dare resist? Sometimes the spontaneous accord of a people, whose convictions reflect the truth and justice of Heaven, establishes a government, which they themselves, and their children, must obey. Why? Because it is right, and the right is divine. These are simple matters of history; and, if one asserts that the power of the individual ruler must be at least mediately through the people, it is to be answered: that there need be no law nor necessity of the kind, because, in point of fact, there are instances to the contrary.

But it may be urged: the power is either immediately from God or not; if not immediately, then mediately, and the people are the medium. Power is received immediately from God by a miracle, as Moses or St. Peter received their commission; and, in other ways, divine power may interpose in an extraordinary manner. But, in the natural order, the due method of power will be in the established nature of things. For example: the vegetable world is governed by the heavenly bodies; the brute creation, in general, by man; in particular, the herd by the bull. Again, the rational creation is administered by the angelic creation; and, among rational beings in particular, the inferior reason or intelligence is governed by the superior; and we must look to facts to know which is the superior and which the inferior, and, this being ascertained, the better reason prevails of right, because it is so appointed by the Author of the constituted universe; which universe, framed by his immediate, miraculous power, contains, as in a mirror, the reflections of his eternal rectitude.

Again, it will be said, there is often a difficulty about the question of fact; and it is not always plain which is the superior or better reason, and which the inferior; in which case, the people solve the dispute, and declare sentence, as the medium, in the last resort, of divine authority. It is to be answered, that, in point of fact, the people often decide contrary to right reason; but their decision cannot make the false to be true, nor convert iniquity into justice. What signifies, then, the will of the people, more than any other will, if it be not a right will? God himself does not create truth. Therefore the popular sovereignty is a phantom, like the divine right of kings, as taught in the early times of the Revolt. Whatever is, is; and what is not, does not exist. If they do right, they are right; and when they do wrong, they are wrong. Let us borrow a ray of light from Holy Cross. It is the glory of angels and of men to serve God; of the inferior to be subject to the higher powers. In this stage of human existence, it has been proved, by the example of our divine Lord, that there is no dignity to be compared with that of humble obedience; no majesty greater than that of the good servant of all; no merit, nor profit, nor honor, like that of administering to another's good. This it is which makes the Ruler glorious before his subjects, the master before his servant; and this, too, is able to exalt the servant to be his master's dear friend; the people, to be the children of God.

15 And the four angels were loosed, who were prepared for an hour, and a day, and a month, and a year; for to kill the third part of men.

As it is not proposed, here, to determine the measure of time of this woe, so perhaps it is not intended by the sacred text to signify a defined period, but the hour, and day, and month, and year denote the fitful, uncertain, and unequal progress of revolutions over society. Or, it might be added, that this manner of counting the time of the second woe, points to the word itself of Revolution. For as the rotation of time is marked by the hour, day, month, and year, so, in the age of moral and social convulsions, do we incessantly pass and repass, from light to darkness, and from cold to heat; and when the pride of progress has made much headway, it is presently turned back; when the insolence of popular sovereignty is swollen to a crisis, straightway it is reversed and prostrated. But this, also, is to be noted in the order of the mutations, that their volume always increases in the ratio of their iteration. Every wave mounts higher than the last; and the commotion which agitated one province, or one horizon, widens its circles, and spreads to other lands, till the whole orb of human existence is at length dragged within its vortex; order, and harmony, and decorum, are swept away, and the times are ended. In the last period men were tormented, but, in this, they are killed. A large part of Christendom is unbaptized; besides this, there is a great number in whom the faith is wholly expired, and who, neither in life nor death, deign to ask for the aids of the church. And because mortal sins have come forth so plainly and unopposed into public life,—and public fraud, public perjury, and public blasphemy, prevails in society, therefore with a vast proportion the private conscience, the natural instinct of justice, of chastity, and of religion, is extinguished; and the memory of one God, the Remunerator, of the Trinity, of the Incarnation, of the eternity of heaven and hell, the four things necessary, *necessitate medii*, is wholly lost. Are not these then dead men? who go and come in our midst, but in whose souls there is not one spark of grace or faith, not a vestige of the cross, nor of eternal life, remaining?

16 And the number of the army of horsemen was twenty thousand times ten thousand. And I heard the number of them.

It is not said his army nor their army, but the army; it is the multitude, the headless mob, the people who have girded themselves to rebellion against the eternal Truth, who are weary of the Christian name, and who are calling for the seditious man, Barabbas. They go forth like mounted horsemen; with them, there is no distinction of gentle and servile; they disdain to go humbly on foot; they despise all order, and rank, and command. And by the mercy of God there is as yet no chief, no Man of Sin at their head. Twenty thousand times ten thousand, or the sum of two hundred millions, is, in round numbers, the mass of the people who pertain to the Latin, or the higher civilization. And I heard the number of them: a most difficult thing is it, to estimate this great army; but it is numbered in heaven, and every action and thought of this vast disorder, is assuredly controlled by a wise Providence. Or, I heard the number: because it is a marked and noted multitude; not aliens and strangers to the Truth, but a familiar people, and the descendants of a sainted ancestry who once served God in the obedience of his Holy Roman and Apostolic Church.

Besides their sins of omission, mentioned above, some notice must now be taken of those of commission, the evils which are plain to the observation of every one. This army of the Democracy, is an army of horsemen also, because of the rapidity of its movements, and because it is so swift to do evil. Its operations may, in one year, or in one hour, as it were, hurl the king from his throne, confiscate the treasures of the State, erase its laws, and invest the seditious man, the scourge of society, with absolute power. Its influence spreads like a contagion from country to country, and successively almost every throne in Christendom is shaken, and everywhere churches, convents, and colleges are desecrated, their ministers scattered over the world, and the patrimony of the poor robbed and squandered in the name of the people. What, then, will be the end, when we know that, in the beginning, the most stupendous crime that ever has been committed, was achieved by the will of the people in the court of Pontius Pilate? When, alas, their clamors have overawed the authority of the mightiest government that ever ruled the world!

17 And thus I saw the horses in the vision: and they, who sat on them, had breastplates of fire, and hyacinth, and of brimstone, and the heads of the horses were as the heads of lions: and from their mouths proceeded fire, and smoke, and brimstone.

The horses, in the vision, are put first, and the riders after; the latter are represented in the defensive, the former in the offensive. The angry passions of the seditious are to be dreaded as the fire; hyacinth is the color of blood; brimstone is the element of hell. Thus, while demagogues excite a misguided people to rebellion, they, themselves, are shielded behind the terrors they inspire, of blood, of hostility, and of infernal cruelty. The horses have heads as lions: the most formidable power of the day is popular opinion; massive and terrible is its aspect; it pursues hotly, and overrides impetuously, like fire; it bewilders the reason, and clouds and overawes the judgment, as with the smoke of the abyss; and as if with infernal terrors, it suffocates and quenches fatally the natural instincts of piety, of honor, and of truth.

18 And by these three scourges was the third part of men killed, by the fire, and by the smoke, and by the brimstone, which issued out of their mouths.

A third part of men is killed, because they are not attached to the Church, even by the slender bond of an imperfect faith. They have no sense of pain, of the scorpion stings of conscience; that is passed away with their faith, and the deadly coldness of indifference is upon them. Overpowered by the enormous delusions of a material progress, of a widespread godless education, of a false civilization, and of a hypocritical refinement of manners, they surrender themselves unresistingly to the tyranny of the popular will; aggressive, insolent, bewildering, and terrible, according as it is spurred and lashed to fury by the brawlers and radicals of the day.

19 For the power of the horses is in their mouths, and in their tails. For their tails are like to serpents, having heads; and with them they do hurt.

It was observed, of the first woe, that its beginnings were subtle, and its end was torment. But this power of an apostate democracy has a double force; formidable by front and by rear; blasting in the beginning, venomous in the end. Or, to follow St. Gregory, by the mouth may be signified their impious doctrine; by the tail, the temporal power which upholds the persecutors of the truth.

Corruptio optimi pessima. This world has witnessed the corruption of the sons of God, and their generation of giants, potentes a sæculo; the corruption of Judaism, the noble kindred of God; but now comes the corruption of Christendom, the generation of the Holy Ghost. The generation that was tenderly reared with holy sacraments, munificently portioned with the price of most precious blood, as if the darling of heaven, for whom the Lamb of God was sacrificed, and for whom he prayed; "Deliver, O God, my soul from the sword, my only one from the hand of the dog. Libera me de ore leonis, et a cornibus unicornium humilitatem meam."[1]

20 And the rest of the men, who were not slain by these scourges, have not done penance for the works of their hands, that they should not adore devils, and idols of gold, and silver, and brass, and stone, and wood, which neither can see, nor hear, nor walk.

In these days, there are many remarkable conversions to the Catholic Church, and many bright examples of holiness within the same; but they are so dispersed and isolated, that they seem like light shining in darkness, to make only more manifest the impenitence of the rest of men. The worship of devils or evil spirits, has its clients, and doctors, and journals. The idolatry of gold and silver, transports nations round the globe. The brazen science of the day is adored as divine wisdom. To the fine arts is commonly applied language which is due to the Deity; and the wonders of mechanics have infatuated the souls of a great part of mankind.

[1] Psalms xxi. 21.

21 Neither have they done penance for their murders, nor for their sorceries, nor for their fornication, nor for their thefts.

If the material goods seem more abundant in this age, so are they more than ever unstable and difficult for the man of integrity. How many motives therefore for the honorable mind to despise them, when he sees them in such unworthy hands, when it is so uncertain how long he shall be left to enjoy them, when he must stoop so low to obtain them! And in an age of homicide, how cold the hearts of Christians if they cannot forget their personal hatreds, when the good should be united against the torrent of evil custom! How dull the man of learning, when he sees to what puerilities, and low sorceries, his science is degraded! How perverse the prodigal, when he knows with what insane and brutal companions he must consort! Sordid and impenitent are the nations where usury and fraud abound, where the market-place is their temple, and where they boast that not now one, but all the peoples are about to be nations of shop-keepers; and that war and peace, the affairs of State, and the welfare of society, are henceforth to be numbered in the institutions of the money-changers.

Morally: As a characteristic of the sixth period, the vice of Covetousness, is to be added to the former ills of Christendom; inasmuch as an insatiable avarice, or love of money, is the main-spring of the actual system of society. To gratify which, the former work of destruction is carried forward into the last resources of nature; exhausting the forest and soil of the earth, devouring the gold in its bowels, squandering human life by its mechanical inventions, and rendering abortive even the laws of generation, through a miserly dread of poverty. On the other hand, the ecclesiastical orders are gradually removed from the converse of society, and repelled back into the primitive poverty. And as the church withdraws her benign influences from the unhappy land, blight, and earthquake, and pestilence, and flood, and drought, prevail more and more.

CHAPTER X.

THE connected historical account of the second woe being ended, here follows an appendix to the same, including some of those preternatural events which are dimly foreshadowed in Scripture and tradition, as relating to the close of the last days.

1 And I saw another mighty angel coming down from heaven, clothed with a cloud, and a rainbow upon his head; and his face was as the sun, and his feet as pillars of fire.

The office of this angel is to announce the end of time: that with the third woe come, the end of the day of grace, and an eternal woe. A personal manifestation of this angel to men, is not to be supposed; but by angelic ministrations, and the counsel of prudent and holy men, a conviction of the approaching consummation may be the actual sentiment of the faithful; if we might not even go farther, and say, that the apprehension of the nearness of that dread moment will be so universal in the Church, that it shall come to have a certainty, like that of an article of faith. But he is clothed with a cloud: for the end is involved in mystery, and however plainly some of the signs may be declared, yet they are but signs, and the day and hour are not revealed, even to angels; and, perhaps, in the nature of things, the relations of the Creator and the creature are so framed, that it is impossible any, but the Eternal One, could know it. Or, the cloud may signify that the truth is always, to the last, veiled and obscure to the worldly-minded, who will be found then, as in the days of Noe, "eating and drinking, marrying and giving in marriage." The rainbow proves that the faithful and true Shepherd of the Church will not forget his promises to his elect, as it is written: "No man shall snatch them out of my hand." Or, if it imports something more than this, it may be, that in the last persecutions the knowledge of the coming end will be as the memory of sweet odors to the faithful, and an abundant consolation, even in torments, according to the words: "See the fig-tree, and all the trees: when they now shoot forth their fruit, you know that summer is nigh."[1] His face was as the sun: because the truth, always too bright for its enemies, shall then be more brilliant than all the delusions of Antichrist. The feet of an evangelist are beautiful, because those of a messenger from heaven, unsoiled by the pursuits of earth; and they are like pillars of fire, by the firmness and force with which his sacred words descend upon the hearts of men.

It does not follow, because the mighty angel typifies, in this awful manner, the end of time, that, therefore, his function is to be removed to a distant age. Not to interrupt the distinct narrative of the second woe, he is described after the same, though his place is within the same; and it is not impossible that the majesty of his stature already overshadows us. For the appointments of Divine Providence do not depend upon the recognizance of men. Thus considered, the cloud of darkness, in our own day, is not without the rainbow of hope, when we see the church adorned with such distinguished examples of wisdom, and of devotion; and Catholic verities gaining daily, in lustre and strength. And this is not incompatible with the presence of great evils in society; rather, there is no bow of consolation without the storm of adversity; and it was in the end of the ravages, amid the vapors and darkness of the retreating deluge, that the rainbow was seen in the clouds. Thus, it follows here upon the end of the first woe, and may, perhaps, attend the evening of this declining life to its close. It may be observed, also, that, in the time of that first desolation, the promise was made: "Seed time and harvest, cold and heat, summer and winter, night and day, shall not cease."[2] The faith of men needs to be re-assured, that the divine intentions may be fully accomplished; for, evermore, the evil goes side by side with the good, and both together seem to prevail. As in the

[1] S. Luke xxi. 29. [2] Gen. viii. 22.

beginning, the earth was watered, not by rain, "but a spring rose out of the earth, watering all the surface of the earth,"[1] and, afterwards, in paradise, "a river went out of the place of pleasure to water paradise,"[2] and before the flood there was no such confusion of storm-cloud and sun, as to produce the rainbow, and men believed not in the coming of the deluge, because there was so little appearance of probability in such an irregularity; yet, almost from the first, "thorns and thistles" were the fruits of an accursed land, and flood, and blight, and drought have so gained upon it that disorder of the seasons seems to be the rule; distemper of the body, and inordination of the soul of man, a law of his condition, enforced with new rigor. And, therefore chastity, and poverty, and obedience, grow brighter to the last; and if they are left to be the virtues of a smaller number, it is of a chosen and beloved few.

To pursue a little farther these reflections: The natural and the supernatural method of human things, may persevere to the end of the world, but yet not without grievous perturbation of the one as well as the other; and since we are invited to study the supernatural by the help of natural signs, some estimate of the degree of faith, that first necessity of man on earth, may perhaps be obtained by the following considerations. It is evident that, in modern times, the rural life is fallen into contempt, and agriculture is in discredit. Whether the irregularity of the seasons be the cause or the effect of their infidelity, so it is, that men will not trust to Providence, but will take their fortune into their own hands. Take, in connection with this, the physical studies and mechanical improvements of the day; that their intention is to render man superior to the inequalities and uncertainties of nature, or independent of divine Providence; and is it not manifest, that even the natural faith of the creature toward the Creator is impaired? But if the natural faith be wanting, how much more the supernatural! When they lack the former, assuredly, they have no sense of the latter.

[1] Gen. ii. 6. [2] Gen. ii. 10.

2 And he had in his hand a little book open: and he set his right foot upon the sea, and his left foot upon the land.

An open book: because the end declares itself; and needs not to be loosed, because of itself it is the dissolution of this present state of expectancy. A little book: because few words describe it, and human discourse has fulfilled its office, and similitudes must now pass into realities. Or if it be regarded as the book of the Sacred Scriptures, which our Redeemer, alone, by his death, resurrection, and ascension, has laid open, as St. Gregory intimates, the conclusion is the same; that now all mysteries are solved, all prophecies fulfilled, and the divine works of creation, redemption, and sanctification accomplished with the end of time. His right foot is upon the sea: because the sea is before the land, in the order of creation. Or the sea is the church, and the land the world; hoc sæculum. It signifies that he stands above the sphere of mortal existences, and holds our transitory state beneath his feet.

3 And he cried out with a loud voice, as when a lion roareth. And when he had cried out, seven thunders uttered their voices.

The divine Savior of men, when his last hour was come, cried for our sakes "with a loud voice." The angel of God, the guardian of our planet, beholding its perils and the last agony of its human race, cries out as a lion roareth, but heaven answers in thunders.

4 And when the seven thunders had uttered their voices, I was about to write: and I heard a voice from heaven saying to me, Seal up the things which the seven thunders have spoken, and write them not.

A voice from heaven, as of a tender Father, commands many things to be sealed up from our feeble understanding, which men would not contemplate, even if they were put in view. "Pondus ejus ferre non potui. His weight I was not able to bear; quia cum supernæ majestatis vim ad judicium venientis terroremque tanti examinis considerando animus conatur exquirere, mox ad semet ipsum refugiens sese expavescit invenisse.[1] For when the mind would attempt to weigh the force of supernal Majesty, and of his fearful advent to judgment, presently it shrinks back within itself, trembling at the knowledge it has gained." It is written, that, in the last days, "there shall be great tribulation, such as hath not been from the beginning of the world until now, neither shall be." Tribulation of body and of soul, pains and temptations of the flesh, fears and anguish of the mind. Here, therefore, curiosity is quenched, and there can be but one impulse of the human heart, to pray that such tribulation may be averted from us, and from our age.

5 And the angel, which I saw standing upon the sea, and upon the land, lifted up his hand to heaven:

6 And he swore, by him that liveth forever and ever, who created heaven, and the things which are therein; and the earth, and the things which are therein; and the sea, and the things which are therein; that time shall be no more:

7 But that, in the days of the voice of the seventh angel, when he shall begin to sound the trumpet, the mystery of God shall be finished, as he hath declared by his servants, the prophets.

The angel, standing between heaven and earth, in the midway of this created universe, swears, by the Creator of all above, around, and beneath, that, at the sound of the seventh trumpet, time shall be no more. If St. Augustine could trace back the beginnings of creation so far into the recesses of eternity, how momentous is the point in time where the vast sequence is closed forever! The long labor and patience of the good God, the ever-increasing and ever-varying magnificence of his works, the prolonged woes of decaying humanity, the swift, unwearied charity of angels, the incessant malice of malignant spirits, the enduring virtues of the just, and the unsparing hostility of the impious; "in a moment, in the twinkling of an eye, at the last trumpet" all is finished. The sands are run, the day, the year, is ended; there is no measure of time; not an hour, not one moment, remains for-

[1] St. Gregory Moral. 21. 36.

ever. There is no longer faith, nor hope, discourse, nor debate, neither counsel nor entreaty; but joy is in heaven, sorrow is shut down in hell. Naturally, the mind recoils from the thought of that last dread moment. The sophist laughs at it, impotently. The man of the world will not grasp it; many an humble soul fears to do so. And yet for this the prophets are sent, the gospel is announced, heaven waits, hell watches, and earth expects, that the mystery of God may be finished, and his adorable ways be vindicated.

The expression, *when he shall begin* to sound the trumpet of the English version, as well as *coeperit* of the Latin, is somewhat ambiguous; as though there might be a series of days when the sound of the seventh trumpet is begun and continued, earlier and later. The Greek μελλη, implies rather the contrary, as thus: that, in the days of the seventh voice, the angel is ready and prepared to sound, but does not sound the trumpet until the appointed time is come. Nothing, therefore, forbids the identifying the seventh with that decisive and last trumpet of judgment, which is elsewhere alluded to in holy scripture, and has passed into the traditions and familiar discourse of Christian nations.

8 And I heard a voice from heaven speaking to me again, and saying: Go, and take the book that is open, from the hand of the angel standing upon the sea, and upon the land.

The heavenly Father, who knoweth the things of which his servants have need, now reserves some, and now imparts other instructions; what the apostle would write of his own motion, was withheld; and the gift he would not have presumed to ask, is bestowed. The book in the hand of the angel, who announces the end of time, relates to the same last days, and is, so far forth, distinct from the book of seven seals; otherwise the appellation *little* would seem to be an expletive. But by synecdoche, it may be the book of sacred scripture, inasmuch as it contains prophetic communications relating to the end of the world, and to the future state; being the compendium, so to speak, of the remainder of the Apocalypse; or, the spiritual nutriment of the Word of God, which was to enable the Blessed Apostle to perform his prophetic office, wherein he publishes the rewards and punishments of divine Justice.

9 And I went to the angel, saying unto him, that he should give me the book. And he said to me, Take the book, and devour it: and it shall make thy belly bitter: but in thy mouth it shall be sweet as honey.

10 And I took the book from the hand of the angel, and devoured it: and it was in my mouth sweet as honey: and when I had devoured it, my belly was bitter.

The good soldier, who is ordered to a post of danger, receives gladly the honorable appointment, though sore distress may follow in the practice of his duty. So the faithful servant receives in a good heart, the Word of God, though it speaks of hell, as well as of heaven, and though it may lead him through much tribulation. The thought of heaven is sweet, though the transit of death is bitter; lovely and desirable is the end, though the agony is under it. Or, as St. Gregory expounds a similar text in the book of Ezechiel: The word of God, which is sweet to the understanding, yet induces compunction of heart while it is ruminated within; that is, according as divine wisdom irradiates the soul, so is the poverty of the latter, and its unprofitable correspondence to grace revealed. Or lastly, while it tastes the divine sweetness, it turns to indignation at the ingratitude of men; and while it praises the blessedness of the elect, it mourns over the obstinacy of the impenitent.

11 And he said to me: Thou must prophesy again to nations, and peoples, and tongues, and to many kings.

Why is it said, Thou must prophesy again, but because that, in the order of narration, we appear to have reached the end? and because, having passed from end to end of universal time, it would seem that all, or enough, has been said. But yet there are many more things to be added, for the instruction of nations, and peoples and tongues; lessons of consolation, and of reproof, to many kings, among whom have been found so often the types of Antichrist.

CHAPTER XI.

IN this chapter is continued the appendix or addenda of certain events which occur in the last days. The history of Henoch and Elias now follows; and if it be asked why it is inserted here, rather than in the visions of the Church Militant, or of Antichrist, or elsewhere, it may be answered: that these venerable names originating in remote ages, one in the middle of time, when the Jewish Church was in its highest prosperity, the other, even before the rite of circumcision was instituted, and far away in an antiquity the most profound of which we can have any notion; they belong not so much to Christian, or even to Hebrew times, as to the compass of all time. For in them will meet the ends of the world, and they "shall turn the heart of the fathers to the children, and the heart of the children to their fathers."[1] And the common humanity of races and languages, however various, and even of religions, (if it were possible,) which have remained at variance, shall in them be reconciled. And besides, it is related in this chapter, that when, after their death, by the beast, they return again to life, and are called up into heaven before their enemies, men are cast into a fear, and will give glory to the God of heaven; and then the second woe is past. As was seen in the end of the first woe, it was said to be past, because there was a reaction, a well-defined revulsion of sentiment toward the ancient and Catholic truth; so here the martyrdom of Henoch and Elias is that point on which hinges the boundary of the second woe; the conversion of men being that crisis which terminates or interscinds the second woe from the third; according to the words of the same Holy Prophet: "lest I come and strike the earth with anathema."

[1] Mal. iv. 6.

1 And there was given me a reed like unto a rod; and it was said to me: Rise, and measure the temple of God, and the altar and them that adore in it.

Before the book of seven seals was wholly opened, and before the last seal was loosed by the solemn consummation of the Cross, the elect were numbered. So here, while the final catastrophe of earth impends, the just are again measured and registered for eternity. But, as if the account were more strict in the last days, the rule of divine justice is like a rod; and, by that true measure, severe, but impartial, none except those who adhere to the temple of truth, who serve faithfully its altars, or who devoutly adore within its walls, none shall endure the scrutiny.

2 But the court, which is without the temple, cast out, and measure it not, because it is given to the Gentiles; and the holy city they shall tread under foot forty-two months.

The court without, is this world wherein God has established his holy temple. Formerly, "God, having overlooked the times of ignorance, now declareth to men that all should everywhere do penance." It is a fearful truth, that from the beginning of the world to the end, the ingratitude of men is aggravated according as the law of God is more widely published, his truth more plainly revealed, and his Church more distinctly defined, with every succeeding year. As the time is shorter, so is the necessity more pressing; and what is it that constitutes the woes of the last days, but the fact, that when Catholic truth is more than ever clearly defined, and its perpetuity most thoroughly tested, at that very time men are most obstinate under the delusions of pride and sophistry. Therefore, at last the herd of the incredulous is abandoned by God, and no measure of them is taken. And what wonder if the multitude of this world perishes, when, for a time, even the holy city, the congregation of the faithful, will be so trodden under foot, that scarcely the elect shall be saved; "and unless those days had been shortened, there should no flesh be saved."

But, before leaving this portion of the sacred text, it may be well to seek a more literal and strict interpretation of the same. The temple is the place of sacrifice; and, as the temple of God in heaven, is the place, or the manner of the divine praises, as they are presented before the throne of God by the heavenly inhabitants, our intercessors; so the temple of God here in this life will be the interior devotion and merits of those actually in the state of grace, as distinguished from the visible fold of the mass, both good and bad. That is, the holy city being the Church, and the temple the place of sacrifice or expiation, the temple of God may be distinguished from the city of God, as that higher and more excellent life, which is found only in the practice, at least impliedly, of the evangelical counsels. And they who adore in it, are measured at the same time with the altar, because their acts are squared and fashioned by the maxims of the Cross. While the multitude of indifferent or imperfect Christians, that is, they who fill the court, or hang like a burden upon the skirts of the Holy Mother, will be cast aside; forfeiting thereby what little grace they may have possessed, and becoming conformed to the Gentile manners, or altogether confounded with the people of the world.

3 And I will give to my two witnessses, and they shall prophesy a thousand two hundred sixty days, clothed in sackcloth.

It is evident, that out of all mankind, two persons, and two alone, have been removed from this visible sphere without death; "and, as it is appointed for men once to die," so it is a common tradition in the Church, that they will return again to human society, and meet the common death. Their resting-place, in the mean time, is supposed to be in the Paradise which "the Lord God planted from the beginning;" For the wise man saith: "Henoch pleased God, and was translated into Paradise, that he may give repentance to the nations." [1]

Of which, it is furthermore recorded: "that the Lord God

[1] Eccles. xliv. 16.

placed before the Paradise of pleasure Cherubims, and a flaming sword, turning every way, to keep the way of the tree of life." St. Thomas[1] shows that the same is a certain corporeal or geographical place, locus corporeus; undiscovered, because inaccessible to men; and it may have been preserved in the time of the Deluge, by the same Power which preserved the life of the prophet Jonas in the depths of the sea. But, however this may be, there is no need of adducing proofs, for a common tradition, that Henoch and Elias will return again among men, and that they are supposed to be indicated by the two witnesses in the text. Forty-two months of thirty days, give a thousand two hundred and sixty days. The time of their prophecy will therefore be simultaneous with that when the holy city shall be trodden under foot. Otherwise it would seem incongruous, that these two portions of time should be mentioned in such close connection. Days, in the prophetic writings, are sometimes reckoned as years, but, in this instance, they must be taken literally, in order to be consistent with Christian tradition, and with the just proportion of events. In the time, therefore, of the Church's greatest necessity, when Satan triumphs over the prostrate souls of Christian people, and the bark of Peter is in its most desperate extremity, these two holy souls, reserved by the divine economy for that hour of need, will be witnesses to that eternal wisdom, which instructed the patriarchs, inspired the prophets, and which ever illuminates the Catholic Church as its appointed resting-place; "in plenitudine sanctorum detentio ejus."[2] But in that time of mourning they prophesy in sackcloth; in the garb of penance, and perhaps in the exercise of austerities more extraordinary than ever before known, being proportioned to their already preternatural subsistence in the mortal life.

4 These are the two olive trees, and the two candlesticks, standing before the Lord of the earth.

[1] Summa. i. 102. 1. [2] Eccles. xxiv. 16.

This is an allusion to a vision of the prophet, Zacharias,[1] in which he beheld a candlestick of gold, with its lights, and two olive branches on either side. Which vision, his angel interpreted, of Zorobabel, the prince, who was then restoring the temple; but to the inquiry made, and repeated, "What are the two olive branches?" the angel answers concisely, "These are two sons of oil, who stand before the Lord of the whole earth." If the life of the just man be a continual progress in holiness, how exalted must be the sanctity to which these have attained, who have stood almost from the beginning, in meek expectation before the Lord of the whole earth! What brightness of wisdom, what noble devotion, what effulgence of charity, and tenderness of unction, must adorn their souls, and illustrate their presence on earth! Worthy, therefore, of these great apostles, is the mission appointed for them, namely, to witness to the peerless and sovereign beauty of the Catholic wisdom, hated and despised as it may be by men, and to restore, again, to its eternal truth, the hearts of the Hebrew people. According to the testimony of Holy Scripture, "Who are registered in the judgments of times, to appease the wrath of the Lord, to reconcile the heart of the father to the son, and to restore the tribes of Jacob."[2] Thus, will the power and goodness of Almighty God be signally displayed, in the conversion of these misguided souls. "For, if the loss of them be the reconciliation of the world; what shall the receiving of them be but life from the dead?"[3] Thus He "reacheth from end to end mightily, and ordereth all things sweetly."[4] And how sweetly ordered is the consonance, the apostle, who tenderly loved his people, argues to us Gentiles; "For, if thou wert cut out of the wild olive tree, which is natural to thee; and, contrary to nature, wert grafted into the good olive tree, how much more shall they, that are the natural branches, be grafted into their own olive tree!"[5]

[1] Zach. iv. [2] Eccles. xlviii. 10. [3] Rom. xi. 15.
[4] Wis. viii. 1. [5] Rom. xi. 24.

5 And if any man would hurt them, fire shall come out of their mouths, and shall devour their enemies: and if any man would hurt them, in this manner must he be killed.

Some pious writers have given, to their interpretation of this text, the literal sense of the same precisely as it reads; which can hardly consist with the fact, that the enemies of the two witnesses will at last kill the witnesses, they themselves remaining in life. Therefore, by that which proceeds from their mouths, it is better to understand their fiery, intrepid words of truth, which will wither and devour the souls of hypocrites. And inasmuch as this fire pierces to the marrow, and to the inmost heart of the man, so is its power more scathing and terrible than that of the material element. It is always dangerous to do an injury to the truth, but in that time when God vouchsafes a testimony so illustrious, he who would impugn such manifest evidence, destroys his own soul. Might it not even be said, that he sins against the Holy Ghost, who then tenders to men, as it were, his last gracious inspiration?

6 These have power to shut heaven, that it rain not in the days of their prophecy: and they have power over waters to turn them into blood, and to strike the earth with all plagues as often as they will.

Among the instances of their miraculous power, most signal and convincing would be that in which they should shut heaven, that it rain not; as the prophet Elias has formerly done in the days of king Achab;[1] and which memorable act of his has remained forever recorded in the pages of holy Scripture. What are the waters of which men drink in the last days? Not certainly the living waters of truth, but rather the fountains of error. And while the error is never unmixed with truth, this very circumstance is their condemnation, and furnishes the occasion for convicting them out of their own mouths. When, therefore, such fragments of holy truth as remain among men, entangled in the mazes

[1] 3 Kings xvii.

of their foolish disputations, are suddenly brought to light and vindicated by the two witnesses; then their own favorite theories and false doctrines are turned to them as blood. And whichever way these holy men may choose to turn, their presence will accordingly be a plague and a torment to the impious; for, while their vocation is attested by miracles in the sensible order, and their venerable appearance will strike the scorners with intolerable fear, their authority will be like that of the testimony of the whole people of God, summed up and embodied in these inspired and glorious martyrs. When men have dissolved the bonds of religion, of patriotism, of morality and subordination in society, how terribly will they be convinced of their profligacy by the austerities of Elias the Thesbite, to whom the fire and the waters of heaven, were obedient! And when charity is grown so cold that they would divide the unity of the race, and sunder the ties of a common humanity; how will their hearts be pierced at the sight of him who can claim a parent's authority over every human being on earth; and from whom one and all alike, may crave an equal and undoubted father's blessing! That Henoch and Elias shall thus appear again, and in a way such that men cannot hesitate to recognize them, seems perhaps to some, a thing altogether incredible. The established order of civilized life appears to them to be founded in a weight so solid, and in a dignity so imperturbable, that an anomaly of this kind cannot be admitted for a moment. But let them not be disturbed; it may pass like other events; and the truth has fallen upon men already, with a shock infinitely heavier than this, when the Lord Omnipotent has himself met them face to face. "Amen," it is written, "the servant is not greater than his lord: neither is an apostle greater than he that sent him."

It should be observed, however, that some authors do not consider it necessary to interpret this passage of the sacred text, personally, of Henoch and Elias; but by the two witnesses, they suppose may be understood two eminent saints, who will come in the spirit or virtue of the ancient Fathers.

On which hypothesis it might be suggested, that they will be two of the Hebrew race, distinguished by gifts of nature, and of grace, whose testimony will be opportune, for the reason that the Jews will be (as it is said) disposed to hail Antichrist as the veritable Messiah. And since, in the mouth of two or three witnesses, shall every word be established, these may be eminently the witnesses of divine truth, inasmuch as their testimony may be supposed to be that of unprejudiced umpires, between the Christian religion and the blasphemies of Antichrist. And, because of their generous defence of the former, they may, in an additional sense, deserve the title of witnesses, when they accept martyrdom, and obtain the baptism of blood.

But, since it is the tradition, as it were, of all ages, both Hebrew and Christian, that Elias, indeed, shall come and restore all things; and, because it might be rash to depart from so authentic a belief, we leave, now, this digression, and resume the exposition in its first intention.

7 And when they shall have finished their testimony, the beast that ascendeth out of the abyss, shall make war against them, and shall overcome them, and kill them.

The beast, or Antichrist, who heads the world in its swift passage to perdition, prevails against even these venerable witnesses, the last defence, and forlorn hope, as it were, of the truth; and then, indeed, the land is desolate, when the resources of Holy Revelation seem to be exhausted.

8 And their bodies shall lie in the streets of the great city, which spiritually is called Sodom, and Egypt, where, also, their Lord was crucified.

It has been thought, by some, that a particular city is here specified, but to this there appear to be insurmountable objections. It cannot be the city of Rome, or of Babylon, because the Savior of men was crucified in Jerusalem. And, again, the literal Jerusalem cannot be intended, because that is never called, in any sense, Egypt, but rather it is the direct antithesis of Egypt. Therefore, in the great city of this World, which, for its abominations, is like Sodom, and for its carnal delights and prodigious enchantments, is like Egypt, in its dusty and crowded highway, publicly, and in open day, where their Sovereign Lord was crucified, here, also, the two witnesses lie slaughtered, by guilty men.

9 And they, of the tribes, and peoples, and tongues, and nations, shall see their bodies for three days and a half; and shall not suffer their bodies to be laid in sepulchres.

Literally, in so short a time how can people of different countries see their bodies? It may be answered, that it is not said all, but some of the tribes and peoples, shall see them. And, if never before, we, in these days, can understand how the facilities of transportation may be so great, that in a moment's notice the representatives of far distant countries may be gathered to a common point. But, mystically, it need not be doubted, that the greater number of mankind, who had never seen them in life, nor desired to do so, but avoided their presence, and studied to drive the intelligence or mention of Henoch and Elias out of discourse, and out of memory, will, at the report of their death, throw off the mask of indifference or pride, and hasten forth to see their dead bodies, though they shunned the living spirits. The spectacle of a bloody death always attracts the attention of the multitudes, but then the curiosity of all men must be strongly aroused, in proportion as the testimony of the two witnesses shall have been luminous, their acts admirable, and their mission portentous.

10 And the inhabitants of the earth shall rejoice over them, and make merry; and shall send presents, one to another, because these two prophets tormented them that dwelt upon the earth.

This proves how universally men will recognize the persons of Henoch and Elias, whether they be willing to own it or not; and, again, their great merriment at the death of the same, shows how grievous will have been their apprehension of the approaching judgment. The same truth, whose brightness refreshes the mind of the just man, is a torment to the soul of the ungodly. It is no fault of the prophet, that he will not swerve or bend the truth to suit the fancy of the depraved; but it is the crime of the latter, and their endless misery, that they will not, themselves, be converted to the sacred love of wisdom. By the death of the two prophets, being sudenly relieved of this anguish of soul, and of the heavy dread of instant judgment; men, for a short time, give loose to the utmost license of blasphemous mirth and revelry, and they congratulate one another, as upon a great danger escaped, or an empty terror wholly exploded.

11 And after three days and a half, the spirit of life, from God, entered into them. And they stood upon their feet; and great fear fell upon them that saw them.

But suddenly all their boasting is hushed, and they relapse into their former fear. Thus are the impious tossed miserably, as with a consuming fever, now elated with pride, now dejected in despair; "Clouds without water, which are carried about by winds, trees of the autumn unfruitful, twice dead, plucked up by the roots."[1] The sacred writer condescends to portray so vividly this last scene of human history, that no words could add to the force of his narrative.

12 And they heard a great voice from heaven, saying to them, Come up hither. And they went up into heaven, in a cloud; and their enemies saw them.

As if the Creator would give to his creatures the fulness of evidence at last, the bodies of the two prophets remain unburied upwards of three days before the world; then, in the presence of their enemies, they stand upon their feet alive; the voice from heaven is heard, plainly, calling them; and they ascend up into heaven; and their enemies see all this with their eyes, and hear it with their ears.

13 And at that hour there was a great earthquake, and the tenth part of the city fell; and there were slain in the earthquake, names of men, seven thousand; and the rest were cast into a fear, and gave glory to the God of heaven.

[1] S. Jude 13.

It is recorded, of many of the saints, that, at their death, and passage out of this life, the earth has trembled; it may, therefore, well be that the land shall quake, when the prophets take their leave of men. By the fall of a tenth part of the city, may be understood a heavy destruction or decimation of the material goods; or grievous disasters to this world, in the temporal pursuits of commerce or agriculture, or of the arts. And the names of men, signifies, either that a vast number of men of note, will perish by the visitation of God, or, that the death of a great number, body and soul, will be so marked that it shall be well known to all it was by a direct judgment of Divine Providence.

Weak and thoughtless minds are always ready to inquire: If the testimony be so plain, if the evidence be indeed sufficient, why do not men believe? why will not the world be converted? A late noble[1] writer has argued that the gospel did not prevail only by force of palpable miracles, that the truth of Jesus Christ has not triumphed over the world merely by dint of evidence, but rather, as man naturally resents a powerful array of proofs, thus it has been seen that the grace of God has overcome the mind of man notwithstanding all obstacles, material, intellectual, and lastly those of his moral nature, or of his perverted will; and, therefore, the truth conquers, not so much by means of its witnesses as over and above, or, as we say, in spite of the same. When, therefore, it is written that the rest of men were cast into a fear, this may indeed be by the force of plain reason; but that they should give glory to God, in this we must admire the free grace and tender love of the Father Almighty.

14 The second woe is past: and, behold, the third woe will come quickly.

Here is the end of the second woe, and of this world's history. At this era the hearts of men begin to be converted again to the service of God, but for how long or how sincerely, who can tell? It is said the third woe will come

[1] Cortes. Enseyo el Catol. i. 5.

quickly: either in mercy to the newly converted, or perhaps in anger at their immediate relapse. Whether the reign of Antichrist will have commenced before the times of Henoch and Elias, or not, it would seem that his power is at its height in that time of forty-two months; and that, from the hour of their martyrdom, commences his downfall. If, then, it may be inferred, from the words of St. Paul to the Thessalonians, concerning the man of sin, "whom the Lord Jesus shall destroy with the brightness of his coming," that the last day will find Antichrist yet in life, perhaps the remainder of time is indicated by the prophecy of Daniel, where it is written, "Blessed is he that waiteth and cometh unto a thousand three hundred thirty-five days;" as if, whosoever will persevere to that time, must needs be saved; since then the hour of probation is ended, and the time of temptation is finished forever.

15 And the seventh angel sounded the trumpet: and there were great voices in heaven, saying: The kingdom of this world is become our Lord's and his Christ's, and he shall reign forever and ever: Amen.

Blessed be God, doth the just man exclaim, that the end is come; and that the long outraged goodness of Jesus Christ shall never be grieved again forever.

16 And the four-and-twenty ancients, who sit on their seats in the sight of God, fell upon their faces, and adored God, saying:

17 We give thee thanks, O Lord God Almighty, who art and who wast, and who art to come; because thou hast taken thy great power, and thou hast reigned.

And all the company of heaven render thanks to God, that he hath come to judgment, and hath again made all his own, the royal power he had entrusted to the sons of men.

18 And the nations were angry, and thy wrath is come, and the time of the dead to be judged; and to render a reward to thy servants the prophets, and to the saints, and to them that fear thy name, little and great; and to destroy them that have corrupted the earth.

Then the angry malice of the nations is overwhelmed by the wrath of heaven, which pierces even to the secrets of the grave. The empty, present joys are scattered, and the far distant and eternal ones are established forever. "A fire shall go before him and burn his enemies round about."[1] Then, purged of every stain, this land remains a spotless portion of the heavenly domain, a garden of the elect, the flowers of sanctity.

19 And the temple of God was opened in heaven; and the ark of his testament was seen in his temple. And there were lightnings, and voices, and an earthquake, and great hail.

In the end, the temple of God is opened in heaven, because the sacramental constitution of things is plainly disclosed, their sacrificial administration ended; and the communion of the saints, of the Church Militant with the Church Triumphant, is visibly completed. How resplendent, then, is the light of truth! How vast the multitude, whose voices bear witness to the eternal wisdom! While even the dull sons of earth are quickened to confess the justice of God, though his goodness is like hail upon their envious souls fixed in the anguish of despair forever.

Within the inmost heaven is seen the ark of his testament, the most sacred law of God, faithful and indefectible. Having traced its action through the bounds of time, the Apostle now returns to the consideration of the same, as it is manifested more specially in the Christian Church; hence we pass to the Third Division of this work.

[1] Psalms cxxix, 7.

PART III.

THE CHURCH MILITANT BEFORE THE WORLD.

Our Creator has appointed this earth for his battle-ground of good and evil. On one side, is his holy church, the company of the faithful; to it are opposed the powers of the world. The latter are of two kinds; the spiritual wickedness of Satan, and the material force of human governments. Of the two chapters which compose this Part, the first represents the church in her conflict with the Adversary of our race; the second describes the exaltation of the political power, and its final supremacy above divine authority. Though the history of the church is, in some respects, the same in all ages, the first six verses of the twelfth chapter will, however, be considered as relating more particularly to the early age of the church; the following verses, as far as the twelfth, which describe the subjugation of Satan, may be understood of her midway course; and the remaining verses pertain to her last struggles with Satan. In which latter period he brings into his service the secular arm; and this leads to the thirteenth chapter, wherein the same power is portrayed briefly in its origin, but more largely in its termination or last result, which is the reign of Antichrist.

CHAPTER XII.

1 AND there appeared a great wonder in heaven: a woman clothed with the sun, and the moon under her feet, and on her head a crown of twelve stars.

It is a great wonder, in this iron world, where brutal strength prevails so often above modest worth, that a woman should be thus exalted; and yet all these gifts, and more, have been truly bestowed upon the Catholic Church and upon its archetype, the Virgin Mother of Christ. In heaven, or upwards, do we look for the heavenly bodies; so the church is lifted up above this world in the sight of all mankind, and is to be sought with upturned face and with uplifted heart. The sun signifies the light of truth; the moon, the ever defectible vicissitudes of time; thus holy church, says St. Gregory, is clothed with the splendor of heavenly wisdom, and holds all earthly things beneath her feet. The stars of the first magnitude, are the twelve apostles, in whose doctrine she is established, and by their acts adorned. Even so, Blessed Mary is clothed, by her inhabiting Son, with immaculate purity, and the stars are blessed that declare her praises, and every creature is less beautiful than her feet.

2 And she, being with child, cried, travailing in birth, and was in pain to be delivered.

Mary is the Mother of Christ, the Church is the Mother of Christians. Her soul was transfixed with grief, and the Church, in tears, labors for our salvation.

3 And there appeared another wonder in heaven: and, behold, a great red dragon, having seven heads and ten horns; and on his heads seven diadems.

Side by side with the marvellous goodness of God, is the

wonderful malice of Satan. He, too, is lifted up, and wanders in high places, between heaven and earth; and thrusts himself between the pilgrim in this valley of tears, and his home above. The dragon is possessed of power beyond comparison greater than any human force. Red, is the color, which seizes most strongly the sense of sight: that chief portal of the human soul. It is the color of Satan's pomps, by which he fascinates and betrays the soul of man; but, by the goodness of God, they pale before the crimson wounds of Jesus Christ, and of his army of martyrs. And, accordingly, it now graces the Prince of the church, by a better right, than it ever adorned the Potentate of earth. The seven heads are the principal empires among which the dominion of the world is successively divided. The ten horns are all other principalities or inferior powers; whether monarchical, or republican, or otherwise. On his heads are seven diadems, because from first to last the grand empires or tyrannies have been his own.

The earth is said sometimes to be the Lord's, or his saints'; and again, the devil is called the Prince of this world. Both propositions may be true, and the two powers be never confounded. So far as it is the Lord's, one divine law and temple, or one faith and one sovereign pastor, is the singular and undivided rule which governs the soul or the spiritual part of the man. But, so far as he revolts from this lofty state of honorable obedience, he falls under the servitude of the flesh and of the material forces, which are not one, but multiple, brutal, and tyrannical. These are the powers of darkness, which touch not the heart; but probe the flesh, or intoxicate the senses; unless, by the grace of God, and almost by a miracle, they are employed in the service of his true worship, as when the State consents to defend and serve loyally the Church. But commonly, the temporal power opposes, rather than promotes, the salvation of men; and therein it is the kingdom of Satan, as distinguished from that of Heaven. Satan is, therefore, thus aptly described, not indeed because he holds personally the reins of government, but because, through the same, his power is derived to mankind in by far the most sensible and formidable manner. For was it not through this means, that the death of our divine Lord was accomplished? and his disciples have suffered and must again suffer, in like manner.

4 And his tail drew the third part of the stars of heaven, and cast them to the earth; and the dragon stood before the woman, who was ready to be delivered; that, when she would be delivered, he might devour her son.

By the stars of heaven, may be understood the angels, or men eminent in the church; who, amid the darkness of this life, were designed, by their Creator, to give the light of holy example, and so fulfil the sentence of the Royal Prophet: "The heavens shew forth the glory of God." But, infatuated by satanic pride, they are led captive in the Dragon's train; and are plucked down from that high estate, into the mire of ambition and mundane glory. A third part is a large part: that is, but little less than a half. For the product of Satan seems almost equal to that of God. How it may be in the secret balance of divine truth, no one can presume to say; Dominus ponderator spirituum;[1] but, to the human estimation, the power and glories of the world appear but little less than those of heaven; and the minions of Satan to outnumber the children of God. "God is good to Israel, to them that are of a right heart. But my feet were almost moved, my steps had well-nigh slipt, seeing the prosperity of the wicked."[2]

The dragon was before the woman: and for long ages had triumphed over the human race. And again, Holy Church is but as a woman, before the secular power; having neither weapons or temporal sword, but trusts to generous hearts, or solely to the Father in heaven to provide her champion in the hour of need. As soon as she is delivered, her son is ready to be devoured: because all the malice of Satan seems light, compared with the malignity with which he persecutes the

[1] Prov. xvi. 2. [2] Psalms lxxii. 2.

regenerated soul. "Son, when thou comest to the service of God, stand in justice and in fear, and prepare thy soul for temptation."[1]

5 And she brought forth a man child, who was to rule all nations with an iron rod; and her son was taken up to God and to his throne.

The First-born of all the living, is the Son of Mary, the Mother of the elect. This is the Man-child, Wonderful, God the Mighty, whose weakness is stronger than men; to whom the Lord hath said: "Thou shalt rule them with a rod of iron;"[2] who hath ascended into heaven, and sitteth at the right hand of God, the Father Almighty. Moreover, every good Christian is as a man-child; for there is no sex in the soul, but the soldier of Jesus Christ, arrayed in the armor of God, and girt about with truth, is terrible to the reprobate; and his holy example in this world, is like a rod of iron upon their necks; and after this life he also is taken up to God, and to his throne.

6 And the woman fled into the wilderness, where she had a place prepared by God, that there they should feed her a thousand two hundred and sixty days.

The wilderness is the world of the Gentiles, to which Holy Church so early turned, being rejected by the Jews. Or, more literally, in the first persecutions, Christians went forth in crowds to the desert, and served God in holy solitude. In some sense, it may be said, that the proper place of the Church is abroad in exile and not in courts; she is a pilgrim on earth, and without a home, flying from land to land; if, perchance, like the dove of the ark, she may anywhere find rest for her foot, and announce the peace of heaven to men of good will. Thus, and only thus, in the twelve hundred and sixty days, the time of her greatest desolation, undoubtedly will she be found, stripped of temporalities, of reverend authority, and of every earthly consolation. Not but that

[1] Ecclus. ii. 1. [2] Psalms ii. 9

even then shall be found a remnant of holy souls, who will feed her by the devout practice of evangelical counsels, and with the merits of martyrdom. But why is that time referred to so early in the vision? Or why is it mentioned once and again, (v. 14,) being repeated in almost the same words? if not to show that first, and last, and always, the Christian must remember his last end; and that the Church in every age is watchful for the end, and ready, in meek obedience, for the tribulations of this life, undisturbed by prosperity, and undismayed by adversity. Or, if a more technical solution be desired, it can be said: that the Apostle surveys the progress of the Church from end to end; and, that the narrative may not be interrupted, sets forth briefly, in these six verses, the whole scheme of the Gospel. But hence, he returns to the consideration of the Church, under a special aspect; and afterwards in a particular relation, to the temporal power.

7 And there was a great battle in heaven; Michael, and his angels, fought with the dragon; and the dragon fought, and his angels.

Sustained by the merits of our Divine Savior, of his Blessed Mother and the saints, the angels of God, together with Michael, the guardian of the Church, meet and do battle against the rulers of the world of this darkness. The name, Michael, signifies, "Who is like God?" as if there were necessary the highest exercise, so to speak, of Divine Power, in order that the cruel tyranny of Satan might be prostrated, and the Church established. The heaven here spoken of, is the same with that before mentioned; being the soul, or the superior part of the man, as distinguished from the body. Over which, the enemy of our race has triumphed almost with entire success, until Christian times. In all times he may have some dominion over the body, and be able to buffet the flesh, but, here, the question is of that which is above, and not of that which is beneath; wherefore the battle is on high, or in heaven.

8 And they prevailed not; neither was their place found any more in heaven.

After three hundred years of battle and persecution, it is evident that the Church of God was gloriously established on earth. And if we consider how transcendent was the change, from the idolatry, superstition, and vices of Paganism, to the pure worship, the truths and the virtues of Christianity; it will appear that Satan has been vanquished, with a defeat, complete and final. The conversion is complete: because what can be more contrary to pride, than humility? what more contradictory to the former rapacity, than the Christian liberality? what more inverse from the coarse delights of sense, than the gentle sorrows of the Cross? And it is final: because it will certainly endure to the end of time; and, however the faith may be impaired, or Catholic truth diminished of its just honors, yet it will not pass away till all things be fulfilled. Or it may, perhaps, be said, that his place is found no more in heaven: because idolatry, which is the distinctive mark of Satanic influence, the public signature of his lofty dominion over men, is banished out of the civilized world. And, whatever vain or impious doctrines may be taught, this gross, visible, worship is scattered forever; and will not be set up again, as the religion of the nations, who have been once made Christian.[1]

9 And that great dragon was cast out, the old serpent, who is called the devil, and Satan, who seduceth the whole world; and he was cast forth unto the earth; and his angels were thrown down with him.

The enemy of the human soul is a monster, hideous to the sight, and enormous in malignity; cunning as the serpent, he steals his way even into Paradise, and yet his bulk is that of the Leviathan. "His body is like molten shields, shut up close, with scales pressing upon one another. Out of his mouth go forth lamps, like torches of lighted fire. His heart shall be as hard as a stone, and as firm as a smith's anvil. There is no power on earth that can be compared with him, who was made to fear no one."[2] And, whereas he seduceth the whole world, and the nations fall down before him in

[1] See Zech. xiii. 8. [2] Job xli.

trembling adoration; the Christian soul has received grace to beat him down to the earth, with the scourge of holy penance. Reared up in the virtues of chastity, poverty, and obedience, she deigns not to notice him; or, with sweet gravity, walks undisturbed amid the turmoil of evil desires; or smiles serenely at his headlong, turbid, suggestions of vanity, or resentment, or fear. But the most signal rebuff, the decisive blow, is that which is dealt against his pride. And if one would but consider how immense and how ineffable is the passage from pride to humility; how sublime is that effect of grace, by which the mind is converted from the insolence of domination, to the meekness of self-abnegation; it must be confessed, that truly there is no achievement of mighty angel more wonderful, no miracle of stupendous power more admirable, than this perfect act of virtue, consummated within the soul, and wrought out in her practice of a holy life. Now, it is to be remembered, that these heroic acts of humility are the very ones which are oftenest repeated in the lives of the Saints. But, since "pride is the beginning of all sin,"[1] therefore, when their head and leader is smitten down, then his angels, the whole train of infernal spirits, are thrown down with him.

10 And I heard a loud voice, in heaven, saying: Now is come salvation and strength, and the kingdom of our God, and the power of his Christ: because the accuser of our brethren is cast forth, who accused them before our God, day and night.

If the angels, in heaven, rejoice over one sinner doing penance, how great is their joy, and how ceaseless their holy admiration, at the spectacle of the Church Militant in her triumphant progress over the domains of her adversary! "Behold, now is the day of salvation," saith the Apostle, which was spoken of by the Prophets. And the day of strength, when "the weak things of the world hath God chosen, that he may confound the strong." Herein is that kingdom and power of the Cross, which many kings and

[1] Eccl. x. 15.

prophets have desired to see, and have not seen them. And a further proof of the Christian's dignity may be observed, in that the loud voice from heaven, as of one glorious in the celestial hierarchy, claims them for his brethren. The angels now rejoice in the redemption of man, as before they were moved to tender compassion at his miseries ; when the accuser spared them not by day, nor night: provoking them to pride in prosperity, to despair in adversity.

11 And they overcame him by the blood of the Lamb, and by the word of their testimony; and they loved not their lives unto death.

A lamb, sacrificed, preserved the people of Israel from the power of the cruel king Pharaoh ; the blood of the Lamb of God, has rescued immortal souls from the fangs of Satan. To this infinite love of our Blessed Redeemer, his disciples have testified by word and work. They hastened to the ends of the world to proclaim it, and they willingly laid down their lives to prove it.

12 Therefore, rejoice, O ye heavens, and you that dwell therein. Wo to the earth, and to the sea, because the devil is come down unto you, having great wrath, knowing that he hath but a short time.

The Church Militant, which is ministered to by angels, and is nourished with a food most heavenly, belongs to heaven, rather than to earth. Not that she has removed, as yet, from this visible sphere, to the one invisible ; but God, having made his tabernacle with men, where the king is, there is his court ; and therefore the apostle says, of the just, " Our conversation is in heaven." Rejoice, therefore, ye heavens, thou holy mother Church, and ye children of God, whose hearts are fixed on high. But woe to the earth, and to the sea ; to the unregenerate infidel, and to the unsanctified believer ; for if before, your enemy was hateful, how terrible must he be in the rage and envy of defeat, under the added losses of an eternal glory, and of a temporal kingdom ; and knowing that not for him, as there might be for you, is there any escape from the speedy perdition of hell. If the goodness of God is great, and the compassion of Jesus Christ boundless, and the truth has been exalted, and the saints have adorned the land, ruling in the heart and mind, the language and the names of Christian people; and if Satan has been cast out from the spiritually-minded, and thrown down from his lofty eminence and domination over the intelligence of man; not for all this does it follow that your snare is broken, and that you are set free. Rather, in his downfall, he clutches at the disobedient and ungodly soul, with a new wrath, and a keener malice; and redoubles his toils, and draws closer his snares, by a just judgment of God, upon those who despise the published truth and the more abundant grace.

Hitherto is the vision of the Church in her full maturity, and in her highest prosperity. Before leaving it, it may be well to consider the difficulties which many find in adapting the prophecies of Holy Scripture to the history of the visible Church; as though her records, thus far, do not exhibit the adequate fulfilment of all those glorious promises, which relate to the joyful flourishing of Christ's kingdom; as though the world had scarcely tasted the sweets of sanctity, but there must be in preparation, somewhere, a kind of millennium of far greater blessings, and of more illustrious privileges, than have yet fallen upon the human race. It is to be observed, in the first place: that no one can pretend to estimate how great a weight of sanctity mankind may be able to endure; but, commonly, they are not disposed to demand more than a very light account, in a computation of that kind. Secondly: the office of the Church is to lead men to heaven; her beginnings are small, but the end is great. To some, she makes it appear as though heaven were already begun on earth; to all she gives abundant assurance, that, if anything is wanting, they may by seeking, find it. Her human aspect may be obscure and lowly, but her living spirit is a vision of paradise: Beata pacis visio. The inception, therefore, of the promises, is on earth, their consummation is in heaven; and as truly as there is a heaven above, so is there a kingdom of God here, within the soul of the just; and it is only by their sense of the latter, that men have a knowledge of the former. Thirdly: If we will not, or cannot, apply the measure of the divine or spiritual rule, or, if we must not go out of the plane of history, the literal narrative of events; then we must resort to comparison, and try to ascertain the relative beauty and holiness of the Catholic age, as it compares with the imperfect light, or with the profound darkness, of other ages. It is true that comparisons are odious, but the odium belongs to those who draw them in their own favor, and not to those who seek to vindicate unhonored merit. A boastful age needs no herald; but it is a sacred duty to yield its meed of praise to the one which humbly shrinks from the noisy ostentation of its own glories. Therefore, "Let us now praise men of renown, and our fathers in their generation."[1] The most Christian age, it is taken for granted, must be that which is the most Catholic. Now, the Middle Age was literally the Catholic age of Christianity; and its Catholicity was so integral and complete, that humanly speaking, the visible, historical dominion of the Church of God was then perfected. And if the argument for the outward perfection of the Church be accepted, it follows, necessarily, that her interior was also consummated in holiness, because, in a perfect organism, the one must be coeval and in unison with the other. What has been now advanced, as it is to be understood of the age as such, so it need not be taken for more than is intended, nor be narrowed down to any idiosyncrasies of persons or things. For example, the dignity of the Apostles and of those nearest to the person of Christ, may be more exalted than that of any others, or the fervor of the Martyrs may have been greater; but when we speak of Christendom itself, in its general career, it may well be presumed that, with its middle age, the heart, as it were, of its existence, it is then in the midsummer of its glories. And a further unavoidable, though regrettable, consequence of the premises will be, that, as before that era, it was always gaining or adding to its strength,

[1] Eccles. xliv. 1.

so, afterwards, it is ever losing more or less of its power over the hearts of men.

This gradation or procession of the Church has its analogies in the other works of the Creator; and not the least obvious is that of the Synagogue, fashioned by the same divine hand. The similitudes, in this instance, may be stated thus: The age of Solomon being the climacteric of the former dispensation, and the Middle age, or more particularly, the thirteenth century, being that of the Christian dispensation, we find: that anciently Wisdom culminated with Solomon, and in the latter dispensation, with the Christian Schools. Before this first epoch, the history of the world was the history of the Jews; before the second, it was the history of the Church. After the first epoch, the pagan history fills the page; after the second, is the renaissance of the same. Before these two points of time, the domain of letters was occupied by the divine wisdom; afterward it is thronged by the crowd of sophists of Greece and Rome, or by the philosophers of a material progress. Before, the works were many, the words few; witness the temple of Solomon, and the Mediæval Cathedrals; afterwards the works are meagre and short-lived, but the declamation and display are astounding. The former dispensation was marked by unity, as one people, one language, one religion; so in the latter, one sovereign Pastor, as God's vicar on earth, presided over the councils of Christendom, and the languages of Europe were so nearly akin, that a citizen of one or another territory, could converse intelligibly with those of almost every other; thus, St. Vincent could preach to all the peoples of Christendom, and be understood by them. At the first epoch, the most grievous sin was idolatry; at the second, the public sense abhorred heresy; after the first, innumerable false gods were brought in; after the second, every conceivable heresy has swarmed over Christian lands. Both periods are marked by the tranquil and sweet repose of the dominions of the Kings of Peace: Solomon, the type, Christ, the reality and divine source of heavenly peace. In both presided the serene gravity of virtue, which stoops not to publish its own praises, though its worthy fruits remain long after it. Thus many of the Psalms, and ancient books of Holy Scripture, are by authors whose names are unknown or doubtful; and the Middle age has bequeathed to us many noble works, whose authors have hidden their names forever from the knowledge of men.

The broad contrast of the nineteenth century, boastful and restless, intoxicated with its acquisitions of the baser wealth, and inflated by its earthly science to indifference or scorn of the supernal wisdom, forces again upon the mind those momentous words: "The devil is come down unto you, having great wrath, knowing that he hath but a short time." In the hurry and whirl of the present age, what is it that men so much desire? What would the soul have, which has forsaken its God? What and where, is this fleeting, mad delight? Is it to obtain, by some worthy sacrifice, a contented enjoyment? Is it a simple felicity, or some singular pleasurable rest? No; not either of these, but one and all, and every pleasure is required to be furnished to every one and at the same time, and in the same manner; and the problem of the day is, not how to reach any given happiness or defined bliss, but how to secure the greatest number of aids, with the shortest route, and least outlay, to the enjoyment of the sum of all the reputed goods of earth; without regard to inequalities of climate, or of temperament, or of mental abilities, or of physical capacities. Why? Because the time is short. And this cupidity of certain modern nations, whose earthly instincts are so keen and vigorous, is spreading rapidly over the world; and this is called civilization; and no one can be permitted to question that it is the gift of heaven, the dawning of a new and glorious era for humanity. Oculi ejus ut palpebræ diluculi. "They pretend," to quote again the prophetic words of St Gregory, "that the night of error is passed away, and that the light of truth is just breaking upon the world; they furnish marvellous signs for proof, and profess to give us better things than the former simplicity could exhibit."

But whatever may be the conquests of the Church Militant, labor and sorrow attend her; her flight to the desert is put first and last in this chapter of the Apocalypse, as though, on every side, and in all times, she must be prepared to suffer persecution for justice' sake, and through many tribulations arrive at the eternal home. We have viewed her in the noon-day of prosperity; let us now behold her in the attitude of grief, and draw near to her in the evening of adversity.

13 And after the dragon saw that he was cast unto the earth, he persecuted the woman, who brought forth the man child:

When at length the darkness of idolatry began to be dissipated, and the public sacrifice to demons to fall into contempt; and when the kings of the earth, from being her enemies, were converted to be the dutiful and affectionate sons of the Church, Satan devised yet other means to persecute the Holy Mother of our souls. After the early heresies, followed the irruptions of the barbarians into Christendom; later in time, the Saracen power began to threaten the existence of Christianity; but his last, and most fatal device is that whereby he tempts the sons of God, to lust after the pomps of this world, to struggle for preëminence of power or riches; whereupon follows discord, covetousness, luxury, neglect of the divine service, and a mournful and perilous relaxation of Christian discipline.

14 And there were given to the woman two wings of a great eagle, that she might fly into the desert to her place where she is nourished for a time, and times, and half a time, from the face of the serpent.

Disorders like those above described, must come at last; "for the imagination and thought of man's heart are prone to evil from his youth." And the wonder should be, not that such a time arrives, but that it could have been so long delayed, and held so long suspended by the power and goodness of the Creator. St. Teresa[1] compares herself to the cloud of dust, which, with favoring winds, is wafted on high,

[1] Cartas de S. T. 8.

but the breeze falling, or the divine inspiration ceasing, she drops suddenly to her native earth. Thus holy Church now beams gladly upon the soul, and anon she flies to the desert; perhaps to revive the divine grace in other hearts more lonely and desolate, or because, repelled by ingratitude, she would gain elsewhere better fruit to God. And thus, for a little while, as it were, the Catholic Church had made her resting-place in the nations of Europe, and had found a sacred and happy home in the house of religion; the monastery, the convent, or the college of canons with its consecrated Pontiff: this was the home and the birthright of her man child, who was to live the life of an angel among men. But now the time has come, when she must set forth to the desert, when her churches and monasteries are desecrated, and her priests and religious are scattered to the four corners of the earth. Why this should be so, what are the causes, or where is the fault, who shall say? Who is able to take up the first stone, and to bring an accusation against the tepidity or negligences of a better age? Irascimini et nolite peccare: Be ye angry and sin not. Satan found his way into Catholic Europe, as well as into Paradise. "The Master sowed good seed in his field, but, while men were asleep, his enemy came and oversowed cockle among the wheat." But if the germ of revolt could exist in a Catholic age, the bitter fruit at length divides from it a Protestant age, decisively, if not forever; and if the good were doubtful before, the evil is indubitable afterward. In the inscrutable wisdom of the Most High God, who "changeth times and ages," the former simplicity gives place to the latter subtlety, the dove-like innocence, to the serpent wisdom. Without stopping, therefore, to explore the vices, the nakedness of Christendom, or to determine the degree of its degeneracy from the first fervor, it is enough to know that a momentous change has passed over the civilized world; and the instruction conveyed by this dispensation of Divine Providence, this is what men should take to heart, and this is what might be, indeed, a salutary counsel to the sober and vigilant mind; even as it is designed by Him "who changeth times and ages, taketh away kingdoms and establisheth them, giveth wisdom to the wise, and knowledge to them that have understanding."[1]

To aid her, there were given to the woman, two wings of a great eagle, that is, wisdom and love. High, and wide, is the eagle's flight; and the wisdom of lofty contemplation was found joined with the works of active charity, in the persons of St. Dominic, and of St. Francis. The mother of St. Dominic dreamed that her offspring was to set the world on fire, with the fervid words of sacred doctrine. St. Francis, while waiting, humbly, on the good pleasure of the Sovereign Pontiff, was seen by the latter, in a vision, supporting on his shoulders, the falling walls of the Lateran Basilica; that Church which was established by Constantine; the Head, the Mother, and the Mistress of all Churches; which stood one thousand years, and then, shattered and rent, by fires and earthquakes, was just crumbling to ruin. Later in time, and in an hour of extreme necessity, came St. Ignatius, with his holy companions; and gloriously did the mighty wings of sanctity and of charity bear them forth into the barren wastes of the secular life, and into the utmost depths of the wilderness of heathendom.

To recapitulate: the home of the Church is manifestly the house of religion; or the religious community of father and brothers, or of mother and sisters, where the evangelical counsels are kept in soul and body. This is the house beloved of God, where they praise him in word and work, and where, with glad heart, they sing: Lætatus sum in his quæ dicta sunt mihi, in domum Domini ibimus.[2] This is that inner chamber, where the Word of God is nurtured in the peace of Jerusalem; whom His beloved spouse sought, by night, in the streets and broad ways, and found him not; and asked for him, of the watchmen, the Prophets of the Lord, and she saith: "When I had a little passed by them, I found him whom my soul loveth; I held him; and I will not let him go, till I bring him into my mother's house, and

[1] Daniel ii. 2. [2] Ps. cxxi. 1.

into the chamber of her that bore me."[1] But men of envious and ruffian hearts have broken down those sacred enclosures, have uprooted the peaceful altar, and have dissolved and scattered that pleasant household over the desert world.

The moral causes of this grand revolution or retrogradation of the Christian world, have been a vexed question, but the efficient cause is very plain. It is the civil government which passes the final sentence of confiscation upon the property of the church; it is the secular arm which throws down her walls, or converts her temples into halls and market places, or banishes the bishop and the faithful priest. Naturally, it is not willing to acknowledge any superior, nor is it accustomed to admit any question of its supreme authority; and, when it found, as in the Middle age, that the church had, with all good will on the part of the laity, obtained the precedence, and had come to possess the land, an evil spirit of envy and avarice seized it. Conscious that its own brute force was great, and, by reason of its innate dulness or poverty of grace, being unable or unwilling to discern anything higher or better, nor to understand how the soul is more honorable than the body, the spiritual order of a dignity immeasurably greater than that of the temporal polity, its covetousness would be contained by no considerations of honor or piety. That is, commonly speaking, such is the character of the secular arm, unless guided by a head endowed with extraordinary virtues of faith and devotion. And such princes were indeed plentiful in the former part of the Catholic ages, but, afterwards becoming rare, many contests arose between Church and State; simony and luxury made their way even into the house of prayer, and the dissolution of its tottering walls, declared in the fifteenth century, and continued ever since, will be consummated when the Church, going forth to the desert, reaches, at length, her place where she is nourished for a time, and times, and half a time, from the face of the serpent. This will be when she attains to the poverty and lowlinesss of her Divine Master: when she has

[1] Cant. iii. 2.

become despised and rejected of men, like Him who had not where to lay his head. How near is that time, may perhaps be inferred approximatively, by observing, first; how almost every day brings some new confiscation and disbanding of a religious establishment, and a new embarcation from the shores of Europe of its holy inmates; and, in the second place: how the work of demolition, begun by kings and continued by aristocracies, is now effected by a form or forms of government which is the expression of the popular will, and the immediate agent of the democracy. And as democracy always tends to tyranny, so the last result of an Antichristian democracy will be the enthronization of the tyrant, Antichrist.

The reign of Antichrist is supposed to be included in the time, and times, and half a time, which is three years and a half, or forty-five months, making twelve hundred and sixty days. This, again, is commonly understood to be identical with the time described by the prophet Daniel in the same phraseology, but which is afterward counted a thousand two hundred and ninety days. The discrepancy is explained by the different modes of reckoning time among various nations. The Jews counted their year by the motion of the moon; and, to make it agree with the solar year, added, at the end of two years, an intercalary month. It is very plain that the prophet, counting from the date of his vision, might have met with one or more intercalations, according as it happened to fall this or that side of the time for such an insertion. But, however this may be, it suggests the reflection, that the computations of sacred prophecies are not always to be narrowed and squared to the precise ways of human calculation, but are to be left in the liberty of him who holds the times in his hand, and who is able, out of seeming irregularity, to educe perfect harmony. Which consideration, moreover, partly meets another objection, which may be framed thus: "If the sacred writer describes the woman as flying into the desert to her place, why is this place of her nourishment divided, by so long a distance or interval from the point of her departure? But it is to be observed that, in the first allusion, (v. 6,) to this passage of the Church, the apostle expresses it in more general terms: And the woman fled into the wilderness, where she had a place, etc.; the flight, and the place, being as if detached events; but afterwards, as the end draws nearer, they are brought in closer connection, as in the present verse, which may read thus: That she might fly into the desert into her place, where she is nourished, etc. But if that hour of darkness seem to be still too much procrastinated, it is to be remembered that no time is long, which may be nigh even at the door, which is most truly hastening fast upon our steps; and, if it be a fact, that the church must decline to the evil days of her humiliation, how worthy of so awful a calamity that it should be long in the preparation; and how earnestly it is to be desired, that it may be still farther removed from our own day!

To return: the Church flies to the desert, when she withdraws from society; to her place, because her portion in this world is tribulation; the time and times, or that fearful period which is the most abominable of all the times of time, is the one in which "the continual sacrifice shall be taken away, and the abomination unto desolation shall be set up." It has been supposed, by some, that the Holy Sacrifice of the Mass will cease to be offered in the time of Antichrist, as if Christ and Antichrist could not be cohabitants of the land; and, perhaps, this is implied in the words of Saint Paul, "And now you know what withholdeth, that he may be revealed in his time." Many have thought, that, to avoid scandal, the Apostle chose to speak in this obscure manner of the fall of the Roman Empire. But there was another subject infinitely sacred, from which the Holy writer would seek by every means to avert profane discussion, as the Believer can well understand. If, therefore, the Holy Sacrifice be wholly taken away from the world, they who will feed the Church may be the two witnesses; even as Elias could once find his own nourishment in the desert; or she may be fed by the consolations of angelic messengers, who will fortify her children for martyrdom. Or, in another way, it may be said, that, as the table of the Church is the altar of the Lord, and her food is the Bread of Life, so, notwithstanding the insolence of Antichrist, who will efface every vestige of the Cross, and of the public worship of the Catholic Church, yet, even then, the sources of eternal life will not be wholly closed; but in secrecy and profound obscurity, the life-giving sacraments will be defended by Almighty God, and protected by his angels, from the face of the serpent.

15 And the serpent cast out of his mouth, after the woman, water as it were a river; that he might cause her to be carried away by the river.

It has been seen, that, in the beginning, the dragon stood ready to devour the child of God, or to persecute the woman, with the terrors of bloodshed and of corporal torments. Afterwards he exhibited the power of temptation, offering to her all the riches and honors of the world. In the latter times, when the Church, despising these bribes, has again set forth for the desert, he has vomited after her a flood of delusions, wherewith to deceive the intelligence of man. It is signified by water: because water is to earth, in some respects, what soul is to body; being a nobler element, endued with subtility and activity, the source of vital humors to the dry land; and therefore it appears to be employed in Holy Scripture in a higher sense than is the latter. This river, which was designed to overwhelm or sweep away the Catholic Church from among men, is an engine, therefore, of Satan's, aimed not so much at the senses or the passions of men, as at their understanding; and therefore it proceeds from the mouth of the serpent, as if having a sound of wisdom, or a show of reason. Historically, what is this river or torrent, but the Renaissance, or, as it is otherwise called, the Revival of Learning, which deserves neither the rank of learning, nor the title of revival. Not of learning, because God hath made foolish the wisdom of this world; and Christendom was already in possession of that sacred doctrine of

Christ crucified, which, though it be "to the Jews a stumbling block, and to the Gentiles foolishness, is, to them that are called both Jews and Greeks, the power of God and the wisdom of God." Neither should it be called a revival, as though it were the reappearance or instauration of human wisdom in Christendom, after the long silence of centuries of ignorance and darkness; for it appears now for the first time among Christian authors or artists, and in all previous ages, from the Apostles, onward, had been held in contempt or as if it were nothing in the world. This modern display of the terrestrial wisdom, had its beginning in an age of faith. It began then to thrust itself forward in the walks of philosophy, of literature, and of the arts; seconded by many inventions, useful, indeed, if they are put to a good use, such as the mariner's compass, and the press, it protruded itself even into the courts of Holy Church; and the minds of many were captivated by its marvellous array of famous names, of polished forms, and by its specious wealth of intellectual graces. It is true, the intellectual goods are valuable, for what can be supposed more powerful to attract, more noble to elevate the mind to the heights of that true wisdom which is "the brightness of eternal light, and the unspotted mirror of God's majesty?"[1] But because of their higher value, therefore, are they more dangerous in the abuse; and the pride which attends them is more hideous, as it is more subtle. Observe one of those minds so common in the latter times; one highly cultivated, and endowed with keen sagacity, and quickness of intellect: if it goes aside to impurity, if it deviates into impiety and blasphemy, if, being organized in a sensibility so delicate that it can detect and appreciate the finest distinctions of propriety and of proportion; if, with all this, it can love a lie, can delight in pollution and deformity, certainly this is the nearest approximation to satanic malice of which we can form a conception. Instantly that it rises into pride, it is transported into the arena of fallen angels; and alas, for poor reason, when matched with

[1] Wisdom vii. 26

the lightning intellect of spirit; then, indeed, is it fallen, not from angelic symmetry, but even below the animal rectitude.

16 And the earth helped the woman: and the earth opened her mouth, and swallowed up the river, which the dragon cast out of his mouth.

Beginning in a Catholic age, even as early as the fourteenth century, it is evident that the river of modern civilization was designed, by the serpent, for the damage of the Faith; and that it reached, as it were, even to the skirts of Holy Church. But presently its ravages were assuaged from her borders; for the sons of earth stood by in gaping wonder, and, with open mouths, they have swallowed down all the unwholesome draught. These, wiser in their generation than the children of light, have seized the gaudy bait, as if their own property; and have hastened on, leaving all others far behind in the march of mundane improvement. Except in proportion as the High Arts of imagination infer religion, or as sound science depends upon faith, all the honors in the domain of sense and of experimental wisdom are now theirs.

In other ways, also, the earth helps the woman, as when the physical activity of the age aids the missionary in his errand of mercy; or according as its restless investigations and its discoveries bring sacred truth more plainly to sight. But beyond this, can it be said that the earth, in some sense consciously, renders good service to the Church? Sometimes a generous resentment fills the human breast, at the spectacle of wrongs and outrage upon the helpless and innocent; or the polite ear is annoyed by calumnies disagreeable and unfashionable; or the refined mind dismisses them with silent contempt; or the busy man of the world is more amiably occupied with other cares; or the scholar is diverted by studies less criminal than the lewd diatribes of the former innovators. In some such ways, perhaps, finding that forbearance toward the Catholic Church carries with it its own recompense, in a certain amenity and repose of conscience, they become thereby happily confirmed in their original good purpose. But, whatever may be the merit of intention, most gladly does the affectionate heart of the woman seize the occasion to prove all her warmth of gratitude and love. And, O, how benignantly has the Queen of high heaven looked down upon the earth in this our day! How gracious the aspect of her Immaculate Loveliness, fully disclosed to our unworthy vision! Surely, never before did the Mother of our souls more kindly invite, more sweetly allure, to the eternal rest. And now, after the flood of infidelity and delusion, has she appeared like a bow of promise in the clouds? betokening a long harvest of immortal fruit? or is it that, like the morning and the evening star, as she adorned the beginning, so she would cheer the end, of the beloved generation of Christ, her Son? Even as the brightness of her purity kindled up the heavens, before the rising of the Sun of justice, even so, perhaps, the splendor of her presence gilds the evening of this day of grace; and irradiates the closing shades with heavenly hope, ere the night falls, and the Man of Sin comes forth from his lurking-place.

17 And the dragon was angry against the woman, and went to make war with the rest of her seed, which keep the commandments of God, and have the testimony of Jesus Christ.

The woman and her seed are not divided, but, like the vine and the branches, they constitute one body of the faithful. When it is said that the dragon went, or, as the original signifies, leaving, went away to make war: this indicates a respite from persecution for the Church and her children, but implies that a formidable assault is, at the same time, in preparation. The rest of her seed, are the last remaining at the end of the Christian dispensation, who devoutly practise a holy life, and are acknowledged, by God and man, to be the servants of Jesus Christ. The Prophets make frequent allusion to a remnant of the people of Israel, who were to be saved in the day of grace, as if the last handful out of a great people. And thus, even to the end of time, there will be found a faithful and distinguished few, who, loving judgment and justice, like the holy brethren of the Machabees, will go down to the desert, or be ready to die, rather than to transgress the laws of God.[1] And with this chosen remnant, gathered out of the four corners of the earth, is the year of grace concluded.

Herein is described a point of time, of deep moment and suspense. When is this time? The response of many a heart will be, that it is our own day. No sentiment has been more common, of late years, than that there must be a struggle soon, a mighty battle, between the city of God and the city of the devil. And even those who are most sanguine of an instant prosperity for the faith, cannot, and do not, succeed in putting this apprehension wholly out of sight; but there is such a disproportion between their words of lofty promise, and the facts of society, that a feeling of mistrust, rather than of security, is inspired thereby.

Out of the great multitude which bear the Christian name, how marked is the number which deserves to be described, as they who keep the commandments! and, were Satan permitted to sift them as wheat, the remnant who have the testimony of Jesus Christ, it is to be feared, would be found small indeed: "gathered as in a vine even to one cluster."[2] The grace of God, infinite in itself, is bestowed not without weight and measure; and who can tell how nearly is the virtue of holy rule, of pious observance, of indulgence, and of jubilee, exhausted? In the increasing confusion of the roaring of the sea and of the waves of this restless age, Satan withdraws, and heaven is silent. Or, if the voice of revelation be heard, as at Mount La Salette, it is with portentous reserve. In such a time, the Christian may well remember the prayer which Saint Louis loved, and pray, as on the feast of the Holy Martyrs, Denis, and his companions, that, for the love of Almighty God, he may despise the prosperity of the world, and fear nothing of its adversity: "prospera mundi despicere, et nulla ejus adversa formidare."

18 And he stood upon the sand of the sea.

[1] 1 Mach. ii. 29. [2] Jer. vi. 9.

It has been already observed that the sea is to be taken in a nobler sense, than the earth. In the beginning, it is written: "The spirit of God moved over the waters." St. Ambrose, quoting the Syriac, reads, The spirit of God embraced or cherished the waters, (fovebat,) animating them to the production of living creatures. Thus the sea has been as the fertile womb of the earth, and, remotely, of its living creatures. Again, in a sense most sacred, Blessed Mary, or the Star of the Sea, has, by the overshadowing power of the Most High, become the mother of Him, in whom all things live and have their being. Moreover, our Blessed Lord frequented the sea, as if he loved its silent depths, and meditated how its bitterness was soon to be made sweet, by his most holy passion. For, as the bitter waters were turned into sweetness, for the children of Israel, when Moses had cast into them the tree which the Lord showed to him;[1] so, by the Tree of the Cross, has the fountain of Baptism been made the source of salvation, to the new creation of the Holy Ghost. Hence, too, Holy Church is compared to the good ship which rides over its waves; and the Evangelist, this is the fisherman, who, with heavenly skill, spreads his nets, and stores her walls with a precious freight of immortal souls, as she voyages toward the haven of eternal rest. Taken in its widest sense, the sea may signify this world, (præsens seculum,) resounding with the cares and occupations of the daily life. But, as distinguished from the earth or dull solid matter, it represents the spiritual forces, and may be understood of the mind of man, fluctuating between life and death, inconstant, vagrant, and contentious, now swollen with pride, now beaten back in confusion, and untamable, except by the grace of Omnipotence. But, on the other hand, when once the mind has received the grace of divine wisdom, it may well be likened to those transpicuous depths, whose silent repose is all undisturbed by the waves of doubt and desire, the incessant ebb and flow of this restless scene of life. Accordingly, in the human mind may be discerned an abyss, or a grandeur, like

[1] Exod. xv. 25.

that of the sea. Therefore, ecclesiastically speaking, the sea is the Christian soul, and, taken collectively, Christendom ; profanely, it may be society, in the common acceptation of the word. In the latter sense, Satan stands by the sand of the sea, when he stands by the margin of human society, and prepares his snares to capture unwary souls of men. By the other interpretation, the sand of the sea, or the outskirts of Christendom, are those unhappy souls who partake of the sacred character, or profess the Christian life, but are inwardly barren of grace and reprobate in sin. This last explication is more to the purpose, because tradition implies that, Judas-like, Antichrist will bear some originally sacred relation to the true religion ; and thus it may be that Satan now waits on the shore of Christendom itself for his coming. Therefore : as the eagle, by the shore, watches the deeps of the living waters ; even so the adversary of our race, looks down into the sea of human passions, explores its dark recesses, and searches for that damned man, whom he will clothe with his own power, to be " the son of perdition, who opposeth and is lifted up above all that is called God, or is worshipped."[1]

CHAPTER XIII.

1 And I saw a beast coming out of the sea, having seven heads and ten horns, and upon his horns ten diadems, and upon his heads, names of blasphemy.

The phrase, secular power, has, for convenience sake, been employed as a generic term ; and, distributed again in the two powers, of Satan, and of men. The latter, that is, the temporal power, is the counterpart of the former, in so far as it is fallible, and characterized by the pride of usurpation, or by the audacity of aggression, and, finally, by tyranny in the persecution of religious truth ; which evil propensities, manifested now and again in the world's history, will be fully

[1] 2 Thes. ii. 4.

developed under the reign of Antichrist, in whom personally will be summed up the whole secular power, both of Satan and of men. Satan is aptly described as a dragon, since he first appeared to men in the form of a serpent; the temporal power is represented in Holy Scripture by a beast, or a mere animal; because its essence consists in the material force of brute strength; in the application of which, it regards the letter, and takes little or no cognizance of the spirit, of the law, but disowns responsibility, and acts bluntly, as if without reason; so that it would be absurd to suggest the finer sentiments of honor or generosity, of piety or charity. Not, indeed, that it is insensible to the interested motives of profit or pleasure; on the contrary, its lively appreciation of such arguments is another instance of the analogy under consideration; for this is also a distinctive mark of irrational animals, that, however deaf they may be to other suggestions, they are easily persuaded by those of commodity or enjoyment; being the creatures of appetite, rather than of reason. The Prophet Daniel, in a vision, beheld "the four winds of heaven strive upon the great sea, and four beasts came up out of the sea."[1] By the action of manifold causes, such as opposing interests, and passions, in the midst of society, is elicited the temporal power; which, in the fallen condition of humanity, is necessarily established for the preservation of the same, in some measure of order and justice. It cannot be doubted that the power is commonly of such a kind as men deserve; when they are brutal, they require an iron rule; when docile a milder sway suffices; and, therefore, the Apostle says not, the powers that ought to be, but the powers that are, simply, are ordained of God. The beast, therefore, comes out of the sea, or is evolved from the womb of society, whether pagan or Christian, because, in the nature of things, it is necessary for the present condition of humanity. Or, from the sea, because its authority is aboriginal, not a creature of earth, nor an invention of men, so much as the ordination of that divine Providence which disposes of all the affairs of

[1] Daniel vii. 3.

time, through purposes wise and good, though oftentimes mysterious and inexplicable by human reason.

But it may be objected: Is it not rash, in an age of insubordination like the present, to point out the infirmities of the temporal power? and is it not unjust to disparage the civil authority, the source of order, and of so many acts of unquestionable utility and beneficence? It is to be answered, in the first place: That, except the True Faith, there is nothing, and there never has been anything on earth, so much and so sincerely respected as the temporal power. Even the most seditious, prosecute their infernal purposes, in the name of order, or of justice, or of the Commonwealth.

It is true the malady of the age, is a want of reverence and subordination in all the relations of life; but the remedy will never be to engage them to the worship of Cæsar, in the hope that greater honor will be rendered to God afterwards. In the second place, Holy Scripture does no injustice in likening the temporal kingdom to a beast, because, apart from all its accidents, such as occasional works of benevolence which are not of obligation, or acts of persecution which are contrary to the law of God, it is in itself a mere unreasoning engine of physical might, appointed for the terror of evil doers; who, when they have degraded themselves below the level of right reason, deserve nothing else than the rude compression of brute force; while, to the just man, it is a thing either indifferent, or merely agreeable; and only by virtue of circumstances extraneous to its ordinary constitution, does it become to him an object of veneration on the one hand, or of terror on the other.

The head is the seat of wisdom, or of political sagacity; the horns signify the pride of office, lifted up in power. It need not be thought incongruous, that skill or prudence is attributed to the beast; for the wisdom of this world, which is infinitely inferior to the true wisdom, is shared even by the brute creation; whose acuteness, foresight, and subtlety are oftentimes found to be more than equal to human dexterity. Commonly speaking, a great degree of skill in schemes of policy and feats of diplomacy, is not obtained by means of a higher progress in the divine wisdom, but rather by descending in the moral order, and by degrading the powers of the soul. The beast has seven heads: because, with the number seven, is accomplished the harmonious measure of time, and the world's history may be divided among seven principal empires. He has ten horns: because the number ten signifies the perfection or totality of powers. Among other expositions, St Augustine thus analyzes this number; seven being the proper number of created things, and three the number of the Creator, or the Trinity, the coherence of creature and Creator gives the sum of ten; which is the number accordingly of the commandments; and, by metonomy, of the rulers, or those who command. If the horns are supposed to be directed and controlled by the head, they may be understood of kingdoms tributary or subordinate to the great empires; otherwise they will represent the temporal powers which are always conspicuous, whether there be, or be not, a universal monarchy at the same time existing.

Upon his horns are ten diadems: because the temporal power is always, or nearly so, adorned with the insignia of royalty; or because might is crowned by men with the highest honors. And upon his heads names of blasphemy: because, in the great empires, or universal monarchies, the sovereign has assumed to himself titles which are appropriate to the Deity alone. History shows how, in proportion to the aggrandizement of their empires, the great tyrants have ended by assuming divine honors, and have ordered religious worship to be paid to themselves or their statues, as if to gods. For which reason, and also because this was a political device to impose upon the understandings of men, the character of blasphemy is attributed to the heads rather than to the horns; though indeed the lesser monarchies have often been stained by the same crime, but notwithstanding, the royalty in the latter is most conspicuous, and the blasphemy is most emphatic in the former. But, in the vision of the dragon, why are the heads, rather than the horns, said to be crowned with seven diadems? and why are the horns undistinguished by any insignia?

It may be answered: that the horns, or the power of Satan, being spiritual in its nature, does not fall under the observation of the senses; or that the material demonstrations of his power, if sometimes they are permitted by God, are what men need dread the least, and what are found commonly to draw after them deserved contempt, by reason of their puerility or vulgarity; while the hidden malice, the unseen potency of intellect, which deludes the understanding, and betrays the mind of man, this is incomparably more fearful; wherefore not the physical prodigies of the dragon, but the capital vices of the spirit, are gilded over by the pomps of Satan. Literally, the seven principal empires may be distributed as follows: First, the Assyrian, from whose dominion Abraham went forth, in obedience to his divine vocation. Second, the Egyptian, from whose tyranny the people of Israel were delivered under Moses. After this last epoch, the people of God were exempt from the domination of the secular power, for about one thousand years; and during that time their own history, is the sole history of the world, every other being utterly confounded with the fables of the pagan mythology. The Third principal empire, and the first universal monarchy in the modern sense, is the Chaldæan, or Assyrio-Babylonian, which culminated under Nabuchadonosor, who carried the Jews away in captivity to Babylon. The Fourth, or Persian empire, soon after succeeded to preëminence under Cyrus the Great, who restored the people of God to their own city. The Fifth, was the Grecian Empire, which came to power under Alexander the Great, the successors of whom cruelly persecuted the chosen race in the times of the Machabees. Sixth, was the Roman Empire. Seventh, comes the Antichristian empire.

Once more, to entertain briefly an objection: How can the temporal power be of God and of Satan at the same time? It may be observed, that the temporal power is of itself good; as we may say of any creature in the natural order, "Fire, hail, snow, beasts and all cattle, kings of the earth and all people,"[1] it is a good thing, and the creature of God. But whereas other creatures may have proceeded from the hand of God as perfectly good originally, yet the temporal kingdoms have never been established in that first innocence, but rather in imperfection, as is intimated in the history of the first king of Israel, when the Lord said to Samuel:[2] "They have not rejected thee but Me that I should not reign over them;" and, therefore, though the powers are of God, and though it is not pretended they are of Satan, yet in so far as they have been derived in the original fault or infirmity of the people, and forasmuch as their evil propensities incline them to sin, rather than to righteousness, they may be said to have their prototype in him, who first of all rejected the rule of God in heaven, and said, "I will be like the Most High."[3] Furthermore, it is to be observed, that this complex vision, or congeries of the temporal powers, may be treated as one Antichrist, because, as has been before remarked, the powers of this world culminate in his person; and there is no reason to suppose, that his power will be something so idiocratical or sui generis, and still less, so out of the natural order, that it should or could be sundered from the common succession of human institutions; but rather that it is bound up with them and is developed from out of them, as the evil fruit of an evil tree. Thus St. Thomas[4] proves that Antichrist cannot be the incarnation of Satan, but simply, that the malice of Satan comes to a head in him; that is to say, the ancient, original, and hereditary vitiosity of the secular power is matured and consummated in his reign.

2 And the beast which I saw, was like to a leopard; and his feet were as the feet of a bear, and his mouth, as the mouth of a lion. And the dragon gave him his own strength, and great power.

The blessed Apostle employs the imagery which is conse-

[1] Psalms cxlviii. [2] 1 Kings viii.
[3] Isaias xiv. [4] Sum. Theol. iii. 9, 8.

crated by the usage of the inspired writers. In the prophecy of Daniel, the resemblances here mentioned, are distributed among four great empires, severally and specifically; the vision of the Apocalypse, as if more comprehensive, blends all in one mass of the body politic, whose collected vices come to an issue in the Antichristian Empire. This empire is likened to a leopard, for its impetuosity and velocity; quæ saltu in mortem ruit, according to St. Jerome,[1] rushing to the death as with a bound. The bear, (following the same holy father,) signifies roughness and severity of discipline in the Spartan manner; or, in the modern sense, it is the morose and gloomy regimen of Puritanism. The first beast in the vision of Daniel, was like a lioness, for its cruelty and lust; the fourth was unlike the other beasts, and distinguished from them, as having great iron teeth. The traits of these two last mentioned, may be considered as combined in the metaphor, the mouth of a lion, signifying cruelty and power. Added to all this brute force of the temporal kingdoms, the dragon confers upon the man of sin his own strength, the subtlety of the serpent.

3 And I saw one of his heads as it were wounded to death: and his deadly wound was healed. And all the earth was in admiration after the beast.

In the ages of pagan darkness long past, the world had been held in servitude successively by the great empires, whose vices are but feebly emblematized in the ferocious traits of wild beasts. But, by the goodness of God, men have been set free in Christian times, from this heavy bondage, "by the freedom wherewith Christ hath made us free;"[2] and it has not been permitted in Christendom, that any tyrant should arrogate to himself a domination over the sons of God, like that of the former despotism; but with the last great empire of Rome, the power of universal monarchy has been broken; one of its heads was wounded as it were to death. It is not said wounded to death, but (quasi,) as it

[1] Comment. in Dan. chap. vii. [2] Gal. iv. 31.

were, to death; for slowly, imperfectly and never irreversibly, are the physical ills of this mortal state assuaged. And though the power of evil seems crushed, and the temporal supremacy over the mind and body of man, has been seen humbled and stricken down almost in death, yet the time is coming when that deadly wound shall be healed. "Le monde est vide depuis les Romains," howled one of the leaders in the French Revolution; and there have been more potentates than one in recent times, who have dreamed of universal sovereignty. When men are inflated with the pride of material progress, when the thirst of riches and the lust of earthly aggrandizement have filled their minds, and have wrapped them in a phantasy of boundless ambition, it would seem that the establishment of a kingdom supreme, far-reaching, and all-powerful, must be the natural and inevitable consequence. It comes, therefore: the sway of that detested man of sin; rapid and terrible, cunning and mighty, in cruelty and in turpitude. And here we dismiss that aspect of the beast, by which it has been regarded in its continuous generation through the times, and proceed to consider it in the personal relation of the man, Antichrist, whose reign is inaugurated when that deadly wound shall be healed, and all the earth, the sordid and the base, shall rejoice at it.

4 And they adored the dragon, which gave power to the beast: and they adored the beast, saying: Who is like to the beast? and who shall be able to fight with it?

It is a condition of mind, that it will not rest in a middle state like dull matter. Upward or downward, it must ever tend in angel flight, or in demon fall, wherein it is impelled by a double force of exterior suggestion and of interior coöperation. The intoxication of the material progress once admitted, it is in turn fomented and aggravated by the powers of the soul, and by that perversity of will which hesitates at no excess, and is ashamed of no disgrace. Thereupon follow fatuity, superstition, and devil-worship; for since man cannot divest himself of soul, and become merely brutal, but, by the necessity of his being, must entertain some commerce with that which is invisible as well as with the visible; he proceeds to confuse the material with the spiritual, and sooner or later to identify the operations of the physical order, with the influences of incorporeal being or existences. And then he may be said to adore the dragon. But, after having adored the fallen angel, it is but a step to adore the fallen humanity, in the person of his agent, that is, the beast; which, however, is even more degrading than to adore the dragon; for, if the worship of the latter, the idolatry of demons, be called spiritual adultery, the worship of the other, might even be termed the bestiality of the soul. When the reason is at length brought to this depth of degradation, there is no longer any place for argument; in its infatuation it holds fallacies for self-evident truths; and the whole power of ratiocination is exhausted in the puerile ejaculations: Who is like to the beast? Who shall be able to fight with it?

5 And there was given to it a mouth, speaking great things, and blasphemies; and power was given to it to act forty-two months.

The Church of God is called a little flock, and its members, little ones. But the Beast arrogates greatness for itself. To the turbid imagination of the ambitious, the simplicity of truth seems to be unworthy of notice, but mundane honors to be of unbounded magnitude. Accordingly, when they have lost their faith in things heavenly, all hearts are turned to the earthly greatness, and all minds are directed to the promises of the impostor, to that voice of Antichrist, which already incites the young to aspire to riches and to the first place, which summons the multitudes to sovereignty, which makes cupidity a law and a duty, the attainment of dignity and preëminence a rule of common obligation, and of most vulgar application; and which denounces those, whether individuals or nations, as poor-spirited and contemptible, who cannot fabricate some greatness for themselves in their day. Not that it makes question any more, about that which is a gift of divine Providence, an emanation of higher and spiritual influences, a unity constructive and harmonious; but it proclaims the greatness which is elaborated in division and disputation, which is a product of the shop and the spindle, which is inflated with the insolence of luxury, of fraud, and of infidelity, or swollen with the coarse bulk of majorities and of material force. Here is the standard of the beastly greatness; and while it advances to power, and challenges the peoples to do it homage, so are the heavenly virtues and sacred institutions which resist its progress, accordingly blasphemed, as superstitious, degrading and infamous.

It is hard to conceive of greater blasphemies than have been already spoken in this world; the just would neither wish nor dare to do so; the impious would have uttered them before this, if it had been permitted. But Antichrist will shock the one, and astonish the other, with new and unimagined blasphemies; and though his doctrine might be contemptible of itself, yet, sustained by the force of the temporal power, it will be rendered terrible. He has the mouth of a lion, for enormous are his lying words, and ponderous is the weight with which they crush the souls of his deluded victims. Forty-two months is the time of his power, that is, his power will be brief; and as history shows how the reign of tyrants is uncertain and their end untimely, so the goodness of God will not be withheld from shortening the grievous tribulation of those days.

6 And he opened his mouth in blasphemies against God, to blaspheme his name, and his tabernacle, and them that dwell in heaven.

The Apostle, St. Paul, says of Antichrist: "He opposeth and is lifted up above all that is called God;" every religious sentiment or affection, which is designed by God to attract the mind toward a better world, or to assuage and subdue the evil passions of the soul, this he will, as if instinctively, seek to exterminate from the earth; to which end he will especially persecute the name of God or the dogmas of sacred truth, his tabernacle or church on earth, and the saints that dwell in heaven. In the last days the infidels have reviled sacred things, at first upon the impulse of wit; more recently, in the cold insolence of pride; it only remains that, in the last envy of despair, they vent forth all their malice, even to the dregs. This last result is a motive of fear; that there is, at this time, a reaction, and the smoke of the abyss has been lifted for a moment, that men may see their danger; this invites us to hope for better things. But the hope which is above is alone certain, and the fear of God alone is salutary.

7 And it was given to him to make war with the saints, and to overcome them: and power was given him over every tribe, and people, and tongue, and nation.

Many have there been who have persecuted the truth, but, of this one, it is said, he shall both make war, and also shall overcome the saints. For on one side the delusion is very great, since St. Paul writes: "God shall send them the operation of error to believe a lie;" and, on the other, the secular power is then in its greatest vigor, so that every dignity and emolument, and every earthly consideration of terror, will be employed against the generation of Christ in every nation.

8 And all that dwell upon the earth adored him; whose names are not written in the book of life of the Lamb, which was slain from the beginning of the world.

Wherefore, many will then fall away from the faith; the indifferent, the timid, and many who practise the precepts of the Church, but yet love the world, and are always able to find excuses for courting its esteem, and are most solicitous that we should always speak tenderly of its excesses, and respectfully of its importance. And, indeed, who will be left that shall not be swept away by the delusions of those days, except those little ones, whose life is a death to this world; such as there have been found, a chosen few from the beginning. For even then, and from the first, this earth has been stained with the blood of the innocent.

9 If any man have an ear, let him hear.

Therefore the world of this darkness, the secular power, has been a murderer. No matter what guise of beauty, or glory, or of virtue it puts on. "The friendship of this world is the enemy of God."

10 He that shall lead into captivity, shall go into captivity: he that shall kill by the sword, must be killed by the sword. Here is the patience and the faith of the saints.

He who leads souls captive in the delusions of this world, or every one who helps to swell the crowd which adores its carnal wisdom, he, the self-same, is binding upon his own soul the fetters of darkness forever. And if he rejoices in some share of the temporal power, and wields it to the injury of heavenly wisdom, he destroys his own life. For what shall it profit a man if he gain the whole world and lose his own soul? Can any glory of men be compared to that of the lily of the field, the poor little flower which the Most High has formed? Does the one ever draw away the thought from carnal, and whisper of eternal joys, like as the other speaks plainly of the majesty of the Creator? He that loveth his life shall lose it, and he that hateth his life in this world keepeth it unto life everlasting. And this is the ancient faith of the servant of God, who walks not according to the flesh: and herein is the patience which is stronger than death.

11 And I saw another beast coming up out of the earth: and he had two horns, like to a lamb's; and he spoke as a dragon.

The minister of heaven is compared to the eagle, or to the angel, because he ministers in the things that are above. The secular power disposes of the things that are beneath; and is said to be derived from the abyss, so far as it proceeds from the instigation of Satan; or from the sea, according as it is the natural production of society, and more or less subtile in its origin, as being hereditary or framed in rights remote and indefinable, but sanctioned by divine Providence; or lastly, it comes up out of the earth, inasmuch as the power is a gross, tangible creation of the human artificer. These latter powers are likened to beasts, because it is their office to minister in things corporal; and since man has a body like the beasts, and a spirit like the angels, they are aptly represented by the animal whose face is prone to earth; while the spiritual authority is as if winged for the flight upward.

The beast from the earth had two horns, or a two-fold power; that is, of mind and matter, being the conjunction of human skill with human industry, or the application of the intellectual energy to the physical experience. And this gives for result, not a spiritual product, but a power of earth, palpable and gross, as was to be expected; because "he that is of the earth, of the earth he is, and of the earth he speaketh." This power has its form or principle in the inductive philosophy, and its substance in the mechanic arts. In other words, the natural sciences being its motive principle or primum mobile, the appliances of human dexterity will be the organ or body of the same. Now as the age of Antichrist is to be that of wonders in the sensible order, and since this is the agent of Antichrist, therefore it is the engine, or organ, by which is brought about the material aggrandizement of the age. It would seem therefore to be no other than the mechanical forces, as distinguished from the moral force of the dragon, and from the political power of the first beast. It remotely resembles a lamb, because to appearance it is innocent, and, abstractedly considered, doubtless it is so; but it speaks like a dragon, for it oftentimes impugns revealed truth, and assumes a tone of superiority, dictatorial, and overbearing, toward the authority of the Church, the depositary and arbiter of revelation. But when is the origin, or what is the precise date of the nativity of this power? The text says simply: that it comes up out of the earth. Not by a suspension of the laws of nature, at some fixed moment of time; for it is not to be expected, as has been already remarked, that, even in the days of Antichrist, there will be any such dilaceration of the common course of events, as but that human nature will be left to its own inherent liberty of eternal life and death. The second beast, therefore, like the first, is of ancient derivation. It may be traced back to the times of Tubalcain; and being thence transmitted with that hereditary stain which imbues the things of earth, its vitiosity comes to a head, in the reign of Antichrist.

But it will be said: Is it not harsh and ungrateful, to qualify, in such terms, the professions and trades which are doing so much for the intellectual culture and physical improvement of the age? It is to be answered: That, while Holy Scripture is no respecter of persons, yet it is not to be doubted that there are many in the professions of art and science, as well as in their correlative, the mechanical trades, who are as amiable in their lives as they are eminent in their reputations, and that they labor with the single intention of the servants of God; but graces like these they never derived from their professions, for they are not the fruits of earth, but of heaven. It is impossible that divine virtues should be derived, through mechanical accomplishments, or should depend upon acuteness of mind. The capital error is, that too many believe that a certain gentleness and refinement of mien, which is so often to be observed among those who are gifted with marvellous ingenuity in the theory, or dexterity in the practice, of the experimental wisdom, is of supernatural worth, and entitles them to eternal life. There are those who have this lamb-like appearance, indeed, but let them speak, and the dragon is declared; truths most sacred are rent and spurned, while errors most detestable are fortified by their countenance and support. Among the arts and sciences, their patrons, or followers, are oftentimes conducted to pride and impiety; each thinks his own divine, and appropriates for it the language which is sacred to religion. And this evil custom, is what makes the telling them they are of the earth, sound rude and paradoxical. But from the beginning, their derivation is plainly traced to the city of the world,[1] as distinguished from the city of God. And again, in the first ages of Christianity, it is well known how the

[1] Genesis iv. 17, 22.

Greeks, the fountain-head of æsthetic skill, were the very ones who always painted our divine Savior as of a miserable, despised appearance; and who, at length, vented their iconoclastic fury against all sacred images, or adornments of religion, as if they grudged their earthly toys to the service of God. The fine arts, therefore, of themselves, are purely things of earth, though, when rightly employed, they are ennobled to render glorious the Church of God, and to preach of heaven to men of good will. The word science is used here in its common acceptation at the present day; that is, it has come now to be employed only in the sense of physical or material knowledge; and one may be a man of science, though quite ignorant of theology, of logic, and of jurisprudence, alike. The modern science, therefore, being essentially material in its constitution, seems tending to materialize the whole method of human society, debasing the tone of art, and elevating that of mechanics, and thus reducing all the operations of the rational man to one vulgar level of mere sensuous existence. And thus it has come to pass, that a purely mechanical production takes rank with the finest achievements of intellect, and even with the dispensations of religion, being denominated as "divine" in the journals of the day.

To recapitulate: the beast from the earth differs from the others, inasmuch as the artificial is contradistinguished from the original powers. It is that power which results from the combined forces of inventive science, and of manual dexterity; being the union of the designer and of the artisan, in one personal representation of the beast with two horns. And, because it is difficult to find a single term which indicates this dual condition, it may be denominated from that aspect of the same which is the most familiar and palpable, namely, the Mechanic Force.

It might perhaps be desirable here, to inquire, what is the affinity, or what the diversity, between this power and the river or torrent of the renaissance. It may be said, that the latter had the sphere of its legitimate effects in the fine arts, literature, painting, architecture, the graces of the mind; the other is observed in the operations of the physical sciences, the accomplishments of the body. The renaissance answers to the *dulce*, the mechanic power to the *utile*, in human life. The one was the hallucination of æsthetic influences over the moral nature, the other is addressed to the animal instincts. The one procured a certain polish of manner to the higher order of talent, the other extends to all alike a certain mock refinement of bearing, or a kind of bastard dignity in the outward and carnal phase of the man. These two agencies, of the renaissance and of the mechanic force, seem, therefore, to differ in kind; but, in point of fact, the latter has nearly absorbed or assimilated the former to itself; whether it has taken advantage of the degenerate condition of the fine arts, to intrude itself into that domain, or whether this has been effected by the natural operation of the inductive philosophy, or from other causes, need not be examined here.

12 And he executed all the power of the former beast in his sight: and he caused the earth, and them that dwell therein, to adore the first beast, whose deadly wound was healed.

That the enormous power of this second beast, already threatens the welfare of society, may be gathered from the consideration: That the material science, having usurped the rank of the liberal arts, and the highest honors of the intellectual order, proceeds now to supply the functions of Christianity itself, and proposes to unite the minds and hearts of men in universal charity by means (horrible to be said,) of iron bonds; substituting, for the gentle yoke of Christ, or the Living Spirit of God, not the vital forces of simple animated nature, but the literal rod of iron and those base powers of the inanimate elements which pertain as it were of right to the infernal spirits. Thus, there seems to be preparing, in the mechanic arts, a ready instrument for the schemes of the tyrant; and the powers of this world, wounded to death by the Cross, will once more revive and make head; and men will leave Christ the Lord, to adore Antichrist the Beast.

13 And he did great signs, so that he made even fire to come down from heaven upon the earth in the sight of men.

"In the times of Antichrist," says St. Gregory, "a sancta ecclesia, virtutum signa subtrahuntur. Not that miraculous signs or virtues supernatural are wholly withdrawn, but, as compared with the wonders of Antichrist, they will seem few or none. Wherefore it is written: Want goeth before his face. In which, by an admirable dispensation, is manifested the divine mercy and justice, forasmuch as the merits of the faithful are augmented according as the Church is humbled before men, since it is then evident that they are held in fidelity by higher motives than the sensible proofs of her divine authority; while the reprobate are the more speedily convicted of infidelity, since they are bound to the things invisible, solely by force of visible signs."[1]

All the testimonies of Scripture and tradition, show that those days will be marked with signs in the material order, or by mechanical wonders. Now fire and lightning, are often used indifferently in Holy Scripture,[2] as if convertible terms. Ignis, grando, nix, glacies, spiritus procellarum:[3] the fire which accompanies hail, is lightning. Therefore if by the fire of heaven be understood the electric fire, this has been already brought down in the sight of men, and controlled to their daily service. To this interpretation it will be immediately objected, that it is puerile and whimsical. But it is evident that none can make this charge, who are accustomed to speak of the invention above mentioned in terms of religious veneration, and in language most sacred;

[1] Mor. Job xli. 13.

[2] The Protestant version frequently renders fire, where the Vulgate reads lightning; and vice versa.

[3] Psalms cxlviii. 8.

while the others who hold it for a thing indifferent and a mere accident in mechanics, must admit, that its intrinsic insignificance cannot mitigate the fact of moral consequences, but if anything aggravates the same, and renders the delusion yet more delusive, the cheat more fraudulent. Assuredly there is no device in the world's history, which points so significantly to the literal fulfilment of this text, as the prospective consequences of a complete subserviency of electricity to the secular power. Compared with this and similar wonders of the day, how grievously is the Science of the Cross diminished before men!

14 And he seduced them that dwell on the earth, by the signs which were given him to perform in the sight of the beast: saying to them that dwell on the earth, that they should make an image to the beast, which had the wound by the sword, and lived.

Abstractly considered, it would seem improbable, that the rational soul should ever be wholly captivated by mere mechanical wonders. But, on the other hand, simple force or feats of strength alone, are not without attraction for the imagination; and if to this be added a cunning, which, in some instances, approximates to diabolic subtlety, it is not difficult to understand how the material advantages may prove at last a seduction powerful and universal; which will sweep over the human race with a success, general and absolute, forasmuch as it appeals not to the select few, more than to the vulgar mass, but to the common nature of one and all alike.

After the flood, when men dwelt in the plain of Sennaar, they said: "Come, let us make brick, and bake them with fire; and they said, Come, let us make a city, and a tower, the top whereof may reach to heaven."[1] In modern times, when society has been visited by the flood of infidelity, and when the grievous effects of the same are so often felt in the convulsions of immorality and insubordination, which threaten its existence, it is an evil symptom that men turn not back to

[1] Gen. xi. 3.

the ancient faith, but rather they repair to the brick and mortar of earthly science, for consolation. With the increasing and renewed conviction of their dependence upon divine Providence, they seem provoked to a greater desire to set their Lord at a distance, and to secure an entire independence against all his righteous interpositions in the affairs of this world. And already they congratulate one another upon the progress they are making, not, as they suppose, to an infinitude of prosperity, but to a Babel of universal disorder. Because at present the progress seems indefinite, it is fondly supposed to be infinite. But there is nothing infinite in the sensible order; there is no infinite spectacle, there is no infinite sound, nor softness, nor sweetness, for the insatiable soul! And yet this phantom perfection, they propose to work out, since other means have failed, with their own hands with axe and hammer. What, then, will be the end of all their labor, but a graven image? Though they use fair, lamb-like words, and pretend that they will effect a conquest of the world, peaceful and bloodless, but mightier than that of the hero in arms, yet they will at last have wrought out but a poor, wooden resemblance of that imperial majesty which ere now has swayed the nations of earth with a tyranny more honorable, if less effectual, than theirs. But this is not all; for they build their image to the beast, who was wounded by the sword of truth, and who will live again; and, therefore, the last perfection of the mechanic arts will be, not a substitute for that universal empire which it imitates, but a mere inanimate tool ready for the hand of Antichrist, who, in his coming, will seize and wield it to the destruction of this wretched world. It may be observed, that, with the first mention of the image, it is called an image *to* the beast, afterwards the image *of* the beast; as if it were prepared beforehand to the beast, that is, to his honor or adoration; and, afterwards, when he takes possession of the same, it is of him or his own. Like the men of Babel, they say, Let us build up a power, which shall be royal as that of Cæsar, and omnipotent as that of heaven. They love the memory of that old pagan might, which was chastised by the sword of the gospel; they would have it restored again, and would rejoice to heal its loathsome wound; and herein they do homage to the ancient imagination of an unlimited human power, consciously and with full intent. Now the embodiment or personification of the beast in Antichrist, is but an accident, or one instance of that same power; wherefore, if they conspire to build up the image, to reconstruct that power in a certain abstract form, so, when it appears in the concrete, they will be also ready to render it their homage.

To proceed now a little farther to trace the analogies of the beast's image. In the first place, leaving aside the intrinsic relations of the Most Holy Trinity, it is to be observed: That every resemblance falls short of its original; and thus the Deity is the resemblance of no other. But of the Deity, there may be a likeness: as we know that man has been made in the image of God. In which, however, he falls short of his original, even as the finite is less than the infinite. In the second place: Of man, there may be found a likeness in the brute creation, formed like him with a spirit of life, and with appetites like his own; and having also an appearance of passions and of reason, though these are only appearances, because the beast falls short of its exemplar, in that it lacks a rational soul. And here also it is to be remarked, how the temporal power, which is like to man, because it is a living force, yet is compared to the beast, because it is inferior to the human soul and subject to it; inasmuch as it must obey the will of the sovereign or the established laws, without distinction of right or wrong, or of any eternal fitness of things. In the third place: As the beast is an image of man, having a sensitive soul, but falls short of its type, in that it lacks the rational soul; what remains for the image of the beast, but that it be a power which seems to live, and yet lacks the spirit of life? an agent, and yet devoid both of the soul rational, and of the soul sensitive; which is endowed with physical strength, and with motion like a beast, but is inferior to the same, because subjected to a more abject obedience, even than the brute creation. And, moreover, as the beast is possessed of a strength vastly greater than that of man, but is yet inferior, because his power is an unconscious and irrational one; so the strength of the beast's image may again be far greater than that of its own exemplar, but yet inferior to it, because it is not only irrational, but also inanimate. Now such an image of brute power is very plainly to be seen, in the organization of the mechanic forces, to a substitution for animal force, or, in other words, in the adaptation of any given organism of inanimate matter to the service of man, in the first instance; and to the service of the secular power, in its integrity or final maturity.

15 And it was given him to give life to the image of the beast, and that the image of the beast should speak; and should cause, that whosoever will not adore the image of the beast, should be slain.

To pursue the interpretation: The giving life, or spirit, to the image, signifies that the appliances of modern science, or the mechanic force, will be brought into such perfect organization and adaptation to the requirements of the temporal power, that it will be as if animated; and the machinery of the body politic will put on the attributes of a personal being, publishing, and at the same instant, executing its decrees, with the celerity and impetuosity of a single will. At present, we are left at liberty (though, it must be admitted, it is a doubtful and inviduous one) to discuss the merit of scientific inventions; but, when they will have been so multiplied as to modify all human acts, controlling them as if by principle, or with an efficaciousness like that of moral habits, then whosoever will not adore the powers of that day, must prepare for a chastisement as summary as it will be brutal and inhuman.

16 And he shall make all, both little and great, rich and poor, free-men and bond-men, to have a mark in their right hand, or in their foreheads.

To refer again to the dual power of the second beast, it was said to signify the union of mental acuteness, and of manual dexterity, that is, of head and hand; and, more particularly, it is the forehead, or the understanding, and the right hand, which is the working hand. When the progress of the mechanic arts has reached the extent it promises, and which indeed is in prospect, then will all, both little and great, rich and poor, servant and master, be stamped with the common mark of the man of sin: the animal man; with instincts strong, but ignoble; astute toward the things of earth, but stupid for those of eternity; no longer erect, agile, free to every impulse of the Spirit of God, but grovelling, sordid, enslaved, and drilled, like the trained beast, to obey the laws of sense and flesh. The philosopher, with all his vanity, cannot refuse an attentive ear to the humble mechanic, for he has become his partner; the rich man and the poor may differ in their professions, and their etiquette, but the one may be as familiar with the gilded saloon, as the other; the master and servant may be divided in their opinions and tastes, but they are equally interested in the success of the mechanic arts, at home and abroad, in hall or closet. The scientific man and the artisan, the orator and the workman, discourse alike in matters of material improvement, and use the same elaborate phraseology, and find their daily employments moulded in the same rigid routine of mechanical law. Thus, as the end draws near, will the mark of the beast, of the corporal refinement, be impressed more and more clearly upon the worshippers of the earthly wisdom; whether they be bound to its service by head or by hand, in mind or in deed. One of the great promises of the day is, that the nations are about to be united by mechanical agencies, in close and endearing ties of sympathy and mutual improvement. To establish a community of faith, hope, and charity, in the souls of men, is the office of the Church of God; fanatics have made desperate, but vain, efforts to fulfil a similar function for society; now, at last, there seems to be approaching, a power which is to bind at least the bodily part of mankind, with its habits, occupations, and pleasures, in a servitude, whose yoke is strong as bonds of oak, and bolts of iron.

17 And that no man might buy or sell, but he that hath the mark, or the name of the beast, or the number of his name.

Suppose, therefore, the mass of mankind thus organized, not on a basis of revealed truth nor of good morals, but in the refinement of mere physical phenomena: he who would dissent from the established order of things, is, by the very fact, excluded from society; not so much by any moral expulsion, as by a necessary inference of the mechanic axioms.

Kindred and tributary to this power of the earth, is Commerce, as it is at present constituted, in a system of usury, insurance, and combinations innumerable and inextricable. Foremost among the worshippers of the image, it boasts of strength more mighty than armies, than the address of statesmen, or than the blood of martyrs. When its results will have become fully developed, and the peoples involved effectually in its perplexities, then, in that "distress of nations," is the weight of its bondage appropriately signified, in that no man may buy or sell, but he that hath the mark of the beast. For as the method of society will be absolutely material, so will its affinities be wholly commercial, its sympathies and affections items of trade. "Membra carnium ejus cohærentia sibi.[1] The members of his flesh cleave one to another. So unanimous are they in their perversity," says St. Gregory, "so concordant in evil, that no disputes divide them, no altercation is able to separate them. As the absence of unity from among good men is deplorable, so is there still greater danger when it is not wanting among bad men."

By the mark of the beast, or the character of the beast, may be understood, therefore, that general feature of mind and person, which distinguishes an antichristian from a Christian people. The mark of the Christian, is the sign of the Cross, whose virtue is impressed upon his soul in baptism, and by

[1] Job. xli. 14.

which he is attracted toward suffering. The character of Antichrist is found in the flesh of that man who abhors the Cross, and who courts the pleasures and pomps of earth. To have the name of the beast, is something more specific. By it may be intended those who control and influence the masses to build up the antichristian power; who invent the name, or the plausible argument, which leads men astray from the truth, to believe a lie; who are able to speak great things which dazzle and incapacitate the mind for the contemplation of divine wisdom, but which lead it captive in error and blasphemy. Whereas, in the middle ages, a false prophet, with his followers, was a local evil, occasional, ephemeral, it is evident that, with the revolt of the sixteenth century, error began to be systematized; or, if that be impossible, began to put on an appearance of system, which is the same thing for a great many. Opinion or human respect, instead of the fear of God, became the corner stone of the new religion. Starting from religion, this principle must, in process of time, be developed into all the modes and operations of society. Men refer to it as to an oracle; they consult it as if the truth did not exist, or as if the entity of simple truth were not a possible object of human intelligence. It is, therefore, a signal of atheistic and antichristian times. It is a kind of instinct of mutual recognition among the demagogues; and these may be said to have the name of the beast, without whose countenance men will not be able to buy or sell, that is, to procure the means of subsistence, or to gain a livelihood.

By those who have the number of his name, remain to be understood the adherents of the personal Antichrist; they who beside the character and the name of the beast have also the confidence of the actual man of sin, and are accessory to his impostures.

18 Here is wisdom. He that hath understanding, let him compute the number of the beast. For it is the number of a man: and his number is six hundred sixty-six.

This text has been regarded by some as the enigma of the Apocalypse, given to test the ingenuity of the wise, or to provoke the curiosity of the skilful. If the sacred writer did indeed intend thus to challenge our wisdom, who could presume to cope with him? But it is not the usage of Holy Scripture, to employ the names of wisdom and understanding in so common, not to say so profane, a sense. Again, it is to be observed, that the holy Apostle concludes the vision of the beast with one word, as it were, of explanation: "It is the number of a Man," which is the first and only indication given, that the whole is intended of a human power, or finally of one human person. Therefore, when it is said, "Here is wisdom," we cannot doubt that an appeal is made to that gift of the Holy Ghost, which is bestowed abundantly upon every humble child of God, wherewith he may be able to resist the delusions of error. And forasmuch as there is a summons to the man of understanding, then and there are the servants of God admonished to be vigilant, to try the spirits, whether they be of God, and to observe the signs of that last day, which shall come as a thief in the night.

For all the rest, the literal number may signify some title of Antichrist, which is probably to be learned only upon his appearance in the world; which distinctive title or attribute of the man, cannot be supposed a secret in the vulgar sense, for it has already been intimated, in the last verse, that his disciples are in possession of it. But what is indeed secret concerning it and hidden from the world, this is that true meaning of the same, which is understood by the spiritually minded; and by him alone, who, strong in faith and firm in patience, discerns the son of perdition even in the midst of his lying splendors; who perceives that his glory is his shame; and in the very title which he boasts, and which exalts him in the eyes of the world, reads plainly his blasphemy, and the sentence of his condemnation.

The conclusion and sum of what has been said, is this: The emphatic word for our own times, or for those which precede the last days, is that it is the number of man; for those contemporary with Antichrist, that it is six hundred and sixty-six. Let us not be deceived by the man-worship of the day, the fond philanthropy, the hypocritical show of goodness and virtue, which is exploded by its very exhibition. And in the last evil days, when, "Faith is lost and taken away out of their mouth,"[1] let the prudent be thankful, if there be left to them a sign of error, convincing and sensible, when the moral and higher proofs are diminished of their worth among men.

We have now reached the end of the Third Part. It will perhaps be thought that many hard things have been said; that honorable professions, and worthy trades, the humanities of this work-day world have been harshly treated; and therefore, it would be better to extenuate and smooth down these asperities, and so leave everything in the comfortable state where we found it. Consider now, courteous reader, whether a word of truth in its rough integrity, is not better than all the gilded phrases of human respect.

God forbid, that any honest calling should be disturbed, or any undeserved humiliation should be invoked upon either one of all the innocent pursuits of this weary life. But at the same time, let each one reckon his goods at the right value. Is there any wisdom, but the truth? Is there any knowledge or science, but that of goodness and rectitude? "Let no man deceive himself: if any man among you seem to be wise in this world, let him become a fool that he may be wise."[2] Can any one really believe that there is danger in thinking too meanly of this world? that its pomps need painting? that the tender mind of youth, requires the promptings of ambition, to arrive at eternal life? that the illusions of vain-glory will better sustain him in the duties of his vocation, than the science of the cross? And yet some worthy persons, forgetful of the rudiments of their Christian discipline, are always casting up the cant exhortations to liberty and philanthropy; and thrust upon us

[1] Jer. vii. 28. [2] 1 Cor. iii. 18.

continually their poor little prescriptions for happiness and success in life. As though it were necessary, to succeed in this world; as though it were a duty, to remain in good health; as though it were of obligation, to be always satisfied with thyself and with the world. The ingenuous mind is not elevated, nor the heart expanded, but rather fretted, confused, and debased, by stimulus like this; in which there is no hint of immortality, nor a thought toward the eternal state. Better, then, to hear the Apostles of Christ saying: "Confess your sins one to another, and pray for one another that you may be saved."[1] And again: "But we entreat you, brethren, that you abound more; and that you use your endeavor to be quiet, and that you do your own business, and work with your own hands, as we commanded you; and that you walk honestly towards them that are without; and that you want nothing of any man's."[2] "And who is he that can hurt you, if you be zealous of good? Be not afraid of their terror, and be not troubled."[3]

[1] James v. 16. [2] 1 Thess. iv. 10. [3] 1 Peter iii. 13.

PART IV.

THE LAST TIMES, OF THE CHURCH AND OF THE WORLD.

The Fourth Part follows naturally upon the preceding ones. In Part II., was considered the manner of the divine dispensations throughout the course of time; in Part III., the same was examined in the latter division of the times, or in those after Christ; in this Part is displayed the last result of the whole, by the summing up of the profit and loss in the divine balance. It comprises three chapters, the xiv., xv., and xvi. The fourteenth chapter describes the fruits of the Church; the sixteenth, the defections of the world. Chapter fifteenth indicates the excellence of the one, and the wretchedness of the other; as if to vindicate, and at the same time to enforce, the opposition between the two.

CHAPTER XIV.

THIS chapter abounds in allusions to the harvest-time of the Lord's vineyard. In the beginning are described the first fruits, to the fifth verse. After the first best fruit, follows that which is of less excellence, or later in time; and because its maturity is uncertain, and in danger from the hazards of the season, words of warning and of consolation are added to the fourteenth verse. Then, when the field is already white for the harvest, the corn is reaped, the grapes are gathered and pressed, and the season of grace is ended.

1 And I saw: and, behold, a Lamb stood on mount Sion, and with him a hundred forty-four thousand having his name and the name of his Father written in their foreheads.

The Lamb is that title of our blessed Lord, which St. John chiefly loved to employ, and is appropriate in this connection, because one signification of the same word, is, virginal or chaste αγνος. Sion may be, (specula vel speculator [1]) the heights of contemplation, and points to the state of Christian perfection. The one hundred forty-four thousand, signifies the full number of perfect souls. Or it may be regarded as a definite number, inasmuch as these are the privileged ones of the elect. As the former one hundred forty-four thousand, (chap. vii. v. 4,) embraced the saints of the old law, so this includes the virgins of the new; as if in the latter dispensation those who have attained to the most sublime degree of holiness, were equal to the whole number of just men under the ancient and imperfect covenant. They have the name of Christ and the name of his Father, because they ascend above all corporal signs, and even above the Humanity of Christ, to the contemplation of the Deity. Not

[1] St. Jer. Heb. Nom.

by any means that the contemplation of the Sacred Humanity is an impediment to Divine favors, [1] but yet the soul may be so elevated by the gift of God, as to transcend the use of the bodily senses, and even of the imagination, and attain to the vision of the divine essence. [2]

2 And I heard a voice from heaven, as the voice of many waters, and as the voice of great thunder: and the voice which I heard, was as of harpers, harping on their harps.

Their voice is heavenly, because in their lives they are so conformed to Christ, that their conversation is rather that of angels than of men. The sound of waters is mingled of sweetness and gravity; and the majesty of chastity is terrible as thunder, to the unclean. By the strings of the harp may be understood the right intention of those who embrace holy perfection; "who, by the affliction of the flesh, are straitened unto another life," says St. Gregory, "and thus, like the extended chords of the harp, are resonant of good example. For the chord is stretched upon the harp, that it may become tuneful; and thus holy men chastise their body, and bring it into subjection; and from the things below, are drawn to those above." [3]

3 And they sung as it were a new canticle, before the throne, and before the four living creatures, and the ancients: and no man could say the canticle, but those hundred forty-four thousand, who were purchased from the earth.

The canticle of the virgins, is a song of the New Testament. The Lord saith, by his prophet Isaias: "Behold, I do new things. I will make a way in the wilderness and rivers in the desert, to give drink to my people, to my chosen. But thou hast not called upon me, O Jacob; neither hast thou labored about me, O Israel." [4] Therefore, the former things have been set aside, and a higher vocation has been announced by the evangelical counsels, as far above the other

[1] Vida de la S. Teresa 22.
[2] Sum. Theol. 2. 2. 180. 5.
[3] Mor. Job. 30. 31.
[4] Isa. xliii. 19.

as is heaven above earth. And historically it is a new one, first practised and honored in holy Church, who best fulfils the sentence of the Psalmist: Cantate Domino canticum novum.[1] And again: Confessio et pulchritudo in conspectu ejus; Praise and beauty are before him, holiness and majesty in his sanctuary.[2] "For since comeliness is attributed to chastity," says St. Thomas; "virginity is therefore of itself the most excellent beauty:"[3] worthy of praise before Heaven, and admirable in the sight of the Masters in holy living, both old and new. O quam pulchra est casta generatio cum claritate, quoniam apud Deum nota est et apud homines.[4]

And no man can say the canticle but the hundred forty-four thousand: because, as it is a thanksgiving for their having been preserved in the integrity of the flesh, necessarily none can participate in that joy, but those who have been thus purchased out of the wilderness of this earth, by the merits of Jesus Christ.

4 These are they who were not defiled with women: for they are virgins. These follow the Lamb whithersoever he goeth. These were purchased from among men, the first-fruits to God, and to the Lamb.

These, therefore, follow the Lamb, the Innocent one, to whom they are so nearly conformed by innocence of mind and of body. And as blessed John leaned upon his bosom, and stood by his cross, and was entrusted with his most holy Mother, so does their purity give them just confidence to adhere to their Lord as his personal attendants, and to follow him whithersoever he goeth. Not indeed that, by virtue of the corporal resemblance alone, they are nearer to Christ; but they are so principally, by the imitation of the mind; and secondarily, by that of the body. Moreover, they are purchased from men, being formed in the common frailty of flesh and blood; and yet the merits of Christ have availed to

[1] Psalms xxxii. 3. [2] Psalms xcv. 6.
[3] Sum. Theol. ii. 2. 152. 5. [4] Wisdom iv. 1.

exalt them high in the angelic ranks. These are the first-fruits, in some sense, even in order of time; for the virgin is first; and the penitent comes after, returning as a second creation, and not now the first. But in a higher sense, divine grace transcends all limits of time, and distinctions of rank, and degrees of talent, and thus Mary, "Blessed among the Blessed, came out of the mouth of the Most High, the first-born before all creatures;"[1] and if the chaste generation be the first creation, she is first among the chaste. Again, this portion of Holy Scripture is the lesson for the Holy Innocents, who have the merit of virginity and of martyrdom; because it is not of him that willeth, nor of him that runneth, but of God that sheweth mercy.[2] And thus, in Holy Church, are we taught to honor innocence wherever the Creator has been pleased to bestow it; not alone the gray hairs, or the gifts of nature, "but the understanding of a man is gray hairs, and a spotless life is old age."[3] Again, the fair generation of the chaste, was found in its fulness in the monastic ages of the Church. The monastery is the established nursery of these best fruits. Instituted by perfect men, and sanctioned by the Head of the Church, to deny that through long ages they yielded a bountiful harvest to God and to the Lamb, would be to make the fabric of Christendom one stupendous hypocrisy.

5 And in their mouth was found no lie: for they are without spot before the throne of God.

But among all the charges that have been made against the ages of the ancient simplicity, that of hypocrisy has hardly ever been preferred. The language of those days is without sophistry, and without guile. "The chaste generation is known both with God and with men." Innocence is manifest by its own artlessness; for it is impossible that the language of innocence should be guarded, distrustful, and suspicious; as it is impossible that guilt should be unstudied,

[1] Eccles. xxiv. 4. 5. [2] Romans ix. 16.
[3] Wisdom iv. 8.

frank, and unaffected in its words. A fair expression, (to take an example,) of the monastic thought, is recorded in the pages of "Imitatio Christi;" whose sentences are household words among the religious orders, and of which it might be said, no lie is found in it, and it is without spot, before the throne of God.

6 And I saw another angel flying through the midst of heaven, having the eternal gospel, to preach to them that sit upon the earth, and over every nation, and tribe, and tongue, and people.

Happy are they who have the grace to follow the evangelical counsels; "But all receive not this word," and there are many others who remain to be gathered into the heavenly garner, with sweat and labor, with greater cost, and commonly with less profit. When, at length, charity began to grow cold, and the time was at hand for the disruption of that ancient fabric of Christendom; when the false prophets were about to arise, and the way of truth was to be obscured and narrowed, by dangerous heresies, and beset with countless perils, and the days of this ungrateful world were numbered, then arose St. Vincent Ferrer, whose mission was to preach, with new fervor, the eternal truths of heaven and hell, and to inspire the salutary fear of judgment, soon to come. He executed his mission, by preaching these words to all the peoples of Christendom; and he proved his divine warrant, by miracles, wrought publicly, in the sight of the Church, the kingdom of Heaven.

7 Saying with a loud voice: Fear the Lord, and give him honor; because the hour of his judgment is come: and adore ye him, who made heaven, and earth, the sea, and the fountains of waters.

He warned the peoples of Christendom of that holy fear which is the beginning of wisdom, and the first step to the honor of God; he discoursed daily, and with miraculous energy, of the approaching judgment, and summoned them to do penance, and thus render worthy homage to Him, who

[1] Matt. xix.

made heaven and earth, the things above and the things beneath; who established his Church in treasures of grace, and supplied it with the abundant rivers of living water. If, therefore, such was the testimony of St. Vincent, publicly and uniformly maintained by him, that he was indeed the angel signified by this text; and if the Church has placed him in her calendar, and appropriated to him these same words of Holy Scripture, in his office of the Breviary, we certainly need seek no better interpretation, than what has thus received the approbation of an infallible authority. St. Vincent did not pretend to say when should be the hour of judgment, nor could he be induced to declare anything more than that it would be quickly: cito et bene cito. The divine decrees are not to be bounded by any figures of human calculation; or, if they are, in some instances, so described, yet even then it is not in the unqualified manner which the impatient human thought would expect, but associated with so much of obscurity, and with a certain degree of conditionality, that the liberty, both of the Creator and of the creature, remains unimpaired. Thus, we may believe, with St. Vincent, that the hour of divine judgment is come; that the way of life eternal is straitened by so many dangers from indifference, infidelity, and persecution, (persecution not the less fatal, because it may have more the appearance of friendship than of hatred,) that the end is at hand; and yet we know not the day, nor the hour.

8 And another angel followed, saying: She is fallen, she is fallen, that great Babylon; which made all nations drink of the wine of the wrath of her fornication.

Here, before the end of the harvest season, are described three angels successively. The first has been already considered in the person of St. Vincent; the third executes his mission manifestly in the times of Antichrist. [See the following verse.] The second, now before us, will accordingly fulfil his office in the intervening period of time. The first warns men that the end is near; the second advises them that this world is already condemned; the third, with severe reproof, and with earnest counsel, exhorts them to be steadfast in the last combat with the man of sin The message of the angels, severally, is of course addressed to the faithful; for it would be useless to tell the unbelievers of an instant judgment, which they always ridicule; or of the overthrow of Babylon, considered literally, as some particular city, since an occurrence of that kind would declare itself.

It has been said, that the message is addressed to the faithful or to the spiritually minded, and, therefore, its meaning is mystical and not literal. Babylon is the city of the world, as Jerusalem is the heavenly city. And if these two names have oftentimes a spiritual signification in the Old, much more will they be so employed in the New Testament writings. The ancient prophets use the same phraseology with that in the text: "Babylon is suddenly fallen and destroyed."[1] "Babylon is fallen, she is fallen."[2] And again: "Babylon hath been a golden cup in the hand of the Lord, that made all the earth drunk." What the literal Babylon was, to the citizens of Jerusalem, such is this world, to the Christian peoples; a place of captivity and of peril for the soul. And by the world is meant, this transitory spectacle of outward beauty, as distinguished from the earth, or the material forces. It is likened to a city, because the glory of this world is always in a crowd, in the confusion of the camp, the streets, the theatre, or the forum. Unlike the city of God, whose glory is within and greatest in solitude, Babylon is fallen, vanished, and extinct, where there is not the praise of men, where there are not the multitudes to wonder and admire. Its power, therefore, is not in any physical coercion, but in the intoxication of the mind. As the woman was seduced because "she saw the tree was good to eat, and fair to the eyes, and delightful to behold;" so the blandishments of this world, like the glittering wine, betray the rational soul, and subvert the understanding; leading it far astray from the

[1] Jer. li. 8. [2] Isa. xxi. 9.

true happiness, to consent to fornication, to unlawful and polluting enjoyments, which overwhelm it sooner or later, as if with a wrath, a frenzy, of lust for the pleasures of this life. But how can it be said that Babylon is fallen, from beforehand, if men are to be eating and drinking, marrying and giving in marriage to the end of the world? Morally, the event has already transpired, as will be seen in a following part of the work. And literally, the sentence is to be understood of an event so near at hand, that now its presentiment is distinctly proved. But again, what need is there of a prophet to tell Christian people, that this world must meet its overthrow at last, that in the end it will fall, since this is a truism which no one disputes? It may be observed in answer, That the fact of the world's final destruction being a truth so familiar, may be in great measure owing to this Revelation of St. John's; and that the imagery in which the holy Apostle conveys the same truth is what has contributed powerfully to impress it upon the mind, and to render the tradition so common and ever present to the thought. And thus, unconsciously, other truths may have obtained much of their hold upon the memory of the Christian, from their having been derived to him through the similitudes of the Apocalypse, in which, because he is attentive chiefly to the figure, he considers not that the authority of a dogma may be contained under it. But in the second place it is to be answered: That, whatever be the substance of the proposition, the manner alone of its announcement may have a very sensible influence upon Christian society, and even upon the world. Perhaps the disorders of the age may be so aggravated, and the dreadful catastrophe may be discovered in such imminent proximity, that the solemn warning of some servant of God may be sufficient to move the hearts of men to penance; even as the Ninevites, heathen as they were, turned to the true God with prayers and fasting. It would seem probable that the present age might be the time for the second angel; consistently with the tenor of this work, and with the rules which have guided it, the conclusion is obvious.

With regard to the personality of this angel, if compared with the text, (chap. xviii. v. i.,) "I saw another angel coming down from heaven, having great power; and the earth was enlightened with his glory;" it would follow that he will be one high in authority who comes down from his exalted state or rank in the ecclesiastical hierarchy, to preach the end of the world with marvellous power of words, and to illustrate his mission with miraculous signs and virtues. But it must be confessed, that, as the three angels are presented in this chapter, there is no hint of any such high prerogatives. It is said of the first that he was "flying through the midst of heaven;" and of the third, that he speaks "with a loud voice;" the second makes but the simple declaration: "Babylon is fallen." It would seem, therefore, that this much, and only this much, can be predicated of the second angel with certainty, namely: that he will be appointed by God to forewarn man of the end of this world, and to proclaim its iniquities: and that he will convince the wise that his mission is authentic, and will thus gain many souls to the harvest of the Lord. "Gracious and plenteous in mercy. Who hath compassion on them that fear him: for he knoweth our frame, he remembereth that we are dust."[1]

9 And the third angel followed them, saying with a loud voice: If any man shall adore the beast, and his image, and receive his mark in his forehead, or in his hand:

The third angel followed them: or is associated with the others in a like office, which is to instruct men concerning the perils of the last days. As it is certain that the Church cannot fail, and the truth cannot perish, so, by the mercy of God, may we hope that, even in the times of Antichrist, the guidance of the Catholic theology, with its marvellous perspicuity and distinctness, of precept and of practice, will safely direct the humble soul through every danger, and that the promise will be good to the last: "Thy eyes shall see thy teacher, and thy ears shall hear the word of one admon-

[1] Psalms cii.

ishing thee behind thy back: This is the way, walk ye in it; and go not aside neither to the right hand, nor to the left."[1] Perhaps, too, there may be deduced from the text another instance of the merciful indulgence of the Church's rule, namely: that the grievous sin, is to adore the beast; but that it is possible one might be in some way implicated in his service, while yet in heart and soul he abhors his bondage, and therefore is not obnoxious to the curse which follows.

10 He also shall drink of the wine of the wrath of God, which is mingled with pure wine, in the cup of his wrath: and he shall be tormented with fire and brimstone in the sight of the holy angels, and in the sight of the Lamb:

Behold the just retribution of a mortal sin; the sin of him who adores the beast, who makes the power of earth his idol, who serves not the Creator but the creature. And if the friendship of the world be always dangerous, more especially is it so in the last days, and eminently in those of Antichrist. Wherefore a double weight of punishment seems implied by the words, mingled with pure wine; that is, mingled, not with water, but with a drink still purer and unmixed, as if the wrath, so far from being mitigated, were, on the contrary, aggravated upon the followers of the man of sin.

11 And the smoke of their torments shall ascend up for ever and ever: neither have they rest day nor night, who have adored the beast, and his image, and whosoever did receive the mark of his name.

It may be remarked that perhaps nowhere in Holy Scripture are the pains of hell enunciated more plainly, and in more minute and connected detail, than in this passage. The sinner who chooses the intoxications of the world while in this life, after death must drink of the wine of God's wrath; and the gift of intelligence, which he perverted to the dishonor of his Maker, is become the means whereby he discerns his

[1] Isais xxx.

own madness, and the fearful pain of Loss. The pain of Sense is signified by fire and brimstone, to which he is condemned in the presence of the Holy Angels, and of the Lord, the Judge of angels and of men. The Duration of the pains is everlasting; their Intensity is proved in that they have no rest, in any moment of that endless torment.

12 Here is the patience of the saints, who keep the commandments of God, and the faith of Jesus.

How can one believe that there is a future state of torment, and yet persist in an ungodly life? Here is the test of faith and of patience: when the just man endures a temporal loss, rather than hazard one that is eternal.

The message of the third angel is now ended; and since his epoch appears to be the same with that of the two Witnesses in Part II., it might reasonably be inquired, in what respect his office is distinguished from theirs? It may be observed: that the two Witnesses are supposed to testify to the dogmas of revealed religion, as held generally by the common humanity. But the third Angel has his mission within the Church: because he is associated with the former two angels; and because the form of his teaching is strictly casuistical, and proper to the Catholic discipline: and, in the third place, because this chapter is occupied with the fruits of the Church, the communion of the Saints. Thus their respective functions are appropriate and distinct.

13 And I heard a voice from heaven, saying to me: Write: Blessed are the dead, who die in the Lord. From henceforth now, saith the Spirit, that they may rest from their labors: for their works follow them.

A voice from heaven says: Write. Record it. For these are indeed heavenly and memorable words. Sweet even to childhood, is their voice above the graves of the departed; and they rest like the warm sunlight of the harvest hour upon God's field.

But chiefly blessed and most illustrious among the dead

who die in the Lord, are the holy Martyrs. And though the merit of virginity is first mentioned in this chapter, (for reasons analogous to those already given under verse 4th,) yet the charity of the martyr who lays down life itself, may be greater than that of the virgin who renounces the delectations of life.[1] Commonly speaking, they who are not defiled with women are virgins; but it is evident that in other ways the body may be violated, and even if the material integrity of the flesh have been kept unimpaired, yet it is the intention alone, the (propositum) determination to be devoted unreservedly to the divine service, which is the form and complement of virginity. And thus the monk who gives up all things, and renounces his own will, proves a higher devotion, than the one who consecrates virginity alone to the Divine honor. In like manner, the penitent may exceed the virgin in charity, and deserve a higher degree or mansion of beatitude, though the aureola of virginity can never be hers.

Thus, while the Lord of the Harvest gathers in the fruit of his dear labor, do the four voices admonish us of the four last things, which should be ever present to the mind. St. Vincent warns us of Judgment. The second Angel tells of Death; of Babylon, the city founded in Sennaar, i. e., in stench. The third declares the pains of Hell. And now the celestial voice shows, that the last resting-place of the Christian soul, is the home in Heaven.

14 And I saw: and, behold, a white cloud, and upon the cloud one sitting like to the Son of man, having on his head a golden crown, and in his hand a sharp sickle.

"The Lord looketh down from heaven upon the children of men;"[2] and if now in the day of salvation his presence be veiled from them, yet it is not with the shadows of despair, but with the white cloud of the harvest hour, while he graciously waits if the people of his pasture will hear his voice, and harden not their hearts. He is crowned with gold: for

[1] 2. 2. Sum. Theol. 152. [2] Psalms xxxii. 13.

this is the Royal Husbandman, who rears up from the dust of earth immortal souls to be made a kingdom and priests to God and his Father.[1] He hath in his hand a sharp sickle: for his purposes are sure, and there is no respect of persons with God.

15 And another angel came out of the temple, crying with a loud voice to him that sat upon the cloud: Put to thy sickle, and reap, because the hour is come to reap; for the harvest of the earth is ripe.

The fields are white already to harvest; and if man prays that the Lord would send forth reapers, how much more does the angel fervently desire that the elect may be gathered to their rest! The temple is the place of prayer; and, by the intercession of holy angels, is the soul conducted through the shadows of death. Or, if this be understood of the end of the world, when the angels shall gather out of his kingdom all scandals, and them that work iniquity; the cry should be one of alarm to the impenitent, lest they have soon to mourn: "The harvest is past, the summer is ended, and we are not saved."[2]

16 And he that sat on the cloud, put his sickle to the earth; and the earth was reaped.

How copious and excellent are the fruits of Holy Church! In what varied magnificence hath the Master displayed his admirable works, when he hath formed the rational soul to be his heavenly kingdom! "Thou shalt bless the crown of the year of thy goodness: and thy fields shall be filled with plenty."[3] The justified soul is the fair return for all his labor, and this he has gathered and will yet gather from out the corners of the earth. "The beast of the field shall glorify me, the dragons and the ostriches."[4] Saint or sinner, virgin or penitent, gentle or savage, black or beautiful, the elect soul shall be led up from the desert of this world, her

[1] Chap. i. ver. 6.
[2] Jer. viii. 20.
[3] Psalms lxiv. 12.
[4] Is. xliii. 20.

"stature like to a palm tree, and her breasts to clusters of grapes." Such is the generation of Holy Church, who holds on her peaceful course through this stormy life, alone faithful, alone sure, and all desirable. Blessed, therefore, is the fruitful Mother in the beginning and in the end; in her virgins, and in the humble multitudes of her faithful people. Venter tuus, sicut acervus tritici, vallatus liliis.[1]

17 And another angel came out of the temple, which is in heaven, he also having a sharp sickle.

After the harvest, comes the vintage. The Lord himself, as if with his own hand, gathers in his wheat, the fair company of his confessors, who are firm in faith, ripe in golden charity, and perfect in contrition. But there remain other souls, weak in the faith, and stained with many imperfections; whose feeble steps, wavering in doubt, or sinking under temptation, are scarcely supported in the narrow way of life, even by the virtue of attrition, and by the wholesome fear of eternal pains. These are the prodigal sons of the Holy Mother, who add nothing to her treasures of merit, but rather impoverish her stores. Who help not so much to bear the burdens of others, as rather they serve to afflict their neighbors, with a double load of care and endurance. Thus the afflictions of holy Job were formerly aggravated by the reproaches of his friends; but, in the end, these were rebuked, and were commanded to offer sacrifice under the intercession of him they had oppressed: "Go to my servant Job," saith the Lord "and offer for yourselves a holocaust, and my servant Job shall pray for you; his face I will accept, that folly be not imputed to you."[2]

18 And another angel came out from the altar, who had power over fire: and he cried with a loud voice to him that had the sharp sickle, saying: Put to thy sharp sickle, and gather the clusters of the vineyard of the earth; because the grapes thereof are ripe.

As the end of the harvest draws near, holy angels are

[1] Canticles vii. 1. [2] Job. xlii. 8.

described as coming out of the temple; that is, from the place of sacrifice, of the intercession and merits of the saints, as the especial motive for the gathering in of the elect; as if, in the course of ages, the increasing and added merits of the saints, prevail to obtain this long desired end. But now another angel is added, as coming from the altar itself; from that which, in the temple of God, is the source, as well as the channel or instrument, of every merit and oblation which can propitiate the favor of a just God. For we come now to those imperfect souls, who abound in the last days; and who are saved only with infinite difficulty, with many prayers, with many interpositions of angel ministers, with sorrow, with pain, and as if by fire.

But if they grievously need these kind offices, so do their fellow-servants, whether in heaven or on earth, with tender compassion, and ardent charity, send up their prayers to him who will not suffer anything defiled to enter the celestial gates; and while the Church on earth offers her earnest petition: ne cadant in obscurum, sed signifer sanctus Michael repraesentet eas in lucem sanctam, the angels with holy zeal guide them in their dolorous way to the distant and long desired rest.

It is seen, from the present interpretation, that the wheat (messis) of the elect, is understood of perfect souls, or of the Church Triumphant; and the grapes (vindemia,) of the imperfect or of the Church Suffering in Purgatory; some reason for which may now be given. These blessed and happy elements of bread and wine, it is true, do equally represent the sacred body of Christ our Lord; but while the bread is more particularly the emblem of his white and virgin flesh, the wine recalls the memory of his heavy wounds, and the bloody stripes whereby we are healed. And since, according to the innocence of a soul, the less of outrage it has offered to the Man of Sorrows; and according to its guilt, the more of pain has it caused to His Sacred Heart; we may be permitted to distribute the former among his stores of golden wheat; and to appropriate to poor souls like our own, the bruised and bloody grape.

19 And the angel put his sharp sickle to the earth, and gathered the vineyard of the earth, and cast it into the great wine-press of the wrath of God.

Those are always formidable words, which show the wrath of God; but even the anger of God is not without hope of pardon, and the continual prayer of his servants: Ne in æternum irascaris nobis, [1] and that of the daily office: Converte nos, Convert us, O God our Savior, and turn off thy anger from us, surely cannot be misplaced in the mouth of his elect. Often do the Holy Scriptures tell of this divine anger, which chastises but does not kill; even as the Lord was "exceeding angry with Aaron, and would have destroyed him, but that his brother prayed for him." [2] The great wine-press of the wrath of God, therefore, cannot be without some fair return, and it may be compared with that of Isaias the prophet: Torcular calcavi solus, I looked about and there was none to help; and my own arm hath saved for me, and my indignation itself hath helped me. [3] By the infinite mercy, and by the riches of God's goodness, his indignation, falling upon his Divine Son, hath become our reconciliation, and itself hath helped us.

20 And the wine-press was trodden without the city: and blood came out of the wine-press, even to the horses' bridles, for a thousand and six hundred furlongs.

Most terrible is the torrent of blood which marks the course of divine justice, and fearful is the chastisement which even a venial sin deserves, and unutterable is the anguish of the soul whose works must be purged by fire; but again this is the blood of expiation, and these are the dolors of sacred penance, rather than the woes of the accursed ones. If he trampled them in his indignation, and his garments were sprinkled with their blood, still it was the indignation

[1] Psalms. lxxviii. 5. [2] Deut. ix, 20. [3] Isaias. lxiii.

which saves, and it was the blood which makes beautiful his apparel; with the accents of love and of hope, and not in despair, we cry with the same Holy Prophet: Who is this that cometh from Edom, with dyed garments from Bosra, this beautiful one in his robe, walking in the greatness of his strength?

The wine-press is trodden without the city: for the imperfect souls now departed, assuredly cannot do their penance in heaven, neither is it permitted in the human society of this life, nor within the borders of Holy Church. Alas! that they profited not by her kind indulgence, but refused her light task; and now they are shut out from heaven above, and from the earth beneath; "neither have they a reward any more, nor is there work, nor reason, nor wisdom, nor knowledge,"[1] but only sorrow and pain in the prison of their purification. The blood is deep, even up to the horses' bridles; for they were nearly overwhelmed by their transgressions, and they drew nigh even to the gates of eternal death. It reaches a thousand six hundred furlongs: that is, throughout the extent of the land of promise; for these are elect souls, children of promise, and the prolific generation of a holy land. Here are ended the labors of the heavenly harvest. Where the fruits are more few, they are the fairer; and wherein they are of less excellence, there is greater gain and an overflowing abundance. Nimis honorati sunt amici tui, Deus; nimis confortatus est principatus eorum. Dinumerabo eos, et super arenam multiplicabuntur.[2]

CHAPTER XV.

In the first verse, and the last four verses of this chapter, are presented seven angels, having the seven last plagues; contrasted with which is the thanksgiving of the elect, in the intermediate verses. The chapter, as a whole, prepares

[1] Eccles. v. 9. [2] Psalms. cxxxviii. 17.

us for the consideration of the reverse of that aspect of the harvest season, which has been just now surveyed; it conducts from the prosperous increment of the kingdom of heaven, to the mournful decrement of this world of sin; and indicates the righteous counterpoise of the fruits of grace, against those of vice; the happy success and flourishing of the just, over against the blight, the decay, and the blasted arrogance of the reprobate.

1 And I saw another sign in heaven, great and wonderful, seven angels having the seven last plagues: for in them is filled up the wrath of God.

From the wrath of God upon the negligences of his own people, the transition is plain to that which falls upon his enemies. The wrath which was considered in the last chapter, that is, the tribulations of the elect, however grievous, is yet but the beginning, the shadow, as it were, of that which is filled up or consummated in the reprobate; for the one being temporal and the other eternal, the difference is infinite. The plagues are seven in number: because the collected vices, with their accursed fruits, may be distributed under seven heads; and the sign is great and wonderful because truly nothing so well deserves the watchful fear of men, as the anathema of heaven.

2 And I saw as it were a sea of glass mingled with fire, and them that had overcome the beast, and his image, and the number of his name, standing on the sea of glass, having the harps of God.

Immediately after the plagues, follows a description of the blessed; and, again, after their canticle of praise, reappear the angels, with the seven plagues; as if there were no hell without a heaven, and no paradise of merit without the terrible retribution of malice. And thus, truly, has the "Father of the world to come" been pleased to ordain us, in a double condition of truth and error, of right and wrong, of heaven and hell, one over against the other. Divest now this stage of human existence, of all its appurtenances of time and sense, and there remains the pure intelligence of truth, with the pure liberty of error. The truth may be compared to a crystal sea, lustrous and transparent; the liberty also is beautiful, quick, subtile, but dangerous as the fire. Upon this sea of glass, mingled with fire, stand the sons of God, who have overcome the temptations of this life; the others, who have preferred their own devices to the love of the Creator, must fall beneath and perish in its fiery deeps.

3 And singing the canticle of Moses the servant of God, and the canticle of the Lamb, saying: Great and wonderful are thy works, O Lord God Almighty, just and true are thy ways, O King of ages.

The sea of this life, the spiritual plane of the human soul, was prefigured for all ages by the Red sea, through which the people of God passed safely, while their enemies perished in its mighty waters. It is red, on the one hand, with the blood of expiation; and on the other, because the innocent blood exasperates the fire of retribution. By the blood of the Paschal Lamb, Moses, the servant of God, and his people, came safely out of Egypt, and through the waters of the Red Sea; and by the blood of the Divine Lamb, the Christian soul is delivered from the bondage of this world, and stands above its temptations.

4 Who shall not fear thee, O Lord, and magnify thy name? For thou only art holy: for all nations shall come, and shall adore in thy sight, because thy judgments are manifest.

The canticle of this chapter, it is to be observed, declares the praises of justice; the ways of God, as they are just and true, rather than as they are beneficent or indulgent. For, after his acts of clemency, his judgments are also to be made manifest.

5 And after these things I saw: and, behold, the temple of the tabernacle of the testimony in heaven was opened.

The tabernacle of the testimony, or the eternal law of God's justice and truth, is deposited within his temple of sacrifice, and is never divorced from his mercy; but, as it would seem now in this time of grace, it underlies, or is contained within it, although it be in fact commensurate and of absolute equality.

6 And the seven angels came out of the temple, having the seven plagues, clothed in clean and white linen, and girded about the breasts with golden girdles.

From the sacred house of justice, proceed the ministers of justice; clothed in spotless white, and girded with golden charity, not only about the reins, the acts of the officer, but even about the heart, the most secret intentions of his mind. Even so, in human affairs, purity in the administration of justice, seems to be the most sacred and necessary of all the conditions of society.

7 And one of the four living creatures gave to the seven angels seven golden vials, full of the wrath of God, who liveth forever and ever.

It becomes the holy evangelists, who first published the truth, to guard it in its progress, and to prosecute its offenders, and to vindicate its purity. The vials or vases full of wrath, signify the fulness of guilt and its consequent penalty; or the narrow vase, may show that it is terrible according as it is contained and pent up from beforehand; or, that even the full wrath of God, is not without measure and rule. The vials are golden: because divine justice is admirable, as well as mercy is also fair to behold.

8 And the temple was filled with smoke from the majesty of God, and from his power: and no man was able to enter into the temple, till the seven plagues of the seven angels were fulfilled.

When the Prophet Ezechiel saw, in a vision, the beloved city of Jerusalem about to be destroyed, one clothed with linen was directed to take coals of fire that are between the cherubims, and pour them on the city; and it is written: "a cloud filled the inner court, and the house was filled with the cloud, and the court was filled with the brightness of the glory of the Lord."[1] The majesty of divine justice is that which we can least endure; with difficulty, and most imperfectly, do we apprehend somewhat of the attribute of divine mercy, when it has been humbled in infinite condescension to our earthly mansion, and to the conversation of men. Thus, with a mighty effort, we attain to a remote appreciation of the weakness of God—quod infirmum est Dei; but his power, and the visitation of his justice, who shall be able to look upon it? It is likened to smoke, or to a cloud, which no vision can penetrate; because, when the goodness and patience of God is withdrawn, guilty man is impotent, blind, and demented to his perdition. And no one [nemo] was able to enter the temple, may signify, that before the divine justice, in respect to its consummation, even the heavenly inhabitants, falling down, dare not, as it were, lift up their eyes to look upon the vengeance of the Most High.

CHAPTER XVI.

WITH this chapter we arrive at the concise narration of the seven last plagues. They are in the spiritual order, what a pestilence might be in the natural order, or a blasting mildew in the vegetable kingdom; and they fall necessarily upon a sinful world, even as diseased food, or a noxious soil, breeds poisonous humors and deadly infirmity. They are seven in number, as the principal vices of the soul are seven; and though doubtless an analysis more worthy of theological art might be described, yet it is sufficient for the present purpose, if their mode of operation be traced, as follows.

When divine truth is presented to the natural man, his first impulse is one of resentment, because he is thereby disturbed in his own estimation, and regards the truth as impeditive of his own excellence; and this is the vice of anger, which may be remarked generally in the treatment of superior merit, by

[1] Ezechiel x. 2.

persons of narrow and prejudiced minds, or by barbarous and uncultivated peoples. But, upon second thought, he pauses to examine the truth; and, prompted by the natural desire of knowledge, he proceeds to inquire and to discuss; and then, inflated by his besetting sin of pride, he divides and changes the truth from its first simplicity, and falls into the vice of vain-glory. Then, in the third place, he becomes weary and saddened in his arduous speculations; and, unwilling to pursue longer the laborious task, his mind is enervated from its former purpose, and conceives a disgust for the higher and spiritual state, which is the sin of acedia or sloth. Wherefore being thus dissipated and wasted in the intellectual account, he turns, in the fourth place, to seek the sensible and private good of his corporal estate; and from the grievous distress of his fainting soul, thinks to find some alleviation in the delights of gulosity. From which he falls into luxury and blindness of mind; and this is a fifth evil. The sixth is avarice, or an unbounded thirst for the material goods; which, being a barren, unsubstantial, enjoyment in respect of the animal appetites, but having its complement solely in the apprehension of the mind, brings us back to the spiritual vices, the last of which is envy. And this may be placed last, because, when all other means have been tried for the attainment of a false good, and to no purpose; and when every violence has been put forth against the true good, and yet it prevails and endures immovably, there remains, in the mind of the reprobate, that inextinguishable envy, which is conspicuous in the fallen angels.

Now if the natural order of the vices, in their generation of one from another, has not been followed, it should be considered that the question here is not about the manner in which fallen man might entertain the gifts of nature, the bounty of the Creator; but what is his conduct, when confronted with the supernatural graces, the mystery of the Cross. It is also to be remembered, that pride is not numbered properly among the capital sins, because it underlies every sin, and is already in possession; and therefore, each and all of the vices may be traced to it, as to a common head; and the plagues severally take effect, not only because of a special vice or because they are bound up with some given evil, but also for the reason that the ungrateful soil itself is accursed, and being already diseased, can yield only the fruits of sin, which at last are found to be rottenness and death. Let it not be supposed, therefore, even if the above account of the capital sins were arbitrary in its derivation, that the reader is consequently precluded from a just appreciation of the seven plagues, for it is to be observed: firstly, that the manner of their announcement denotes, that these are evils of the utmost magnitude; secondly, that nothing deserves the name of evil but sin; but, in the third place, all sin may be summed up in seven principal vices; which are to the rest, as is the head to the body, directive of all their movements. Therefore the seven plagues correspond substantially to the seven sins, which in turn are contrasted with the seven-fold grace of the Holy Spirit of God.

Some reference must now be made to the seven trumpets, in the former part of the work: the resemblances to which, of the seven plagues, are very close, as the reader will easily ascertain, by comparing the two portions of the sacred text. The phraseology in both is all but identical, and it might reasonably be asked, whether the ground-work or rationale laid out for this chapter, have not been already occupied? or, where is the divergence, between the trumpets and the vials? It is to be observed, that the sacred writer himself distinguishes the plagues, as being the last; in which the wrath of God is filled up or completed. Therefore, the trumpets are not the last plagues; but they herald the progress of truth through the latter ages of time, in loud and solemn tones; while the plagues fall in mournful silence, upon the infatuated sons of men. The seven seals might be regarded as simple representations or the shadows of coming danger; the trumpets, as threats; but the plagues are the curse itself. The seven trumpets, moreover, are evidently distributed throughout a succession of distinct events; but the plagues are enumerated without any such note of demarcation, and therefore they may be understood as simultaneous in point of time. It was declared positively that, with the seventh trumpet, time should be no more; that is, historically, it shall be ended; and in that end, it has been seen there was joy in heaven; but, with the last plague, men are left in the horror and confusion of guilt, and the conclusion is impenetrably obscure, and there is no consummation of times, nor of events, nor of works, but only of wrath divine. Therefore the plagues need not be deferred to the end of time, or to some distant age, but we will now proceed to examine them by the experience of this present generation; and to consider whether their baleful influences are not already at work in this day: the day alone of all the times, which concerns us, which we can call our own, which is of virtue infinite, and of consequence eternal.

1 And I heard a great voice out of the temple, saying to the seven angels: Go, and pour out the seven vials of the wrath of God upon the earth.

The great voice of divine justice, proceeds from the temple of truth, and when it is least apparent to the outward ear, it is most audible to the guilty conscience suspended in secret apprehension within. The vials are poured out upon the earth, inasmuch as they take effect upon the earth; for whatever may be the tribulation of the Church, or the persecution of the truth, all the evil therefrom accrues solely to the earth.

2 And the first went, and poured out his vial upon the earth: and there fell a sore and most grievous wound upon the men, who had the mark of the beast, and upon them who adored his image.

The Greek text implies that the wound is an old one, fretted to ulceration. John d'Avila, writing in the sixteenth century says: "Do we not see fulfilled before our eyes that which St. Paul prophesied of the last times; God shall send them the operation of error to believe a lie?"[1] Here is the grievous wound which has been inflicted upon men for the punishment of their indifference, and as yet it is unhealed. The operation, or the efficacy of error, still wastes and corrodes the souls of those who have gone out from the fold of the Church, because they were not of it. It has fallen upon all who have the mark of the beast; who love this world even to adoration, and who hate the glories of the Cross. The ulcer may be secret, yet it has become most painful by the lapse of time, and now it will no longer endure to be touched. It has been remarked by wise and learned writers of late, how, in their social intercourse, men will converse upon any topic whatever except one; will discuss any religion or argument, or folly whatever, but there is one forbidden subject which cannot be entertained; there is one august and sacred science of catholic and apostolic truth, which must not be mentioned. Or if they make some approaches to it, suddenly again they draw back—you have said enough—you have chafed that dolorous wound which will endure no pressure, even of a friendly hand. The memory of that "ancient beauty ever new," the Church of the fathers and of the saints, radiant as the sun, and gracious as the gentle virgin, rises up before them; and, like a burning light, it shows them that they are outcasts. Thus, the division between the Catholic Christian, and all others, the cruel wound which has been festering in neglect, or suffering under the brutal treatment of unskilful pretenders, or, of treasonous apostates, this is felt like a sore which will not be forgotten, which cannot rest. And so grievous is the evil, that even some of the faithful, out of a mistaken kindness for the sufferers, and by dint of an exaggerated sympathy, have come to be as tenderly sensitive as if the wound were their own. Thus every way is the evil aggravated; it sorely needs healing, but it is not healed; it smarts for a remedy, but it will not be handled.

[1] Trat. audi filia. c. 48.

3 And the second angel poured out his vial into the sea: and it became as the blood of a dead man: and every living soul died in the sea.

It will be remembered that the first vial is poured out upon the earth, or upon humanity in its carnal aspect; and the first plague is afflictive, by reason of the absolute repugnance of the flesh to the mortification of the Cross. But the second is poured into the sea: which represents the spiritual forces, or the human understanding in its Christian aggregation; that is, Christendom. The second plague, then, has fallen upon Christendom as such; for whereas formerly Christendom and Catholicity were synonymous terms, that sacred ideal is obscured; and is as the blood of a dead man, because there is at present little or no promise of its restoration. And every living soul died in the sea: because from the fact that one is a member or a habitant of Christendom, it by no means follows, that he has the guaranty of truth and of the means of salvation. The face of Christendom is now changed and disfigured by that vain-glory, which makes the multitudes to set down the ancient simplicity for a folly and a darkness, and to exalt their own century as absolutely the age of light; so that their highest aspiration of gratitude is one and the same with that of the Pharisee: O, God, I give thee thanks that I am not as the rest of men. Thanks, that their age is not like the former ages; thanks, for the singular privilege by which they have been born in these days, and by which they were not born, and may not be counted, in the humble family of the Catholic obedience.

4 And the third poured out his vial upon the rivers, and the fountains of waters: and they became blood.

The rivers and fountains, are considered to be the tributaries or branches of the Church Catholic. Every day is revealed the indifference and langour of the faint-hearted peoples, when we see the national churches one after another, rent from the apostolic obedience, by laymen who dare to usurp a divine authority over the prelates, the sacraments, and the discipline of religion: and as often do we witness the tearful remonstrances of the venerable Pontiff and Father of the Christian families, who beholds the sweet waters of truth thus polluted, and, from sources of life, converted into channels of error and of death.

5 And I heard the angel of the waters saying: Thou art just, O Lord, who art, and who wast, the Holy One, who hast judged these things:

As the angel guardian of some reprobate soul, confesses the justice of God, though as if with sorrow that his holy office has been made void; so the angel, or the patron saint of the Christian nation, discerns and confesses the purity of the divine motive, which decrees these disorders of particular churches.

6 For they have shed the blood of the saints and prophets; and thou hast given them blood to drink; for they deserved it.

Here it may be objected: Where in these days do we find that men shed the blood of the saints? To which it may be answered: that the outrages committed by revolutionists against the church in certain countries, are never unattended by many acts of personal violence toward the ecclesiastical body; and always with the greater atrocity, according as individual prelates or pastors are especially devout and faithful in the defence of religion, and of its time-honored institutions. But, since it is said in this same connection: Thou hast given them blood to drink; it is proper to interpret the blood of the saints and prophets, according to the antithesis which is furnished by the text. Now the blood which men have to drink, is the boastful and impudent promises of these intruders in sacred things; who brave the anathema of heaven, and, in the name of public good, plunder the revenues of the Church, the property of the poor; who interpose between the pastor and the flock, despoiling of authority those whose office it is to guard the truth in its integrity, but granting every license for the propagation of heresy and infidelity; who usurp authority in the administration of sacraments, obstructing the channels of grace, but promising an abundant material prosperity, and a marvellous light of earthly wisdom; who, for bread to the immortal soul, give it a stone; and for meat, reach it a scorpion. And again, men have deserved these plagues, when they neglected the service of the saints and prophets, when they began to despise their humble virtues, their holy precepts, and the precious merits of their blood, which has, perhaps, watered the soil of those very countries. When they began to weary of these things as if they were ancient fables, and to envy the godless liberties and hollow glories of less favored nations, then they made the merits of holy martyrs void, and their wounds to bleed afresh.

7 And I heard another from the altar, saying: Yea, O Lord God Almighty, true and just are thy judgments.

When some bodily injury befalls him, man is not so quick to question the justice of Providence; but even the profligate, sometimes churlishly, sometimes with a better grace, will finally acquiesce in the common physical ills of life; because they are hereditary, and in the natural order of cause and effect; and because of the instinctive perception by contrast of the dignity of the soul, which is better than the body. But when the soul is touched, when the spiritual blight befalls, when the way of life eternal is obscured and graces are withdrawn; when the oil of charity is wasted, and the lamp gone out, and the Bridegroom is shutting against us his heavenly gate: oh, then is the anguish inconsolable, and man's perturbed vision can discern no justice, and will confess no proportion in that awful ordination. But the voice from the altar, even that of the Victim, the Crucified One, declares the judgment just and true. For may it not be said of him, who despoils the Church of God and of his own fatherland, wherein he has received life-giving sacraments, "That he hath trodden under foot the Son of God, and hath esteemed the blood of the testament unclean, with which he was sanctified, and hath offered an affront to the spirit of grace?"[1] And therefore, upon such men it seems not unjust to denounce the remainder of that apostolic sentence, "If we sin wilfully after having received the knowledge of the truth, there is now left no sacrifice for sins, but a certain dreadful expectation of judgment, and the rage of a fire, which shall consume the adversaries."[2]

8 And the fourth angel poured out his vial upon the sun: and it was given to him to afflict men with heat and fire.

The sun, which is the source of light and warmth to the universe, in divine things will be the light and power of sacred truth; or, perhaps, the sacred minister, who is its organ and representative; or again, according to St. Gregory, sapientium intellectus—the intellect of the wise man. In the latter interpretation, the plague falls upon the wise man, when overcome by the weight of persecution or of temptation, he countenances the evil acts of the feeble-minded, and, by his bad example, adds fuel to the fire of their concupiscence. Suppose, for example, in a time like the present, when great calamities are threatened to society, when short-sighted men are so ready to subvert the ancient institutions and safeguards of the public good, so eager to mitigate all fines and penalties, so active to deride creeds and ceremonial observances, to sweep away forms, diplomas, and professions, to extend unqualified liberties and privileges, to offer a larger license of impiety, of usury, and of sensual indulgence; suppose, in such a time, that the wise man affects to discover, in these evils, the ripening fruits of goodness and truth, that he even elevates them into an additional good and a new advantage; that he binds them up in the tenacity and vigor of a theory, to prove that the Church will have the greater prosperity according as the temporal power withdraws itself from her service, that the ministers of religion will be apostolical, according as they lack the means to adorn her altars or to

[1] Heb. x. 29. [2] Heb. x. 26.

feed her poor, that they will be respected the more, according as there is the less reverence required; that, in a word, the solid, stable establishment of religion, of morality, and of government, is to be secured by the very means which would naturally be employed to extirpate the same; then, indeed, might we not say, there is a plague upon the wise man? and that he afflicts us with heat and with fire?

But, in the second place, if by the sun be understood the Pastor, whose office it is to give the light of good example to his flock; it is plain how he has power to afflict men, since one unworthy act of his, is able to kindle a flame of earthly desires in the minds of thousands, and to wring the hearts of faithful men, torn by the contending emotions of respect for his holy office, and of indignation for their unholy life.

To resume the first interpretation, the sun being considered simply and purely the light of truth, the Church, which is the pillar and ground of the truth, also afflicts men; not indeed by any infirmity of hers, but by the luminous force of her dogma, the unshaken and indefectible purity of her practice. All the errors of Protestants, the blasphemies of infidels, the clamors of the malevolent, and the injuries of men in power, have only gained new triumphs for the Catholic truth; and it seems now to beam forth upon men with a lustre and certainty, positive and irresistible.

9 And men were scorched with great heat: and they blasphemed the name of God, who hath power over these plagues; neither did they penance to give him glory.

Men seem to have been scorched and oppressed by this great weight of the truth, when they make such mighty efforts over all the world, to counteract its influence by the dissemination of pernicious errors; and when their personal repugnance for the minister of truth is such, that only the sight of the humble ecclesiastic in their streets, is enough to make them turn pale, or to burn with scorn and hot resentment. And accordingly many are the blasphemies which have been spoken against the name of God: against all religion whatever, against all morality, against every hierarchy and order, religious or civil. And now, if for the moment these clamors are hushed, as if before the presence of the Immaculate Mother of Divine Grace, what means the silence, if men do not penance to give glory to God? What does it purport, if they do not accept the proffered grace, and return to obedience of the truth? Would to God they might show this repentance, and rejoice the affectionate hearts of those who hope for better things, and make all these ungrateful arguments fall to the ground.

10 And the fifth angel poured out his vial upon the seat of the beast: and his kingdom became dark; and they gnawed their tongues for pain:

It might be supposed that, by the seat of the beast, is signified the chair of Antichrist; but the relative *they* proves rather that the indiscriminate mass of the impious is intended. The beast being the secular power, its seat or throne is this world; and its kingdom, are the servants of the world at enmity with God. It may be observed, that this vial is the converse of the former one, and in opposition with it. The plague which is derived to men through the sun or the truth, is the great light and vehemence of the same; that which is induced upon the service of this world, is the darkness of the same, in its last intensity. Men take refuge from the oppressive fervor of truth, in a natural or affected dulness of apprehension, which is the evil fruit of gulosity. Blindness of mind is attributed to luxury; for as the flesh is adverse to spirit, so the pleasures of sense are the darkness of the soul. The maxims of the carnal, are the contradictory of those of the spiritual life. The former draw it downward in a closer and ever nearer assimilation to the mire of earth, the latter elevate it to the angelic sublimity. And when we descend earthward, darkness besets us; and when we ascend heavenward, light attends us; the region of profoundest darkness is beneath, but the firmament above is always in light. Now to estimate the darkness of the world, we must consider what is the force of a maxim in the moral order; how it enters into the soul, and possesses it as a law and condition of its being; or, like a habit, enfolds and wraps it up, and seems to act spontaneously, and shows as if it were greater than the inhabiting soul. This is a great evil, when it is an evil. If it were a good habit of faith, hope, and charity, it would sustain the soul even in the agony of death, when it has lost all hold upon the faculties of sense, and is suspended between time and eternity; but, on the other hand, "If the light that is in thee be darkness, the darkness itself how great shall it be!" If the false principle gets possession of the mind and becomes the rule and measure of its operations, the spring of countless modes and relations of thought and action, of speculation and practice, then follow ruin and desolation which can only be compared to that spoken of by the Prophet: That which the palmer-worm hath left, the locust hath eaten; and that which the locust hath left, the bruchus hath eaten; and that which the bruchus hath left, the mildew hath destroyed.[1] And thus this last blight leaves the soul in darkness compared with which, all other evils are less: palmer-worm, locust, and fire, all are but shadows and emblems inadequate.

In the next place, to ascertain the degree of this darkness, we must observe what is the outward manifestation of the carnal maxims in the public sentiment; what is the expression and manner of the popular sympathy, in point of fact. The entity of popular opinion, once so vague and indefinite, is now fixed in the conditions of a substantive, bodily, organism; that of the Press. And, while it waxes stronger and louder day by day, and in the nature of things, is swift to publish calumny and falsity, but slow to repair injury and to acknowledge itself a liar; so is it to be feared that this evil must grow with its growth, and strengthen daily with its strength. As the last degradation of the immortal soul is, when she seeks her good absolutely in the limits of this

[1] Joel i. 4.

putrid flesh, so popular opinion occupied about itself, adoring itself, is able now to procure its own worship. Does human nature love praise? the incense of the press is wafted forward in clouds. Does nature love honors and dignities? the press pronounces the sovereign greatness of the people. Does it grieve upon losses or temporal calamities? its own organ promises, with the progress of science, infallible remedies and sure preventives; and drowns all apprehension of sin and danger, in a torrent of witticism and caricature. Does it love knowledge? its echo tells it that men shall be as gods. And has it any misgiving that this is not the straight and true way of knowledge, that the good fruits do not as yet appear, and that perchance it is wandering miserably in a vicious circle? the voice assumes a tone of triumphant confidence, and promises, that not one or more shall be made wise, but the literal multitude shall be a nation of sages. In circuitu impii ambulant. Vana locuti sunt unusquisque ad proximum suum; labia dolosa, in corde et corde locuti sunt. [1]

It will be objected, that these things cannot be so; that they are contrary to common sense, and that humanity is not altogether so demented as this. This much indeed is true, that, however fondly men may cherish the delusions of the age, they cannot, nor will they ever be permitted, so to deface the image of God in the soul, that a lie shall be its sufficient food, or furnish it one moment of true happiness; wherefore it is said: They gnawed their tongues for pain. That is, inwardly they suffer with doubt concerning the truth of these earthly promises; or about the value of their possible reality, since they are transitory; or, if there were no other anxiety, still there will be the gloomy presentment, that perhaps the coming good, will not, after all, bring that precise satisfaction, upon which their own heart is set. Again, the pain is referred to the tongue, and justly, because by the tongue is this great evil of popular opinion propagated.

[1] Psalms xi.

11 And they blasphemed the God of heaven, because of their pains, and wounds; and did not penance for their works.

It was said above, that, in order to appreciate the moral darkness of the age, we must also examine the manner of the popular sympathy. There is in the human body a certain connection of parts, technically called the Consent of Parts; so that when one given organ is distressed, it is found that another also suffers, as if out of sympathy with the former. Thus, in society, we detect its secret wounds and pains, by the public expression of its sympathies. Now these are on the side of error, of revolution, and of usurpation; and are not the consent of heavenly virtues, of order, of obedience, and of truth. "The wisdom of the flesh is an enemy to God: for it is not subject to the law of God, neither can it be." And if the law of God be onerous, so does the flesh naturally resent the human authority and subjection of order. This is seen in its morbid tenderness for the suicide and the prostitute; for the culprit, that he be not subjected to the rod, that his flesh be spared; and, for the great criminal, that he be kindly housed and warmly clothed. But the great clamor of the day betrays its sympathy for the seditious man. Chastise proselytism or the aggressions of heresy and infidelity, prosecute the demagogue of sedition and revolution: and that moment society writhes; it smarts to the core. And because of these wounds they blaspheme the God of heaven, the God of order.

12 And the sixth angel poured out his vial upon that great river Euphrates; and dried up the water thereof, that a way might be prepared for the kings from the rising of the sun.

The sixth plague invites a more literal interpretation, and seems to have a special significance for the present age. The river Euphrates denotes the security, plenty, and placid repose of the city of the world, and, by implication, of Christendom, so far as it lies within the terrestrial limits. And it may be called the great river: because of the marvellous abundance of temporal blessings, which God has bestowed upon his people, over and above those that are eternal. It has been seen under the sixth trumpet how this river was the occasion of mutiny in the social order, inasmuch as it provoked the bad passions of the multitude, lusting with carnal desires. The city of Babylon resisted, however, all the shocks of war, till king Cyrus drained or dried up the river which flowed through it; and then, in the night time, and in the midst of feasting and debauchery, the judgment of divine Providence permitted its lamentable downfall. Thus, under the sixth vial, it is found, that this river is at last wholly dried up. That is, the ancient tranquillity, the calm contentment of Christendom is passed away; and one by one, each of the nations is daily admonished that the anarchy and dangers lurking within its bosom are ready for instant explosion. Not that the industry, or the riches, or the furniture of civilization are consumed; but its form and complement, the peace of the Holy Ghost, is vanished. The fruit of peace, says St. Thomas,[1] imports two things: that we be not disturbed in its enjoyment by exterior influences, and that all the desires be set at rest in one fruition; for he, whose heart is perfectly at peace in one true good cannot be molested by any other thing, but the others are as nothing to him; wherefore it is said: Pax multa diligentibus legem tuam, et non est illis scandalum.[2] Thus the peace of the Gospel to men of good will, may be discerned in the former repose of Christendom; and the discord of the latter generations, in the scattering of the same over the face of the earth.

It may be said: that the former ages possessed not peace, because they were more distracted by strife and bloodshed than our own. But to this, it may be answered: that, however much the disorders of those times may be magnified, yet they possessed the peace of Christ, because, non illis scandalum —those evils did not disturb them, but they were contented to rest at home, in the land of the saints, their ancestors.

Again, it may be said: the moderns do not go abroad

[1] Sum. Theo. i. 2. 70. 3. [2] Psalms cxviii. 165.

because they lack peace at home, but because they would improve their fortunes, and perhaps embellish the original homestead. But this is a contradiction in terms, that one is perfectly contented with his home, and yet prefers to go abroad. Again, it may be objected: The Christians of the Middle Ages, did not, in fact, possess contentment; for they left their homes to crowd by myriads, in their foolish crusades to the Saracen dominions. It may be answered: They set forth to the Holy Land, either from a supernatural motive of spiritual good, or from a natural motive of material advantage. If the latter was their purpose, men in these days would consider the crusades to have been by no means quixotic, but prudential in the highest degree. And, therefore, some endeavor to vindicate them, upon the ground of a wise temporal policy; which, however, is a difficult argument to establish; for the poor, mutilated soldier, returning in rags from his campaign, is but little suggestive of the material improvement; while the tear or the sob we yield him, proves how strongly he appeals to the nobler sentiments of the heart and soul. And therefore, a better and a sufficient account of the crusades is, that those expeditions were inspired by the love of God, of which love the peace of the gospel is a consequence; and when the crusader impoverished his estate to furnish out the equipage of war, and left his home for a distant and dangerous land, the inference is, not that he loved his home less, but that he loved God more; not that his peace was withered, but his charity abounded; and the fruit of his enterprise was the acqusition, not of material wealth, but of spiritual treasures to the memory and understanding of the Christian soul; which reads, in his acts, the fulfilment of the prophecy of Isaias: And his sepulchre shall be glorious.[1]

To resume now the definition of the Euphrates: it signifies the peace of the Christian soul, as it subsists in the nations of good will. And, though not a material good, yet it is a sensible blessing, so far as it is the confidence of divine

[1] Isaias xi. 10.

truth infused upon, or informing, the natural advantages and accomplishments of human society. In a word, it is the sentiment of tranquillity, or contentedness of mind; which, being first disturbed, and finally exhausted, there follows anxiety, and a restless roving of the peoples over the face of the earth. This may be that distress of nations, which is aptly expressed by the "pressura gentium" of the Vulgate; and still more significantly by the Greek συνοχη, i. e., the complication and binding of the nations one upon another. Which disorder of society, it may be here observed, if it is to be referred to one vice more than to another, seems especially due to the capital sin of avarice. For this is the opposite of liberality, that virtue by which is procured the free, unselfish enjoyment of the bounties of the Creator, signified by the fruitful river Euphrates. While, on the other hand, the magnitude and multiplicity of the evils which cause the distress of nations, have their adequate source in the vice of cupidity, which is the root of all evil: radix omnium malorum.[1] For as pride is the beginning of all sin, in respect of the mind's aversion from God; so in respect of its conversion to a mutable good, avarice is the root of all evils; since, like the root to the tree, it furnishes the aliment, or the instrument, i. e., riches, for the perpetration of every other evil; according as it is written: "All things obey money."

To resume the sacred text: this agitation of society prepares the way for the kings, from the rising of the sun, from the remotest regions of the East. Beside the peace of Christianity, which is supernatural, is the natural tranquillity of heathendom, which is signally displayed in the Asiatic repose. The subtraction of the former, leads to the perturbation of the latter; and the expiration of the Christian peace, prepares the way, or opens a way and communication with the distant powers of the earth. Now this event follows, as the effect follows the cause, for a two-fold reason; firstly, Christian people would never betake themselves to the ends of the earth,

[1] 1 Tim. and 1, 2, Sum. Theol. lxxxiv. 1.

unless they had first lost their own peace at home. And, secondly, the nations of the remote East would never of themselves seek intercourse with the Western people, since their inveterate customs and severe laws prohibit it; and it is comparatively easy for them to perpetuate constitutions of their own creation, while it is most uncertain, when and how the others may forfeit divine blessings. The second of the above propositions needs no proof; to the first it may be objected: that it is not necessary to suppose cupidity to be at the root of the commotion of modern society; but, rather, this is to be regarded as the wholesome agitation of the active charity, which would extend the blessings of Christianity and of civilization, to the ends of the world; according as it is written: "This gospel of the kingdom shall be preached in the whole world for a testimony to all nations: and then shall the consummation come." To this it may be answered: that the propagation of the gospel of peace is effected by the man of peace, who goes forth not to destroy, but to save; and as the Divine Master himself disturbed not the powers of earth, so never has it been seen, that the preaching of his holy truth, by the missionaries of the Catholic Church, has subverted a single political institution, or for one moment weakened, in the least, the hands of the powers that be. Now that process of civilization which is at present under consideration, is the reverse of this; and is accomplished through human means, at first by the promise of a material improvement, but afterwards the personal violence; and now, while these lines are written, the cannon of Christian Europe is thundering on the shores of by Eastern world

Formerly, Christendom was ever in the attitude of defence; exposed to the irruptions of barbarians, and harassed by their insolent usurpation of her territories: and then many nations were converted to the obedience of Christ. But now that method of the Cross is wholly reversed; the Christian peoples are the aggressors, and the heathen tribes throughout the world are vexed by the rapacity, corrupted by the vices, and aggrieved by the cruel injustice of those who go forth from the centres of civilization, of light and liberty: and now no nation is converted to the charity of the Gospel.

Again, though Christianity encourages social intercourse, and promotes friendships, and multiplies affinities, yet it respects the ancient landmarks of language, race, and climate, loves order in its variety, and heralds its advent by the gentle missionary, the angel soldier of the Cross, who carries neither purse, nor scrip, nor shoes, and who salutes no man by the way. Truly, such is not the pioneer of the material progress, who publishes his schemes on every side, and who goes forth freighted with earthly toys, of books, or of idols as it may be, with the protecting cannon of his country to wait upon his side, and to follow him to the uttermost parts of the earth. Christianity favors the commerce of nations, both ecclesiastical and civil; but the mere carnal operation of colonization, is no part of her office. So far as it is a thing indifferent, and procuring natural advantages, the human development is the first dictate of nature, as was signified in the beginning, by that precept of the natural law, Increase and multiply and fill the earth. But when, prompted by the desire of riches, or of dominions foreign to the parent country, it transports peoples, and substitutes races of hot for cold, of white for red, and of black for white; these are the achievements, not of the gospel, but of a mongrel and vicious civilization. The Pagan nations have practised the same kind of colonization, and under the Romans it seems to have brought about that crisis of human misery, which engaged the most holy Redeemer to come down from heaven for our salvation; and even so it may be that the Christian republic is preparing that accumulation of evils, which will deserve his second coming to judge the earth. It is true, indeed, that there is a promise, the gospel shall be first preached in all the world; but it is nowhere said, that all shall accept it. Often has the truth been announced in the Eastern world, and as often has it been rejected or lost; and there seems now about to be fulfilled another sentence: "I am come in the name of my Father, and you receive me not; if another shall come in his own name, him you will receive;"[1] for it is evident that a corrupted Christianity is gaining in those regions a crowd of deluded followers. Because the transactions of the modern civilization are not engendered by pure religion, therefore, it is not to be expected that the propagation of sacred truth will follow; but rather the operation of error, a spurious philosophy, and a mutilated Christianity. And such a result is plainly indicated in the following verse:

13. And I saw from the mouth of the dragon, and from the mouth of the beast, and from the mouth of the false prophet, three unclean spirits like frogs.

The dragon is the Devil; the beast is the secular power, or the World; the false prophet panders to the desires of the Flesh. The false prophet supplies the concupiscence of the flesh, the beast fosters the concupiscence of the eyes; the dragon furnishes the pride of life. "For all that is in the world," saith the Apostle, "is the concupiscence of the flesh, and the concupiscence of the eyes, and the pride of life." St. Thomas[2] shows how to these three, may be reduced all the passions which are the cause of sin. The inordinate desire of good, in the first instance, is the cause of every sin. And good is in two ways the object of the sensitive appetite, in which are these passions of the soul; one way, absolutely, according as it is the object of the concupiscible in man; the other, in respect of its being difficult, and as it is the object of the irascible power. Again, the concupiscence is two-fold; one, natural and common with the brute creation, relating to the conservation of the body, whether by food or drink, or by the copulation of the sexes; and this is the concupiscence of the flesh. The other is the concupiscence of the mind, which brings no direct carnal delectation, but relates to those things which are apprehended by the imagination as delectable, such as money, lands, jewels, and the like; and this is called the concupiscence of the eyes; either because it is of the vision, the lust of curiosity, or because it is of the things visible, the

[1] John v. 43. [2] Sum. Theo. 77, 5.

desire of riches. The other inordinate desire of the good which is arduous, pertains to the pride of life, which tends to things lofty and high above the proportion or merit of the individual.

Now it is plain that these three unclean spirits proceed severally as follows: the spirit of pride, from the mouth of the dragon, of him who said "I will be like to the Most High." The spirit of the world, from the mouth of the beast, which is sovereign lord of the things visible; whose it is to regulate and dispose of the temporal riches, distributing or withholding, accumulating or confiscating them, with the resistless force of brute power. And lastly, the spirit of lust proceeds from the mouth of the false prophet, who comes up from the earth, who prescribes for all the desires of the flesh, the earthly part of humanity; and who is like a prophet, because he promises a perfection of corporal enjoyment; but falsely, because the tangible good is always superficial, and absolutely does not extend beyond the surface of things. Snch is the general application of the three, in the abstract, but of late, these evil principles have issued forth from the mouth of a corrupt society, almost as personal, concrete existences. They are named Liberty, Equality, and Fraternity. The name of Liberty thus employed, means liberty to do wrong, liberty from all restraints of Church or State; so that one may be free, not to embrace the truth, but even error also; not to accept absolute certainties, but to take a choice of doctrines, even though they be false. That he may be free from political subordination, independent of the heads of government; that he may be permitted to control their acts, patronizing them by his favor, reproving by his frown. Free to know all things, good or evil; to speak all things, wise or foolish. In a word, liberty to be self-governing, self-subsisting before God, and in the face of men. The inordinate desire of Equality, is the concupiscence of the eyes. By the eternal law of order, it is necessary that inferior existences be administered by the superior ones. But the discontented mind rebels against this dispensation of the Creator, and beholding, with malignant eyes, the vast variety and endless gradations of his bounty, he clamors insanely for an impossible equality; an equal division of the soil, of honors, and of privileges; an absolute equality of the riches and pomps of earth; an equal knowledge, and health, and strength, for all, little and great, male and female; an equal dignity and authority in all things, natural and divine, political and religious. And this unclean spirit proceeds from the mouth of the beast, because, when he has by fair words seduced the rational mind, and prostituted it to the idolatry of his mundane chattels, he himself shall sit in the temple of God, showing himself as if he were God. From an equality of riches, the carnal mind passes to a Fraternity of pleasures. There is, in the communion of the saints, a love and reciprocity of kind offices, more than sufficient for all the wants of man. But, by reason of gross indulgence in the baser joys, the sensual man is become stupid and incapable of spiritual friendships, and he demands of mankind a place, not only in their memory, but in their flesh; not only in the affections of the heart, but in those of the body also; and because the spiritual ties have lost their virtue for him, he itches for a larger share in the convivial joys of his species, and strives viciously to aggravate the flames of concupiscence, till all shall be bound up in one accord of the luxurious life. And herein is detected the odor of the false prophet, the earthly stench of the animal man; which betrays the baseness of his origin, the ferment of his short existence, and the instant corruption of his inevitable death.

The three unclean spirits are like frogs: which are a filthy animal, noisy, impudent, lurking in low and stagnant places; which, in the night time, is intolerably clamorous; but is not easily seen at any time, and plunges down headlong to avoid approaching footsteps. Even thus there is, at this day, low down in the dregs of society, an impure herd of seditious men, whose obstreperous clamor for liberty, equality, and fraternity; whose impious doctrines of revolution, by means of conspiracy, regicide, and general bloodshed; whose audacity, avarice, and interminable bombast of swelling words, can only be equalled by the obscurity and perversity of their dark designs; to accomplish which, they lurk by the margin of infidel societies; or are of uncertain residence, as they leap about from city to city, and are known by the pertinacity of their impudent falsehoods, rather than by any public manifestation of their hidden schemes.

14 For they are the spirits of devils working signs: and they go forth unto the kings of the whole earth to gather them to battle against the great day of the Almighty God.

The three unclean spirits are plainly of infernal origin, if, indeed, it might not be said they are personal existences, or the individual spirits of three malignant demons, who have so deluded the understandings of men, by their signs of progress in liberty, prosperity, and sensuous enjoyment, that many are as if possessed with the persuasion, that they will at length be free from all authority, endowed with all riches, and secure from all evil, in the strong animal friendship of their species. These spirits, proceeding from the centres of civilization, have gone forth unto the kings of the whole earth: so that, from north to south, and from east to west of either hemisphere, their voice is already heard, and a new ambition is already enkindled in the minds of heathen people the most distant and most hidden from the intercourse of nations. Now the friendship of this world is the enemy of God; and, when the kings of the earth, or the powers of this world, are banded together in this fraternity, which is not of heaven but is of the earth, not the fruit of Christianity, but of infidelity and rebellion; then there must be war between the Creator and his creatures, and this will be, not alone the battle of his servants, but the battle of the great day of the Almighty God.

15. Behold, I come as a thief. Blessed is he that watcheth and keepeth his garments, lest he walk naked, and they see his shame.

Observe how unusual and how abrupt is the transition.

The blessed Apostle warns us not of a voice from heaven; not of angel, nor of eagle messengers: but the conscious soul recognizes the interposition of the Personal Deity. These are the words of Him who cometh to judge the earth; whose "day shall so come as a thief in the night: for when they shall say peace and security, then shall sudden destruction come upon them."[1] But, blessed is he that watcheth against the delusions of error, who keepeth his faith in the things not seen and eternal; and, while his soul is free to the conversation of the heavenly wisdom, holds his body and his senses wrapped and guarded from the contact of earth; lest, while intent upon the cares and follies of this life, his garments of faith and charity be loosed from him; and then suddenly, and in his greatest need, he be seen destitute of the habit of heavenly virtues, but naked in his former gracelessness. Mundus transit et concupiscentia ejus. Qui autem facit voluntatem Dei, manet in æternum.[2]

16. And he shall gather them together into a place, which is called in Hebrew Armagedon.

Again, the construction is abrupt, and there is no antecedent of the one who gathers the kings together. Perhaps to signify, that, as the majesty of Christ is incommunicable, so is the malice of his adversary Antichrist, solitary and singular, according to the words of Daniel, the prophet: "And none shall help him." The place of their gathering, whether it be understood as a specific locality, or as the watchword and pretext of their conspiracy, is called Armagedon. This word is interpreted by St. Jerome[3] variously; one signification is "consurrectio tecti" or "consurrectio in priora," which is synonymous with a amiliar phrase of the present day, viz.: the reconstruction of society. It is admitted, that, with the progress of the material civilization, there is also an increase of moral evils; and, if both its friends and opponents feel already the necessity of some fundamental reconstruction of society, so, when this

[1] 1. Thes. v. 2. [2] 1. John ii. 17. [3] Heb. Nom.

necessity is come to its extremity, then may Antichrist appear, the impostor, who will pretend to restore all things, and to this end will combine the powers of earth to execute his will. Another, is the Hill of Robbers; or the rendezvous of these outlaws from the kingdom of heaven, the thieves and robbers who enter not by the door, but climb up another way than that which has been divinely appointed for the restoration of fallen men. Another meaning is "mons globosus," which may point to the centralization of the powers, and their tumid ambition to exalt themselves above the humble dispensations of the Church of God, which alone can assuage the ills of human life, and conduct to true happiness.

17 And the seventh angel poured out his vial into the air: and a great voice came out of the temple from the throne, saying: It is done.

When the blight has passed upon all the fruits of earth, the air itself is finally tainted, and there is a pestilence for the souls of men in the very breath they draw. Christendom has been compared to a soil enriched with the merits of the saints, and with the traditional grace of ancient institutions, of multitudinous and time-honored customs, consecrated by the usage of the servants of God, and by the indwelling spirit of truth. And it is feared now, that, after so many years of desolation, that fertile soil is exhausted; that men have thus far reaped of its bounty, and have been satisfied, but now they are about finally to abandon it, and to mark out for themselves another fortune in their own way. The very atmosphere of society is tainted, when, beside the defects of particular institutions or functions, there is an organic malady of the public thought, which is the breath of its life. Suppose, for example, one or another odious, unnatural, vice or affectation shows itself in society, and acquires wide influence from the general vogue; till at length common good sense revolts against it, and there appears one on the scene to give battle to the evil, promising, with fair words of generous effusion, to trample it in the dust as it deserves. What now are we to think of this champion, if, while appearing to crush the vice, he only screens it under a monstrous pile of new sophisms? or bewilders the popular understanding with a cloud of other kindred, but more inveterate cant? while his heaviest blows, falling upon sacred truth, his hypocritical conduct in the face of the original, perverse sentiment, only makes it the more offensive, and proves him a coward out of a thousand. Somewhat like this is the popular author of the day.

By the nature of the case, a spiritual blight does not admit of palpable proof; and therefore it is difficult to do more than suggest the symptoms of the disease, while even these cannot fall under the cognizance of the one implicated. When the insensibility of the patient, the torpor and indifference of the peoples is the complaint, then the evil itself seems to preclude a remedy, and, humanly speaking, to be final. And, therefore, when judicious men so frequently express their apprehension that a catastrophe is at hand, they mean the final one, if they mean anything. Otherwise their fears would seem an affectation, and out of proportion; for a political crisis of things temporal, is unworthy of contemplation by the spiritual man; and Holy Church is absolutely secure of hazard, and beyond the reach of revolutions, for, with her generation, (and not before nor after,) are all things fulfilled. Finally, it might be objected, that, however numerous, and however grievous the symptoms of danger for society, yet they are after all only symptoms; and in point of fact we see all these evils of themselves counterbalanced and continally repaired, by the influence of contradictory good, or of other counteracting evils. But, in the first place, the argument would prove too much; for, down to the end of time, there must be a probation by temptation, and, as long as there is a state of probation, there must be a certain equipoise of good and evil, or there could not be a true liberty of choice, nor a condition of merit. And, in the second place, it ignores the question, whether this detrition itself, of good and evil, is not wearing away the fabric of Christendom, and determining all things to that final dissolution which separates forever the elect souls, from the ungrateful crowd of the reprobate.

Thus, side by side, do the cities of God and of Satan run their course. And, at last, the one is filled with the riches of his mercy, but in the other is consummated the wrath of God. When upon the latter the angel has emptied the last vial of wrath, and the voice of divine Justice, "It is done," declares the fulness of the plagues inflicted by heaven, and the breath of the unhappy city seems heavy with danger and death, then there can be no other name given for its restoration than that which has been given; but the plagues it has deserved, must work out their issue; and how nearly they may be spent, or how far the hope of sinners may be permitted to protract the train of evils, who shall dare to say?

18 And there were lightnings, and voices, and thunders: and there was a great earthquake, such as never hath been, since men were upon the earth; such an earthquake, so great.

These are days when sacred truth is known and seen to flash like lightning upon the souls of men. It is seen in the testimony of modern science to the historical veracity of Holy Scripture, and of Christian tradition; in the testimony of learned men, who, by their writings, have vindicated the wisdom of the Catholic Church, or who have given yet more distinguished proof of their sincerity, when they have renounced the dignities and profits of the pharisaical creeds, to embrace the poverty of the Apostolic Faith; and when the humility, which exalts before God, is made illustrious by the example of him who descends from prelatic eminence in the congregation of the arrogant, to become the least in the communion of the saints; "choosing to be an abject in the house of God, rather than to dwell in the tabernacles of sinners." Also the brightness of truth is revealed in that logical necessity, which is incessantly felt, and most frequently confessed, of the authority of Holy Church to define the first principles of moral science, and to restrain the passions of men in the bounds of reason and of order.

In these times have been heard the voices of the faithful servants of God, warning men of the impending dangers of the last days; and while as if yet speaking, they have been abruptly withdrawn from this mortal scene, as if the world were unworthy of their words of wisdom; or as if their prescient mind beheld, and was about to declare, more than was meet for the learning of their weaker brethren. The thunders which startle men in the midst of riches and careless indifference about religious truth, are those appalling outbursts of depravity, the murders and suicides of the day, and the revelations of Satanic malice furnished by the secret societies; the narratives of which, being propagated by the industry of the press, reverberate with fearful echo upon the tender minds of the rising generation.

Modern times have been distinguished by earthquakes in the physical order, but now much more the moral order and the foundations of human society, are disturbed. The disorders already enumerated, if summed up, are a sufficient account of this great earthquake. The dissolution of the quiet life ecclesiastical and secular, the uncertainty about objective truth, the contempt for a visible means of salvation, the audacity of blasphemy and of perjury, the paganism in education which has exalted ambition, to be counted among the heavenly virtues; these, and similar defections of the age, would lead to the conclusion that the last vice of envy, with the whole train of grievous sins, have finally deposited their dregs upon this shore of human life. In the most peremptory manner, is the vice of ambition enforced upon the mind as a necessary virtue, the love of money defended as the spring of prosperity, while, at the same time, the clamor for equality and fraternity, waxes daily more vehement, till, like mingled fire and oil, the passions are inflamed and exasperated by every insane and contradictory maxim the world can produce. If when a single individual aspires ambitiously to preëminence envy is created, how much more when the whole herd are stimulated with the same desires; and how will not the offspring of envy, slander, and detraction, be multiplied, till the highest enjoyment of one, is proved in the fall of another; and his deepest affliction, in his neighbor's exaltation! Hence that excessive eagerness to diminish the Church of her honors, and to divorce the clerical influence from all part in human affairs. Hence, too, the recourse to evil spirits, and to demon worship; for, in the last resort, they who reject the ministrations of Holy Church, recur always to the patronage of Satan and the powers of darkness. "By the envy of the devil, death came into the world, and they follow him that are of his side."[1]

The manner in which the blessed apostle describes the earthquake: "Such as never hath been since men were upon the earth, such an earthquake, so great," calls to mind the words of the Prophet: "And a time shall come, such as never was from the time that nations began even until that time."[2] And when Daniel inquired further concerning these things, and when answer was given to him, yet he says: I heard, and I understood not. The magnitude of the crisis can only be compared with the profound uncertainty of its issue. It might be argued: that, at this present moment, there is certainly no just cause of complaint, since the devout man is left to his liberty, and every one is encouraged to serve God each in his own way. But alas for the concordate between good and evil, between truth and error, between faith and infidelity! If the momentary and inconstant peace of the day were inspired by a good spirit, all would be well; but, if the fitful pauses of the earthquake are the secret treachery of the Evil One, then all is rottenness. "Soundness of heart is the life of the flesh, but envy is the rottenness of the bones."[3]

19 And the great city was made into three parts: and the cities of the Gentiles fell; and great Babylon came in remembrance before God, to give to her the cup of the wine of the indignation of his wrath.

If by the great city be understood Christendom, it is evident that this has been grievously rent; and remains divided

[1] Wis. ii. 24. [2] Dan. xii. 1. [3] Prov. xiv. 30.

between three parties, Catholics, Protestants, and Infidels. But, if it be interpreted simply of Holy Church, the visible city of God, this is naturally divided among the infirm, the strong, the perfect; "the blade, the ear, afterwards the full corn in the ear;"[1] and, in the last days, when the powers of the world begin to be arrayed against divine truth, and the beast prepares to resume his absolute dominion over the energies and resources of earth, and the souls of men are grievously tried by his seductions, it would seem necessary that the distinction be developed, and become more forcibly marked with the advent of temptation. There are always traitors in the great city, and it cannot be construed to the injury of Holy Church, if it be here said that there are those now in her visible fold, who appear to be ready to adore the power of the beast; who have been so carried away by the delusions of the age, that they regard the doctrines of progress, of popular sovereignty, of revolution, of liberty, equality and fraternity, with the same reverence as they do the articles of their faith; and, while they esteem them as of equal certainty, so do they to appearance, render them a devotion even more genuine. Opposed to whom, are they whose judgment of the earthly maxims is the direct reverse of that just described, and who watch their formidable prevalence with sorrow and dismay. Between which two is a third class, who aim to keep a just mean; moderate in their zeal for the prerogatives of the church, but exercising a more cheerful liberality towards the requirements of the age. But if these distinctions appear outwardly in the visible city, yet it is impossible that the perpetual unity of the church should be divided; nor does the Greek text imply any violent sundering of the city, but (εγενετο—μερη,) a distinction of parts or classes, rather than a division of essence. Because one is zealous outwardly for the honor of God, it does not follow that he participates in the interior grace; and when another appears to be attached strongly to the worldly affections, it

[1] St. Mark iv. 28.

cannot be concluded that he is deprived of that invisible bond of unity. They who appear nearest to perfection may be of slender virtue, and those whose imperfections would seem more than enough to overwhelm them, may, notwithstanding, be possessed of a spiritual vigor equal to their necessities. The conclusion, therefore, is, that though the great city cannot be broken nor destroyed, yet, inasmuch as she is established on earth, the throes of the mighty earthquake are felt even within her peaceful walls; and the distress of our common race is reflected on her human aspect.

But if the great city is shaken, the cities of the Gentiles are utterly fallen. The heresies of Protestantism, the schism of the Greek Church, Mohammedanism, and the false religions of the East, are shattered and crumbled to the dust. It is a common observation, that, whatever of virtue or fragmentary truth they once possessed, is now wretchedly dissipated, their vigor wasted, and their vitality lost. And great Babylon, the glory of this world, begins to sicken and fade; and the pride of the worldling is broken, when, faster than the imperfections of his planet can be repaired, new deficiencies are declared; when the cold North draws closer upon his borders, when the worm and the rust corrode the fruits of his land, and when his greatest achievements begin to look more like defeat than victory; his godless education giving death to the soul, and his mechanical improvements making slaughter of the body of man.

20 And every island fled away, and the mountains were not found.

And now there is hardly a place on earth which has not been invaded by the sound of progress; the most sacred seclusion of ecclesiastical or of domestic life, the noblest establishments of Christian or of pagan polity, are no longer a security for peace, nor conservative of the natural analogies and common maxims of human prudence, or of revealed wisdom, which presided in all antiquity.

21 And great hail like a talent came down from heaven upon men: and men blasphemed God because of the plague of the hail; for it was exceeding great.

Sometimes the natural bounties of the Creator are found perverted to the detriment of the creature; and the dews of heaven, when they encounter the frozen heart of the obstinate, fall like hail upon his unfruitful soul. Thus the temporal goods of the age, innocent in themselves, seem to be the occasion of torment to the impious; and their murmurs against authority, and their blasphemies against divine truth, are exasperated in proportion to the tranquillity and good order of the one, and the benignity and patience of the other. Or, again, the angel having poured the seventh plague in mid-air, at the last there comes hail: by the disorder and inequalities of the moral atmosphere, the waters of truth are discharged like arrows of ice upon the perverse mind. Mittit crystallum suum sicut buccellas.[1] Or, the hail may be compared to a talent: when the great gift of Christian civilization has been degraded by men, to subserve their temporal fortunes; and when the wisdom of Christ has been debased by the material philosophy, and counterfeited by the mercenary science of earth. For who can conceive of a greater anguish for the rational soul, than that the shattered truths of Christianity, should be conveyed to the mind with the admixture of fatal errors, and with the deadly force of carnal motives? Because the Gospel promises liberty, the sophists say that obedience is a slavery, and all must be released from it; and, when they have left none to be subjects, immediately they propose that every one shall be a commander and a sovereign. Now they shew that ambition and pride are virtues all desirable; and again, that a perfect equality is absolutely necessary; that poverty with rags is a detestable vice; and anon, that a fraternity of animal friendships is all pure and redolent of celestial odors. When the human understanding is thus lacerated and stunned; when the orator involves himself in

[1] Psalms cxlvii. 17.

such giddy circles that every sentence is a self-falsification or a mere inanity; and when poor, laboring men are seen to gibber and drive askance with the same ambitious speculations; then it is to be feared lest the heart of man be daily hardened, the understanding obscured, and the affections seared, till the tender sentiments and noble devotion of the Cross be finally blasted and wholly withered from his soul.

Here is the end of the Fourth Part; and here we cease to explore the tendencies, or to probe the miseries, of the present age. The most painful and laborious part of the journey is accomplished, and henceforward the vision leads to less obstructed walks, and to passages of broader scope, though the unworthy traveller pursue them with faltering step and with feeble sight.

PART V.

RETROSPECT OF THE WORLD'S DESTRUCTION.

THIS Part describes the iniquities and the fall of Babylon. This is the city whose beginning was from the earliest ages, built to the defiance of Almighty God, which held his people in captivity, and was denounced by the Prophets. This name of evil odor, coming from a remote antiquity, so long familiar in the usage of the inspired writers, and having in the Old Testament a local and particular signification, would naturally be employed in the New, in a mystical sense. Thus it is found applied, in the Epistle of St. Peter,[1] to the city of Rome, while yet the city of Satan rather than of God; but, taken in a wider sense, it may stand for this visible World, which, by means of the senses, seduces the mind from the worship of God, and leads it captive in the servitude of the devil. Babylon has been supposed by some to indicate a particular city in the end of the world; but to this there are the following insuperable objections: First: she sits upon the beast, who was and is not, and upon the seven mountains or kings, some of whom are long since fallen, and others not yet come; that is, from first to last, while monarchs come and go, and empires rise and fall, she is exalted always in the sight of men. And in the second place: it is said all nations have been deceived by her, and in her hath been found the blood of all who have been slain upon earth. Therefore, Babylon being this world, and the beast the secular power, the former is distinguished as

[1] 1 Peter v. 13.

the beauty, (cosmos,) the latter as the physical strength, of the same. The former is a harlot, who seduces and intoxicates; the latter is a beast, who inflicts death (occidantur,) or loss of property (ne quis . . . . emere aut vendere. chap. xiii.) The one is addressed to the concupiscible in man, i. e., the common desire of good in its simplicity; the other to the irascible power, by which he pursues a good which is difficult of attainment or extraordinary. But the concupiscible is first and last; for the passions of the irascible, take their rise in the concupiscible; to which they superadd a certain effort and elevation of the mind toward a good which is arduous, and, this being secured, they are terminated again in that rest or enjoyment, which is the property of the concupiscible.[1] Thus the glory of this world, like the blandishments of the harlot, encompasses and cherishes all its pomp and power, as well as its vanity and its impotence.

But this specious bloom of life, which, in Holy Scripture, is compared to the grass that withereth; this Babylon ever falling, which is threatened, by the prophets, with ruin and desolation, in the Christian dispensation is regarded as already destroyed; and the spiritual man is not curious about its fortunes, nor anxious about its issues, because he esteems it as grass which is parched, its flower fallen, and its beauty perished. The prophetic vision beholds things distant as if present, and thus the blessed Apostle displays the downfall of Babylon, not as a theme of argumentation, but as a fact accomplished, before which we need not toil in disquisition, but may rest in contemplation. Wherefore, the Fifth Part is denominated a Retrospect of the World Destroyed. It comprises two chapters (xvii. and xviii.) in one of which, are described the inherent qualities and the crimes, together with the affinities and the accomplices of the condemned harlot; and, in the other, is witnessed the execution of her wretched doom.

[1] Sum. Theol. 1. 2. 25.

CHAPTER XVII.

1 AND there came one of the seven angels, who had the seven vials, and spoke with me, saying: Come, I will show thee the condemnation of the great harlot, who sitteth upon many waters.

After the weary journey through this valley of earth, one of the seven angels who have concluded its last plagues, invites the Apostle to come aside and behold the issue of its ungodly courses; and the condemnation of the great harlot, now brought to misery, to rottenness, and to hell's door. Who sitteth upon many waters: oppressing, with her foul enchantments, the multitudes of our human race.

2 With whom the kings of the earth have committed fornication: and they who inhabit the earth, have been made drunk with the wine of her prostitution.

The kings are put first among her paramours, for by virtue of their office, the lords of the land sustain and enhance the glories of the same. These are her favorites, and the admired of this world; "whose sons are as new plants in their youth, their daughters decked out, their storehouses full, their sheep fruitful, their oxen fat; there is no breach of walls, nor passage, nor clamor in their streets."[1] And while they are praised and envied because of the abundant opportunities which serve their lust, their state is, of all others, the most perilous, and commonly their vices are the most numerous. They, however, are not the only ones, but the common multitude of mankind have been made drunk and giddy in her dalliance; have panted after mundane joys, and have been corrupted from their innocence: the rectitude of the rational soul, which is an eternal joy.

3 And he took me away in spirit into the desert. And I saw a woman sitting upon a scarlet-colored beast, full of names of blasphemy, having seven heads and ten horns.

[1] Psalms cxiii.

The harlot is called a city: and we must go into the desert to see it; not indeed the desert of barren fields, the solitude of the hermit, and the place of prayer, but in spirit we enter the city life, the metropolis of earthly pleasures, where the prostitute makes her market, and where wanton joys abound; whose streets are adorned with the corruptible riches, but are destitute of the celestial goods, and void of the fruits of the Holy Ghost. Or in another way: The city of this world, this scene of human life, what is it but a desert, a hard and stony highway, between hell and heaven, where there is no true home nor rest, till the journey be ended, and all have passed upward or downward, each to his eternal abode?

The visible beauty of this world is compared to a woman, because it is stamped with the traits of the feminine vices in all their virulence. Vain, petulant, fickle in favors, and rancorous in malice, her chief delight is, to behold her victim enthralled, unmanned, and powerless before her. Thus, the youthful mind takes his first lesson in life, when, reaching eagerly after the painted pleasure, he finds himself suddenly repulsed. Or, he hears the world praised, till he is persuaded he owes it his love; and, when he would join his tribute of flattery, is spurned for his pains. He becomes silent and indifferent, and then the world more than ever displays her favors, or ridicules him for his ignorance, and derides his simplicity. Again, he pursues, with new ardor, and perhaps obtains some disgusting proof more than sufficient of her baseness. He is too sincere as yet, too faithful to the natural impulses of his aching heart. What he would have, he has not; and what he would not, that he has. But when, at length, his heart is hardened, his innocence blasted, and his mind attempered to the conventional hypocrisy, then the world and he will be at peace.

She sits upon the beast: for the secular power upholds her splendors, and she in turn adorns the beast. It will be remembered that, in a former part of this work, the secular power was distinguished in two kinds, viz., the power of Satan and the political power; represented, the first by a dragon, the second by a beast; as if the two forces were independent, one of the other. The reason of which may be, that the dragon, or Satan, is primarily the adversary of the church; but the political power is so, only in a secondary and casual manner; and, therefore, when the church was represented as opposed to the world, (Part III.,) her spiritual combat with the powers of darkness, which is the combat by excellence, is delineated apart, and exclusively of other agencies of less moment. Afterward, however, are displayed her struggles with the temporal power, and with its coadjutor, the third beast, which came up from the earth. But now, in this division of the work, where it is treated of the city of the world, of that evil influence which, since the fall of Adam, pervades and possesses all this sublunary sphere of life as with an atmosphere of witchery and illusion, in this Part, the two powers seem blended in one. As the city is one, and its beauty one, so in this connection its strength is comprehended in one secular power.

There is no question of the Church; for the sacred Spouse remains not in the presence of the harlot; and the third beast, the false prophet, being accidental, or entirely of artificial derivation, is left out of the account. We have, therefore, the two grand forces of this world; the powers of darkness, and the political power, combined in one image of the scarlet-colored beast, full of names of blasphemy, having seven heads and ten horns. The color of the beast is the same with that formerly described, except that, in the first instance, the red was (πυῤῥος) flame-colored, as befitted the distinctive sphere of Satan; but here it is scarlet, as being more dazzling, and directly attractive to the human imagination. There is no mention of the diadems, for the harlot sits not upon the beast in respect of his royalty or civil authority; but it is full of names of blasphemy: because her exaltation is in virtue of his infirm humanity, and eminently by reason of his impiety and infidelity.

It is not supposed, in what has been now laid down, that the wickedness of Satan, and the power of the civil government, are identified or confounded. But since history shows plainly that they do sometimes act in concert, and since there is nothing, in the essence of the civil polity, which determines it to the side of revealed truth, but rather the contrary, even as human nature is inclined to evil; therefore this world being considered spiritually, and by the light of the cross, its beauty is only that of a harlot, unworthy of the aspirations of the soul; and its power is only that of a beast, which extends not to the volitions of the rational creature. And, if we would sum up the whole power of the world in one term of the Secular Power, it is impossible to exclude the satanic influence, which evidently enters into the account of human affairs. And, furthermore, lest any prejudice should be thought to accrue from this interpretation to the Christian Prince, or to any lawful authority whatever, it is easy to observe and keep in mind a distinction between the mere physical force and the just authority of the same; between the fact and the right. The vice of the age is, that it hates authority; but it by no means hates power or force; on the contrary, the great struggle which convulses society is the struggle for power, right or wrong, as before it has been a struggle for liberty, good or bad.

And again, and finally, it may be observed: If the civil government be compared to a beast, this is in respect to its physical force; but, if its jurisdiction be also valid, and on the side of rectitude, then, and so far forth it of course partakes of the attributes of reason. And if to this be added a strict devotion to the Christian Faith, it hardly deserves to be ranked in the category of the beast; or at least only so far as it is composed of body and mind, constituted with animal functions as well as with Christian attributes. Wherefore it is said, the beast "was and is not;" for, under the Christian dispensation, it is as if the beast were eliminated, and did not exist; and the Christian monarch who serves God in his Church, is not to be compared with the unbelieving tyrant, or the infidel government, whose power is merely brutal.

4 And the woman was clothed round in purple and scarlet, and gilded with gold, and precious stones and pearls, having a golden cup in her hand, full of the abomination and filthiness of her fornication.

In the fulness of its glory, this world is arrayed royally in purple, brightly in scarlet, and richly in gold and precious stones; in the privileges of rank, beauty, and wealth, are comprised its best gifts. The felicity it gives is not a substantial food to be ruminated, but a draught to be swallowed greedily; and though outwardly it seems inviting in its golden cup, yet in effect it is polluting and most offensive to the life of grace in the soul. Like the harlot, all her glory is on the surface, while she is in fact filthy, and utterly void of intrinsic worth. The true good is communicative and diffusive; but her goods are the reverse, and excellent, in proportion as they are contracted and confined. The one who was accounted rich among his neighbors, will be deemed insignificant among those who are more opulent; the one who was supposed to be beautiful, pales with envy before another more beautiful; he whose neck was stiff with the pride of circumstance, is humbled and broken before another of higher rank. Would one admire earnestly her riches? he is naturally suspected for a thief; is he attracted by her beauty, and does he confess that it is desirable? it is the beautiful one who is the most scornful of his devotion; would he render profound homage to her magnates? then let him annihilate himself. Thus all the earthward aspirations are incessantly thwarted, checked, and repulsed; so that, instinctively as it were, men do not give the world entire, unqualified praise. We hear of a magnificent prince, of a bright day, of beautiful scenery; but to take the world and its contents in the gross, it is not, nor has it ever been, a familiar form of speech, to designate it as beautiful, or lovely, or noble. For a mind of high order to do so, would be an affectation; he may have many words and modes of praise, but a heartfelt affection for his footstool of clay, is impossible. And, in minds of a low order, we read, by their lives, what is the real estimate they set upon it: for their boast is, not that they are desirous of the world's goods, nor that they are dazzled or astonished by her enchantments, but, on the contrary, they disdain the expression of surprise and wonder; and they consider that to despise a given vanity, to pass it by as a trifle of no value, is evidence, of itself, that they have the advantage of other men, that they have already proved and enjoyed it; and therefore they, the favorites of fortune, may glorify themselves, because they can afford to make light of her favors; because, for a little moment, for one instant, as it were, they can despise the goods of earth as they deserve.

But what wonder, if the minds of men are thus divided about the excellence of this world? when we know that it has been purposely so contrived, that they must perforce derive from it some knowledge of evil, as well as of good. The first parents, in the bliss of Paradise, may not have had a knowledge of anything but the good; they added to it, however, the knowledge of evil; and this is the inheritance of good and evil which is transmitted to their posterity. We may say the stars are beautiful, for we know nothing of them but their splendor; but the moment we touch upon our own planet, and come home to ourselves, we are diffident and guarded in our language, and the just man hesitates to pronounce that beautiful, which has in it the seed of death. St. Gregory, describing a certain nun who was in danger from temptation, says, not that she was beautiful simply, but she was "beautiful according to this putrid flesh." It were absurd to deny that, from our earliest infancy, the sense of evil is so enforced upon the observation, that it is impossible for the most favored son of earth to withhold his testimony to the presence of much that is displeasing and most offensive in the various relations of life. Throughout the brute creation, there is no appetite nor sensation so strongly marked, as this, by which they evince the instinct of danger; even so the intelligent mind is compelled to acquire, through and by means of its mortal experience, the perceptions of wrong as well as of right, of foul as of fair, of hell as of heaven; and the natural understanding is able to deduce from the facts and condition of its own being, a presentiment of beatitude, but also an apprehension of horror everlasting.

5 And on her forehead a name was written: A Mystery: Babylon the great, the mother of the fornications and abominations of the earth.

A mystery is that which is mute or secret about its own interior and real meaning; and so this world, wherein the creature is made subject to vanity, is a fearful mystery; it is smiling, silent, plausible, and yet it betrays the soul; it promises happiness, and it renders back sorrow and death. Babylon signifies confusion; and the plain of Sennaar, where it was built, signifies (excussio,) that it was rejected by God, or (fetor eorum,) their own stench; or again, according to an opinion[1] of the Hebrews, (excussio,) because the dead bodies of men, after the deluge, were drifted, or settled down in that place, by reason of its low, depressed position. Thus, the city of the world is a vast Babylon of universal confusion; blooming with a brief prosperity, in the midst of corruption and stench; abounding in hollow and short-lived joys, but crowded with real and enduring miseries. As the holy city is the mother of graces, so this one is the mother of fornications, to the soul. Impregnated with that concupiscence which propagates the abominations of earth, she brings them forth and nourishes them, as if with her own breast. She is the evil mother, who invites to sin; who encourages the first steps in iniquity, and who paints in glowing colors to the tender mind, untried in vice, the joys of flesh and sense.

6 And I saw the woman drunk with the blood of the saints, and with the blood of the martyrs of Jesus. And when I had seen her, I wondered with great admiration.

She is foremost among the enemies of holiness, and persecutes, with bitter hatred, the fair virtue of the chaste generation. She has made their blood to flow in torrents,

[1] Malv. de Antichrist, v. 4.

and never ceases to deride and scourge them, with calumny and drunken ribaldry. Wonderful, therefore, is this mystery of life! its visible beauty, and its secret filth; its hypocritical kindness, and its effectual cruelty.

7 And the angel said to me: Why dost thou wonder? I will tell thee the mystery of the woman, and of the beast which carrieth her, which hath the seven heads and the ten horns.

It is written of Babylon, in the beginning: "That the Lord came down to see the city and the tower, which the children of Adam were building." The flower of this world is a phantom, which has no being, only as it is seen; if not seen, it does not exist. And yet, it strikes the human heart with admiration, and causes it to throb with fond surprise, and hope of instant enjoyment; so that no one, unaided by the grace of God, can withstand the flush of prosperity, its strong and sudden flow, and its precipitate, drunken impulses. But now, before the simplicity of sacred truth, this skeleton is laid bare of its gay disguise; and all the power and glory of the world are known for their real significance, and are set down at their right value.

8 The beast, which thou sawest, was, and is not, and shall come up out of the bottomless pit, and go into destruction: and the inhabitants of the earth, (whose names are not written in the book of life, from the foundation of the world,) shall wonder, seeing the beast, that was, and is not.

The beast, or the secular power, was, and is not: formerly, it was the grand power of the world, but, with the advent of Christianity, it is so no longer. The former is the natural force of the creature, the latter is the supernatural virtue of the Creator; of course, where the latter is present, the former retires; and when the latter withdraws, the former prevails. The secular power is mighty, oppressive, sensual; and outside of Christianity, there never has been any force to compare with it, except the occasional and partial manifestations of supremacy by the prophets and kings of Israel; and it cannot be proved that any mythology, or priestcraft, or philosophy, or refinement of the arts, or wisdom of Socrates, or greatness of Cicero, have ever in like manner swayed the world; or have extorted from the human mind a homage so sincere, as this which they naturally render to the secular power. But now the gentle influences of Christianity, and the divine authority bestowed upon the Church, have constituted a force incomparably greater, and infinitely honorable, for all to whom it reaches. And this moral strength of Christianity has been well proved, in that men recognize its supremacy, and sacrifice for it gladly their property, and their lives, and all worldly considerations.

But the secular might will again prevail; and it is to be remembered that this time the beast comes up out of the bottomless pit, and by virtue of diabolical agency. Whatever may have been his origin formerly, does not much concern us; but that now, in the year of grace, he should regain his ascendency, and triumph over the soul, which has been once illuminated by evangelic truth, and ennobled with the freedom wherewith Christ hath made it free, this cannot be in the course of nature, so much as by the preternatural action of satanic influences.

And why is it said, they shall wonder whose names are not written in the book of life? but because those who have not the grace of God, cannot understand, how anything can be greater than the secular power; they cannot believe that the moral force is stronger than the physical, that spirit is better than flesh, that faith is greater than sense. If they have not the truth, the sufficient object of the understanding, the divine Word in a good heart, then no reason nor philosophy can save them; but they wander, helpless vagabonds, on the shore of eternity. And because they are the slaves of sense, and because they worship the sovereignty of brute power, so will they wonder at the sight of its personification: the beast, who appears to supply the fearful void of their souls without God.

9 And here is the understanding, that hath wisdom. The seven heads are seven mountains, upon which the woman sitteth, and they are seven kings:

The mountains are the high places of the earth; and the earth is the woman's seat, the sphere of worldly joys. The high places of earth are the inventions of carnal men; for the heights of evangelical perfection are lowliness in this life. The seven heads, or mountains, or kings, signify seven principal empires, as has been already anticipated in Part III.

10 Five are fallen: one is; and the other is not yet come: and when he shall come, he must remain a short time.

Five were already fallen in the times of the Apostle; one, that is, the Roman Empire, then flourished; the other, that is, the empire of Antichrist, is not yet come.

11 And the beast that was and is not, the same is also the eighth, and is of the seven, and goeth into destruction.

The Greek text would permit a reading a little different, thus: "The beast that was and is not, the same is also an eighth king." That is: the seven heads of the beast, are seven kings, and the trunk of the beast is also an eighth king. Which latter eighth is of the seven: that is, the octave of the same; or, manifestly bearing a certain relation to each of the seven heads, which they, as distinct heads, do not bear reciprocally to one another.

Here we must take patience, with the blessing of God, and return to the distinction which has been suggested (Part III.,) of the secular power. The brute force of earth, lies within the dominion of Satan; and though the temporal authority is of God, yet its exercise, or the administration of temporal power, is more or less subject to the sway and suggestions of the devil. Unlike the indefectible integrity of the ecclesiastical hierarchy, its human institution is obnoxious to many corruptions; and history shows how the instigations of Satan have commonly pervaded the whole body of human society. And therefore the power of this world, or the secular power, is sometimes taken for a principle of evil in respect of its relation to the demons, the rulers of the world of this darkness; but, at other times, as a power animal, and merely indifferent or imperfect on the side of its human administration. Now, in the text, all these relations of the secular power, the whole corpus of satanic and of human agencies, are summed up and distributed in one and the same construction. The body, this is the power of Satan; the head is the principal organ of the body, and these seven heads are the principal empires of earth; the horns spring from the heads, or depend upon them, and these are the inferior powers, tributary to, or derived from, the great empires. And because we are considering now, not the virtues but the vices of the world, which lead on its destruction, the powers of the world are justly cited as the chief offenders; and if every human government, even of limited jurisdiction, is an imperfection, so the seven empires may be called capital evils; and the wickedness of Satan is at the bottom of all, pervading the whole mass, and instigating to all the sins of the whole world. Wherefore, it is said, he is of the seven: he is their body or trunk; and, besides, he is an eighth, not indeed visible, but yet as real and as potent as the human tyrants, and of equal rank with them. He is all that they are, and more; he is beneath them, and above them; he is first and last, the horrid diapason of the whole octave.

One difficulty yet remains: It is said, the beast was, and *is not;* and, of the heads it is written: some are fallen, but *one is;* as though, at one and the same time, the secular power did not exist, and yet one of the great empires flourished. The answer to this, will be a recapitulation of what has been already laid down. The secular power is two-fold: one is the power of Satan, spiritual, invisible, preternatural; the other is that which is human, visible, corporeal; these, and these alone, are the grand agencies which move in the sphere of Babylon, in the impure medium typified by the harlot. Now the body of the beast being appropriated to Satan, and the heads to the visible polities, the secular power, so far as it appertains to Satan, was and is not; but the temporal power of the human polities, still exists. This is the plain statement, and the solution of the problem taken in its liberal sense, and in regard of its general outline. But because of its remote bearing upon some other points, established by the sacred writer, it becomes necessary to add some qualifications. And in the first place: although the body is referred to Satan, and the heads to the visible empires, yet this is not absolutely so; for the beast, as a whole, is commonly taken for Antichrist throughout the Apocalypse. But the beast is also taken for Satan, since it is said the beast is an eighth; and this eighth is the invisible kingdom of the devil;. or otherwise, the satanic influence would have no part, root nor branch, in the beast; which were absurd, and contrary to tradition, as well as to common consent. It would seem, therefore, in the last evolution of the secular power, that the seventh head and the eighth, the visible Antichrist, and the invisible Adversary of the human race, do concur and issue in one conjunction of the visible beast; for it has been said, "they shall see the beast and wonder." Nor does it follow from this, that Antichrist is an incarnation of the devil, (which St. Thomas[1] shows to be impossible;) for it is not said, that the beast is absolutely the seventh head, but that he is an eighth. Now Antichrist is the seventh and last head, to which is associated, as it were insensibly and mysteriously, an eighth, as if the octave of the whole, or the ghostly duality of the last. And thus there remains, not a perfect or hypostatic union of the two; but they are said to be united, because the invisible malice of the one, and the visible power of the other, are developed in the sole visible head of Antichrist.

To sum up and conclude this part of the argument: The beast of Holy Scripture, in general, is the secular power. The beast of this prophecy in particular, is Antichrist. To pass beyond the visible order of things, and come to their principles or motives, which indeed are obscure, because less apparent, but are of a grander influence, because of their spiritual character, then, from this aspect of the secular

[1] Sum. Theol. iii. 8. 8.

power, the beast is Satan. While Christianity is supreme, the beast is wounded, or dying, or dead. But in the last days, both the satanic and the temporal powers are revived and fused in one living, visible, agent; and though this is, strictly speaking, the beast as Antichrist, yet the same term of the beast may be, and in this instance is, predicated of Satan. Wherefore it is repeated of him, he goeth into destruction: for, however it may have been with the former heads or kings, yet, in the last result, whether considered as the abstract power of this world, or as Antichrist the last visible head, or as Satan the invisible octave of the whole, thus considered, the beast shall inevitably be thrust down in hell.

In the second place: though it is said the temporal power still subsists, yet this is not without modification. The same cause of Christian revelation, which destroyed the tyranny of Satan, also impaired the arbitrary human despotism, and weakened its bondage upon mankind. It is true, that in the times of the Apostle, the Roman empire did exist; but from that time it began to decline, till at length it quite disappeared from the earth; even as all things are appointed in the natural order, wherein the end is reached inevitably, though it may be with many delays, and sometimes even unconsciously. And this is according to the analogy of human reason, which proceeds to its conclusions, not immediately, but discursively, tardily; while, on the other hand, the angelic intellect beholds, intuitively, all that is within its range, and there is no gradation nor succession in its knowledge, nor in its manner of existence. Wherefore, it is said positively, of the power of Satan, "it is not;" for, in spiritual things, (as for example, the divine grace in the soul,) absolutely it is, or it is not; and that, instantaneously. But in human affairs, or in the moral order, a proposition cannot always be enunciated so peremptorily; but, if the enunciation is to be comprehensive, it must be with detail and circumlocution. Now, this detail was not necessary in the present instance; first, because the falling of some of the heads, the solitary existence of another, and the brief duration of the last one; that is, the mention of the past, present, and future tenses in the text, sufficiently indicates the transitory and defectible nature of the temporal power; whose uncertain and troubled existence is more a dying than a living one, and though it is not said to be extinct, yet it is as if wounded to death. And, in the second place, it was unnecessary; because the Roman empire would have fallen if there had been no Christian religion; and the Apostle would not give us to understand that the power of the Cross, which subverted the dominion of Satan, does, in the same sense, militate against the impious human tyranny; because the latter is in a different sphere, while the force of Satan is in the same plane; that is, the spiritual and incorporeal one.

The conclusion is, therefore, briefly this: In the condemnation of the harlot, that virtue of divine truth, which overwhelms her, and which confounds the secular powers that uphold her, this same truth is directly antagonistic to the Satanic influence, but incidentally hostile to the temporal power; and the destruction, which is predicated absolutely, of the beast, is also implied on the part of its heads.

12 And the ten horns which thou sawest are ten kings; who have not yet received a kingdom, but shall receive power as kings one hour after the beast.

It is worthy of notice, in how unusual a manner the ten kings are described. Whence come these kings, who have not yet received a kingdom? or how can they be kings, if they have never been possessed of any dominion? Commonly, the kingdom awaits the king, but here the kings wait upon the kingdom; commonly, the throne is from beforehand, and the king coming possesses it; but here the kings are first, and the thrones are not yet built. In Christian times, when the beast is thrown down, and the heads are wounded to death, the horns also are divested of much of their power; and, even now, such is the spectacle which Christendom presents. The kings of these days, who have succeeded to the fallen

Roman empire, are kings in name, but they are much more dependent on popular will, than the public good, or the action of government is to be traced to them as to its authentic source; and, in some of the modern polities, the head of government is so far from being considered the real governor, that, on the contrary, he is supposed to be the one governed, and the people are regarded as his masters. But they shall receive power as kings one hour, or shortly after the beast. When Antichrist comes, and when it is evident that his iron rule is established upon the necks of the people, then the others also, supported by the weight of his example, will usurp a like authority; and the abominable tyranny will be multiplied tenfold.*

13 These have one design; and their strength and power they shall deliver to the beast.

Instead of uniting to oppose the wickedness of Antichrist, they will seek each their own interest by promoting the aggrandizement of him who lends them countenance in iniquity, and whose despotism constitutes a precedent of such force, that they cannot, or will not, resist the temptation of copying it. Thus they will have one and the same evil intention; they will contribute their strength to the power of Antichrist; and will be bound to him as integral parts of the tyranny of the man of sin.

It is written in the prophecy of Daniel,[1] concerning the ten horns, "I considered the horns, and behold, another little horn sprung out of the midst of them, and three of the first horns were plucked up at the presence thereof;" that is, "after the ten kings, another shall rise up, and he shall be mightier than the former, and he shall bring down three kings." If this be interpreted of Antichrist, it would appear

* An illustration, (and a harmless one, if it please the reader,) of this progress and extension of despotism, may be found in the acts of him who was borne to such a height of power on the waves of democratic commotion, in the beginning of the present century; and who shortly afterward appointed kings for many of the other states around him beside his own.

[1] Daniel. vii. 8. and 24.

that his kingdom will not be derived from one of the ancient and hereditary monarchies, but will mount up suddenly, as a new power in their midst, and will bring down three of the former principal powers. The ten, comprises the whole number of kingdoms, whether more or less, since it would be impossible, in any period of the world's history, to ascertain precisely ten powers, and neither more nor less, which should be entitled to the rank of kings. And, therefore, when he is said to bring down three kings, it would follow, not that he humbles three of the lesser powers taken at random, but three conspicuous and leading kingdoms; such as would bear the proportion of three parts out of ten, to the whole temporal power of Christian countries.

14 These shall fight with the Lamb; and the Lamb shall overcome them; because he is Lord of lords, and King of kings; and they that are with him are called, and elect, and faithful.

Wherefore is this mighty array of the powers of the world? and who is the dread enemy, that is deemed sufficient to unite their discordant minds at last in one single purpose, and to engage them in the unity of a common action? It is no other than the Lamb; the gentle, and lowly Christian truth, the religion of him concerning whom it is written: "Tell ye the daughter of Sion: Behold thy king cometh to thee, meek, and sitting upon an ass, and a colt, the foal of her that is used to the yoke." Yet he will conquer them, for he is the King and Lord of all the kings; and they that are of his side, are the precious souls whom he has loved with an everlasting love, who know the voice that has called them from darkness to light, and who will follow it gladly, even to death.

15 And he said to me: The waters which thou sawest, where the harlot sitteth, are peoples, and nations, and tongues.

The human soul is signified by water, because, as compared with the body, which is akin to the dull clod of earth, the former is of a quality more subtile, nimble, and of far-reaching activity. The place of the harlot is amidst the waters: for the glory of the world germinates and thrives in the assemblies of men, in the court, the market place, or wherever there is the concourse of human wit and skill. The countless diversities of tribe, and nation, and language, combined with the outward graces of beauty and strength, of form and action, offer a scene most fascinating to the mind; and when gathered within the fold of Holy Church, as the Patriarch gathered the living wonders of creation in the safe enclosures of the Ark, it becomes, indeed, a spectacle more resplendent than the firmament, and full of wonder and delight to the angels in heaven. But if void of the grace of God, if inspired by no breath of the eternal life, what is it but an empty show! a painted harlot, a wretched illusion!

16 And the ten horns, which thou sawest on the beast; these shall hate the harlot, and shall make her desolate and naked, and shall eat her flesh, and shall burn her with fire.

It has been seen, that the kings of the earth have made dalliance with the harlot; and, in the following chapter, they bewail themselves at the sight of her torments; and certainly if the human felicity is prized and cultivated anywhere, it is in the courts of princes. But in order to understand how the kings may, nevertheless, hate the harlot, the analogy of the libertine and his paramour will suggest some considerations. The libertine courts his mistress, and lavishes upon her his best gifts, and when he has habituated himself to riotous excesses, so is his anguish great if he be deprived of her society, and of the means of pleasure. But on the other hand, it is impossible that he can have any sincere friendship, or real esteem for his partner in vice; and if it be considered how frequent are the brawlings, the blows and brutal usage, the hideous ribaldry and paroxysms of rage, which harass her daily life; how soon she is brought to want, and consumed with hunger; or inflamed with the ferment of her corruption, and parched with the ardors of fever; this assuredly would argue more of hatred than of love, and her paramour might be justly esteemed her most cruel enemy. Thus the political tyrant, the master of this world, though he depend upon it for the sum of his pleasures, and though he have no enjoyment out of this life, yet, by his cruelty, he is often proved to be the greatest enemy to the world, even in the low sense of its material prosperity. Did he love truly his mistress, he would cherish her graces, economize her pleasures, and husband her strength. But if he hastens to vulgarize and bring into contempt her honors, if in a frivolous age he is foremost in frivolity, if among infidels the boldest in impiety, among hypocrites the chief of liars, then he is not a friend but a traitor to the state; who betrays her good name, corrodes her vigor and grace, and exhausts her resources; till all the land is vexed with his presence, racked and ruined with his profligate and reckless excesses.

Many are the pangs of the harlot, even in life, and before her career is closed in death; and many are the woes of this world, before its final dissolution is determined forever. And if the kings of earth have often been found to be its worst enemies, especially will the Antichristian kings prove to be a heavy curse to the worldly prosperity. The Catholic truth which deals equal justice to all, and holds them in equal estimation before God; which teaches the prince to wash the feet of the poor of Christ, and to kneel with him on the same religious level: this alone can establish the true charity and forbearance of master and servant; and according as society departs from it, or loses its benign influence, so these distinctions are founded on hatred, rather than on love; arrogance taking the place of dignity, and servility that of reverence; and a distinction of classes is a sign, not of mutual dependence, or reciprocity of good offices, but only of estrangement, of a haughty independence of interest and animosity of sentiment. When, therefore, the kings have rejected the Catholic truth, have renounced the Christian name, and are abandoned to the full license of godless power, consternation and distress must needs follow; and while a vicious and turbulent society detests their rule, so will a bitter personal hatred and jealousy of their people, be the retribution which they will repay upon the heads of their restive and unhappy subjects. For, if the extravagant claims of the regal prerogative, signified as the divine right of kings, once caused fearful scenes of revolution and regicide; can it be doubted that the pride of popular sovereignty will one day receive its chastisement? According to the magnitude and extension of the vice, so, may it well be supposed, shall the retribution be terrible in proportion.

But now it appears to result from this interpretation, that the harlot is nothing more nor less than the populace, and that she remains undistinguished from the multitude of our common race; wherefore it seems desirable to seek a clearer and more explicit definition of the term. The whole account of the harlot may be summed up in the words of holy scripture: "All flesh is as grass, and all the glory thereof as the flower of the grass." To distinguish the harlot in matter and form: her material element is this corruptible flesh, which, substantially, is nothing more than the grass of the field; and her spirit is the glory thereof, the perishable flower of this brief human life. Concretely, she is the life of the flesh in its outward manifestation of color, sound, motion, and the like; or, in other words, the carnal life in its thousand combinations of the animal energies, or sensuous forces, natural and artificial. Now this predicament of the flesh, might, in some sense, be extended to embrace the whole animated nature, and even the inanimate; but, properly, the flesh which is as grass, is put for humanity, for we can suppose an animated nature and a visible creation, with or without human life; but there cannot possibly be a Babylon without the hand of man, the human agent. And, since it is written: "she sitteth upon many waters," and "the waters where she sitteth are peoples," therefore the sphere of the woman is the carnal humanity; and she herself is its glory, the lumen which irradiates it, and with tinsel art seems to transform the foul to fair, the bitter to sweet, and woe to mirth. Therefore the common humanity, on its weak side, that is, its carnal aspect, being represented by the harlot; in the next place, (by the figure of speech, in which a part is taken for the whole,) the simple multitude, which is to the select few as is the woman to the man, or as the feminine to the masculine order, may be represented by the same term: in so fär, that is, as a vicious multitude will inevitably be vexed by a wicked few. For, whether consciously or not, it is nevertheless most certain, that in effect the people are controlled by certain leaders, whose power over them is precisely analogous to that of the male over the female, or of the villainous man over the frail woman.

In some sense, therefore, the harlot seems to be confounded with the peoples, as indeed the sacred text saith, "the waters where the harlot sitteth are peoples." And the figment of popular sovereignty, so often quoted in these days, or the popular will, or the popular opinion, or that spirit of the world, no matter by what name it may be called, which is always a proverb for fickleness, petulancy, venality, and treachery; this is, in truth, the spirit of the harlot. But if her affinities are obscure and disgraceful, on the other hand, her differentia is perfectly clear and well marked; and the dignity of human nature, within the reasonable bounds appointed by the Creator, remains unimpaired. For, by the nature of things, the plurality of human wills cannot be aggregated in one essence, nor assimilated in one hypostasis; wherefore no one ever has defined, nor ever can define, the popular sovereignty, so as to shew that it has, in itself, any real concrete existence. For if you, or I, or any other, choose to protest and divide, that hypothesis is at once exploded. Behold an instance, how one rational soul is better than the whole world! In this connection, moreover, it may be remembered, how the Apostle elsewhere compares the company of redeemed and perfect souls to the voice of many waters; and does not employ, for the purpose, a symbol such as might be taken for an individual or a simple unit, but, even in Paradise, the heavenly spirits conserve their distinct personality, in a harmonious unity. And thus also, the voice of the Son of Man, is compared to the voice of many waters, because, inasmuch as the Creator approaches the human nature, he acquires to himself the variety of the creature. But the perfect Unity is in the Holy Trinity alone; and thus also there is a real unanimity and concord of human wills, only so far forth as they accede to the divine order, and accordingly participate of the heavenly harmony and the eternal simplicity.

Therefore the dictum of popular sovereignty requires a qualification, and it becomes necessary to introduce another element, before it can have any consistent, substantive form. Accordingly, statesmen resort to the brute force of majorities, or to tradition, or to the accidents of age and sex, of property, of birth, or length of years. And if, by the blessing of God, the good sense and virtues of the people permit the State to proceed in tranquillity and prosperity, the efficient cause of the same, is immediately referred to one of the aforesaid or similar expedients; according to that shallow and common judgment of things, by which men mistake the husk for the substance, the instrument for the agent, or the operation of the creature for the inspiration of the Creator. But neither one nor all of the inventions of men, can secure the perfect harmony, nor compel the unanimity of human wills. There is one divine right of God's truth and his Providence, and there is no other on earth nor in heaven, which can establish them in solid worth and dignity. When the people, by acclamation, make St. Ambrose their Bishop, it was said, "Vox populi, vox Dei." But why was the people's voice, the voice of God? Was that voice divine, because it was the people's voice, or because it was God's voice? Assuredly, the action was divine, because it proceeded, not from the people, but from God. Here, then, is the royal method, by which a people becomes honorable and sovereign, when it is made the people of God; and, in this way, may every soul of man maintain his individual sovereignty, when he lives, not upon the breath of the world, but by the Spirit of God.

To return: It has been seen how, literally and politically, there may be hatred between the kings and the harlot on the side of her corporal affinities; but, morally, how can they be said to hate the spirit itself of the world? the glory of the age? The good Christian, indeed, who hateth his life in this world, abhors the harlot; but how, or why, should the reprobate kings hate their mistress? In the first place, the flower of this world is so fleeting and vain, that naturally man conceives at intervals a certain disgust for it, and occasionally he assays a stoical indifference to its charms; but presently some metamorphosis of the ever-changing scene occurs, and reason totters, fancy whirls away the understanding, and the heart is again bewitched with the silly illusion. And whereas from beforehand he did not apprehend the charm, and after it is passed he cannot retain it, so in the height of enjoyment he did not fully possess it; nor is it in his power ever to seize, analyze, and give a rational account of it. For precisely as the glory of the carnal life is in the ascendant, and in proportion to the force of its influence is reason displaced, thrown down, and rendered incompetent to its office. Again, where there is pleasure, there is presumed to be love; but the joys of the world are so vile, so wretched a counterfeit and mockery to right reason, that, if they be supposed to have any hypostasis whatever, that is, if they be personified by a harlot, as in the text, this will be a principle, not of love, but of hatred; or certainly a complex form, of false love and of real hatred. And therefore where the earthly felicity is most exalted, we know that envy abounds, and that for every throb of carnal pleasure, there shall be a pang of anguish to the fevered heart. This suffices to show how the hatred is possible, and it only remains to consider its probability. To come, therefore, to the point of the inquiry: it may reasonably be conjectured, that according to the actual, historical, decay of the world, according as much of the aliment of temptation is removed from the observation of men, and the occasions of boasting are subtracted from human life; even so, this, which must be a subject of congratulation for the well disposed, will elicit no sentiment of gratitude from the breasts of the impious; but, on the contrary, will harden them in cold despair, or goad them to bitter hatred toward the age in which they live. And when, for example, they see the world verging on ruin, the harlot running to decay, they vindictively speed her downfall; and, whether through wanton malice, or as if by the last excess of reckless profligacy, they thrust onward to her ruin the wretched creature which is insufficient for their lust, and who seems about to vanish from their dreams of happiness.

Men have now, these many years, been left to run riot in a large liberty, both political and religious, and they find that the fruits are not so pleasant as they expected. The flower of this world begins to fade; its treasures of art, of imagination, of philosophy, of truths sacred and profane, have been rifled and dragged, sifted and searched, till their charms have sickened and waned in the sight of the common mind. And if, at such a crisis, the kings come to power, if, at the very moment when they obtain that long coveted boon, they are to be thus defeated of a great measure of the earthly glory upon which they had counted; assuredly they will not hesitate to speed the ravages of the degenerate age, nor spare to plunder the decaying harlot, till she is left desolate and naked; her stock of worldly toys all broken and wasted, her festive apparel of joyous plenty all tattered and despoiled, while her nakedness, her loathsome vices, are only too apparent in the midst of a corrupt society. Let the kings take in hand this material progress, which is now the speculation of usurers, let them bind the people in the servitude of factories, and corrode them with schemes of sordid industry, till their strength and health are wasted, and famine and distress lower above the crowded haunts of city life; let them thus pursue the popular joys, the chimera of a progress earthward and downward, and behold, then they are eating the flesh of the harlot. Or let them urge on this diffusion of knowledge of good and evil, let them stimulate this thirst of wisdom without truth, of science without God, till all the evil passions are kindled, and the whole mass is hot with ferocious lust and insatiable cupidity; let them prosecute a jaded society, with the incubus of these infernal embraces, and then and there, they burn the harlot with fire.

In the preceding account of the ten kings, no mention is made of the beast; but what is said of the one is to be understood of the other. In the Greek text, the verse reads: "The ten horns, which thou sawest, *and* the beast," thereby including all alike in the same vicious action. But following the reading of the Vulgate as given above, which makes no such distinct enumeration of the beast, it may be said, that it was not necessary to do so, because Antichrist is especially the enemy of Christ; and the hatred which he may bear to the world, or to his fellow-men, is a small matter as compared with his malignant persecution of divine truth. It is however to be inferred, that, if the kings persecute the harlot, much more will Antichrist afflict her, as is evident by the following verse.

17 For God hath given into their hearts, to do that which pleaseth him; that they give their kingdom to the beast till the words of God be fulfilled.

These words suggest the apology of what has gone before. Even as it would appear, at first sight, strange that the kings should hate the harlot, so doubtless, that hatred, however it may be interpreted, is in some sense unnatural, and makes against their own interest; wherefore this singular obliquity of the kings is, in the last account, and when other reasons fail, to be ascribed to the will of God, who disposes of all events with sovereign power. The will of God cannot be the cause of any evil; but it permits evil, and sometimes gives it fearful license, for the chastisement of men. And, in a little while, and for a short time, till the words of God be fulfilled, Satan will be let loose again on earth; and the beast, his representative, the perfection of his malice, will become the great power of the world; and all other of the kings, whether wilfully or blindly, whether infatuated by hatred of the truth or by worldly ambition, will effectually build up his power; and so rivet the fetters, which bind their own souls in the slavery of hell.

18 And the woman which thou sawest, is the great city, a kingdom which hath dominion over the kings of the earth.

Again it is said, the woman hath power over the kings of the earth. They embrace the woman, and yet they hate her; they uphold, and they torment her. Whence this insanity, this pitiful madness of the kings? but because they are bound in the toils of a harlot. It were to be expected, that in the last days, the magnates of earth would fall into dotage, and into that folly which is foremost among all the follies, namely, that of him who saith in his heart, There is no God. But into this folly they are seduced by the woman. Corrupted in the great city, the crowd of worldly glories and lusts, they cease to be the ministers of justice, and the servants of heavenly wisdom; but become the minions of a harlot, and the slaves of the beast.

Here, therefore, is the indictment of the guilty woman; and in the following chapter, is the account of her condemnation, and the scene of her last torments.

CHAPTER XVIII.

IT has been observed, how Holy Scripture oftentimes compares the human life to grass, for its frailty and brevity. These similitudes are collected, as it were, in one text of the Apostle St. Peter, the first clause of which has been considered in the last chapter: "For all flesh is as grass; and all the glory thereof as the flower of the grass;" and now the second member of the same sentence; "the grass is withered; and the flower thereof is fallen away:"[1] these words give the whole sense of the present chapter. The Christian is taught

[1] 1 Peter i. 24.

not to love, but to despise the world, as already withered; and if it be a wholesome thought for him to remember his last end, and a noble act to discard all earthly cares, in order to attend to the things that belong to the Lord; much more would it be reasonable that the multitude of mankind, the intelligent creation, should consider the earth as unworthy of their esteem; not merely with some speculative contempt for the things that are beneath, but in the certain conviction, that the world itself is withered, and its glory fallen away. It would be an impudent thing, to praise the charms of her whose cheeks are hollow, whose skin is shrivelled, and whose breath is tainted with a life of vice; and who can deny that the world is diseased, and shaken with storm, and pestilence, and earthquake, and that society is distracted with the fever of infernal passions rankling at its vitals? In its flower and its pride, it is unworthy of the rational mind; how much more should the wretched weed, when withered, be cast aside, and the soul engaged to higher and to heavenly interests!

Every one knows that the world will finally abandon him, and leave him in the common death of man and beast, and therefore the honest heart renounces the service of the world, accepts none of its flattery, but receives, as the angels of God, those who disclose its baseness, who bring to nought its empty boasts, and who prevent him of its cruel desertion in his last necessity. Thus the angels now fulfil their office. The chapter is found to be divided accordingly in three principal parts. The first angel denounces the vices of Babylon. The second voice, (v. 4,) degrades her from her false honors, and strips her of her pomps. The third, (v. 21,) shows her utter destruction, and the extinction of all her enchantments. To these divisions, moreover, may be supposed to correspond severally, three forms of objection which might be urged against the condemnation of the city of the world. The first is that of the philosophers, who resent it as an injustice and a misproportion. The second is that of the clients of civilization, who remonstrate that it would be needless severity, and a deplorable violation of economy. The third is that of the democracy, who menace, with the terrors of brute force, the accuser who should dare to appear against their wondrous Babylon. But in very truth, this is not the time for apology, nor mitigation, nor commutation of the sentence. With the spiritual man, there is no question nor solicitude, how to save the city, or to defer her downfall, for the cause is already finished, her life expired, and her beauty perished.

1 And after these things I saw another angel coming down from heaven, having great power: and the earth was enlightened with his glory.

The hour of earth's greatest necessity, is the one when heavenly truth is radiant with majesty. In the time when the sources of terrestrial felicity are dried up, when the graces of human life are dissipated and levelled to the vulgar experience, which robs them of all their value; when the flower of this world is a thing of history, in the past, and not in the future, and which will never return; then the eternal goods begin to resume their value in the eyes of men, and the heavenly messenger appears in the surrounding gloom, as a glorious counsellor of the celestial wisdom. Qui docti fuerint fulgebunt quasi splendor firmamenti.[1]

2 And he cried out with a strong voice, saying, Babylon the great is fallen, is fallen; and is become the habitation of devils, and the hold of every unclean spirit, and the hold of every unclean and hateful bird:

With a strong voice: because he speaks with authority and fortitude; or because his message is a formidable one, and of itself falls with energy upon the mind of the hearer.

Literally, the angel who comes down from heaven, might be interpreted of some one exalted in the ecclesiastical hierarchy, who condescends to preach to men of the last days; and whose official dignity, joined with personal merit, renders his message most grave in import, and luminous in certainty; and who, though he be not the same with the angel spoken

[1] Daniel xii. 3.

of in chap. xiv., v. 8, yet endorses or confirms the mission of the one aforesaid. By the earth, may be meant the human race: not so much as it pertains to Holy Church, the heaven of this world, as to the common and secular life which is exterior or independent from the Catholic obedience. And this may be said to be enlightened by his glory, when his example and teaching appeal to men, even on the side of their temporal welfare; or when even their earthly pursuits and projects are compelled to testify to the truth of his mission, and so reflect the glory of God. As if, for example, the angel were one who condescends to the patronage of arts and sciences of human invention; or were so devoted to their desires, and so attentive to their schemes for the amelioration of the physical and moral ills of the day, that even their own plans and theories are found to be already forestalled and occupied by him; so that the most gross and material minds must own him their benefactor, and join the acclamation of his praise.

But, if these conjectures are gratuitous, it may be said that the intention of the blessed Apostle is sufficiently appreciated by the devout meditation of the narrative of the vision; as by his mediation, it is here communicated in the pages of Holy Scripture.

The tenor of this denunciation, is the same with that uttered by the ancient prophets against the former Babylon. Only that now the Christian Prophet enforces, with greater vehemence, the malediction of the city of the world. It was said of the former: "It shall be a dwelling place for dragons;"[1] but now, it is written: "It is become the habitation of devils." And assuredly the apostate Christian may be more justly compared to a devil, than to a wild beast. And if the Chaldæan or the Philistine sinned through ignorance or brutal lust; the other, "who has been once illuminated, and has been made partaker of the Holy Ghost," this one is guilty with the malice of Antichrist. And the world is become the habitation, the established abode, of these enemies of the Cross; and the stronghold of every unclean

[1] Jer. li. 37.

spirit, of false doctrine and heresy; and of every unclean and hateful bird, so that, whether in science, or in literature, or in the arts, every avenue and portal is watched and garrisoned by the ministers of infidelity, of every detestable error, and of every incentive of luxury.

3 Because all nations have drunk of the wine of the wrath of her fornication: and the kings of the earth have committed fornication with her: and the merchants of the earth have been made rich by the abundance of her delicacies.

There is no injustice, therefore, in the condemnation of the world, nor can there be any question of equity, for when the peoples and the princes of earth are corrupted by the blandishments of material prosperity, then in point of fact the city is fallen, because it is become the scene of vices and crimes. It is not said, that the merchants have been corrupted, but that they have been made rich: and when they have been made rich, when the means of luxury have been accumulated to excess, of course it needs no words to show that their corruption follows as a matter of course; for where affluence of riches is the rule, the common order of society, it is not in human nature to resist the abundance of sensual delights. Even as in the gospel, there is no accusation brought against the rich man in hell; but it is said that he received good things in his life-time, and Lazarus evil things, and now he is tormented, and the beggar is comforted.

4 And I heard another voice from heaven, saying: Go out from her, my people; that you be not partakers of her sins, and that you receive not of her plagues.

The voice from heaven, which calls forth the elect people by name: My people; this may well be the voice of the Divine Savior and Shepherd of our souls. The heavenly wisdom, in all ages, requires the people of God to go out from the city of the world. The name of the Father of the faithful, Abraham, signifies "transitus;"[1] as of one who

[1] St. Ambros, de Abraham, l. 2, c. 1.

remains not in the world, but passes to a holy life. The Paschal solemnity commemorates the passage of Israel, from a sinful land of bondage; and of Christian people from the darkness of this world to the light of Paradise. The ancient prophet also cries out against Babylon: "Go out of the midst of her, my people, that every man may save his life from the fierce wrath of the Lord."[1] And what is there in the present age of the world, that renders it less dangerous than ever before? But there are some Christian men who so boast the advantages of this age over others, that it is hard to discover wherein they distinguish between the material goods and the evangelical beatitudes. But when these things are so, more than ever is the contact of the world perilous to the life of grace.

5 For her sins have reached even to heaven: and the Lord hath remembered her iniquities.

The worldling always argues that the temporal riches are a mark of spiritual prosperity, and an evidence of divine favor; but, in fact, they are a presumptive proof of injustice, that the laborer has been overworked and underpaid. While they are a sure warrant of pride, the beginning of all sins. Wherefore the age of riches is the age of sins, and of iniquities or injustices.

6 Render to her as she also hath rendered to you; and double ye the double according to her works: in the cup, wherein she hath mingled, mingle unto her double.

The gospel commands us to love our enemies; but not their vices; rather to hate every way of iniquity. The city of the world is the capital seat of vicious joys, and as such, has brought sorrow and death to the human soul. Justly, therefore, do the elect render back the hatred which is its due. The earthly friendship may have the name of love, but if its fruit be sorrow and sin, then it cannot be without malice; and he who has been liberated from its snares proves

[1] Jer. li. 55.

the highest charity when he repays the hatred in kind. When the strong man of Israel had been captivated by the arts of Dalilah, he suffered most cruel treason; but when, returning from the ways of folly, he renewed his strength, then he proved his zeal against the enemies of God more than in all his life before. The harlot has procured for the elect soul perhaps a temporal loss; he will therefore render to her the double when he spurns her now and forever, and thrusts her forth to present miseries and to eternal loss. She has so artfully mingled her cup of pleasure, that it seemed to challenge the finest sensibilities of tender compassion and of gentle affection; and since she, of all others, is least able to endure rebuke and privation, therefore is the emancipation of the Christian soul a double torment to her, by reason of her necessity and of her cupidity.

7 As much as she hath glorified herself, and hath been in delicacies, so much torment and sorrow give unto her: because she saith in her heart: I sit a queen, and am not a widow, and sorrow I shall not see.

Happy is the state of poverty, since the poor who love God have the more abundant reward; and if they be deprived of the divine love, yet is their loss not so great as theirs who boast themselves in riches and in worldly glory. For the torment of the latter must be in proportion, not to the real value of the material joys, but to the estimate which they set upon them; and it is well known that they esteem them of more worth than the joys of Paradise.

8 Therefore shall her plagues come in one day, death, and mourning, and famine: and she shall be burnt with fire; because God is strong, who shall judge her.

Nature loves honors, but abhors sorrow. In her heart she esteems herself of royal dignity, and in the moment of prosperity arrogates the prerogative of immortal beings. Hence the world always prompts the extravagant dreams of the ambitious; and asseverates to tender youth, that they shall one day come to eminence and have the first place; and promises royal honors to the multitude; and to all, immunity from sorrow, this which it deems the great and only evil. But here is the turning point of her downfall. In this presumption, this ecstasy of her joy, lies the madness which causes her dissolution; and that which seemed to be her strength, is the wreck of her safety, and the engine of her perdition. For, immediately after an access of prosperity, the city of the world always falls back into deeper misery; and is desolated with pestilence, or wasted by famine, or blackened with fires, and with the evil passions which have been inflamed by its sudden affluence of vulgar riches and base delights. And thus, in one day, and with sudden vengeance, will a just God purge with fire the frame of this visible world.

9 And the kings of the earth, who have committed fornication, and lived in delicacies with her, shall weep, and bewail themselves over her, when they shall see the smoke of her burning.

It is possible for one to live in the midst of delicacies, and yet be in spirit detached from them; but the common humanity is incontinently seduced by them, from the love of God, to the impure friendship of the world. And how commonly this is so, none ought to understand better than the ungodly, since they ridicule the former proposition as absurd and incredible.

10 Standing afar off, for fear of her torments, saying: Wo, wo, that great city Babylon, that mighty city; for in one hour is thy judgment come.

Especially, therefore, do the great ones of earth, suffer in the calamities which befall this human life. Cruel is the separation which rends them from the spectacle of earthly glory, from the refinements of luxury, from the delights of an obsequious society, the adulation of courtiers, and the feminine applause. Coarse and rude is the shock of popular commotion, which disturbs them for a moment from their security, but in one short hour all the stage of life is passed, and they, afar off from every joy, mourn and bewail themselves over the shadow of a phantom, the memory of a dream.

11 And the merchants of the earth shall weep, and mourn over her: for no man shall buy their merchandise any more:

The temporal goods are either natural or acquired. If the kings represent those who are born to greatness, the merchants may stand for those who acquire importance by purchase, or otherwise. When their traffic is neglected, they suffer; when this busy life, the market-place of mundane glories, is closed, then their greatness is laid low forever.

12 Merchandise of gold, and silver, and of precious stones; and pearl, and of fine linen, and purple, and of silk, and scarlet, and all thyine wood, and all manner of vessels of ivory, and all manner of vessels of precious stone, and of brass, and iron, and marble,

Perhaps the philosopher smiles at this enumeration; perhaps the humble servant of God blushes at the childish catalogue of the Holy Apostle. Happy for them if they would! Let them do so with a good heart and be wise indeed. For here is the whole account of the treasury of earth.

13 And cinnamon, and of odors, and ointment, and frankincense, and wine, and oil, and fine flour, and wheat, and beasts, and sheep, and horses, and chariots, and slaves, and souls of men.

Trinkets of gold and silver to adorn the body, robes to cover its shame, vessels for its service of vanity or of hard necessity, odors and sweets, meats and drinks, behold the treasures of earth! the end for which its multitudes toil and sweat, or the means by which a few are built up in transitory splendor. Goods that are valuable, as they may be consumed; odors that are pleasant, as they are dissipated; ointments that are useful, as they are wasted. Or, if they are long in use, and slow to decay, they must be transmuted or else thrown aside. Or if some of them seem more noble than others, yet those who trade in the souls of men, can derive no honor to themselves, by an act which is a fraud and a robbery; while the soul which can be bought and sold, is in truth compared to the senseless beast, and is of no higher value than the other chattels of earth.

14 And the fruits of the desire of thy soui are departed from thee; and all fat and goodly things are perished from thee; and they shall no more find them.

Even the soul has its certain capacity; much more then is the body constrained in a measure so strict that it deserves to be called a prison-house of flesh; and as it rarely happens, under the Providence of God, that either man or beast is wholly deprived of what is sufficient for his wants, so, by no means, can he appropriate more than is enough for his sustenance. If a scant supply causes suffering at times, much more does a superabundance bring disquietude of mind, and countless pains of body. We cannot conceive of a utility smaller, therefore, than this of the riches of earth; whose whole purpose is the least service of all which can be rendered to the rational soul, while it subsists for a little while in the body. Uncertain and perishable, hard to obtain and easy to lose, they wholly vanish when death and eternity draw nigh. Made only to be consumed, why is it not good that they be at last ended, and heaven begun? When Blessed Magdalen wasted her precious ointments, the sweet odor of her good works is carried forth into all the earth. Happy would it be for the world if all its treasures could be spent, and all its wealth so poured out, that her children might flourish in immortal health, and in eternal joy.

15 The merchants of these things, who were made rich, shall stand afar off from her, for fear of her torments, weeping and mourning.

In the time of prosperity, the kings are gracious, and the merchants draw nigh; but when adversity supervenes, they suddenly remove, and like feeble children, they fly in terror, weeping over the reverses of fortune. They have studied how to procure pleasure, but they are unlearned in sorrow; they are wise in the enjoyment of the present life, but ignorant of any other good; they are trained in the practice of self-indulgence, but they have no skill nor vigor to suffer tribulation.

16 And saying: Wo, wo, that great city, which was clothed with fine linen, and purple, and scarlet, and was gilded with gold, and precious stones, and pearls:

In the temporal calamities, therefore, of this world, the social disorders and political revolutions, they stand afar off: as if the farthest of all, removed from any enjoyment; for new men of coarser quality, who are not so difficult in their tastes, rush in for the plunder of the falling city, and even find a reckless joy in the sight of its burning. In such times, moreover, the great ones must stand afar off, because they are hated more than others, and are in great danger to be trampled by the envious mob. And again, they have reason to fear, because these disorders of the last days, have been in a measure provoked by themselves. In seeking too greedily their own aggrandizement, they meet their ruin. By abusing the prerogatives of rank, or by forcing the resources of society and of nature, they hasten on the catastrophe, the sudden downfall, which follows a great height of prosperity.

Morally, it may be added, that as they are never without fear of temporal reverses, nor without some apprehension concerning the eternal issues of this life of probation, so will the remembrance of the worldly glory, hereafter be a torment from which they would fain escape, and a terror from which they would willingly be removed.

17 For in one hour are so great riches come to nothing. And every ship-master, and every one that sails into the lake, and mariners, and they that work at sea, stood afar off.

The mariners are the retainers of the ship-masters, who are the subalterns of the merchants, and they suffer with them. They who work in the sea are those actively employed in the secular affairs of this stormy life. And they who sail into the lake, or, (according to another reading,) from place to place, are a type of those restless souls, who, like the Athenians, are always striving after something new and better, who compass sea and land to make one proselyte, but who are empty of solid worth and void of interior virtue.

18 And cried out, seeing the place of her burning, saying: What city is like to this great city?

Therefore, being occupied about the exterior glory, and exploring only the surface of this painted existence, they find marvels in small matters, and they extol, with swelling words, the city which, to their feeble apprehension, seems wonderful.

19 And they cast dust upon their heads, and cried out, weeping and mourning, saying: Wo, wo that great city, wherein all were made rich, who had ships at sea, by reason of her prices: for in one hour she is made desolate.

And when they meet with temporal disaster, they assume the attitude of mourning, the garb of penance, and all the circumstance of grief, which were due only to eternal loss.

20 Rejoice over her, thou heaven, and ye holy apostles, and prophets: for God hath judged your judgment on her.

On the other hand, the just man smiles at the material losses, and mourns only over the spiritual detriment, in grief too heavy for words; and his joy begins, where that of the other ends; and the kingdom of heaven prevails, when the kingdom of this world is crumbled to the dust.

21 And a mighty angel took up a stone as it were a great millstone, and cast it into the sea, saying: With this violence shall Babylon, that great city, be thrown down, and shall not be found no more.

The imagery in the text, is analogous to that of the prophecy of Jeremias,[1] who commanded Saraias, when he had made an end of reading his book, to fasten to it a stone, and to throw it in the river Euphrates, saying: "Thus shall

[1] Jer. li. 63.

Babylon sink, and be utterly destroyed." As the stone sunken in the Euphrates was a figure of the annihilation of the city built upon its shore, so the mill-stone hurled by the mighty angel into the depths of the sea, signifies the final and utter destruction of the Babylon which sitteth upon the great waters of human life. In this chapter the first angel denounced the world; in the second place, the heavenly voice called out from it the elect; and now, at the voice of the third angel, it is abandoned, to sink, by its own weight, in the overwhelming deeps of the abyss.

22 And the voice of harpers, and of musicians, and of them that play on the pipe, and on the trumpet, shall no more be heard in thee: and no craftsman of any art whatsoever shall be found any more in thee: and the sound of a mill shall be heard no more in thee:

At length the glory of this world is wholly passed away; its songs and vanities, its varied show of ease and pastime, its stirring feats of war and statesmanship, its marvellous skill and lavish beauty of art, its cunning devices and combinations of mechanic power, all are gone.

23 And the light of a lamp shall shine no more in thee: and the voice of the bridegroom and bride shall be heard no more in thee: for thy merchants were the great men of the earth, for all nations have been deceived by thy sorceries.

Vanished is all its pomp of learning, its pride of intellect, and the palace windows are deserted and dark, and the splendor of assembled manhood, and youth, and beauty, is quenched, and the bridal mirth, and the voice of love, are heard no more forever.

For has it not been seen how all its glories are venal, how its honors may be bought and sold, how its mighty men are but sordid traders, who thrust upon us paltry wares, which are an insult to the immortal soul? And all have been deceived by its sorceries, mocked and derided by its fleeting joys, which no bar, nor bolt, nor sentinel can keep, which shift and change in every successive moment of time, and are never again the same forever.

24 And in her hath been found the blood of prophets and of saints, and of all, who were slain upon the earth.

To its folly, alas, is added vice; and to its empty vanity, dark deeds of crime. And when the sun shines brightly over it, he looks down from heaven upon a field of murder.

PART VI.

RETROSPECT OF CHRIST'S VICTORY.

The end of the vision draws near; even as the end of all things is nigh at hand. The earth, created in primitive beauty and excellence, was corrupted and decayed; man, built up in the image of God, was fallen and accursed. And again, Christ our Lord has overcome the world of sin, "He hath showed might in his arm; he hath scattered the proud in the conceit of their hearts." After the abasement of the proud, follows the exaltation of the humble. He has blessed the land of his saints: "He hath visited and wrought the redemption of his people; salvation from our enemies, and from the hand of all that hate us." Here is the time of his glorious victory, the year of grace; now is the day of salvation, the harvest-time of good hope. Afterward there remains nought but the day of his judgment, and the eternal doom.

According to the title of this Part, as given above, the Victory of our Lord Jesus Christ is regarded as already accomplished, though some of the events indicated in the following chapter, are not yet fulfilled. But while one day is as a thousand years to the divine Ruler, who obtains his ends oftentimes after long intervals, and not without the delay of second causes, yet for this his acts are not the less decisive, and are now and again determined in the majesty of Absolute Power. Such an act is this of the Victory of Christ over sin and death; an act so well achieved, so perfectly consummated, that they who look for any other conquest, any other like interposition of Sovereign Power, except the final one of Judgment, seem to be deceived with the folly of Millenarians, and to make too little account of what has been already fulfilled; compared with which, all that remains of human history is but a small matter, that of itself can neither impair nor enhance the trophies of his glorious victory.

CHAPTER XIX.

THE division is a brief one, and composed of a single chapter. In its details are comprised, (v. 1,) the happiness of the Faithful; (v. 7,) the marriage of the Divine Spouse; (v. 11,) the revelation of the majesty of the God of armies, and (v. 17,) the perdition of his enemies.

1 After these things, I heard, as it were, the voice of many multitudes in heaven, saying; Alleluia: salvation, and glory, and power is to our God.

Alleluia is the word of divine praise: Laudate Deum.[1] It is proper to the Lord's Day; the day of his resurrection and triumph over death, and over sin, which is the ghastly principle of death. From that time forth it is the song of the people of God, and is heard, as it were, in heaven: because their conversation is in heaven, whether they be yet in the body or already departed to the home of the blessed. The divine praise transcends our human language, and in this life there are not words nor space to satisfy its sacred demands. Therefore, in this brief note of joy, the mystic alleluia, is meant to be conveyed the fulness of that praise, which swells the grateful heart of the Christian, though it falter on his lips. By the first alleluia, the saints praise the mercy of the Creator, which has gained salvation for his creatures; but they also adore his justice as it follows accordingly:

2 For true and just are his judgments, who hath judged the great harlot, which corrupted the earth with her fornication, and hath revenged the blood of his servants, at her hands.

We know that the earth has been corrupted, because heavenly truth is offensive to the human mind. There might be

[1] St. Aug. in Psalms cxlviii.

an earthly enjoyment which would yield health and strength of soul to weary mortals, and quicken their desire for supernal joys; but when the advent of the kingdom of God fills them with sorrow, when the evangelical doctrine is a scandal to them and a reproach, then it is evident that they have been seduced from the charity of God, to an unlawful love of the world. If one mourns because he is deprived of an indulgence which was injurious to him, it is all the more necessary that the rigor of his discipline be enforced. If the worldling howls because his riches fall away, or his schemes of pleasure are baffled, true charity would seek to detect the fraud of those uncertain joys, and so detach him from the causes of his hurt. Now this has been accomplished by the maxims of the Cross; the world has resented it, and has raged against the holy martyrs; but yet the truths of Christianity have prevailed; its testimony is everywhere, and before it the worldly bliss is convicted of falsity, and condemned for a harlot.

3 And again they said: Alleluia. And her smoke ascendeth forever and ever.

Therefore the elect again praise God, because of the chastisement which has fallen upon the harlot. And herein is the Christian like to a good soldier, whose manly heart exults in the confusion of his Lord's enemies, and rejoices in their downfall; for otherwise he were a coward and a traitor. The harlot smarts under her punishment, and her companions would fain redeem her from her woes; would build up again a temporal felicity, would cover the land with a harvest of material joys, and crown the nations with an overflowing abundance of carnal delights. But that will never be. The sorrows of a decaying humanity will not be hidden; the turmoil and sweat, the empty joys and the solid miseries of this weary world will not be repaired; but the ferment of lust which shall never find rest, the smoke of the harlot, ascendeth forever and ever.

4 And the four and twenty ancients, and the four living creatures

fell down and adored God that sitteth upon the throne, saying: Amen: Alleluia.

The third alleluia is that of the princes of the heavenly court, who take up the song of praise begun on earth; and thus the alleluia of the servants of God, is carried before his throne on high by their holy patrons, the Fathers in the faith.

5 And a voice came out from the throne, saying: Praise ye our God, all his servants, and you that fear him, little and great.

Whose is the voice from the throne, that calls upon the little as well as the great, to sing alleluias to God, but that of our gracious Lord? who hath shared our sorrows, that we might be partakers of his joy and praise.

6 And I heard as it were the voice of a great multitude, and as the voice of many waters, and as the voice of great thunders, saying: Alleluia, for the Lord our God omnipotent hath reigned.

To him the universe of his heavenly creation make response. The multitude of holy angels, the Christian peoples whose voice attuned by grace, is like the the sweet murmur of living waters, and the voice of great thunders, of sacred preachers, these fill up the alleluia of celestial harmonies. The holy evangelists and sacred doctors are compared to thunders, like the Boanerges, because their unwelcome words of truth fall like the shock of sudden blows upon the careless minds of the incredulous. And as they have spoken in times past, so is their voice now heard on every side. And they have supplied all that is to be found in these pages, which is of any worth.

7 Let us be glad, and rejoice, and give glory to him: for the marriage of the Lamb is come, and his wife hath prepared herself.

The marriage of the Lamb, is the union of Christ the Lord with his spouse, the Church. Of the one it is said: "Speciosus forma præ filiis hominum. Thou art beautiful above the sons of men; grace is poured abroad in thy lips." Of the other it is written: "The queen stood on thy right hand, in gilded clothing, surrounded with variety."[1] The spouse leaves father and mother, to be joined with his wife; the Son of God leaves his home in heaven, and the Church departing from the Synagogue, the joyful union of the Creator with the creature is accomplished in the sacred womb of the Immaculate Virgin. And the praises of Holy Scripture are due to this blessed event; the glorious promises of the prophets, the hopes of the faithful, and the desires of the angels have taken their rise in its auspicious purpose, and find rest in its consummation. Prevented by divine grace, his wife hath prepared herself, when the Gentile world has become obedient to the Divine Spouse, and she that was barren has been made glad with many children. The Omnipotent God has reigned, when his royal standard of the Cross has been lifted up; and the nations have "gone forth to see the King in the diadem, wherewith his mother crowned him in the day of his espousals, and in the day of the joy of his heart."[2]

8 And to her it hath been granted, that she should clothe herself with fine linen, glittering and white. For the fine linen are the justifications of saints.

The assembly of the arrogant assumes for itself the garb of holiness; and appears just, outwardly. But the true spouse has received authority and grace, to put on robes of spotless white; for in her alone are found interior virtue and heroic sanctity.

9 And he said to me: Write: Blessed are they, who are called to the marriage supper of the Lamb: and he saith to me: These words of God are true.

Write it, that is, record in perpetuity this memorable truth: That they are blessed who are called to the marriage supper, the banquet which our Lord Jesus Christ has set forth in his Church. "Wisdom hath built herself a house, she hath hewn her out seven pillars. She hath slain her victims, mingled her wine, and set forth her table."[3] And it is true,

[1] Ps. xliv. [2] Cant. iii. 11. [3] Prov. ix. 1.

that they who are invited to it, shall be royally fed with the living bread that came down from heaven; and the veracity of a God is pledged, that he who eateth this bread shall live forever. Neither prophet nor king in all the ages, have been so blessed as the least one of those who worthily partake of this heavenly feast, set forth amidst the pillars of wisdom in the house of God. Nor is there any true happiness to be found elsewhere on earth, nor dare we say that any other is blessed, than he who is thus called to the infinite joy, which the spouse hath lavished on his happy guests. It may be said: that the marriage supper should be referred to the final beatitude, that last supper where they are indeed blessed who shall sit down and take their rest, after the labors of this life are ended. But if the joys of heaven deserve praise, so do the graces of the Christian Altar deserve no less; and if it be true that there is a heaven, it is equally true that here is the gate of heaven; and he will not pass there, who has not entered here; but, if he enter here, and keep the grace of God which is committed to him, he is now already blessed, as the Truth himself has said: "If any man keep my word, he shall not see death forever."

10 And I fell before his feet to adore him. And he saith to me: See thou do it not: I am thy fellow servant, and of thy brethren who have the testimony of Jesus. Adore God. For the testimony of Jesus is the spirit of prophecy.

The blessed Apostle, considering the riches of divine goodness, how an infinite treasure of heavenly gifts has been bestowed even in our human measure, falls down in the fulness of his joy to adore the angel, through whose ministration he has been instructed in sacred wisdom. And herein he did no wrong, or it would follow that the gifts of God corrupt, rather than purify the heart. But the illusions of Satan, disguised as an angel of light, these alone disturb the soul and inflate the mind, with inordinate motions of pride or false devotion. Therefore it may be said: first, on the side of the Angel, he disclaims the homage of the Apostle, because the saint always avoids honors; as many examples are given in the life of their Lord, who, when he was himself praised, or when his blessed Mother was commended, referred the homage to the eternal Godhead. And also, because the dignity of the Christian is elevated to an equality with that of the angels, wherefore he calls himself the fellow-servant of John, and of all those who confess Jesus Christ. In this connection also, it has been observed by the Holy Fathers,[1] how in ancient times we read, that just men adored angels, (Gen. xix. 1, and Jos. v. 15,) and were not prohibited; but, after the advent of our Redeemer, the angels decline their homage, since they behold the humanity which was once beneath them, now elevated far above them in the King of heaven; and they cannot disdain man for an equal, since they now adore the Man who is God. In the second place, and on the side of the Apostle, his adoration is resisted, not for his reproof, but for his consolation. It is necessary that the just man should humble himself, although the humiliation is not the end; but rather the glory which is under the self-abasement, the exaltation before heaven, this is the end for which he was created. So long as one seems cold to pay the reverence he owes to virtue or to merit, we regard him with distrust, and are disposed to enforce the claims of just desert; but if he submit to the requirements of pious observance, inclining meekly, and with heartfelt respect, instantly we reverse our purpose, dissuade his generous courtesy, and desire for him better things, namely: that he may have for himself true honor; and the true honor is that which is in God.

It is not then an impulse of blind enthusiasm, but a habit of solid virtue, which makes the just man docile and prompt to acts of veneration; and, in Christian times, we look for the full maturity of this virtue, as well as of every other; that the superabundant charity of God falling upon the soul, the soul also shall overflow in love to the friends of God. Before our Lord's incarnation, the divine goodness was contained and held in reserve, until the appointed time. The

[1] St. G. Hom. in Evang. viii.

creature was as yet unblessed by the personal union of the Creator, and its homage was circumscribed accordingly. But, with the advent of the Son of Justice, the darkness of idolatry is scattered, and the intelligent mind, instructed by faith, discerns the goodness of God in his saints, the power of God in his apostles and their successors, his wisdom in the sacred doctors, and his justice in the martyrs, or in their relics, or in the sign of the cross; and where he finds these vestiges of the divine Majesty, there he adores. The dishonor, the insults of the Creator, he finds only in the malicious mind of the reprobate; and that alone he hates. The relative worship, then, is the dictate of sound reason, the effusion of a great and generous heart, which is not anxious for itself, but is thoughtful about others. The ambitious man who aspires to the highest seat, this is the selfish soul, fearful lest another's good be its own irreparable loss. The one who is too proud to humble himself, this is the shallow mind, of contracted resources, which cannot afford to communicate of its goods to others, but is niggardly of its virtues because they are few to spare; and even so he judges that the Creator is parsimonious of his graces, and jealous of his angels, and suspicious of our offerings. But the one strong in virtue, and fearless in the simplicity of a holy intention, would diffuse his benedictions, as the blessings of God are also extended to him. Thus the Apostle, for the heavenly favors bestowed on men, offers the homage of his mind to the heavenly habitant nearest to his side; the latter, as becomes his angelic office, directs him to the throne of God; which proves not ignorance in the worshipper, nor resentment in the one worshipped; but the sagacity of the one, and the sanctity of the other. And the sanctity of the latter is a proof of the former's sagacity; for if he did not refer the homage to God, it would show that he did not deserve it, and that the former was guilty of superstition; but, since it terminates in God, it is plain that God was the final cause of the pious act. Had the act originated in ignorance, like that of the Lycaonians[1] who wished to offer sacrifice to Paul and Barnabas, it could not have been from God; for a good word falling on bad ground, or a false doctrine falling on good ground, in either case the product cannot be good. But in the instance before us, it is plain that the grace of truth is bestowed in an upright mind, which is illuminated, and not blinded, by the ministration of the angel; and therefore it cannot furnish a pretext, for those who would excuse themselves from the veneration of the saints, but on the contrary, it constrains them to draw the following inference: If the Apostle, in his greatness, humbles himself before the ambassador of heaven, how much more ought they, in their littleness, to render homage to the friends of God!

There remains, then, on one side, the diffusive charity of a grateful heart; on the other, the humility of true holiness. If there is any contention between them, it is a contest of humility. If there is any emulation, it is to make some worthy acknowledgment of divine goodness, and to render to Almighty God the service which is his sovereign due. To conclude this point: if one be willing to reverence a finite holiness for the sake of its holiness, this proves, not that he is unmindful of the infinite holiness, but on the contrary, that he will be ready much more to adore it, with a supreme act of worship. And even thus will the created holiness infallibly refer the just man to that which is Increate, through all his pilgrimage on earth, and till that day "when the Son also himself shall be subject to him, who subjected all things to himself, that God may be all in all."[2]

But to leave this digression: it seems most probable that the purpose of the sacred writer, in recording this passage, was to demonstrate finally, and by actual example, the sublime dignity of the Christian soul. The angels are the fellow-servants of those who confess Jesus Christ, because the testimony of Jesus is the spirit, or as it were the essence, of prophecy. For if the prophets were to be honored because they foretold, or prepared the way, to the Son of God, the

[1] Acts xiv. 12. [2] 1 Cor. xv. 28.

Christian is above them, since he is in possession of the blessing which they could only promise; and if they were great because they showed its possibility, how much greater is the privilege of those who can exhibit the reality, the good in its essentiality! Or again, the testimony of Jesus is the spirit of prophecy: because, since no man can say the Lord Jesus but by the Holy Ghost, he who confesses Christ before men, is inspired by the Holy Ghost; and, if inspired, he has the spirit of prophecy, and the office of a prophet is the office of an angel. Wherefore St. Peter hesitates not to address, to the flock of Christ's fold, the titles of royalty, of priesthood, and of sanctity, saying: "You are a chosen generation, a royal priesthood, a holy nation, a purchased people;" while their angelic or prophetic office is indicated in what follows: "that you may declare his virtues, who hath called you out of darkness into his admirable light." [1]

11 And I saw heaven opened, and, behold, a white horse: and he that sat upon him, was called Faithful and True; and with justice he judgeth and fighteth.

Behold the Bridegroom! the sacred Head of the Church, the Conqueror over death and hell! whom we have seen in the beginning ride forth gloriously to execute his eternal decrees, and whom we confess with heart and soul to have fulfilled his promises, to have supplied his people with blessings innumerable, and to have defended them with virtue infallible. The temporal monarch, who is truly great, must be a wise legislator, and a formidable warrior; he must know to dispense justice at home, and to chastise his enemies abroad; to maintain order and contentment among his people, and to inspire terror to their foes. So the divine Majesty, when he has established his kingdom on earth, the land infested with perils and with scandals, with daring enemies and with secret traitors, he also with justice judgeth and fighteth. Guiding his own in the paths of wisdom, appointing to each according

[1] 1 Pet. ii. 9.

to his need, the graces of authority or of obedience, of action or of contemplation, of liberality and magnanimity, or of poverty and patience, he moreover reveals the strength of his arm against the adversaries of the truth, when their rage is made vain, their counsels derided, and their boasting confounded; while his Church still prevails, his ensign of the Cross is yet exalted, for the consolation of his people and the terror of their enemies.

12 And his eyes *were* as a flame of fire, and on his head many diadems, having a name written, which no man knoweth but himself.

Who can flee from the eye of God? "If I ascend into heaven," saith holy David, "thou art there; if I descend into hell, thou art present. Darkness shall not be dark to thee, and night shall be light as the day."[1] In the hour of temptation, in the heat of persecution, by night or by day, the eyes of the divine Master are over the just man; like a flame to enlighten him in adversity, or like a wall of fire to bar him from the foul thought of sin in prosperity. And for the sinner, in his lonely hours, in the security of darkness, or in the silence of seclusion, the eyes of God are upon his guilty soul; like burning truths of justice and judgment to come.

On his head are many diadems: for the titles are numberless of the Lord of angels and of men. Who in this life shall be able to declare, how gloriously he reigns above the celestial hierarchies? Among men, he has proved himself in the former ages, "the Lord of hosts, and the God of the armies of Israel;" and now, as the Prince of Peace, his gracious rule is yet more happy and glorious. He is the King of heaven, and of the visible universe; Sovereign before all above, and Sovereign among all below. He is the King of Glory, to whom the eternal gates are lifted up; and he is the King of the Jews, transfixed beneath a crown of thorns. In joy or sorrow, in power or infirmity, in majesty or obedience, in manhood or childhood, he is the Leader who bears his part

[1] Ps. cxxxviii.

royally, and there is none like him. The kings of earth have adored him, and have gone over seas to give their lives for the honor of his sepulchre; and the publicans and sinners, more blessed than kings, have entertained him at their own tables, and have sat down with him. He who can fill up all these various and untold relations of power and goodness, of majesty and grace, is the Infinite One: whose name no man knoweth, nor can angels comprehend it, but he alone, the Omnipotent God.

13 And he was clothed with a garment sprinkled with blood: and his name is called, THE WORD OF GOD.

When our Almighty Lord has condescended to enter into battle with his enemies, he returns victorious; but, as becomes the generous warrior, not without honorable wounds. In himself no sorrow can molest him, but when he has come forth from the eternal mansions to appear in the warfare of our human life, his innocent body, the sacred clothing of his divinity, is sprinkled with blood, and all wounded with the transgressions of a sinful race.

The written name of the inaccessible Godhead, no man knoweth; but he is called the Word of God: for in him God speaks to the soul, and appeals lovingly to our human heart, and through him is all our conversation with the adorable and ever-blessed Trinity: to whom belong all power, and praise, and glory, now and forevermore.

14 And the armies which are in heaven followed him on white horses, clothed in fine linen, white and clean.

"The burden of Babylon," saith the prophet Isaias.[1] "Upon the dark mountain lift ye up a banner. I have commanded my sanctified ones, and have called my strong ones in my wrath, them that rejoice in my glory. The Lord of hosts hath given charge to the troops of war, to them that come from a country afar off." Upon the high land of this earth, exalted by the goodness of God, but wrapped in the

[1] Isaias xii.

darkness of ingratitude, is the battle between good and evil. Though the victory be gained, the war is not finished; and, though the combat be fast hastening to its close, yet it is not wholly ended. But the God of armies gathers his hosts, and prepares all things for the final separation of good and bad, and for the extermination of all iniquity from his dominions. And they that are on the side of heaven, the cause of justice and truth, of order and religion, these deserve to be numbered among his troops of war, and to be marshalled in the ranks of the Lord of hosts. These are clothed in fine linen, white and clean, because of the simplicity of their intention, and the purity of their affection. And, like their victorious Lord, they follow on white horses, as conquerors and partakers of the King's glory. For thus it is, that, whether in heaven or on earth, a sublime greatness, a sacred liberty, and a true success are the privilege of those who are engaged to the cause of divine truth, and whose warfare is conducted by the Word of God. While, on the other hand, the followers of the world are led in chains by a tyrant, who requires them to toil and sweat for honors, which are only another burden; or who makes it of obligation for them to become distinguished and successful, to no purpose; as though always the things most difficult or impossible, were, at the same time, the very ones which are of the most strict necessity, and enjoined by the most rigorous claims of duty. Behold, what a slavery is the glory of this world! For not only does man find its goods difficult of attainment, not only are its high places arduous, but even its deep places, its mire and its slime, will not always receive him; but, when pressed by temptation, he would cast himself downward, then also by the awful goodness of God, is he oftentimes baffled and prevented from his purpose. Does it follow, therefore, that man is not a free agent, that he is not endowed with the liberty of a free will? On the contrary, he has been created in such honor, that the world is unworthy of him; and therefore, to be disencumbered of its glories, is the only true freedom, as was abundantly proved, even by the Cynic philosopher. But much more are we assured by divine revelation, that he has the highest liberty, and the noblest claims, and a paramount duty, to pursue a good which is better than the whole world, because it is eternal; in which the rivalry of his compeers cannot forestall him, because its capacity is infinite; and which cannot possibly deceive nor elude him: for this true good, have we not seen it nailed, hand and foot, so that no man can fail to make it his own, if he will but stretch forth his hand, and take, and eat of the tree of life? The sign of this great good, is the Word of the cross; that word which is at the same time the beginning and the end, the experiment and the conclusion of Wisdom; with each and every induction of which, shall the soul be irradiated by that light of Truth, which discloses infinite consequences, and follows them even into their eternal state. This is indeed, the experimentum crucis, whose instances are as simple as its occasions are liberal. The world's riches are narrow, obscure and difficult; but humiliation and poverty are free in perfect liberty. For when one seeks the first place, what envy and heart-burnings are stirred up; but let him take the lowest seat, and what peace and tranquillity does he impart to every breast! If he aspires to the friendship of the prosperous and great, he will be scorned; if he turns to the lowly and the destitute, he will be received with benediction. If he lay hold on the carnal delights, he will be chased out with indignation; but if he would embrace chastity and obedience, neither God nor man can withhold him. If he thinks to overcome wrath by wrath, and to outbrawl the railer, how insignificant does he become by failure, or how ignominious by success! But let him, by a mild answer, allay the storm of insolence, and he becomes an honor for his neighbors. In a word, if he aims at the earthly good, his spirit is filled with confusion and bitterness; but, if he aspires to the eternal good, his acts are noble, his aim is sure, his paths are peace, and his end is a crown of joy. O marvellous likeness of man to God! Thou, also, hadst no power, sweet Lord, to overcome hatred by hate, contempt by scorn, nor arrogance by pride. Thou hadst no liberty to fill thy omnipotent spirit with a finite joy, nor to find any rest in the perishable riches. But thine was the power, and the liberty, and the grace, to be made subject to poverty, to obedience, and to the heavy burden of our transgressions. And by the same royal road, and in the footsteps of thy Majesty, are we also permitted to follow to the true glory and the eternal greatness.

15 And out of his mouth proceedeth a sharp two-edged sword; that with it he may strike the Gentiles. And he shall rule them with a rod of iron: and he treadeth the wine-press of the fury of the wrath of God the Almighty.

The God of armies brings peace to men of good will, but not the earthly ease which carnal minds fondly expect to follow on the diffusion of heavenly favors; wherefore it is said to these: "Do not think that I am come to send peace upon earth; I came not to send peace, but the sword."[1] His sword is not the dull weapon of temporal power, but the sharp sword of the spirit, which proceedeth from the mouth of the Word of God; and it pierces irresistibly, and divides infallibly, between good and evil. It smites the Gentiles, the strangers to sacred truth, the unconverted infidel, and the hardened sinner, who love darkness rather than light, who hate the distinction of right and wrong, and who dread the division of heaven and hell. And therefore whithersoever the standard of the Cross is advanced, it carries sorrow and dismay to the foolish multitudes of the world, and they groan under its gentle rule, as if it were an iron bondage.

But not only is he formidable to these, his justice is also strict and impartial toward his own. For the time is that judgment should begin at the house of God. Now, in the day of his victory, when we have been delivered from our enemies, when the riches of his goodness, and patience, and long-suffering have been poured out upon men, now is the time when the worthy fruits of virtue will be strictly required of his people.

[1] St. Matt. x. 34.

To estimate the vehemence of the wrath of God, we must remember the magnitude of his mercies. How the one who treadeth the wine-press of his justice, has been himself tormented in the night of his agony. He himself is the victim in the Christian sacrifice, an infinite treasure; but it was a crime infinitely heinous, to inflict the wounds he received in his sacred body. Who has ever believed that that body was of the Person of God the Almighty, and has doubted that there is an infinite woe? Who has ever adored the chalice of salvation, and has doubted that there is an infinite joy? Therefore the Christian soul, however sorely pressed by the anguish of grief, or by the burning heat of temptation, dares not refuse his cross, nor forsake the strict ways of eternal justice; but should it waver for a moment in the occasions of sin, then, even then, is it constrained by the weight, and fast bound by the formidable apprehension, of the fury of the wrath of God the Almighty.

16 And he hath on his garment and on his thigh written: King of kings, and Lord of lords.

A garment, as something superadded, may denote an acquired good; the thigh, which signifies the order of generation, indicates a possession by inheritance. When our blessed Savior, in the clothing of his humanity, has humbled himself, becoming obedient unto death, even the death of the cross; he has therefore deserved to be exalted, and to receive a name which is above every name. But also by his eternal generation from the Father, he is the Son of God, and the Sovereign Lord of heaven and earth. Moreover, by his human generation, he is the son of David, and descended from those who were first in dignity, among all the kings of the earth. And thus, over all his creatures, angels and men, by right divine, by virtue of inheritance, and by grace of merit, by possession and by conquest, in the beginning, in the end, and forever, he is King of kings, and Lord of lords.

We come now to the last section of this Part, in which is described the final scene in the combat between heaven and earth. And, because it cannot be fulfilled but with the end of the world, it may again be objected: that this Part is misnamed a Retrospect, when it comprises events which are prospective, and yet unaccomplished. But it is to be remembered that, in the beginning, (chap. i. v. 19,) the apostle was directed to write the "things which he had seen, and which are and which must be done hereafter;" that is, the things which subsist eternally, which are now in this day, and those which will be. Now since the book is written for the instruction of Christian people, it might perhaps be said, that these conditions of past, and present, and future, are to be traced in the prophecy, in every part of it, and in all times, to the end of the Christian generation. But it is sufficient for the present purpose to observe, that nothing forbids our applying the aforesaid rule to this Part, which manifestly describes Christ's victory: as a whole and substantially, it has been and is accomplished; accidentally, and in some of its details, it may not be finished. But of course it is to be named according to its general complexion, and not from any particular feature; even as the battle is always named from the capital point of action rather than from some combat at the extremities of the field of war, or from particular exploits of some single battalion. It remains, then, to consider now the closing scene in that great struggle which the Creator has so long maintained with his unworthy creatures. Conquered by his goodness, confounded by his majesty, they pretend to defy his authority to the last; they even think to reunite their broken and scattered forces, and once more make head against his resistless power. This it is which brings the end itself; and that mysterious point in time, when the last act of man is blended with the advent of Christ in the last judgment, when, it may be added, the whole compass of events and of second causes are numbered in the past; and the apothegm of St. Jerome, "that this book contains as many mysteries as words, and Christ alone can unfold it," will be proved good; since then indeed we must look back upon them as no longer things that are to be, quæ futura sunt, so much as things fully accomplished, quæ fuerunt; which have been mysterious, but which are so no more thenceforth forever.

17 And I saw an angel standing in the sun: and he cried with a loud voice, saying to all the birds that did fly through the midst of heaven: Come, and gather yourselves together to the great supper of God:

That any object should be interposed between us and the sun, impresses the imagination unfavorably; if a material body, some sinister influence over the animated nature, is instinctively attributed to it; but when the pûre spirit of the angel makes his station in the sun, this prognosticates not a sensible hurt, but, what is much more grievous, a spiritual disaster to the souls of men. When they prepare to array their human forces against the powers of heaven, they prepare their own destruction. They seem to make good progress; heaven is silent, the sun shines brightly on their unholy armament, and their eyes glisten with the insolence of a brief prosperity. But high above, the minister of divine justice, in brightness and purity undisturbed, forecasts a retribution, summary and perspicuous, as the very light in which they rejoice, and wherein they boast themselves so audaciously, as if they were the creators of that which is the very grace of their existence. As the vultures follow the armies to battle, and hover over the ghastly bodies of the wounded and dying, so the evil spirits who wander in the high places of this world, discern from afar the ills which threaten the souls of men. And while these, blinded by prosperity, lie basking in the license of impiety, the demons more astute and quick to malice, with mind ever prescient of the judgments of God, watch them from the shades of air, and perceive the moment is at hand to stoop upon their prey. Though they repose in an outward security, and in a brutal stupidity to the things that are unseen, yet, in their secret heart, men know that God is just, as well as good; that he has a banquet in heaven for his angels and the company of the blessed, and that the devils also have their terrible nourishment, when they are permitted to devour the spirits of the reprobate. The great supper of God's justice, is that last hour of temptation, when all the demons in mid-heaven are gathered together and swarm above the apostate nations, to buffet and to rend them, for their manifest impiety and the abundance of their iniquity.

18 That you may eat the flesh of kings, and the flesh of tribunes, and the flesh of mighty men, and the flesh of horses, and of them that sit on them, and the flesh of all free-men and bond-men, and of little and great.

Here is the enumeration of a society whose ranks are unblessed by the grace of Christian discipline, but are according to the natural or mere pagan order. The kings represent monarchies; the tribunes, popular governments; the mighty men are they, who are able to control the public affairs to their private good; the horses may be the achievements of science, or art, or commerce; and those who sit on them, are they who are enabled, by such pursuits, to take the advantage of others, and override the common herd. The bond and free, masters and servants, little and great, make up the mass of this human race: composed in such variety, and strength, in such affluence of numbers, and skill, and experience, that the worldling, who ventures not to contemplate the things invisible and within his soul, but who looks abroad for consolation, reposes in it all his trust; and scorns the thought, that it will one day be made desolate, and fall as carrion back to its native earth.

19 And I saw the beast, and the kings of the earth and their armies gathered together to make war with him that sat upon the horse, and with his army.

Scripture and tradition show: that first there is an apostasy of the nations from the Catholic truth, and afterward, their impiety comes to a head in the man of sin, whose reign, though terrible, will be brief. By his instigation, all the powers of earth conspire against the divine authority; but this will be the occasion of their instant destruction. According to the present narration of the sacred writer, when they begin to marshal their forces, the birds of prey prepare to devour their flesh; when they are fairly arrayed against the powers of heaven, they are utterly destroyed; and there is no mention of any great action of longer or shorter duration, no mighty combat of doubtful issue or of rapid success either way, but only the annihilation of the rebellious herd. For how should the victorious Lord of the Church condescend to enter into altercation with those who would crucify again the Son of God, and make a mockery of mercy itself? Nor will he suffer his own to be tempted "above that they are able;" wherefore, if the temptation is more vehement than they are able to bear, then the motive of the divine economy in the institution of this human existence ceases; nor is there any reason why the reprobate should be suffered to abuse his goodness a moment longer. The means by which this great insurrection of the nations is propagated, has been suggested in a former Part, (IV.;) and we have not now to review the insolent array of its congregated forces, but the same is here considered only in its relation to him that sat upon the horse: the Lord, mighty in battle, of whom it is written: "The earth trembled and was still, when God arose in judgment, to save all the meek of the earth."[1] "As wax melteth before the fire, so let the wicked perish at the presence of God."[2]

20 And the beast was taken, and with him the false prophet; who wrought signs before him, wherewith he seduced them, who received the mark of the beast, and who adored his image. These two were cast alive into the pool of fire burning with brimstone.

As those who rebelled against the first establishment of revealed religion, went down alive into hell,[3] so the leaders of the last rebellion against the Church of Christ, are cast alive into the same place of torments. They are the beast, or the secular power as personified in Antichrist, and the false prophet, or the power of earthly science, perverted to the service of error and against revelation. This text

[1] Ps. lxxvii. [2] Ps. lxvii. [3] Num. xvi. 33.

would seem to imply that the false prophet is not only an abstract power, but a distinct person. If it is to be so interpreted, the false prophet may be the one who, in the time of Antichrist, stands at the head of all those who are engaged in the pursuits of human industry, as contained in theory or practice, and who therefore has the preëminence of a master, surpassing the rest in the temerity of his speculations, or in his success of experiment; whereby he will seduce, from the love of sacred truth, those unhappy souls who are infatuated by the things of sense, but are indifferent to those of faith, and who therefore have the mark of the beast: the mark which has been seen in men from the days of Cain, the founder of the city of the world, but which is broad and terribly distinct in the antichristian times. For they have the mark of the beast, who love the world; as those have the mark of Christ, who love God. And all mankind are divided between these two sects, and there are in truth but these two kinds alone. One is the reasonable, faithful, and honorable generation, which lives by faith in the things that are eternal; the other is the servile race, who are in bondage to sense; and as the beast goes bowed to the earth, with its breast between its feet,[1] even so the men who mind earthly things, and whose heart is never lifted up erect to heaven, are justly compared to the senseless brute. Gladly would the sceptic persuade himself that there are more than these two classes, that there are a thousand kinds of reason, and ten thousand divided truths; that right and wrong are of no fixed or certain essence, but that there is an infinity of variations either way, which are neither right nor wrong; that the good are but little better than the bad, and the bad but little worse than the good, and hereafter heaven will not exclude the one, and hell will not swallow up the other. Outwardly, there is this seeming confusion of good and evil, but he who abides by the testimony of sense, and refuses to follow where reason invites the way, he, like the stolid beast, is strong in the

[1] St. Ambrose Paradis 15.

instincts of the flesh, but is coarse and dull to the sacred impulses of the spirit.

The image of the beast may also be of ancient derivation, though it be of little note in history. But the devices of human ingenuity, even innocent in themselves, and receptive of the benedictions of the Church become however an image of Antichrist, and an occasion of idolatry, when men are seen to render to them an adoration greater than that which they pay to the truths of the gospel, and when they do not hesitate to compare the puerile wonders of mechanic force, or material industry, to the miracles of almighty power, and to reckon the latter as insignificant by contrast. If there be many Antichrists, there may be also many false prophets. Truth does not require us to judge any but one son of perdition and one false prophet; but, if these two are certainly condemned to the pool of fire burning with brimstone, is it not to be feared that they who imitate them in their blasphemy, must also copy them in their miserable end? though, indeed, we may not be without hope, that they will yet repent of their impiety.

21 And the rest were slain by the sword of him that sitteth upon the horse, which proceedeth out of his mouth; and all the birds were filled with their flesh.

St. Paul calls Antichrist "the wicked one whom the Lord Jesus shall kill with the spirit of his mouth, and shall destroy with the brightness of his coming."[1] From which it would appear that he will be destroyed as if by the only presence of Christ the Lord; before whom the earth opens to swallow up the wicked one, both soul and body; his soul already killed or accursed from the presence of God; his body, if living, yet condemned to the death whose agony has no end. The same holy Apostle calls "the sword of the Spirit the word of God;"[2] therefore that divine virtue, which proceedeth out of the mouth of the Word of God, and which kills the beast and the false prophet as by a direct interposition of mirac-

[1] 2 Thess. ii. 8. [2] Eph. vi. 17.

ulous power, is the same sword of sacred justice by which are slain the rest of the impious, who are on earth at the time of his coming; though the destruction of the latter be not marked by such signal vengeance, but is as if by sentence of judgment, and in the ordinary course of divine justice. And then all the birds are filled with their flesh: because the envy of the demons is at length satisfied. For in that last wreck of the world, when so few are saved, the multitude of the reprobate is as it were sufficient for the malice of devils. Or in another way: their envy of man, so far as he is a being in the possibility of eternal happiness is then concluded forever, when the year of grace is ended, when there is no longer a hope for the impious, and when there is no fear for the just, who have passed away from the reach of their temptations, to the kingdom prepared for them from the foundation of the world.

PART VII.

THE DAY OF JUDGMENT.

In the beginning God created heaven and earth: a heaven of angels, an earth of men. The Creator remains immutable, but there is no created being which has not been subject to mutation. Thus, of the angels, some have stood, others have fallen; and among the human race, changes the most profound are oftentimes repeated in one and the same person. Moreover, that the intelligent mind may be fully convinced of its vanity, and learn to stand in fear, the Creator has declared that the first shall be last, and the last first. Lucifer, first among the angels of heaven, is rejected; and the lowly Virgin of Nazareth is exalted to be the most glorious of the works of God. "The princes of the nations, the merchants of Merrha and of Theman, the searchers of prudence have not known the way of wisdom; nor the giants that were from the beginning, hath he chosen;"[1] but the publican and the sinner he converts to be sons of God, and the poor he lifteth up out of the dunghill to place him with princes, the princes of his people. That the mouth of the scoffer may be stopped, he not only calls being out of nothingness, but even produces goodness out of evil. He then can suffer no loss, because he can make loss itself a gain. But reverses to infinite loss, or conversions to infinite good, these are the daily record and the whole history of the creature.

Again, the Creator is eternal, but the creative act is produced in time. In some respects, the creation is finished and good; as God rested on the seventh day from all his works, and angels and saints have passed to their rest; but, as long

[1] Baruch iii. 16, 33.

as inferior causes continue to operate, and from every point of time is incessantly evolved a new mutation; "while the spirit goeth forward surveying all places round about, and returneth to his circuits, while the rivers run into the sea,"[1] and to the place from whence it came, the river of existence returns to flow again: the end is not yet; the creation is not completed in its integrity, nor perfected in its parts. "He hath made all things good in their time, and hath delivered the world to their consideration, so that man cannot find out the work which God hath made from the beginning to the end."[2] The mighty chain of second causes reaches throughout, and while we labor painfully in its consideration, we know not the beginning nor the end. The expectation of the creature waiteth for the revelation of the sons of God; the elect, who have the first fruits of the spirit, wait for the redemption of their body; and even angels, (with joy,) watch and labor for our salvation, and know not the day nor the hour. Therefore the time, the manner, the measure of that last day, which is above time, and is measured by no space, these pertain to the judgment of the Creator, and to him alone. Whether the higher and the lower causes proceed in such unison that the revolutions of the natural creation will complete the mighty cycle, and the sun and stars shall stand again in the place of their first creation: whether that day reveals every act in time to every created mind: whether, in the nature of things, there is such fitness and coherence of all which happens under divine Providence, that no one act can be perfectly comprehended, till all that go before, and all that follow after, are conducted to the period of a universal judgment; these, and every question, or doubt, or hope, that can be devised, receive their answer with the Day of Judgment: the day when all things return to the repose of their First Cause: when the immutability of the Creator is extended to his works: and when time is swallowed up in eternity.

But if the divine decrees are so veiled that not one of

[1] Eccles. ii. 6. [2] Eccles. iii. 11.

them can be fully comprehended, yet perhaps it might be said, there is no sacred mystery so absolutely and on every side hidden from the servants of God, (to whom it is promised the spirit of truth shall teach them all truth,) but that they may have some apprehension of the same, though imperfect and obscure. We know that now is the judgment of this world, and that a divine retribution is already awarded to some, who, visibly or invisibly, are within the sphere of earth. While, therefore, the day in which we live, looks forward to the last judgment, so the day of doom recalls the times of the past; and the present hour will be reflected in that which surveys all the former ages, as well as it discloses the eternity of the future. For there is no guilt of devils, nor idle word of men; no virtue of angels, nor aspiration of humble penitents, which will be omitted from the divine balance in that last account; but the justice of God, in the beginning and in the end, will be proved one and undivided: in æternum omnia judicia justitiæ tuæ. [1]

Then every created intelligence will be assembled, to vindicate the equity of the Judge of angels and of men. By the temptation of the fallen angel, man has fallen; and by the guardian care of the good angel, he is brought back to virtue; one generation of men is bound up with another, their virtues redound to the advantage, their vices to the detriment of their neighbor; and thus the whole rational creation, celestial and terrestrial, is involved in one cause of heaven or hell. And, even if some have already passed to that state of happiness or of torment, still their reward is hitherto a temporal one; for, while time endures, by time it may be measured; and the day which divides it from eternity is necessary to transmit it to the ages everlasting.

The day of judgment then relates to the past, as well as to the future. The mind cannot comprehend it as a whole; but in its parts, no truths more vividly impress the soul, than the judgments of God which have already come to the

[1] Psalms cxviii. 160.

knowledge of men, or which may be apprehended by faith. If, therefore, the blessed Apostle would instruct us in that last period of all which is transitory, he must discourse of the things of time, to those who exist in time ; and compare the judgments temporal, with the doom which is eternal. The remaining chapters of the Apocalypse are comprised in one Part, with the title above given, because they relate to the remuneration of rewards and punishments. If they contain some events which are measured by years, and are concluded apart from the general judgment of the last day; yet these are enumerated manifestly in respect of their juridical import, and according as they are signal instances and integral parts of that distributive justice which reaches from end to end. Or, again, if some of the details appear to be narrative of temporal transactions, rather than declarative of any actual sentence: yet these are coincident to the main purpose, and pertain as it were immediately to the crisis of a final retribution.

The analysis of this part shows, (chap. xx. v. 1.,) the temporal punishment of Satan ; (v. 4.,) the temporal beatification of the saints ; (v. 7.,) the end of the year of grace ; (v. 9.,) the beginning of the day of vengeance ; (v. 11.,) the supreme act of judgment ; (v. 14.,) the damnation of the reprobate ; (chap. xxi. v. 1.,) the salvation of the elect; (v. 6.,) the end of the works of God ; (v. 9.,) the final beatitude of the elect ; (chap. xxii. v. 6.,) some words of exhortation, of admonition, of holy ejaculation and benediction, conclude the book.

CHAPTER XX.

1 AND I saw an angel coming down from heaven, having the key of the bottomless pit, and a great chain in his hand.

The Judgment of God begins with his first creation; the bad angel first offended, and by the good angel he is chastised. While the demons always bear about with them the pains of hell, yet, by the advent of Christianity, another temporal penalty is added to their eternal one. When the Lord, the just Judge, came upon earth, they, conscious that the hour of his judgment was drawing near, already began to beseech him that he would not command them to go into the deep. But by the ministration of holy angels, their malice has been restrained from the Christian peoples, and they have been thrust down, and bound in the chains of hell, even before their time. And these are the fetters which make our adversary like to the chained mastiff, according to the comparison of St. Augustine; so that, though he may bark, he cannot bite; and though he howl, he has no power to harm any but the fool who wilfully comes within his reach.

2 And he laid hold on the dragon, the old serpent, which is the devil and Satan, and bound him for a thousand years:

The first offender, therefore, summoned to the awful bar of divine justice, is he who was once first among the angelic hosts; who, in the splendor of his beauty, said: "I will ascend above the height of the clouds; I will be like the Most High." But suddenly all his glory was blasted, the grace of the Creator departed from him, and his own malice remained with him. Like a devouring dragon, he drew multitudes with him in his fall; and like a serpent, he has since tempted the multitudes of our human race to the same perdition. And, whereas he was designed to make virtue lovely, he is now worthless, except to make vice hideous; like a foul reptile, good only to startle the nobler mind to a holy horror of the things that are beneath, and to a watchful trust in those that are above. From a patron of the just, he has turned to be their adversary, the devil, and accuser of all that is innocent and good ; and, for some time, has rejoiced in the miseries of the human soul, but again, for a time, he is beaten down from his seeming triumph, by the power of the Cross; dragged in chains, and degraded to be the most infamous among the accursed, according to the mournful sentence of the Prophet: How art thou fallen from heaven, O Lucifer, who didst rise in the morning? how art thou fallen to the earth, that didst wound the nations? Formerly, Satan had license to wander round about the earth, and to walk through it, and could thrust himself among the sons of God, exulting miserably in the ruin of those who were made to fill up his place in heaven; but in the Christian times, he is held fast in the torments of his own envy, while he has no power over the happy throngs who hasten from the courts of Holy Church to their home above, and who, for long years, have now in countless numbers pressed onward through her open door, to that eternal rest which is the sure inheritance of every one who chooses to enter, and to walk in her paths of wisdom. Here is the beginning of the judgments of God; and this is the condign chastisement of Satan: the act of sin, committed in time, but with infinite malice, receiving its temporal, as well as its eternal, punishment.

3 And he cast him into the bottomless pit, and shut him up, and set a seal upon him, that he should no more seduce the nations, till the thousand years be finished: and after that he must be loosed a little time.

The question now presents itself: How can Satan be bound in hell and yet be able to tempt men on earth? It cannot be said that he is in both places by virtue of his angelic capacity, the application of which might be extended to earth and to hell at the same time; for, even if that were possible, yet the text seems to imply that he is restricted absolutely to the abyss, being shut up and sealed therein. Nor can it be supposed that the thousand years are to be some time when the evil spirits will have no power whatever to vex mankind; since there is nothing in Scripture, nor in reason, to warrant the expectation, that a moral agent in our human order, while placed in a state of probation, will ever be deprived of the occasions of merit by temptation; but the sentence of the prince of the Apostles: "Be sober and watch; because your adversary, the devil, as a roaring lion, goeth about seeking whom he may devour;" this is addressed to the congregation of the faithful for every age. While the good angels always sustain and defend them, so the fallen angels are ever ready to exercise them to tribulation, the test of virtue; that thus even the evil spirits may not be without some utility among the works of God.[1]

It remains then to consider the bondage of Satan for a thousand years, as figurative merely of the comparative tranquillity of Christian times; or else literally, as an actual imprisonment of the prince of devils, who, as the head and leader of the apostate spirits, is personally restrained from the molestation of the nations, for the even number of one thousand years. According to the former interpretation or allegorically, we know that, with the promulgation of the Gospel, the outward manifestations of satanic power began to be less frequent and at length almost wholly to disappear. According to the words of sacred Truth, "I saw Satan as lightning falling from heaven,"[2] it were impossible that the powers of darkness should not be dispersed by the triumphant progress of the true light of the gospel; and in some part extirpated, though it is not necessary that the free moral agent be wholly exempted from their solicitations. And this must continue to be the common order of things, nearly to the end of the world, and throughout that goodly number of years, which measure the full span of the generation of Christ. During which time, the proper place of torments for the evil spirits, is the deep; and because of their unbounded malice,

[1] Sum. Theol. l. 1. 64. 4. [2] St. Luke x. 18.

it is a bottomless pit. And this abyss, according to St. Gregory, may be found in the hearts of the reprobate, wherein Satan is shut down and constrained in anguish, while he dares not come forth and manifest the fulness of his malice. Also, the abyss may be called a bottomless pit, because of that unfathomable mystery which attaches to pride, or to the origin of evil. For example; any given natural virtue of honor, or skill, or strength, or beauty, when innocent, may be disregarded; while, if to the same, there only be superadded a proportion of pride, and the stamp of a haughty mind, instantly the beholder is attracted, is challenged to admiration, and presently is stimulated to an emulation, which, as fast as it is kindled, devours and despoils his heart of every peaceful and kindly affection. Thus we see, in some modern societies, how the display of these traits of pride and disdain, have passed into the manners, even of tender youth; and their countenances, while yet blooming with the first freshness of life, are already distorted with affected, if not real, arrogance, and ambition, and concupiscence; conventional graces indeed, but nevertheless germs of rebellion, and of infamy everlasting.

But to proceed now to the historical interpretation of this passage of Satan's bondage: It is appropriate for the spirit of an angel to be in place; and also to be in one place, and not in many, at the same time. As the angel, however, is measured by no bodily dimensions, he is not said to be in place circumscriptively, but according as he pertains in any whatsoever manner to that place; and as the soul contains the body, properly speaking, and not the body the soul, so he possesses his place, rather than he, himself, is contained by it. And, as all that to which he virtually applies himself, whether greater or smaller, farther or nearer, corresponds as one place to his spiritual nature, [1] it might perhaps be said, that Satan is even present to earth and to hell, at the same time. But since, beside the reasons drawn from the sacred text, and given above, it seems incongruous for the same finite

[1] Sum. Theol. 1. 1. 53. 1. and 2.

being to be present to both, as to one sphere of operation, it is to be remarked, that the name of devil is common to the evil spirits,[1] but that the name of Satan is proper to their leader or prince. When, therefore, Satan is cast to the earth, and when his angels are thrown down with him, (as in Part III., chap. xii., verse 9,) their ranks are broken and scattered, and their evil designs frustrated. But in the present instance, somewhat more is added; for it is said of Satan, though not of the others, that he is shut up and sealed in the bottomless pit; and whether a greater or a smaller number of his companions remain on earth, and whether some are, or are not bound with him in hell, the literal meaning seems to be: that, by a signal judgment of Heaven, he himself is absolutely withdrawn from the high places of the earth, and for one thousand years, the demons who remain upon it, are left to wander without a master, as if without power, or without any united purpose to contrive the perdition of the Christian nations. Accordingly, in her public ritual the Church does not commonly exorcise Satan by name, but rather the accursed one, the devil, or the unclean spirit[2] which may be present to the subject offered for her benediction; while she alludes, as it were, only remotely to Satan, the personal chief of all reprobate spirits. Or at least it may be said, that Satan is not exorcised in the baptism of children, which is the common office of a perfected and continuous Christian generation, but only in that of adults, which, generally speaking, is proper to an incipient or an interrupted Christianity.

The time of his bondage may, perhaps, have a precise date; but it need not be determined with the mechanical accuracy of human events, for the operations of spirit are not manifested like human actions; nor would Satan's disappearance from, or his return to, this mortal sphere, be cognizant necessarily, even to the faithful or to their pastors. The libertine, who plots the corruption of some innocent mind, often shrinks

[1] St. Aug. Quæst. Nov. Test. xc.

[2] Præcipio tibi. . . .quicumque es, Spiritus immunde. Rituale Romanum.

back, and conceals his purpose, and the very victim he desires is, unconsciously to herself, a terror to his guilty soul. Now the human race, compared with Satan, is like a feeble and helpless maiden; and before its simplicity and ignorance, how much more must his hideous depravity of spirit be abashed and confounded? As the artless words of little children sometimes probe the conscience of the old transgressor, so do the infirmities and susceptibility, the credulity and ingenuous freedom of the human nature, startle him in his perfidy, and cause him to writhe under the greatness of his own guilt, the incomparable malice of his unclouded intellect. Therefore the approaches of Satan are compared to those of the serpent, who glides towards his prey, without notice of sight or sound. And moreover, according to the venom of his malice, will he be the more guarded; even as the vehemence of his delusions in the last days, is best proved by the very security in which they are accepted, and by the temerity with which they are maintained and propagated. Wherefore, without pretending to fix the precise boundaries of the time of his bondage, it may be said, there is no one period of a thousand years in human history, to be compared with the Middle Age of the Christian religion, whether considered as a unity of faith and sanctity, or as a uniformity of worship and repose, under a Catholic moral discipline. Before and since that period, the Christian religion has seemed multiform and fragmentary to the natural understanding; but then, there was one round number of a Thousand years, which no sophistry can divide, no heresy can overlay; and in, and through which, Satan has no power to beguile a mind docile to the voice of truth. Wherefore, in the sixteenth century, when men openly revolted from the Catholic Church, this mighty barrier of a thousand years, serene and immovable, confronted them, and constantly opposed to all their projects of impious reform, the majesty of a sainted ancestry, whose countless numbers reached, unbroken, through all that length of ages. Then it was, that the argument of "a thousand years" passed into the familiar discourse of Christian people, and in the controversies of those times, it is found an established phrase; for the Catholics, a consolation and a help to their sorely tried faith, for the Reformers, a stain and disgrace, which they were not afraid to invoke upon themselves, at the peril of their own infamy. The question was put plainly before them: The Thousand years; was it of God, or of Satan? And when they found it in their hearts to say it was of Satan, then indeed it is to be feared the thousand years was finished, and Satan has come forth again from his prison.

4 And I saw seats, and they sat upon them: and judgment was given unto them: and the souls of them that were beheaded for the testimony of Jesus, and for the word of God, and who had not adored the beast, nor his image, nor received his mark in their foreheads, nor in their hands: and they lived and reigned with Christ a thousand years.

Simultaneous with the temporal punishment of Satan, is the temporal exaltation of the Saints; who live and reign with Christ, exerting a princely authority over the lands of Christendom where their memory is held in veneration. Preeminent among the thrones of the Church Triumphant, are the seats of the twelve Apostles. An instance how well their authority is recognized by the faithful on earth, may be remarked in the sacred formula, whereby the Sovereign Pontiff, in every age, threatens the disobedient with the indignation of the blessed Apostles, Peter and Paul, at the same time with that of Almighty God. Besides these, are the martyrs who have suffered for the name of Jesus, or for his sacred truth; and the saints in every age who have not adored the powers of the world, nor its pomps; or, if they have dwelt in the midst of its vanities, have not been defiled thereby in mind or in body, but have lived as strangers and pilgrims on the earth, detached from the common joys, and separated like outcasts from the multitude, whose glory is in the carnal life. And if the example of such on earth is a reproach to sensual men, so is the memory of their beatified spirits in heaven, much more a discipline to the conscious soul; adjudging peace to the innocent, and terror to the guilty. Thus, in the cause of good and evil, which comes before the tribunal of heaven, the just are not merely suitors with, or competitors of, the unjust, but they do effectually sit in veritable judgment over their enemies. The thousand years of their beatification is like a temporal reward, because it is superadded to their eternal one. It may be interpreted mystically of the whole time of the New Testament, which is a thousand years and more, for the assembly of the Blessed, taken collectively, though not the same equal number for each particular one, who is added with succeeding years from the unfailing generation of Christ the Father of the world to come.

5 The rest of the dead lived not, till the thousand years were finished. This is the first resurrection.

Those who confess not Christ, but oppose divine truth, and all everywhere who serve the world, the flesh, and the devil, are dead in sin; and if they depart out of this mortal state impenitent, they are dead till the end of the world and the day of the general resurrection. But the others anticipate that day, and their beatified spirits already live in the vision of God. Thus there are two deaths, that of the body and that of the soul; and two resurrections, one of the soul, the other of the body. For the reprobate, there is a double death, now, and also in the day of judgment; for the elect there is a double resurrection, one now, and one in the last day. In the first resurrection, the reprobate have no part whatever; though, in the second, and general resurrection, they partake of the life which restores to every one his natural faculties, for joy or woe, according to his desert. In the second death, the elect have no part whatever; though they participate in the first death, so far as it affects the body. Thus the works of God are designed in such wisdom, that they hasten to their consummation with every moment of time; and, even before they are ended, it seems as though their ultimate perfection were eternally present to them.

6 Blessed and holy is he that hath part in the first resurrection:

in these the second death hath no power: but they shall be priests of God and of Christ, and shall reign with him a thousand years.

After the brief temptation of this life, the saints pass to a rest which will never be disturbed, and to a life which is above the power of death forever. And in that holy estate, they become the intercessors of the Christian peoples on earth, and, like priests, they minister to them in heavenly graces. The dignity of a Priest is such, that no other is to be compared with it, and for him who lacks it, there is something yet to be desired. Hence we see, in their translations of the Holy Scriptures, how fondly the sects appropriate for themselves the priestly dignity, whenever it can be referred to their society in the gross; although they enviously expunge every term which would give it a distinct and individual application, to any person in the Church of God. But a better illustration, is the example of St. Louis of France, who wished much to be invested with the sacerdotal honors; and cherished the intention that, if his Queen should die before him, he would procure for himself that sacred office. It was otherwise ordered, however, by Divine Providence; for doubtless it is a much greater miracle that a king should be a saint, than that a priest should be eminent for sanctity, who almost in the course of nature, is bound to manifest the fruits of holiness. But now, in the courts of the Church Triumphant, all are consecrated like priests, to the divine service; and much more than when on earth, do they abound in treasures of grace, overflowing to all who abide in the communion of the saints.

It remains now to interpret this section of the chapter literally, and to examine if the thousand years' reign of the saints, historically considered, will coincide with the abasement of Satan for the parallel term of years, as before described. The mystical does not conflict with the historical interpretation, but by an admirable disposition of the inspired text, seems to hold it enclosed within its ample bounds; and if there are some reasons which require us to enlarge the signification, there are others which invite a more literal application of the same. Thus the thousand years may be predicated, generally, of the saints, but since, according as the end of the world approaches, there must be holy souls, who would have little or no part in those happy years, it may be permitted in another way to seek a meaning better accommodated to our human exigency. And this will be obtained by leaving aside, for the time, the investigation of the celestial rewards which are ordered in a measure wholly above the natural comprehension, and by turning our regard to that which more nearly concerns us here in this present existence, namely: in what manner the saints stand affected toward our own salvation, or how they instruct us about the one thing necessary. When, by the good providence of God, this world has been conducted to such fruitfulness of sanctity, that the minds of men seem to have been united about one common good, the eternal welfare of the soul; when the means of salvation, as well as the end, was unanimously accepted by them, and held the first place in the public veneration; when perfect souls of men, whether on earth or in heaven, possessed the affections, guided the understanding, and directed the affairs of prince and of people, in peace and in war, in prayer and in study, in labor and in recreation, then the saints have reigned: for they have exercised a rule beneficent and effectual to the one true and eternal good of the human race. In this manner the saints have occupied the middle age of the Christian religion. That the vices of humanity had their place in those times as well as in others, only proves that the saints may reign even over this sinful earth; and that the grace of God can abound unto justification, more than sin unto death. But now the question is not, what age has been most stained with crime and injustice, but which has been most adorned with the memorials of sanctity, and so impressed with the supernatural energy of the servants of God, as to render their example and their acts the most prominent, and almost the sole recorded facts in the history of the time. So far, therefore, as the edification or the true civilization of the human race is concerned, then the saints have sat in judgment, and have reigned with Christ, when their names, their insignia, and their lives have been displayed in the public and domestic relations of Christian people. And their authority has, for a thousand years, been prodominant, their thrones established above the powers of the world, when of these two the Church and the world, the former was the strongest; and when, although the latter was not without force, yet the spiritual was in effect more mighty than the temporal power.

Some analogies which favor the literal interpretation of the thousand years, may be found in the other periods of the world's history. It has already been suggested, (c. xiii. v. 1.,) that under the former dispensation of the Old Testament, the people of Israel were for one thousand years an independent power; and in their full maturity, they were undoubtedly distinguished as the most excellent and renowned of all the nations of the earth. And secondly, even the brief record of the antediluvian era, furnishes ground for ascertaining a consimilar period of time, when the worship of Almighty God was maintained in its highest honor. In this instance, it may be dated, from the days of Enos, of whom it is written: "This man began to call upon the name of the Lord." It being evident, from the fifth chapter of Genesis, that Enos was born in the year 235 of the world's history, therefore we may suppose the prosperous age of that first era, to have been initiated in or about the year 300, A. M. The middle term, or climacteric of the same, will coincide with the days of Henoch; who, for his full maturity of sanctity, deserved to be translated to Paradise. This was about seven hundred years later, or in the year 987 A. M. Sixty-nine years afterward, was born Noe; of whom it was said: "This same shall comfort us, from the works and labors of our hands, on the earth which the Lord hath cursed;" as if then the fervor of devotion began to be abated, and as if religion were beginning to decline somewhat from its late happy and prosperous condition. But if three hundred years, or less, be added to complete the round number of one thousand, this brings us to within three centuries of the Deluge; when the decadence of the race had become manifest, and when its corruption threatened to become universal.

Another reason why the thousand years may be interpreted historically, is because it is said: That after they are finished, Satan must be loosed a little time; that is, there must be an interval between the thousand years and the end of the world. And though it is said: The rest of the dead lived not till the thousand years are finished, as if, after that, were the day of the general resurrection, yet this does not prove that there is not the interval implied above. Because, firstly, Holy Scripture often employs this manner of expression, which is narrative of facts unto a certain period, but leaves whatever may be thenceforth future about them wholly indefinite. As for example, Noe sent forth the raven, "which went forth, and did not return till the waters were dried up on the earth;" that is, it did not return again to the Ark. Hence, it does not follow that, immediately after those years, the dead live again; but it is expressly affirmed, that they do not by any means live before that time. But, secondly, it may be said: That in truth all the time of those who are dead in sin, whether in the body or out of the body, is not worthy of being remembered, and all the time of Satan's active malice is but short, even though it were centuries; for the latter, it is but a little thing, for the former, it is nothing. Such as it is, however, it is sufficient to constitute a distinction, and to preclude the application of the thousand years, absolutely to the whole Christian times; that is, in the full sense of all its parts, the term of the thousand years fails to meet the requirements of either interpretation, taken singly, but seems to need both, in order that its stores of meaning may be distributed, and be suitably applied.

In conclusion, it may be observed, that it is not necessary even by the conditions of a literal interpretation, to fix the precise dates of the beginning and end of the Middle Age of the Church. "The spirit breatheth where he will; and thou hearest his voice; but thou knowest not whence he cometh nor whither he goeth; so is every one that is born of the spirit."[1] The moment in which his grace possesses, and that in which it abandons the soul, are far removed from the natural observation; but yet there are signs which argue his actual presence, because they could proceed from no other than his own indwelling virtue. As early as the fourth century, may be traced the beginning of the prosperous era of Christianity, when St. Augustine[2] describes the marvellous change which had passed over the world; "lately adoring idols, now adoring God; then serving the things itself had made, now him by whom the world itself was created. When the remnant of the Pagans trembled, seeing the Churches crowded, their temples deserted; the one become illustrious by the concourse of the people, the others neglected and left to solitude." But by the sixth century, the Middle Age is unquestionably inaugurated. Then St. Gregory[3] shows how the secular prince, formerly given up to the mire of sinful pleasures, and like the rhinoceros, abandoned to the field of his desperate courses, was brought, by the goodness of God, into obedience. "Shall the rhinoceros be willing to serve thee? or will he stay at thy crib?" By grace was wrought a conversion much more wonderful, "when," says the Holy Father, "we see the potentates of this world willingly receive, and constantly study the divine precepts; and everywhere depart not from them, but as if domesticated to the enclosures of sacred truth, remain contented to receive a heavenly nourishment, and to be enriched with the food of life eternal. Alligabis rhinocerotem ad arandum loro tuo? Canst thou bind the rhinoceros with thy thong, to plough? or will he break the clods of the valley, after thee? Behold the earthly prince," in the better days of holy Church, "bound in the thongs of faith, and harnessed, to toil patiently in the field of religion, and to labor for the prosperity of the kingdom of heaven. And the clods of the valley, those obstinate souls, who suffocated the good seed, and who, trusting under the former infidelity of tyrants,

[1] St. John iii. 8. [2] Enarr in Psalms xliv.
[3] Mor. in Job. xxxix. 9.

defied the gentle discipline of the Church, behold them broken and scattered by the secular prince; who, not now exasperated with the fury of unbridled power, but submitted to the mild influence of religion, yet with fervent zeal, bruised and pulverized those obdurate spirits, till they were left no longer to oppress others, but were themselves made to germinate the seed of the Word of God, received at length in an humble mind." Then all hearts were glad, when king and bishop vied in humility and in mutual deference, with a united mind, and a single intention, seeking first the kingdom of God and his justice. But after those years, and in the sixteenth century, it was thought a shameful thing, that the prince should be obedient to Holy Church; degrading for the son to pay filial reverence to the father; prodigal and rash, to jeopardize his mighty honors in condescension to the servant of servants. Alas! the pride of these last days, and the strife for precedence, have been the only irreparable injury to the kingly honor, which has fallen in Christian times.

The temporal judgments of God having been set forth in these two most signal instances, the abasement of Satan, and the exaltation of the Saints; the one high in the celestial ranks, the others lowly and insignificant, the refuse of this wretched world: what remains but that the eternal judgment be finally pronounced? The justice of the Creator having been vindicated, his goodness demonstrated, and the purpose of his creation seemingly accomplished, the few remaining years bring us quickly to the end, which changes not forever.

7 And when the thousand years shall be finished, Satan shall be loosed out of his prison, and shall go forth, and seduce the nations, which are over the four quarters of the earth, Gog, and Magog, and shall gather them together to battle, whose number is as the sand of the sea.

If Satan be at liberty, he is assuredly able to seduce the nations, and if the reprobate be permitted, they will certainly conspire to set up a kingdom independent absolutely of the divine government; and so doing, they, by the inherent force of their fallen nature, hasten all things to dissolution. In the ages of the former ignorance, the guilt was less; but now it demands the advent of the Son of God, not again to repair their evil works, but to bury them forever in the darkness of the abyss. The distinctive excellence, so to speak, of the Christian religion is, that it is Catholic: the understanding being instructed in all truth, the mind nurtured with the grace of perfect virtues, and the soul enlarged to a sovereign charity, the human creature is regenerated a child of God, and partakes of the universality of the Creator. To apostatize therefore from this inheritance, will be an infinite loss; and hence we see in the last days, that the wants of ungodly men are immeasurable; their desires leap to the ends of the earth, and they yearn after a carnal felicity which is to be as universal as the Catholic verity. Now it is evident that an evil like this must be propagated indefinitely. It could only be originated among the Christian nations, but once conceived, the vicious impulse is naturally communicated to the barbarous nations; and by force of the superior energy of the former, the multitudes out of the four quarters of the earth are also seduced, with the promises of an infinite prosperity, to violate their ancient and cherished associations of patriotism and religion, and to renounce every tradition and principle which is opposed to the progress and thrift of the age. And so far forth, they all stand ready to battle against sacred truth, either explicitly or implicitly: perhaps the known truth of revelation, perhaps the natural truth written in the heart; here the express injunctions of Scripture, there the spontaneous convictions of the common understanding. Every conceivable form of hostility to sacred truth, may be thus appropriated to one of two categories: the secret, or the open hatred, of the law of God; which is the plain signification of the words Gog (tectum,) and Magog (de tecto,) or odium tectum, and odium detectum, as commonly understood by the Holy Fathers. Gog is the more malignant enemy, who lurks within the pale of civilization; Magog, the wild, untamed, heathen. The former is wrapped up in the sophistry, and sheltered under the conventionalism of a refined society; the other, rough, uncouth, and ignorant, is without method or order in his hatred of the Cross. Which ignorance or simplicity of the latter, is aptly indicated by another variation of the second definition, namely: quod tectum?[1] as if expressive of the doubt, or scorn, or wonder, of the untutored infidel. Considered as a unity, this insurrection of the nations, will be that vast and motley aggregation of the classic and the barbaric peoples, which, in numbers and physical advantages, outvies the Christian civilization. And because there appears to enter into it much of the Christian character, or many Christian traits, it also simulates the interior and secret virtue, which is proper to the religion of the Cross. In a word, it is that universal civilization, which is the counterfeit of the Catholic Evangelization; that earthly aggrandizement, which is at war with the spiritual edification of the human race. And now, in respect of the end itself, may there not already be discerned, in this progression of the nations, a preparation for the advent of the Divine Master? The herd of the Gentiles is about to be gathered within what is called the "pale of civilization." The pale of civilization, however, is not the fold of Christ, and therefore it does not follow that they will be aggregated to the Christian Church. And at the same time, though not Christianity itself, this civilization is, nevertheless, a sound of the truth: it is an echo of God's Word, it is an intelligence of his Gospel, which inevitably and inextricably shall cleave to it, and attend it to the uttermost parts of the earth. But when all have heard the tidings of salvation, when the times of ignorance are wholly scattered, and when the Word of the Cross has been made familiar to the race, then may the consummation come, and the sign of the Son of man appear in heaven.

The Prophet Ezechiel[2] was directed to denounce "Gog, the land of Magog, the chief prince of Mosoch and Thubal,"

[1] St. Jer. Heb. Nom. [2] Ezechiel xxxviii. and xxxix.

and to him it was said, "Thou shalt fall upon the mountains of Israel; thou and all thy bands." Of Magog, it was added: "I will send a fire on Magog, and on them that dwell confidently in the islands; and they shall know that I am the Lord." Under the ancient dispensation, the cultivated and the barbarous nations of the earth, alike dwelt apart from the people of God. But the former, that is Gog, is addressed in the first person, because he came at times into actual collision with them, while the other nations remained at a distance, gross and insensible as the dull earth. Considered relatively with one another, and both with the people of God, Gog was the type by excellence of the whole wide world, or the land that lay in darkness; and the chief prince of Mosoch, (folly,) and Thubal, (all things,) that is, of all earthly vanities. But he was to be overthrown upon the mountains of Israel, where the salvation of mankind was achieved, and to fall before the power of the Cross; while even the uttermost parts of the earth were also to be disturbed from their false security, by the fire of charity, which was carried by the evangelists to the ends of the world. Formerly, then, the land of Magog was merely a title of Gog; and because of its profound rusticity or obscurity, treated as an impersonal appendage or property of the other. But in the last days, it is brought into closer communication with the Christian peoples; and now it is made to stand up on its feet; that no man may be excused, but that side by side with the progress of human knowledge and of human arts, the standard of the Cross may be advanced, and every soul be admonished of a judgment to come. Gog and Magog, therefore, are the children of this world, far and near, black and beautiful, the old Gentile race who secretly or avowedly are the enemies of evangelical truth; whose numbers are as the sand of the sea, and in respect of their numbers alone, have they any title to be compared with the faithful generation, the seed of Abraham and of Christ.

8 And they ascended upon the breadth of the earth, and surrounded the camp of the saints, and the beloved city.

In the last confusion of the nations, it would seem that they are not to be concentrated at one common point or term of space, but rather, they ascend upon the breadth of the earth; they everywhere rise up from that repose, which is common with the animated nature, to that active industry which aspires after an independence or immunity of divine control. They are assembled together to battle, when their minds are united in one purpose: to perfect the material knowledge, whereby their first parents were deluded; and to crush the evangelical wisdom, which forbids us to be solicitous about earthly goods, about the morrow, or any one of all the days of this life, which are as it were without a future, without any perfection, or solid progress, but are only transitory as the smoke, and worthless as the dust.

If the camp of the saints be the tents of Holy Church, whose faithful soldiers maintain the Christian warfare in every land, and guard her distant outposts in heat, in cold, and in want, the beloved city may be the fortress itself of sacred truth, the rock on which the Church is built, the cherished citadel, our strength and our last hope in all the changing scenes of this life. As when St. Peter was imprisoned, the Church prayed for him without ceasing, so when his successor in the Roman see is oppressed, do the faithful everywhere suffer with him; and their love is proved when they guard his honor with filial reverence, when they cherish his divine rights and his sacred person, as the apple of their eye.

Now, at last, the camp and the city alike of Holy Church, are surrounded with the overwhelming numbers of the reprobate; but the gates of hell shall never prevail against it, for, when its defenders are so trampled, and their life so nearly spent, that there seem to be scarcely any left to confess the name of Jesus, and to carry his cross on earth, then the year of grace is ended, and vengeance long delayed begins.

9 And fire came down from God out of heaven, and devoured them: and the devil, who seduced them, was cast into the pool of fire and brimstone, where both the beast

10 And the false prophet shall be tormented day and night forever and ever.

"Let God arise, and let his enemies be scattered: and let them that hate him, flee before his face."[1] "A fire shall go before him, and shall burn his enemies round about."[2] Before that awful presence, the earth is purged by fire, and the powers of this world are suddenly swept away. First, Satan, who seduced the human race from its innocence; and afterward the beast, the earthly tyrant or Antichrist, who has had power in his day to destroy the souls of the multitudes, by the terror of his law; and again, the false prophet, who has usurped the office of a heavenly teacher to deceive them with false hopes of earthly happiness, and has taught them to adore the mundane glories with divine honors.

11 And I saw a great white throne, and him that sat upon it, from whose presence the earth and heaven fled away, and there was no place found for them.

In the last day, "The powers of heaven shall be moved."[3] "The elements shall be dissolved with heat, and the earth and the works that are in it, shall be burnt up."[4] The celestial spirits are moved to admiration, at the new order of created things; the celestial bodies, though they suffer no change of their intrinsic properties, have this mutation from their present condition, that they are forever put to rest. In this lower sphere of human life, the heavens and the earth, the air and the dry land, "which were out of water, and through water, consisting by the word of God,"[5] these, which constitute our visible world, are purified by fire; the elements, so long polluted by the contact of a sinful race, so infected with the continual alternations of heat and cold, of generation and corruption, are renovated to their last perfection, and to a certain proportion with the glorified bodies of the just. Of the intelligent creation subsisting here within this world,

[1] Psalms lxxvii. [2] Psalms xcvi. [3] Mat. xxiv. 29.
[4] 2 Peter iii. 10. [5] 2 Peter iii. 5.

Satan is instantly cast into the pool of fire and brimstone, because for him there is no other state of transition possible; the rest of the reprobate then on earth, are to be tormented with him, but this is not affirmed of them absolutely in the same instant of time, because, being destroyed by the fire of judgment, they may immediately after be revived in the resurrection for their final doom; while Satan, as a pure spirit, is subject to none of these transmutations of bodily life and death. In a former chapter, it is said, the beast and the false prophet are cast alive into the pool of fire; as if the perfection of their malice merited a punishment as instantaneous as that which falls on Satan; now since this were something more than the common death, it may be supposed to include the natural dissolution of the body and soul, just as the destruction of the whole necessarily implies the destruction of a part; and, therefore, the distinction just defined, in regard to other reprobate souls, is in some measure applicable, if not strictly so, to the beast and the false prophet. The bodies of the just being dissolved in death, will also be instantly renovated in a joyful resurrection to life eternal. When it is said the earth and heaven fled away, and there was no place found for them, it is not supposed that their substance is annihilated, but their visible form, and this present scene of animal existence, are scattered forever.

The thought of judgment is formidable even to just men, but they confide in the justice of the Son of God, that, before his sacred throne of spotless white, no virtue can possibly suffer loss, nor the least good work fail of its eternal reward.

12 And I saw the dead great and small, standing before the throne; and the books were opened: and another book was opened, which is *the book* of life; and the dead were judged by those things which were written in the books, according to their works.

How tremendous is the moment of judgment, when all that have ever lived and died, are summoned before the throne of God! When, at length, the acts are proved, the cause is ended, and the irrevocable sentence is pronounced forever! The countless works done in the body, both good and bad, are signified by many books; but the single intention of the just, is not divided among many, but is inscribed in one book of life. The book of life is one, as truth is one; but error is manifold, and the acts, even of good men, are not every one in uniform accordance with the law of God, while the evil deeds of the bad are contradictory with truth, with charity, and with one another.

13 And the sea gave up the dead, that were in it: and death and hell gave up their dead, that were in them: and they were judged every one according to their works.

Those who are dead in the sea, may be the souls of the faithful, who have been buried with Christ in the waters of baptism; or, all who have passed from this life by the peaceful death of the just, and who rest as it were in the waters, inasmuch as their spirits partake of life, which is signified by the element of water. But those who have died in sin, belong wholly to death; and those in hell, complete the full number of the reprobate, whether spirits of devils or of men.

14 And hell and death were cast into the pool of fire. This is the second death.

Death, to the common understanding, seems merely a negation of life, a nonentity; but, if this be true of the body, it is not so of the spirit, and death would hardly deserve the name of death, were it not for the real anguish of the lost soul, which endures the penalty of death, not for a moment, but forever. And as hell would no longer be hell, were it not for the malice of the damned, so death and hell, (which are here employed figuratively, the effect being put for the cause,) will signify respectively: the human beings who are dead in soul and body, and the fallen angels, who, though not obnoxious to the death of the body, are yet subject to that spiritual perdition of hell which is even more grievous; and which contains the other, as the greater the less; or as being itself the term and last result of death.

All these unhappy and accursed beings, as their works deserve, are condemned to the place of endless torments, which is the second death. And here it is to be observed how the blessed Apostle makes no singular mention of any resur rection or death, except the first resurrection, and the second death; for on these alone depend the eternal state. He who has part in the first resurrection is saved forever; he who deserves the second death is lost forever. The first resurrection is that which we must desire, and for which we must diligently labor; the second death is that which is indeed terrible, and infinitely to be dreaded. The first death can do but little harm, the second can do none to the just. The second resurrection will not disturb the rest of the saints, nor will it solace the woes of the impious.

15 And whosoever was not found written in the book of life, was cast into the pool of fire.

Moreover, there are some, even among the people of God, whose souls have been consecrated in baptism, and who have been called to the inheritance of the blessed, but who have secretly despised the lowly way of the Cross, or have neglected to adorn their souls with the wedding garment of virtuous works, and therefore are condemned at last to be cast into the exterior darkness. "There shall be weeping and gnashing of teeth. For many are called, but few are chosen."

CHAPTER XXI.

THE condemnation of the guilty being pronounced, the impious are banished from the presence of God, and from the scene of this fair creation, which is henceforth renewed in the splendor of holiness; while the universe of his spiritual inheritance, is established immovably in the salvation of the sons of God.

1 And I saw a new heaven, and a new earth. For the first heaven and the first earth was passed away; and the sea is no more.

The principal divisions of the physical world are three: heaven, earth, and sea; or substances, fluid, solid, and liquid. In the new creation of the future state, the two former are renovated in perpetuity; but the latter ceases to exist in its own order, being resolved by fire into one or the other of the two remaining classes. That is, literally speaking, such appears to be the sense of the text; and there seems to be analogy for it, in that common order of things by which they proceed from imperfection to perfection, or from that which is less perfect, to that which is more perfect. The water has been regarded hitherto as a nobler element than earth, but this was in respect of its activity and volatility, and as it is an emblem of the human life. But in itself, stability is better than instability, and therefore, in things heavenly, the sea has been described as a sea of glass, or a sea of crystal; and as we approach the eternal state, the resemblance of the restless element of water to the soul which has passed away from this life, ceases accordingly. Therefore to leave aside for the present, the former signification of this emblem, and to pass beyond and outside of the whole scene of active life, it may be said that in the order which proceeds from the imperfect to the perfect: The waters were first. Afterward, the waters were divided, by the firmament, from above to below.[1] Again, the lower sphere was subdivided, between the dry land and the seas. The sea, therefore, (which, in Hebrew, is all waters, fresh or salt,) remains always as a waste or residuum, which, by a further development toward perfection, and by a final distinction, may be wholly reduced to the other classes of substance above designated.

Again, in the former ages, when it repented God that he had made man on the earth, and in sorrow he desired to call back the work which he had made, we know that the waters of the deluge returned upon the world, and it perished

[1] Gen. i.

beneath the waves. But afterwards, when the sacrifice of Noe ascended as a sweet savor to heaven, it was promised that there should "no more be waters of a flood to destroy all flesh."[1] For the sake of just men, the present order of this world shall not be turned back, but shall persevere to its consummation; which consummation is by fire, for "the heaven and earth that now are, are reserved unto fire against the day of judgment."[2] Therefore, beginning in water, and perfected in fire, the world, in its progress to maturity, is first emancipated from the hazards of the waters, and finally disengaged or wholly liberated from every vicissitude of the same, being fixed in a condition of absolute stability. And indeed it is easy to conceive a heaven and earth that shall be immutable, but a sea without motion, or without any volatility whatever, is not agreeable to the imagination, even if it were possible for the mind to abstract this property of liquidity or instability, which seems to pertain so nearly to its very essence.

But however these things may be, the mystical signification is plain. The new heaven and new earth being the sanctified spirits, and the glorified bodies of the just, who are then conducted "unto the perfect man, unto the measure of the age of the fulness of Christ,"[3] the sea is no more: because the voyage of life is ended, its perils are passed, and the soul is fixed in that true happiness which can never be lost, nor can ever fluctuate for a single moment in the least uncertainty. Again, if by the sea be understood the waters of Baptism; that sacred institution is no more, when the faithful, once buried with Christ, are finally risen to his divine life, and are reformed like to the body of his glory.[4] Or if it be human society in respect of its spiritual qualities; this is no more, when the passions are now at rest, the office of faith fulfilled, and reason no longer step by step toils after the truth, which is then beheld in the intuition which transcends time and sense. "For we know in part, and we prophesy in part. But when that which is perfect shall

[1] Gen. ix. 15. [2] 2 Peter iii. 7. [3] Ephes. iv. 13. [4] Phil. iii. 21.

come, that which is in part shall be done away."[1] Or finally, the sea as Christianity is no more; when the office of the Roman Church is ended, and the Church militant gives place to the Church triumphant.

2 And I John saw the holy city the new Jerusalem coming down from God out of heaven, prepared as a bride adorned for her husband.

Unlike the productions of the natural order which proceed from beneath to above, and from the seas or the earth aspire upward to the light of day, the new Jerusalem, the peaceful city of the Blessed, comes down from God and condescends to men: even as "Every best gift, and every perfect gift, is from above, coming down from the Father of lights, with whom there is no change nor shadow of vicissitude."[2] Therefore it rests graciously upon the little ones of the earth, who are to God, as a bride to her husband; who exalts not herself, nor is elated by any merit of her own; but whose glory it is, that, adorned with perfect virtues, she deserves to be loved by her Sovereign Lord, to be cherished by him who alone gives value to her graces, and to be defended by him, who alone can make her adornments a reasonable service, due to his sacred honor.

3 And I heard a great voice from the throne, saying: Behold the tabernacle of God with men; and he will dwell with them: And they shall be his people: and God himself with them shall be their God:

Thus the relation of the Creator to the souls of men, is more sacred and blessed than any the most tender and intimate friendship which the heart could devise, or the mind dare to conceive. And the great voice of revelation has declared plainly this truth, and has impressed it upon the conscious soul with such lustre, that the man of good will may thereby rejoice as in the light of noon-day: In sole posuit tabernaculum suum.[3]

[1] 1 Cor. xiii. 9. [2] James i. 17. [3] Psalms xviii. 6.

4 And God shall wipe away all tears from their eyes: and death shall be no more; nor mourning, nor crying, nor sorrow shall be any more; for the former things are passed away.

As the natural prudence which toils in want that it may afterward rest in affluence, is amiable; so is the humble penitent lovely in her tears, and wise unto eternal life. For soon the former life of shame and grief is passed away, and the justified soul succeeds to an inheritance of joy and an everlasting name.

5 And he who sat on the throne, said: Behold, I make all things new. And he said to me: Write, for these words are most faithful and true.

Born in sin, and reared in sorrow, the beloved of God are renovated in that ineffable life which is stronger than death, more mighty than the woes and insults of a world of malice. No pain nor decay can touch them, no burden oppress, no distance weary them; nor a desire, nor an imagination can bring one shadow of delay or doubt over the brightness of their perfected nature, henceforth resplendent in the salvation of our most Holy Redeemer: who liveth, and reigneth, world without end.

Because of our human infirmity, it is said again: Write, for these words are most faithful and true. The joys of heaven are so far removed from the natural experience, that human language falters in the description, and labors in feeble negatives; wherefore there is necessary a repeated assurance, that the mind may be sustained, and kept in the remembrance of things so salutary and important. For if men argue and divide upon the common truths, which are published and vindicated in the visible example of good men here on earth, it were to be feared that they are quite thoughtless about the heavenly truths, which transcend both observation and discourse alike. But now, in the year of grace, they are admonished, by word and by act, of the reality and the magnitude of the salvation which is dispensed in Holy Church, in an abundance so excellent, that it seems an anticipation of heaven itself. So obvious, indeed, is this conclusion, that it has been a vexed question, whether these first five verses of the present chapter are not applicable to the Church, rather than to the Paradise of the Blessed. It is certain, that the blessings of Christianity cannot be over-estimated by any power of imagination, nor exaggerated by any language. Now, if the praises of Holy Scripture are inadequate, both to the joys of heaven, and to the sacred mysteries of the Christian dispensation; this, at least, is evident: that, of the two, they fall short of the former, more than they overrun the value of the latter; and hence they will, generally speaking, be better proportioned to these, than to the heavenly joys. It is true, that following immediately after the condemnation of the reprobate, this passage of the salvation of the elect seems to pertain also to the eternal state; but by the goodness of God, grace abounds unto life, more than sin unto death, and while damnation is incident to the end alone, salvation takes possession of the soul from beforehand; and heaven is even nearer than hell, to the pilgrim in this valley of death. Inasmuch then, as the Church is the depositary of salvation, and of the merits of eternal life, it is the inchoation of heaven, or of that true felicity which all naturally desire; and which, being of itself far removed from the notice of a sinful race, is yet brought so near to mankind, that the kingdom of heaven is said to be at hand, or it is within the souls of the just; not merely by desire, but by possession, and only the fruition is not consummated in this life. Therefore, let us review these words of the inspired text, and compare their meaning with the tokens of the Catholic Church, and once more repeat the praises of our Holy Mother.

"And I saw a new heaven, and a new earth. For the first heaven and the first earth was passed away, and the sea is no more." There was a new heaven for this world, when, with the new revelation of the Christian religion, the minds of men were instructed in the fulness of divine wisdom; and a new earth, when the evangelical counsels reformed their manners to angelic purity. And the first heaven was passed away, when the sphere of the intelligence was purged of a devilish mythology, and of the fatal errors of a pagan philosophy, and when idolatry and demon worship gave way to the pure worship of the one true God. The first earth was passed away, when the former vices which infested the bodies of men, and suffocated the life of the rational mind, were chastised and driven out; when ferocity gave place to clemency, rapacity to charity, and incontinence to virginity. And then the sea was no more, because the storm of evil passions was hushed, and it was impossible that they should waver in the least uncertainty of precept or of practice, whose faith was confirmed like the solid rock.

"And I, John, saw the holy city, the new Jerusalem, coming down from God out of heaven, prepared as a bride adorned for her husband." Within this fair world of Christian truth, is established the new Jerusalem, the holy city of the Church; which is no abstract scheme of a possible religion, but is the visible channel of salvation to the souls of men. To which the Apostle testifies: I, John, saw; and in every age do the successors of the Holy Apostles, audibly invite their fellow-men to contemplate the beauty of the Spouse of Christ, to behold her precious jewels, the unsullied blood of her martyrs, the merits of her confessors, the wisdom of her doctors, and the piety of her virgins: to behold them, and so discern that she is indeed from God, and as a bride, prepares herself for the advent of her omnipotent Lord.

"And I heard a great voice from the throne, saying: Behold the tabernacle of God with men, and he will dwell with them. And they shall be his people, and God himself with them shall be their God." Here is the tabernacle, where God condescends to be really present with men, and where they are elevated to be the temples of the Holy Ghost.

"And God shall wipe away all tears from their eyes; and death shall be no more, nor mourning, nor crying, nor sorrow shall be any more; for the former things are passed away." In this holy estate, the just man is released from the common grief of the sons of earth. If he perseveres in the life of grace, he is secure against the terrors of death forever. The remorse and shame of mortal sin, are impossible for him. If he makes but such progress in a holy life, as is the reasonable service of gratitude and an ordinary prudence, one by one the sorrows of this life are trodden under foot, and his heart is fixed on the things that are above. And if any tribulation should for a moment disturb him, yet this is not so but that tribulation itself brings joy to his heart, above measure greater than the sorrow, and his tears of love are prized as a precious gift of heaven. An order like this is the rule, the common law of progress in the Christian life. And if there be some, or many feeble souls, who in the beginning are afflicted and cast down with pains of mind or of body; or other frail ones, who relapse into sin and spend their days in tears and despondency; yet this cannot make void the divine constitution of the Church, whose virtue is proved by the examples, not of her degenerate, but of her perfect children.

"And he who sat on the throne said: Behold I make all things new. And he said to me: Write; for these words are most faithful and true." The saints testify how all things are new, when the carnal maxims are by them wholly reversed; and when they are known to seek humiliations and to shun honors, to refuse pleasure, and to embrace suffering, to despise the life, and to sigh after the death of their bodies. And if this be an unearthly life, so is it a heavenly one, for otherwise it would not be heavenly. Thus do heaven and earth meet together, and it is true that even here, in our midst, is the holy city where God dwells with men; which, because it rests upon earth, does not therefore suffer any detriment of its celestial beauty, but itself adorns the land upon which it is built; transfusing life, and vigor, and grace to all around, in the kind and degree of which they may be capable; here attracting some through the medium of a chaste and lofty imagination, now addressing the intellect with the wisdom of its doctrine, and again engaging the heart by its copious fountains of unction and piety. Accordingly, in every age, its influence is felt; in some, it is acknowledged and praised; but if not always recognized, as the life of our human generation, yet never at any time without some attestation of its vital energy, even among its enemies. Hence, the statesman, the poet, the artist, each render their tribute to the holy city, to which they are indebted for so much which adorns their works; while the philosopher, who is most rancorous in infidelity, does not refuse some testimonial of its excellence of proportion, of splendor, or of some utility. There are those, whose life and writings contain nothing which is derogatory to the honor of the Church; there are none who do not lend some evidence of her benignant influence. There are many whose works are her unqualified praise; there are none whose acts and words are filled up with unqualified censure and dishonor to the Mother of our souls. And again, their sentences of respect, are those which are best remembered, while the ribaldry is forgotten; for, when they frame their words to declare her virtues, then from the very subject do they derive harmony of accent, and grace of language, and dignity of meaning; and the simplicity of truth, which finds a sweet response in the human heart, causes their sound to be prolonged, and in the end, perhaps, to admonish of heaven, more than their discordant, short-lived notes of error, had once inveigled minds to perdition. Therefore, as the soul beams forth in the action of the body, so does Holy Church irradiate the human society, imparting health and strength by her presence; but when she withdraws, society languishes, and the Christian generation approaches its term; then man ceases to struggle after the eternal life, and the works of God are ended.

6 And he said to me: It is done: I am alpha and omega; the beginning and the end. To him that thirsteth I will give of the fountain of the water of life, gratis.

Behold the purpose and the end of the works of God: the

Revelation of his goodness, and his Judgment according to truth. And He is the beginning and the end, who issues the eternal decree, and who executes the last sentence ; who has created all that is good, and has paid the debt of all that is bad ; who reigns gloriously in heaven, and prosperously from the tree of the cross ; the one all lovely ; beloved of angels and men, and the one Beloved in the most sacred Trinity, for the Father loveth the Son, and hath given all things into his hand.

7 He that shall overcome, shall possess these things : and I will be his God, and he shall be my son.

With him are the certain rewards of salvation, or of condemnation. To every one who desires it, eternal life is freely offered ; and to him who overcomes the temptations of this world, nothing is refused which a God can bestow.

8 But to the fearful, and unbelieving, and the abominable, and murderers, and fornicators, and sorcerers, and idolaters, and all liars, their portion shall be in the pool burning with fire and brimstone, which is the second death.

On the other hand, there is no loss which can be suffered, no depth of woe, like the pains of the accursed, who are driven from his presence. These are the cowardly ones, who are ashamed to confess the Son of man ; the infidels, who openly deny him ; the abominable, whose life is that of the cattle, without any sense of an eternal state ; the murderers and fornicators ; the sorcerers, who worship the spirits of demons ; the idolaters, who adore the pomps and riches of earth ; and all liars, who love darkness, and hypocrisy, and treason, and who hate the plain words of truth : this is the dreadful catalogue of the reprobate ; each one of whom, taken singly and apart, how insignificant and pitiful is he, even in his own eyes ! And, though their numbers seem formidable, yet are they as nothing : "Being born, forthwith they ceased to be ; and have been able to show no mark of virtue."[1]

Here is the end of the works of the Creator and of the

[1] Wisd. v. 13.

creature: a sure eternity of infinite consequence to the rational soul. What is the gain to the inaccessible Godhead? What is the loss in the darkness of the abyss, who can say? Altitudinem cœli, et profundum abyssi, quis dimensus est? [1] But steadfast and resplendent is the sacred truth, which makes lovely the way of virtue, which abhors the pit of vice; which seeks justice, but shuns iniquity; and which irradiates the understanding, with an eternal conviction: that ONE THING IS NECESSARY, and they who choose it shall live forever.

Now the blessed apostle passes hence to the contemplation of the heavenly city: and thereupon the inquiry naturally presents itself, why should there be this second rehearsal of the beatitude of the elect? Or, if it be something more than a repetition, how is it distinguished from that consideration of the same, which has been already entertained? So sweet is the thought of the true happiness which all naturally desire, that it may well be deemed a happy privilege to return to its meditation; and a sacred duty to repair often to those higher joys, only the anticipation of which is able to refresh the mind, wearied and stained with this warfare of life. But again, there is another reason for the twofold consideration of the heavenly kingdom, because it pertains, in some sense, both to time and to eternity. To the time of this life, because every man that cometh into the world has been enlightened to some sense of his true happiness; and those secret inspirations of the beauty of virtue and of the sacredness of truth, which enter his soul, are a sure copy of the beauty and purity of the supernal joys. And after this life, though these may be held in full possession by the saints now in heaven, yet the final beatitude deserves to stand apart, distinguished from every other, as the eternal rest of that heavenly Sabbath, which is marked by neither time nor change, which is the perfection and divine fruition of every good without end. Wherefore, if it please the reader, the following section might be regarded as an eighth division of the work, or

[1] Eccles. i. 2.

THE OCTAVE

of these sacred visions, in the vision of divine glory.

9 And there came one of the seven angels, who had the vials full of the seven last plagues, and spoke with me, saying: Come, and I will show thee the bride, the wife of the Lamb.

The holy angel, who instructs the apostle in the divine joys, whether those of the church, (as was before noticed, chap. xix., verse 7,) or of the final beatitude, its counterpart, is one of those who poured out the last plagues upon the earth; as if the defection of earth, and the increment of heaven, were correlative; or as if the perdition of the flesh were the rapture of the spirit.

10 And he took me up in spirit to a great and high mountain: and he showed me the holy city Jerusalem, coming down out of heaven from God.

To contemplate worthily the peaceful beatitude of the heavenly Jerusalem, the mind must be detached from earthly things, the heart denuded of every carnal affection, and the soul must ascend far above the common consolations; for though the Sacred Bride be always worthy of her Lord, yet does her final beatitude transcend all her former graces.

11 Having the glory of God; and the light thereof like unto a precious stone, as it were to a jasper stone, as crystal.

The holy city has the glory of God, when God is "all in all;" or it has a divine glory, because it rests in the vision of God. Its light, like the jasper stone of various colors, and yet as crystal: may signify the beautiful variety in perfect harmony, of its many virtues.

12 And it had a wall great and high, having twelve gates; and in the gates twelve angels, and names written thereon, which are the names of the twelve tribes of the children of Israel.

The wall great and high shows its perpetual immunity from every harm; or it shows with how great care it has been prepared from the former ages, and with how great diligence it has been built up. The twelve tribes of Israel are written on the gates, because they were at the entrance to the city of God. And the Holy Angels are associated with them: for they from the beginning led the way; and by their ministration, is all our human race conducted unto the eternal gates.

13 On the east three gates; and on the north, three gates; and on the south, three gates; and on the west, three gates.

This holy city has been designed by God to gather together in the confession of the Most Holy Trinity, the souls of men from out of the four quarters of the earth; and to yield, on every side, a free and abundant access to its mansions of bliss.

14 And the wall of the city had twelve foundations; and in them, the twelve names of the twelve apostles of the Lamb.

It is established upon the foundation of the apostles: that foundation which has been planted deep in our own lowly borders, the domain of Christian and Apostolic Truth.

15 And he that spoke with me, had a measure, a golden reed, to measure the city and the gates thereof, and the wall.

Heaven itself is framed in golden measure and order: the city, the gates, the wall: the end, the means, and their application; or the mansion of bliss, its approaches, and those who are acquired into its sure possession.

16 And the city is situate four-square; and the length thereof is as great as the breadth: and he measured the city with the golden reed for twelve thousand furlongs: and the length, and the height, and the breadth of it are equal.

The square signifies rectitude; for, on every side, the perfect man will show the exact measure of well-balanced virtues. As also Holy Church, however viewed, or by whatever tribulation it may be tried, can be convicted of no deformity; but is proved ever true to the rule of divine equity, both in the length of her patience, in the breadth of her charity, and in the height of her holy intention. The heavenly city measures by twelves of thousands: because its pastors are twelve, and their flocks are thousands.

17 And he measured the wall thereof a hundred forty-four cubits, the measure of a man, which is of an angel.

The number twelve, which represents the totality of the patriarchs, or prophets, as also of the apostles, may be supposed to embrace the whole former and the whole latter times; and thus the multiplied merits of angels and of men, gives the measure of the wall; which, compared with the city itself, is as the cubit to the furlong. The latter signifying the large liberality of the Creator, the former and lesser measure is nearer to the capacity of the creature. In one, is displayed the magnificence of the divine Architect; in the other is recognized the hand of his workmen. And herein the measure of the angel and of the man are equal; for if the man has been made a little less than the angel, so now his Christian dignity may well be deemed sufficient to fill up the former minority; while both on earth, and from the realms of heaven, has it been proved how the saints may exercise a celestial skill and an angelic office, in the edification of the faithful servants of God: the little ones who are "built upon the foundation of the apostles and prophets, Jesus Christ himself being the chief corner-stone; in whom all the building fitly framed together, groweth into a holy temple in the Lord."[1]

18 And the building of the wall thereof was of jasper-stone; but the city itself pure gold, like to clear glass.

The distinction between the city and its wall, which is indicated in the text, may have its reason in the exterior good works of the saints, as distinguished from the interior and supernatural motive of the same. The former are as it were the sacramental matter, of which an eternal felicity is the form. Outwardly, how various are the works and merits of the elect! who are gathered from out of the universe, celestial, terrestrial, and infernal; of angels, of saints, and of imperfect souls, whose works in part, suffer loss. But

[1] Ephes. ii. 20.

within, the pure golden charity which endures forever, is one and the same in all; and though now, when one "knows not whether he be worthy of love or hatred,"[1] it seems the most secret and hidden of the virtues, yet then it will be as transpicuous, as it is ever lovely and precious.

19 And the foundations of the wall of the city were adorned with all manner of precious stones. The first foundation, jasper: the second, sapphire: the third, a calcedony: the fourth, an emerald:

What shall be found to compare with the merits of the just, so well as the things which are most precious in the eyes of men, those whose qualities are most rare of purity, of incorruptibility, of undying beauty and lustre? These are the precious stones, in which are expressed the essential properties of the solid rocks: the firm foundations of the earth, and the pillars of its everlasting hills. Therefore the solid virtues of the just, are likened to jewels, for their value; and they are set in the foundations of the holy city, because of the magnitude of that eternal reward, which takes its rise from them, and is proportioned to their just desert. Like the precious stones of the Rational, in which were written the names of the twelve tribes of Israel, these, in the text, may be attributed severally to the holy apostles, in whom the assemblage of Christian virtues was manifested to the world. Briefly, they may be thus applied: The jasper, which is of various colors, and distinguished by its hardness, may represent St. Peter, the rock upon which the Church is built; and with whom is also to be associated St. Paul, his colleague. The sapphire, reminding us of the blue of heaven, is like St. Andrew, who led his brother to the Messias, and to the good hope of eternal life. The red of the calcedony, may signify the zeal of St. James, who, with his brother, were called the Boanerges; but the latter, St. John, is better known by the love which we may suppose to have tempered his impetuosity to that gentle condescension, which is denoted by the emerald.

[1] Eccles. ix. 1.

20 The fifth, sardonyx: the sixth, sardius: the seventh, chrysolite: the eighth, beryl: the ninth, a topaz: the tenth, a chrysoprasus: the eleventh, a jacinth: the twelfth, an amethyst.

The sardonyx, of red and white mixed, as referred to St. Philip, who was especially in the confidence of his Divine Master, may be an emblem of the prudence which unites in itself both wisdom and simplicity. The sardius, a flesh color, suggests the patience of St. Bartholemew, who suffered such cruel torments in his martyrdom. The gold color of the chrysolite, corresponds to the charity of St. Matthew, the publican; who, doubtless, loved much, because much was forgiven to him. The sea color of the beryl, is an emblem of St. Thomas, who, from the dejection of incredulity, passed to the confession of an exalted faith, in the divinity of his Lord. In the yellow of the topaz, may be discerned the maturity of many virtues, which gained for St. James, the son of Alpheus, the title of James the Just. The chrysoprase is green, the color of faith; it may be applied to St. Simon the Zealot, whose active faith was proved by his holy indignation against those who dishonored their Christian profession by unworthy lives. St. Jude, whose fortitude was evinced by his fearless denunciation of the heretics of his day, as well as by his bloody death, may be indicated by the jacinth, whose color is blood-red, or red mingled with yellow. The amethyst, which is violet, or the color of penance, may stand for the cardinal virtue of temperance, and be referred to St. Matthias, who was distinguished for his mortifications, and who would never cease to chastise his flesh and bring it into subjection, remembering the downfall of the apostate Judas, into whose place he had been assumed.

21 And the twelve gates are twelve pearls, one to each: and every several gate was of one several pearl: and the street of the city was pure gold, as it were transparent glass.

It has been said before, that in the twelve gates were twelve angels. The simple substance of the angelic nature is aptly represented by the undivided pearl, whose pure white, and perfect round, will not suffer correction, nor admit embellishment from any but the hand of its Creator. And not unlike the holy angels, were the prophets, whether as regards their sacred office, or the kindred purity of their souls; as is implied by those words of Scripture, which describe the Precursor: "Behold, I send my angel, and he shall prepare the way before my face."[1] Which way of truth is the golden street of wisdom; not as now obscured by the perversities of the human mind, but in that heavenly state, transparent with the glory of God.

22 And I saw no temple in it. For the Lord God Almighty is the temple thereof, and the Lamb.

This text constitutes a grand distinction between the final beatitude, and the present bliss of the saints. For, in the beginning of Part II., chap. vii., verse 15, it was said of the saints now passed to their rest, where they shall not hunger nor thirst any more, and where God shall wipe away all tears from their eyes, it was said of these: "Therefore they are before the throne of God, and serve him day and night in his temple." That is, amidst the glories of heaven, they still continue to intercede for us, and to send up continual aspirations to the throne of God, for the welfare of their fellow Christians now on earth. But, hereafter, these petitions must cease; for, when all have passed into the eternal state, there can be none for whom any oblation is again to be made. Then there will be no longer a temple, nor a sacrifice, nor the service of intercessors; but without any second causes or means, without any intervention of measure or condition, the Lamb will be the temple of his saints, the Lord God Almighty will be their glory and their absolute end.

23 And the city needeth not sun nor moon to shine in it: for the glory of God hath enlightened it: and the Lamb is the lamp thereof.

The light of heaven, the Lumen Gloriæ, is not a created cause, but the glory itself of the Creator; in the midst of

[1] Malach. iii. 1.

which, the humanity of our divine Savior shines with gracious lustre, for the perpetual joy of the Creature.

24 And nations shall walk in the light of it: and the kings of the earth shall bring their glory and honor into it.

The Christian religion has furnished not one people, but numberless nations, to the service of God; and under its benignant influence, the kings of the earth have submitted to the Son of God, their crowns and all their royal honors; and with their whole heart have hastened to embrace the evangelical counsels, and to run the way of eternal life.

25 And the gates thereof shall not be shut by day: for there shall be no night there.

This is the true Jerusalem, where is the perfection of peace; the heavenly home, which knows neither darkness nor danger, but whose gates stand open, and forever free from hostile fears.

26 And they shall bring the glory and honor of the nations into it.

How blessed are they who shall enter with the happy throng, which gathers in its train all that is good and amiable, all that is honorable and glorious, of the nations of the earth!

27 There shall not enter into it anything defiled, or any one that worketh abomination, or a lie; but they who are written in the book of life of the Lamb.

Assuredly, their happiness is none the less, because nothing defiled can enter with them; because they pass away from those whose sordid life is loathsome to the spiritual mind; and because they hear no more forever, the words of traitors who profess the eternal truth, yet are enslaved in the base friendship of the world. But they go rejoicing, in the company of the sons of God; and, on every side, they behold none but chosen souls, predestined from the ages of ages, to dwell amid the splendors of the saints.

CHAPTER XXII.

1 AND he showed me a river of water of life, clear as crystal, proceeding from the throne of God and of the Lamb.

God and the Lamb do reign from one equal and etérnal throne of the Father and of the Son; and from the Father and the Son proceedeth, with coequal majesty, the Holy Ghost, the Lord and Giver of life; who, in the beginning, moved over the waters, quickening them to the generation of this visible world; who has again regenerated the souls of his people by the waters of baptism; and who, in heaven, is the fountain of eternal life; not as now, wrapped in most sacred mystery from the human apprehension, but the river, clear as crystal, which maketh joyful the city of God. Fluminis impetus lætificat civitatem Dei.[1]

2 In the midst of the street thereof, and on both sides of the river, was the tree of life, bearing twelve fruits, yielding its fruit every month, and the leaves of the tree for the healing of the nations.

In the midst of the golden street of wisdom, stands the tree of the Cross, which is on both sides of the river; not alone deriving virtue from the waters, but itself constituting or determining that channel, through which the same sweet waters of life are derived to our souls. For the Father hath established the heavens, through his divine Son, and in the virtue of his Holy Spirit. Verbo Domini cœli firmati sunt, et Spiritu oris ejus omnis virtus eorum.[2] And, as the Church's calendar is adorned with the memorials of the saints, through every month of the Christian year, so does the Tree of the Cross crown the circle of eternity, with perennial fruits of sanctity, while its leaves are for the healing of the nations that even now are, in this our day: inasmuch as their safety rests not upon the things present, but is

[1] Psalms xlv. 5. [2] Psalms xxxii. 6.

suspended upon that distant and eternal state, which shapes all the ends of the servants of God. The nation, certainly, is not less than the man; but what is possible for an individual, is possible for a people. Now the wise man puts not his trust in princes, but is strong in divine faith, which is the true health of the soul; even so the nations that would be healed of their disorders, must cease to take counsel from the "wisdom which is earthly, sensual, devilish," and repair to that higher science which ends not in a temporal welfare, but pursues the common weal which is unseen and eternal. To be protected by divine Providence, is the true prosperity; to be estranged from its control, is to be accursed: and what art of men, or skill of ages, can invigorate the sinews, or empower the steps of him who staggers by his own weight, who reels by the force of his own act, who dashes his own feet and stumbles headlong, at every struggle to plant himself upon an inheritance which is not and cannot be his? Assuredly, he who would be prospered, must be sustained by Him in whose hand is every blessing; they who would be safe, must be bound by hope, as by a good anchor, to that distant shore where stands the tree of eternal life; the nations who would be healed, must lift up their hearts, and maintain the glory of that Most Holy Cross, which is the health of our human race and its everlasting joy.

3 And no curse shall be any more: but the throne of God, and of the Lamb shall be in it; and his servants shall serve him.

Then is fulfilled the universal prayer of the creature: Thy kingdom come; and then there is no more a curse, when God reigns in all, and there are none to breathe a thought of opposition to his holy will.

4 And they shall see his face: and his name shall be on their foreheads.

As the throne of God, and of the Lamb, is one; so, with the Holy Spirit, is their face one vision of the Most Holy Trinity in Unity. Beholding which, his servants are filled with an eternal joy; and in the presence of his majesty, are transformed to his likeness, and bear upon their brow the impress of his divine radiance.

5 And night shall be no more: and they shall not need the light of a lamp, nor the light of the sun; for the Lord God shall enlighten them; and they shall reign for ever and ever.

As the souls of the just are thus illumined with the uncreated light of the Godhead, so will their bodies be made more resplendent than the sun, and brighter than the most brilliant of the glories of this visible universe. And the servants of God reign forever and ever: when, being exalted to this great glory, the conscious soul discerns, also, its own capacity; that the all-wise Creator has given to it all things, and has done no injustice; has greatly magnified it, and has committed no disproportion; has set it up on high, and has still appointed to it its proper place; has invested it with the royal honors of a celestial throne, and has therein accorded to it its proper inheritance; through our beneficent, and ever glorious Lord and Savior, who liveth and reigneth, world without end.

6 And he said to me: These words are most faithful and true. And the Lord God of the spirits of the prophets sent his angel to show his servants the things which must be done shortly.

How easy it is for man to promise himself a temporal happiness! notwithstanding the countless obstacles and hazards of earthly ambition, still he puts no limits to his dreams of greatness, but, like Lucifer, he leaps insanely toward the utmost heights of grandeur, which can be surveyed within this sublunary sphere. On the other hand, he is timid and faint-hearted for the true greatness, faithless and cold to the peaceful aspirations which prompt him to expect, above measure exceedingly, an eternal weight of glory in heaven; wherefore we are again admonished that these words are most faithful and true, and this by the voice of our Divine Lord, who now speaks in his own person. He, in his infinite goodness, has sent his angel to instruct the beloved Apostle in the spirit of all the prophets, to complete the volume of his Holy Scripture, and to charge his servants that they stand ready for the fulfilment of his decrees.

7 And, behold, I come quickly. Blessed is he that keepeth the words of the prophecy of this book.

Blessed are they, who, in deed and in truth, await the coming of God to judgment. He has promised it shall be quickly, and his Christian generation has ever believed it. But it is the evil servant who says: "My lord is long a coming. And in the hour he hopeth not," when he has promised himself another good, when he thinks he has the earnest of his finite joys: then his lord cometh, his lofty schemes are laid low, and his insolent presumption is suddenly quenched.

8 And I, John, who have heard and seen these things. And after I had heard and seen, I fell down to adore before the feet of the angel, who showed me these things:

Before the contemplation of these sacred truths, how is the mind affected? What has the just man to say of himself? What is the trembling response of our human heart? "And I, John, who have heard and seen these things." The little one, before the awful compass of sacred truth. The feeble sigh of the mortal, before the boundless ocean of the Infinite. And as if languishing under the weight of his prophetic office, again he falls meekly at the feet of his heavenly companion, and acknowledges the lowliness of his service, and presumes not to stand in the company of the prophets.

9 And he said to me: See thou do it not: for I am thy fellow-servant, and of thy brethren the prophets, and of them who keep the words of the prophecy of this book: Adore God.

But the power of God is perfected in the weakness of men; and he, in his humility, is exalted to declare the marvellous works of the Lord of angels and of prophets. In which, he is the fellow-servant of the angels; and they also who keep the words of this prophecy, are like the angels, when they meditate the things unseen.

10 And he saith to me: Seal not the words of the prophecy of this book: for the time is at hand.

The words of this book are not to be sealed, because they are of immediate use; they are not to be laid aside for another age, but they are of instant and continual application to the Christian times.

11 He that hurteth, let him hurt still: and he that is filthy, let him be filthy still: and he that is just, let him be justified still: and he that is holy, let him be sanctified still.

The habits of vice are as inveterate as those of virtue are solid and constant. Commonly, the unjust man is uniformly unjust, and the virtuous one, uniformly virtuous. It is certain, also, that, in the passage of this life, no one remains inert and destitute of merit; but the compass of his acts as a whole, bears him nearer to heaven, or with every moment, drifts him downward to perdition. Let the unjust then persist in their injuries, and the filthy in their obscenities, provided the just abound in good works, and the virtuous advance in sanctity; for it is better that the good fruit be cultivated to its maturity, than that the bad be drugged to its counterfeit. We read how shipwrecked sailors, in the jaws of death, and when all hope of life is gone, sometimes abandon themselves to the vilest excesses of lust and intemperance; so in times of crime and disorder, we may judge how insensible infidel men are to the awful retribution of sin, when every suicide is an occasion of mockery, every murder furnishes a new jest, and every new scandal to chastity, is accepted with conscious gratification, as a proof of the nonentity of virtue or of the hopeless absurdity of a human sanctity. On the other hand, as little children sometimes have a deep insight of spiritual things when death is upon them; so the religious mind, as the end of the world draws nigh, is perhaps quickened to a clearer perception of the unseen things, and to an instinctive sense of the near approach of its Divine Judge; wherefore it hastens the preparation of good works, and yearns to renew its strength, in a more active and heroic practice of Christian perfection in the Catholic obedience.

12 Behold, I come quickly, and my reward is with me, to render to every man according to his works.

When the just are more strenuous in virtue, and the reprobate more obstinate in vice; when the tribulation of the one is greater, and the perversity of the other more grievous; then there is a double reason that the Lord, the just Judge, should render quickly to each according to their works.

13 I am alpha and omega, the first and the last, the beginning and the end.

He is the Alpha, who displays his magnificence for the visible instruction of our earliest years; and the Omega, who reads the hidden secrets of our inmost soul. He is the first to begin the Christian generation, and the last to end it, when, coming to Judgment, he enters this world, where no man shall enter afterward forever. He is first and last in the universe of existences, when none have been so high in glory, none so lowly in tribulation, as he.

14 Blessed are they that wash their robes in the blood of the Lamb; that they may have a right to the tree of life, and may enter in by the gates into the city.

Blessed are they who, in their humble measure, imitate the Lamb, whose blood taketh away the sins of the world; they who do no wrong, but who suffer injuries; who speak no lie, but are themselves reviled; who commit no violence, but are strong to endure the shock of injustice; for they are clothed with the precious merits of Christ, and they deserve, by virtue of his Holy Cross, an everlasting inheritance, into which they enter, not with the pomp of human wisdom, not in the pride of the human intellect, but, like little children, obedient to their spiritual guardians, the angels, the prophets, the apostles, and the pastors of their souls.

15 Without are dogs, and sorcerers, and the unchaste, and murderers, and those that serve idols, and every one that loveth and maketh a lie.

The difference in their degrees of merit, even between souls who are both in the state of grace, may be so great that the saints to whom it has been revealed, have been terrified at the vision. How vast, then, must be the contrast of the reprobate, who are utterly void of the life of grace! Compared to the former, they are as the wild beast to the innocent lamb. Like dogs, they stand without, howling enviously at the good they will neither accept for themselves, nor suffer others to hold in peaceable possession. These are the sorcerers, who dare to bring in their own inventions, or even the utterances of demons, for messages of divine wisdom. They delight in their own uncleanness, and find more joy in the hatred, than in the love, of their brother. They are the slaves of the earthly goods, of the paltry honors of this world, which savor of rottenness and the grave; and, in their secret soul, they blush at the ignoble servitude which gives no hope of liberty forever. They love the dark ways of craft and hypocrisy better than the open words of sincerity; they grope in the tortuous paths of error and treason; and shrink back from the light of truth, as if their very life were suddenly to be blasted. For, alas, they are without any purpose, when God is not in their intention; they are in fathomless confusion, when the heavenly order does not reign in their hearts, direct their acts, and guide their lives, in the paths of rectitude and of true honor.

16 I Jesus have sent my angel, to testify to you these things in the Churches. I am the root and stock of David, the bright and morning star.

He who first established the Church in his own blood, will have his Churches in every land and in every age, to remember in what numberless dangers of secret and of open enemies, in what reverses of splendor and poverty, of secular honor and of secular hatred, they must battle for his sacred truth; that while empires rise and fall, and peoples, and languages, and nations, follow in ever-changing succession through the restless scene of this world, they honor him who is the Priest forever, the Maker and the Royal Son of the Prophet King: that when the night of infidelity and the storm of persecution descend, they watch for him who is the bright and morning star, that will scatter every cloud of fear and sorrow; the true light that announces the glorious morning of resurrection to the life and joy that have no end.

17 And the Spirit and the bride say: Come. And he that heareth, let him say: Come. And he that thirsteth, let him come: and he that will, let him take the water of life, gratis.

O, what loving voices invite us to that heavenly home! How gracious are the inspirations of the most sacred Paraclete! How sweet the intercession of departed saints; how affectionate the gentle entreaties of holy Church; how cheering the fervent words of those who have proved the way that leadeth to eternal life! If one have but the desire of it, blessed is he in that sacred and honorable thirst. If the multitudes will only not refuse it, the infinite gift is freely their own. Truly this time of grace, is the day-star of heaven's perpetual light. "This is the day which the Lord hath made, let us be glad and rejoice in it."

18 For I testify to every one that heareth the words of the prophecy of this book: if any man shall add to these things, God shall add upon him the plagues written in this book.

How formidable is the anathema which guards this sacred book! He who presumes rashly in divine things, must suffer the penalty of his sacrilege: ignominy before the just, and derision among the reprobate. Wherefore, if I have exceeded in this work the measure of divine order, or the limits of my human subjection, I beseech the reader to take compassion; remembering my grievous necessity, which needs not the added burden of his censure, but which may be mercifully alleviated by his charitable prayers.

19 And if any man shall take away from the words of the book of this prophecy, God shall take away his part out of the book of life, and out of the holy city, and from these things which are written in this book.

Truth will not suffer any excess, nor any diminution. And whether one seems to exaggerate its purpose, or to impair its integrity, the bitter consequence is always to him the detriment of his own good. In the present work, if there are some profitable thoughts, the reader may be assured that they have been already uttered by better men, and he may rest in them with confidence. But all that is feeble or rash, this is my own; if the proper authority deign to reprehend it, may the author have grace to retract it.

20 He that giveth testimony of these things, saith: Surely I come quickly: Amen. Come, Lord Jesus.

As the other volumes of Holy Scripture pertain to the coming of the Messias, and to the institution of his Church, so this book of the Apocalypse regards principally his second coming to judgment. Therefore, since from first to last, this awful consideration has been presented, and continually represented to the Christian mind, behold now, the conclusion of the whole matter, the last word of God to men, recorded in the inspired pages: SURELY I COME QUICKLY. Assuredly, the good Christian, believing it, in every generation, watches for the fulfilment of this promise. And though the mind be sometimes swayed by the hope of temporal blessings, and distracted with the flattering promise of a better progress, and of some perfect order in human things, yet always it must return at last to the truth which is alone most sure: The Day of Judgment is at hand. Moreover, let the world deride it as it may, that frame of mind which meditates the last things, is most consonant to the Christian character, as it is also most worthy of a prudent understanding and a sound philosophy. Man does not need, nor even does he care, to.

be always cheered with sensible consolations in his pilgrimage; he is not made vigorous, only by the perpetual stimulus of the active life, he demands repose; now the soul will find rest, not in the things present, but in those that are final and eternal. The anguish of dissolution, the awful dangers which forerun the wreck of this world, none can dare to contemplate; but where is the rest? where is there any good hope? if not in the end itself, and in the promise of his coming. Therefore, in the virtue not of any human dictate, but of the Christian intelligence, elevated by faith, and instructed in the Catholic and Apostolic doctrine; as is our bounden duty, looking for and hasting unto the coming of the day of the Lord; and confiding in the goodness of the Almighty Word, who is pleased to desire our love even more than our fear, we will most humbly and faithfully respond: "Amen. Come, Lord Jesus."

21 The grace of our Lord Jesus Christ be with you all. Amen.

May the benediction of the Beloved Disciple be with us in life, and protect us in death; and may you, beloved reader, obtain of his merciful intercession, the pardon of the author's indiscretions, and of the vast imperfection of his labor: through the merits of our Lord Jesus Christ, to whom is the Honor, the Praise, and the Power, forever and ever. Amen.

GLOSSARY

OF THE

SYMBOLICAL TERMS OF THE APOCALYPSE,

ACCORDING TO THEIR GENERAL SIGNIFICATION.

ALTAR. Christ himself, is both the victim and the altar; or the Cross is, by excellence, the altar of the created universe.

ANCIENTS. The spiritual progenitors of the faithful under the former and the latter covenant, who represent the elect souls of the human race.

ANGEL. The minister of heaven, whether his nature be purely spiritual or merely human.

BABYLON. The World.

BEAST. Generically, the secular power; specifically, Antichrist.

BIRDS. Demons; spirits of evil.

BLOOD. False doctrine; that which is offensive or pernicious to the understanding; being to the mind, what bloodshed or murder is to the body of man.

BRASS. Incorruptibility.

BREASTPLATE. Obduracy; hardness of heart; contumacy.

BRIDE. The elect; the Church, either militant or triumphant.

CAMP OF THE SAINTS. The Church militant.

CENSER. Ministration of Angels.

CITY. The holy city signifies the Church; the beloved city, the Roman Church, or the capital of Christendom; the great city, the World in general, or even the Christian world.

CUP. The ecstasy of worldly delights, on the one hand; of the torments due to sin, on the other.

DAY. It sometimes stands for one year.

DIADEM. Preëminence, royalty.

EAGLE. The elevation of the soul, by detachment from the world; a lofty devotion for the science of the Cross.

EARTH. The material order.

EARTHQUAKE. A moral perturbation; a convulsion of society.
EUPHRATES. The tranquillity of order. (St. Aug.)
EYE. The providence of the Creator; the watchfulness of Christ, and his secret inspirations; the plenitude of evangelical doctrine.

FALSE PROPHET. The teacher of earthly wisdom, as opposed to that which is heavenly.
FIRE. Charity, zeal, persecution, divine vengeance, lightning.
FIRST RESURRECTION. It is of those who depart out of this life, in the grace of God.
FOREHEAD. The intention.
FOUNTAINS. The ministers of religion; the sacraments themselves, the sources of life.

GOG AND MAGOG. The secret and the open adversaries of the truth; the refined and the barbarous nations.
GRASS. The multitude of the simple; the innocent, the frail.

HAIL. The reverse of charity, hatred of the truth, obstinacy, despair.
HALF-HOUR. An interval or interruption of time.
HAND. Works; human acts.
HARLOT. The personification of Babylon; the spirit of the world.
HEAD. The seat of authority; a monarchy.
HEAVEN. The spiritual order; the region of the intelligence, in general, of the Christian intelligence in particular; the realms of the blessed.
HORN. Power.
HORNS OF THE ALTAR. The strength or virtue of the altar.
HORSE. In a good sense, active, triumphant; conversely, aggressive, offensive.
HORSEMEN. Democracy; the people in power.
HOUR. A short, indefinite time.

IMAGE OF THE BEAST. The mechanic forces, moulded to a likeness or subserviency of the temporal power, under Antichrist.
INCENSE. Intercession of the Saints.
IRON. Irresistible power.
ISLAND. Such human institutions, usages, or traditions, as are most retired from common observation, and therefore supposed to be least in danger from moral or political disturbance.

JERUSALEM. The kingdom of God, whether on earth or in heaven.

LION. Power; cruelty with power.
LOCUSTS. The infidel philosophers.
LIGHTNINGS. The force of truth.

MARK OF THE BEAST. The character of the worldly-minded; of those who are actuated by the carnal motives, as contradistinguished from the evangelical maxims.
MONTH. Thirty years.
MOON. The Church, the reflected light or mirror of divine truth. Or sometimes, it signifies merely the vicissitudes of time.

MOUNTAINS. Empires, high places, and by inference, pride, heres y.

NUMBERS. The number Seven is the harmonious measure of action, and of the principles of action. Ten denotes the symmetry of order and law. Twelve declares the summons, the vocation, or the testament of the Creator to his creatures; hence the Apostles are twelve, and the Patriarchs are twelve; and Twenty-four is the company of their united numbers in heaven.

RIVERS. Particular or national Churches; branches of the Church Catholic.

SEA. In general, the age; præsens seculum; the mass of human society. In particular, Christendom.

SEA OF GLASS OR CRYSTAL. Truth; intelligence of truth; the intelligent and celestial creation.

SEAL. That which is obscure or mysterious in the dispensations of the Creator.

SEAT. One's place; throne; sphere.

SECOND DEATH. It is of those who die impenitent in mortal sin.

SERPENT. The devil.

SIGN OF GOD. The Cross; the evangelical character.

SMOKE. The darkness of a delusion; "the operation of error."

SMOKE OF THE TEMPLE. The inaccessible majesty of divine justice.

STARS. Particular Churches; the lesser lights; doctors in the Church.

SUN. The light of truth.

SWORD. Evangelical truth.

TABERNACLE OF THE TESTIMONY. The eternal law of God.

TAIL. Moral sequence; final consequence.

TEETH. Ferocity; malignity.

TEMPLE OF GOD. The constitution or method of things, by sacrifice; the vicarious merits of the just; the divine atonement.

THOUSAND YEARS. The whole time of the generation of Christ; the same in the time of its highest prosperity, and of its literal supremacy.

THUNDERINGS. Evident tokens of divine admonition, reproof, or anger.

TIME. Annual period; a year.

TREES. Men of eminence in virtue, or learning, or dignity.

TRUMPET. That which is manifest in the divine ordination, and compels the attention.

VIAL. That which is most grievous, most obscure, and, at the same time, most terrible, in the effects of the divine displeasure.

VOICES. The testimony of just men, the admonitions of the prudent; the counsels of the wise.

WATER. The human life which is transacted in time; remotely, the life which is eternal; in a sense still more remote and final, the third person of the Holy Trinity, the Lord and Giver of life.

WATERS. The peoples; the common humanity; ecclesiastically, the Christian peoples; and, by synecdoche, the heavenly graces or sacraments which are the life of the people; anagogically, the spirits of the blessed in heaven.

WILDERNESS. The world; the secular life.

WINDS. Agitation of the moral or political order; the vicissitudes of human passions.

WINE. The intoxication of carnal joys; the retribution of eternal pains.

WINE-PRESS. The rigor of justice; the severity of the time of probation.

WO. An epoch of disorder, and of spiritual calamity.

WOMAN. The Mother of Christ; the Church.

WRATH. The madness of lust; the penalty of sin. The divine displeasure.

YEAR. A time indefinitely long.

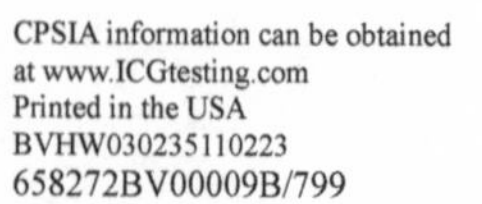

CPSIA information can be obtained
at www.ICGtesting.com
Printed in the USA
BVHW030235110223
658272BV00009B/799

9 783375 138684